PYRAMID OF THE ANCIENTS

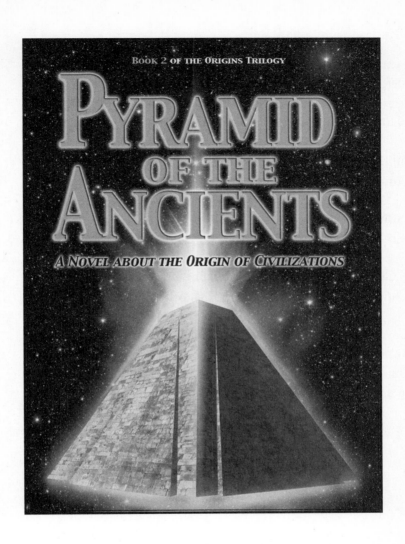

BOOK 2 OF THE ORIGINS TRILOGY

PYRAMID OF THE ANCIENTS

A Novel about the Origin of Civilizations

KEITH A. ROBINSON

DEFENDER

CRANE, MISSOURI

Pyramid of the Ancients: A Novel about the Origin of Civilizations
Defender
Crane, Missouri 65633
©2010 by Keith A. Robinson

ISBN 10: 0984061134
ISBN 10: 9780984061136

A CIP catalog record of this book is available from the Library of
Congress.

Cover illustration and design by Daniel Wright.

Unless otherwise noted, Scripture quoted is taken from the New
International Version.

DEDICATION

To my two adventurers, Alejandro and Sebastián.
I pray that my fictional stories will inspire you to dig deeper
into your earthly father's faith and help you realize that
science and religion are not at odds with each other.

ACKNOWLEDGMENTS

First and foremost, I must give all honor and thanks to my Master and Savior, Jesus, who gave me my gifts and talents. May my efforts bring you pleasure, Abba. Solo Dei Gloria.

To Kevin, Aimee, and Tim Chaffey—my "proofreaders, editors, and story consultants"—thank you for all of your time, your advice and your comments.

To Angie Peters, my editor—for doing so much to improve and clean up the text of this novel. Thanks for catching all of my repetitiveness. You taught me so much about my own writing style through this process. Without you, Rebecca and the others would have been moving a lot more "slowly," and things would have been happening to them more "suddenly."And in case I forgot, thanks for catching all of my repetitiveness.

To Pamela McGrew, my typesetter—for her patience with all of the changes Angie and I kept making along the way.

To Daniel Wright, my cover artist—thanks for capturing the essence of my story in one picture. Who says you can't judge a book by its cover?

To Tom Horn, my publisher—thank you for taking a chance on me. I hope you feel it has been worth it!

Due to my own oversight, I failed to include any acknowledgements for *Logic's End*. So, I would also like to thank Samuel Schlenker for his amazing sketches and Steve Warner for his cover art. You both really helped bring the bizarre aliens from Ka'esch to life! My gratitude goes to my editor, Michelle Warner, as well—for a great job on getting the manuscript in shape.

To all of my friends and family as well as all those who purchased and enjoyed *Logic's End*—your support has been vital. Without your enthusiasm and positive encouragement for *Logic's End*, I don't think we ever would have heard from Rebecca and the others again.

And finally, I must give special thanks to Mom. You have believed in me from day one, and have helped me ever since. Thank you for all you have done to support my writing—proofreading, editing, story suggestions, book sales, website building, and financial backing! You are definitely the one whose shoulders I have been standing on to achieve my success. I love you.

CONTENTS

THE PYRAMID OF THE ANCIENTS

2nd Floor

Control Center

1st Floor

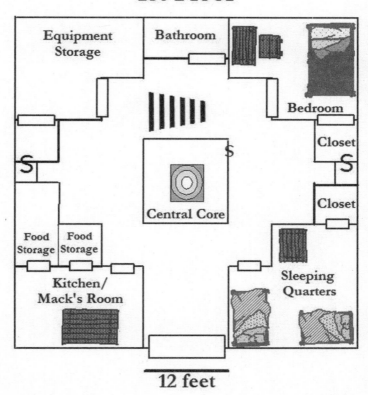

Equipment Storage

Bathroom

Bedroom

Closet

Closet

Central Core

Food Storage

Food Storage

Kitchen/ Mack's Room

Sleeping Quarters

12 feet

PROLOGUE

THE SHAFT OF light pierced through the blackness of the chamber like a ray of morning sunlight breaking through a dense canopy of storm clouds, its brilliance accompanied by the rumble of stone grating against stone. As the artificial thunder intensified, the shaft widened and grew until the brightness revealed the full outline of a doorway. The large stone door came to a grinding halt with a loud boom that echoed throughout the chamber beyond.

Slowly and gracefully, an odd-shaped object floated into the opening, its cylindrical torso momentarily framed by the radiance from the chamber beyond. Two pinpricks of light hovered over the torso like a pair of disembodied eyes, while beneath it, three legs spaced apart in a triangular formation kept it aloft on cushions of air. The gentle whir that accompanied the intruder as it entered the chamber was joined by the sound of metallic gears as two spindly arms rose up from the sides of the torso.

The soft blue glow being emitted from the spinning disks on the circular ends of the legs was suddenly overpowered by a beam of iridescent light that shone forth from just above the beady eyes, its rays causing a ring of dim white to suddenly appear on the far wall of the chamber more than forty feet away. Slowly and methodically, the beam began to probe around the room, steadily sweeping the area in a counterclockwise motion.

"Incredible. Absolutely incredible."

Behind the droid, a yellowish, spherical lantern flared to life, held by a figure dressed in a solid black T-shirt and blue jeans. The shirt fit snugly to the person's body, revealing a form that, while not overly muscular, was one that had spent at least a few hours in the gym. The man had a medium build and slightly above-average height, and carried himself with an air of confidence. The light from the glowing sphere held in his left hand reflected off his tanned skin as his intelligent eyes swept over his surroundings. Stepping carefully into the room, the man raked his right hand through his shoulder-length, dark brown hair in amazement and let out a low whistle. "Jerome, come on in. Dr. Eisenberg, are you guys getting this?"

"That's an affirmative," came a reply. "The picture is crystal clear."

A moment later, the figure of a tall man passed through the open doorway, his own lantern preceding him into the room. His forest green polo and khaki pants were damp from perspiration, and his dark skin glistened with sweat. Reaching up with his free hand to wipe his brow on the back of his glove, he moved farther into the chamber and joined in the examination. "Jeffrey, what is this place? This chamber looks as if it hasn't been disturbed for hundreds of years."

"Probably much longer than that," his companion replied. "The masonry and stonework are definitely the same as the antechamber, but it's too early yet to make any guesses as to what this room was used for."

"Ugh! What an incredible smell you've discovered," a third voice commented from the doorway. "It smells worse in here than a Hutt's backside. Whoa, would ya look at the workmanship on this door frame? And this engraving is flawless," the man stated in awe, his lantern held inches from the wall as his gloved right hand caressed the markings etched into the rock. Setting his spherical lantern down, he grabbed the bill of his baseball cap and took it off, revealing a mop of wavy black hair. Using his right sleeve as a handkerchief, he wiped beads of sweat from his brow. His unkempt hair was matched by a pair of dirty jeans and a wrinkled brown T-shirt that looked as if it had spent one too many nights in a heap on the floor. Replacing the cap on his head so that it faced backward, he leaned closer to the wall and resumed his inspection of the door.

A fourth person, a woman, brushed past him, nearly knocking him over as she stepped into the room. The newcomer, tall and dark-skinned, held her lantern high, adding noticeably to the brightness fending off the encroaching darkness. With a nearly six-foot frame, she was dressed in a sleeveless, gray, one-piece jumpsuit cinched at the waist with a black belt. Her ebony hair, pulled back tightly into a ponytail, combined with her high cheekbones and chiseled features to make her seem like an ancient obsidian statue that had somehow been imbued with life.

The droid, seemingly oblivious to the entrance of the others, continued to scan the room with its searchlight as the four humans fanned out behind it. As they walked, their boots kicked up small clouds of dust that covered every inch of the smooth stone walls and floors.

"Elmer, give us a report on da dimensions of da room," Akwen commanded the droid, her voice thick with the heavy Cameroonian accent of her heritage. As she spoke, she worked her way across the room toward some objects on the floor several feet in front of her.

The droid responded even as its searchlight continued sweeping the room, its clear tenor voice echoing off the nearby walls. "The main portion of the chamber is a perfect forty-five feet square, and the additional back portion of the room measures twenty-seven feet wide by fifteen feet. The ceiling is a uniform fifteen feet in height. Two doors are set into the northeast and northwest corners of the main chamber."

"There is a lot of debris on the ground," Jerome said once the droid had finished its report. Circling around a four-foot wooden table lying on its side, he stooped down and picked up one of the many smaller items strewn across the floor. "What are these things?" he asked, his brow furrowing. "They look like pieces of machinery. And there are broken glass, tools of various kinds, and containers everywhere. Here's one that still has some kind of liquid in it."

Akwen bent down to examine the jar in Jerome's hand, but she suddenly stood and turned to face the droid, which had ceased to probe the room with its searchlight. "What is wrong? Have you found someting, Elmer?"

The circular disk on the droid's rear left leg angled outwards slightly, propelling it at a forty-five degree angle towards the eastern wall. All four humans stood frozen in place like marble statues as the droid stopped in front of what appeared to be a large table set against the wall. In its usual calm voice, the droid replied, "It seems I may have found one of the former occupants of this chamber."

Like sprinters just released by the crack of the starting pistol, the humans moved simultaneously toward the droid and its discovery. As the others approached, Elmer floated up and to the side to make room for them. In the light shining down from the droid, they saw a large, hooded form slumped over in the chair, its upper torso resting face down on the tabletop.

"Look at the size of that thing!" Mack said in awe as he moved in closer for a better look. "It's as big as a Wookiee! It's gotta be seven feet tall, at least."

Withdrawing a large brush from a bag hanging from his shoulder, Jeffrey began removing the dust from the still form. "Have any of you ever seen cloth like this?" Without waiting for a reply, he removed his right glove and ran his hand along the corpse's back where he had brushed off the dust. "It feels as soft as silk. And watch how it shimmers in the light. The whole robe appears to be the same."

Growing excited, he looked up at each of the others. "Cloth that is made out of an unknown material, masonry unlike anything we've seen before, the book we found in the antechamber written in a language no one's ever heard of—"

"—although it has similarities to Hebrew," Mack chimed in, interrupting Jeffrey.

"—and most importantly," Jeffrey said, without skipping a beat, "it contained instructions on how to build technology we've never seen before. Lady and gentlemen, I think we may be looking at the real thing here." Even in the yellowish light of the glowing spheres, his brown eyes sparkled with passion and exhilaration.

Jerome looked up from the body to stare at Jeffrey, his own excitement evident in his face. "Its body shape looks human, but—wait. Look at the hands!"

"Those definitely don't belong to any human," Jeffrey said. Leaning over the table, he used his brush once again to dust off the portion of the corpse's hand not covered by the sleeve of its robe.

"I don't know," Mack said with a smirk, "you obviously haven't met my Uncle Joe! He's the hairiest man I've ever seen."

"Okay, so *other* than your Uncle Joe, I don't think there are any other humans with that amount of hair on their hands," Jeffrey replied with a chuckle. "But even that aside, these hands look like animal claws, except that most animals I know don't take time to trim their nails."

Akwen, standing on the right side of the body, pulled a file and small container from her satchel and took a sample of skin and hair from the right hand. "If dis chamber has been sealed for tousands of years, den why hasn't da skin rotted away?"

Jeffrey shrugged. "That outer anti-gravity seal we had to break through must have also kept the chamber vacuum sealed. Brace yourselves, everyone. We're about to get our first look at an extraterrestrial. Dr. Eisenberg, are you still with us?"

"Yes. Elmer's feeds are still coming through crystal clear," came the reply from the commlink on Jeffrey's wrist. "Are you ready to make history, Jeffrey?"

"Oh yeah," Jeffery replied with a grin. "Here we go. Ready, Jerome? Let's tilt the chair back. On three. One, two, *three!*"

On cue, they pushed the body backward, causing the ancient marble chair to tip. With Mack holding on to the back of the chair, the four of them lowered it and its occupant to the floor. However, the stiffness of the body—combined with the odd angle at which it had been resting—caused it to fall sideways to the left, toward Jeffrey. Instinctively, he reached out to try to catch it. As his right arm reached around the shoulder to cradle the head, his fingers tangled in the hood, pulling it back from the corpse's face. The sightless eyes and monstrous features that stared back at him became the source of nightmares for months to follow.

The figure's facial structure was unmistakably human-like. However, its large brows, deep-set eyes, sharp teeth, and cranial shape seemed much more suited to that of an ape-like animal. Coarse, brown hair lined the sides of the face and swooped low over the massive forehead, but was notably absent from around the eyes, mouth, and cheeks.

Stumbling backwards in shock, Jeffrey released his hold on the corpse and let it fall to the dust-covered floor of the chamber with a dull thud. The body fell onto its left side and lay still, lifeless eyes staring up at Jeffrey as if mocking his lack of nerve.

"Okay, I'm officially weirded out!" Mack said, nervousness still apparent in his voice. As he looked at Jeffrey, a smirk slowly crept across his features. "Man, you moved faster than a greased pig being chased by the butcher on Christmas Eve!"

Jeffrey let out a tense chuckle. "Yeah, and I bet you'll make sure I don't live it down anytime soon," he said, recovering his voice. His initial fear having dissipated, he leaned closer to the corpse to examine the face in more detail. "Is it just me, or does this thing look familiar? What does it remind you of?"

Crouching next to him, Jerome studied the still form intently. "It kind of looks like those artists' sketches of Neanderthals, except this thing is hairier, and a little more ape-like. Do you think there's a connection?"

"Sure!" Mack chimed in excitedly before Jeffrey could respond. He stood to his feet and began gesturing with his hands as he spoke. "I mean, aren't they always saying that aliens might have placed life here on earth and then helped with evolution? Maybe they took some of their own DNA to begin the process. Or maybe after humans were evolved enough, they began reproducing with our ancestors to produce the Neanderthals!"

"Has anyone ever told you that you watch *way* too many sci-fi movies?" Jeffrey asked dryly.

"Don't knock 'em. Many times, reality copies fiction. I mean, just look at our flying Swiss army knife over here," he said, pointing to the hovering droid, which had begun moving about the room once again to continue its search. As it floated overhead, the blue light from its gravity control outputs revealed the outline of an open book near the right edge of the table.

"Hey, what's that?" Mack asked, rushing over to the table. Like a mother picking up a newborn, he gently lifted the ancient manuscript and caressed the worn leather spine. It was as if he expected his very touch to be sufficient to pierce the binding and absorb the treasured contents within. Jeffrey, Jerome, and Akwen gathered behind Mack, looking over his shoulder as he studied the book by the light of his lantern, which now rested on the table.

"So, are you going to open it or just stand there petting it?" Jerome asked impatiently.

"Sorry," Mack said, as if snapping out of a trance. Reverently, he grabbed the corner of the dark metallic blue cover and opened it. He began leafing slowly through the pages, examining their contents.

"Can you read it?" Jeffrey asked, his voice just above a whisper. "Is it in the same language as the one we found in the antechamber?"

"Yes!" Mack replied, his voice quivering in excitement. "And it seems to contain more diagrams, schematics, and instructions on how to build...something. I can't quite tell yet."

"Do you tink dis creature could have written bot' books?" Akwen asked quietly, glancing back at the corpse resting on the floor behind them. "If so, why? Was dis place some kind of workshop or laboratory?"

"Maybe," Jeffrey said. "It would certainly explain the tools on the floor and some of the other objects. But what was he building, and why? Let's finish checking out the rest of the chamber before we start jumping to conclusions. Mack, you joining us?"

Mack was so intent on studying the ancient book that it took Jeffrey several tries to get his attention. Finally, Mack looked up and shook his head. "No. You guys go on. This stuff is amazing. I feel like a caveman who just discovered fire! From the looks of it, this could be the find of the millennium! I mean, if the technology in here is anything like what was in the other book, then it could change the course of human history! It may be too early to say, but I think these are plans to build a spaceship far faster than any of our shuttles!"

"Are you sure that isn't just wishful thinking?" Jeffrey asked.

Mack gave him a serious look that left no doubt that, for once, he wasn't exaggerating. "Okay," Jeffrey continued, "call us if you discover anything revolutionary." Moving away from the table, Jeffrey, Akwen, and Jerome headed over to join Elmer near the door in the northeastern corner of the chamber.

As they approached, the droid's head rotated 180 degrees to face them. "The door in the northwest corner led to a storage room that was almost completely empty. There were traces of oil and grease on the floors and walls, and several pieces of strange metal and ceramics were scattered around the room."

"—More confirmation that this was some kind of workshop," Jeffrey said, looking at Jerome. "Well, let's see what's behind door number two." Expecting the door to be stuck from countless years of nonuse, Jeffrey grabbed the plain metal door handle in both hands and pulled hard. To his surprise it opened easily, nearly causing him to hit himself in the head with the edge of the door. Stepping to the side, he pushed it the rest of the way open and held up his lantern to illuminate the interior of the room.

The onlookers' hearts, already beating rapidly from excitement, went careening into high gear in response to what they now saw before them. Filling the center of the nine-by-fifteen-foot room was an enormous, hairy monstrosity. The dead creature lay sprawled on its back with its feet closest to the door. From where they stood, its head seemed tilted to the left at a sharp angle, as if broken. Its oversized limbs lay straight, giving Jeffrey the distinct impression that it had been dragged into this closet. The massive arms were complemented by claw-like hands that looked capable of ripping a small animal in half with a simple twist.

Although its twelve-foot height, heavy build, and fearsome claws were more than enough to inspire awe, it was the monster's facial expression that caused Jeffrey's body to go cold. Like the corpse in the main chamber, this one looked like it was part human, part animal. But compared to the other body, which seemed more like a human with animal features, this one appeared as if some angry, pagan god had twisted a rabid wolf or wild dog into the semblance of a human. Its canine-like snout was mangled into a vicious snarl that sent shivers down Jeffrey's spine.

Taking a steadying breath, Jeffrey stepped into the room, leaving Akwen and Jerome standing in the entrance. Picking his way carefully around the body, Jeffrey stopped near the head, bent down, and held his lantern closer to the creature's face. "It looks like his neck is broken," Jeffrey stated, his features splitting into a grimace. "He sure is ugly." Looking over at the others, he smirked. "I'm sure glad he's dead! I'd hate to run into one of these on a dark street. Then again, I'd hate to run into one of these in broad daylight surrounded by an army…" Noticing the look on Akwen's face, he paused, his humor fizzling. "Hey, are you okay?"

The dark skin on Akwen's forehead was creased with worry lines. "What are dese tings, Jeffrey? Dis…beast…is not human. It is one ting to speculate dat aliens might exist, but it is difficult to grasp the reality when faced with cold, hard evidence." Shaking her head and closing her eyes, Akwen turned away from the corpse for a moment, her left hand coming up to cup her head. Jerome, watching her with concern, hesitantly placed a comforting hand on her shoulder.

Akwen shrugged off Jerome's hand as she lowered her own. Turning, she stared at each of them, her normally stoic face etched with worry. "I don't like dis. Someting feels wrong. Can you sense it? Dis whole place seems…oppressive. Dere is someting here…almost like a dark presence."

Standing up, Jeffrey tried to force a smile. "Akwen, stop. You're scaring me—"

"I am not joking, Jeffrey!" Akwen stated, her voice rising as she shot him a withering glance. Sobered by her reaction, the crooked smile on Jeffrey's lips faded as Akwen continued. "Where did dese tings come from? Dey don't look friendly. What happened in dis chamber? What if…what if, after all dese years, we disturb someting that could…I don't know…call others of deir kind back here."

"Now you're beginning to sound like Mack," Jeffrey began. Akwen's eyes narrowed and her face darkened further, causing Jeffrey to quickly add, "but you're right. We should be careful. Besides, there's nothing to worry about. All we've found are a couple of dead bodies and a book."

"Yes, and what is in da book?" Akwen pressed. But before she could say anything else, Mack came running up behind her, bringing their conversation to an abrupt halt.

"Jeffrey! I think I found something!"

Mack's face appeared just above Akwen's broad right shoulder. One glance at the contents of the room, however, and his face disappeared almost as quickly as he tumbled backward, tripping over his own feet. "Sweet mother of Gene Roddenberry!" he exclaimed as he picked himself up off the floor. "What is that thing? It looks uglier than a Klingon on a bad hair day!"

"Never mind that," Jeffrey said as he retrieved Mack's baseball cap from the floor and placed it back on his head. "What did you find?"

Unable to tear his eyes away from the creature on the floor, Mack replied as if in a trance, his mind clearly not yet focused on the task of speaking. "The…uh…the book has a…it…there's a drawing…. Man, that thing is huge!"

Grabbing Mack by the shoulders, Jeffrey forced his colleague to look at him. Speaking slowly, as if talking to a child, Jeffrey asked again, "What...did...you...FIND?"

Finally coming to his senses, Mack's enthusiasm came rushing back. "Oh! Come here. Quick! I've gotta show you this!"

Leading the others over to the table where the book rested, Mack pointed down at a drawing of a triangular object. "See that? What does that look like to you?"

Mack moved out of the way so Jeffrey and the others could get a closer look at the diagram. "It looks like an Egyptian pyramid, or a ziggurat," Jerome said, sounding puzzled.

"That's what I thought, too," Mack said.

"So what are you getting at?" Jeffrey asked, looking up from the book.

"There was this sci-fi show many years ago that talked about how the pyramids were landing pads for triangular-shaped alien ships. What if there was some truth to that? But instead of being landing pads, what if all of these ancient cultures built these pyramids and ziggurats to copy the design of the spaceships?" Ignoring the skeptical looks, he continued. "I believe, based upon what I can read of the text and the diagrams, that this book gives instructions on how to build one of these spaceships!"

As the four stood contemplating the import of Mack's last statement, a low rumble put an end to further discussion. In unison, they jerked their heads toward the north end of the room to see Elmer quickly floating towards them.

"Dr. Nancho, I believe I may have inadvertently tripped some kind of mechanism," the droid said, its voice calm despite its rapid movements.

As they watched in astonishment, the entire northern portion of the wall slid upward, leaving a gaping black opening in its void. As the dust settled, the four explorers—still frozen in place—slowly began to stir. Jeffrey picked up his lantern and quietly made his way forward, the hairs on his neck standing straight up. His heart pounded thunderously in his chest from a mixture of adrenaline, fear, and excitement. With each step he took, Akwen's words flowed through his mind, causing inexplicable fear to come over him.

Setting his will against his feelings, he forced his legs forward until he stood at the threshold of the new chamber. Raising his lantern into the air, he simply stared at the sight spread out before him bathed in the yellowish glow of light. Sitting in the center of the new, larger chamber was a two-story pyramid with a flat top and steps leading up the sides. Directly in front of him, a twelve-foot-wide corridor led into the interior of the pyramid, the shadows within seeming to call out to him with promises of adventure and discovery.

So enraptured was he with this new sight that he didn't even realize that his colleagues had joined him until Jerome spoke. "This is it!" he said in an excited whisper. "Congratulations my friend, you just made history." Placing an arm around Jeffrey's shoulder, Jerome stated more firmly, "And now, here is the man who brought the world into a new era of space exploration by his discovery of an alien spacecraft. Jeffrey David Evans!"

1

REBECCA'S ARRIVAL

THE JEEP ROCKED wildly to the side, causing Rebecca to reach up once again and grab the door frame in order to keep her head from bumping against the side of the vehicle. She had driven over many lousy dirt roads near her home in the Midwest, but this one definitely took the prize for being the worst. The fact that she had been riding on it for more than forty-five minutes only highlighted the road's many flaws.

But according to her driver, this was the *best* way to get to the dig. *If this is the best way, I would hate to see the others,* she thought sarcastically.

"Please be careful!" she called out for the umpteenth time, leaning forward so the driver could hear her better from where she sat in the back seat. "NASA has gone through a lot to get this package delivered. It's vital that it arrives undamaged."

Her concern was met with the same response as her previous efforts: nothing.

"Relax," the soldier sitting beside her remarked nonchalantly. "We secured the package very carefully."

Trying to hide her frustration with the others' seeming lack of concern, she again addressed the driver. "Can you at least tell me how much longer it will take?"

"At our current speed, we should arrive in another fifteen minutes," the driver said in lightly accented English.

Fifteen minutes. Her heart began to pick up its relaxed pace as her stomach performed its customary acrobatics that signaled the onset of nervousness. *What will he say? Will he be happy to see me, or angry that I surprised him at his precious dig?* Her thoughts had traveled this familiar course for so long, asking the same questions over and over, that she wouldn't have been surprised to learn that they were forever etched on the inside of her skull.

Ever since she had started speaking regularly about the topic of the origin of life, her relationship with Jeffrey had gone from strained to almost nonexistent. In fact, this would be the first time she would see him in person since the night he had walked out at the end of one of her speeches. That was over ten months ago. Since then, she had decided that if their marriage had any chance of succeeding, she would have to go to Iraq to be with him. *Look at me,* she thought as she glanced down at her clothing. *My new shirt and jeans are completely covered with dust, this blasted midday heat is causing my hair to curl out of control, and I smell like diesel fuel. I probably look like something out of a horror flick. I want Jeffrey to notice my appearance, but this isn't exactly what I had in mind.*

The minutes seemed to drag on inexorably, Rebecca's thoughts bouncing back and forth as if trying to compete with the hole-ridden road. At long last, the perimeter of the military encampment came into view as the vehicle crested another hill.

According to the driver, once the Iraqi government realized the importance of the discovery, they had quickly—and quietly—set up a military presence to guard the dig. From a military perspective, they couldn't have chosen a better location. The entire compound was near the base of a mountain in an uninhabited section of the country. With the mountain at their backs and the dry plain in front of them, they would have plenty of notice if anyone came sniffing around.

In the center of the rear section of the compound was a large structure Rebecca assumed housed the dig itself. Due to the secret nature of the discovery, the government had erected a temporary building around the entire site, which was nearly as large as a football field. The structure was unusually shaped—probably because it followed the formation of the dig, Rebecca surmised—and was built out of a kind of off-white, plastic material. The length of the dig stretched in a more or less northeasterly direction until it almost literally ran into the side of the mountain.

The outer perimeter was marked by a heavy-duty, fifteen-foot electrical fence nearly two hundred yards from the dig site. Between the fence and the central structure, several prefabricated buildings of various sizes dotted the landscape. Three guard towers were positioned in a triangular shape: two along the northern sides of the encampment near the mountain, and one farther down the slope, in the southern section next to the main gate. The entire setup reminded Rebecca of a twentieth-century concentration camp.

Jeffrey, what did you get yourself into? She found herself wondering this for the hundredth time. In her mind, she could once again hear the words Jeffrey had spoken to her during their last "heated conversation": "This discovery will blow all of that religious junk back to the Middle Ages where it belongs!" he had said. She could still hear the conviction in his voice and the sheer certainty of his statement.

The jeep Rebecca was riding in was fifth in line in the convoy of trucks and military vehicles bringing fresh supplies and cargo to the compound. As the first truck approached the main gate, located just west of the southern tower, two pairs of high-powered laser rifles pointed in their direction from each of the three towers. Rebecca's seven years of service as a gunnery sergeant in the Marines caused her to wonder what other security measures were in place that she couldn't see.

One of the soldiers standing in front of the gate held up a hand, signaling the driver to stop. Detaching himself from his post, he stepped cautiously toward the driver's side of the lead truck. Reaching down with his left hand, he unclipped an electronic device from his belt while his right hand rested comfortably on the handle of his holstered pistol. Leaning back in her seat, Rebecca tried to relax while the guard finished the security check on the four preceding vehicles. Finally, after what seemed like an eternity, the car in front of the jeep moved on through the gate and it was their turn.

"Please prepare for retinal scan," the guard stated in a crisp, military fashion.

Holding the device up to within inches of the driver's face, the machine emitted a blue beam that quickly scanned his left eye. Within seconds, the soldier had moved on to Rebecca and the other occupants of the jeep. In less than a minute, they were instructed to proceed. Moving slowly, the driver edged through the heavy metallic gate and into the compound.

Once clear of the entrance, the driver steered the vehicle toward the left. The entire place was alive with activity, seemingly oblivious to the rapid approach of evening. Several times, Rebecca and her fellow travelers were forced to slow down or stop to let a group of scientists or technicians pass by. Each of them, Rebecca noted, wore shirts or jackets emblazoned with the NASA logo. Finally, the driver brought the vehicle to a halt fifty feet from the skirt of the mountain, on the northwest side of the slanted dig site. As the other members of the convoy were cleared through security, they were directed toward various other areas of the compound.

"All right," the driver said, his voice cold and business-like. "Let's get this thing unloaded." Glad to be getting out of the uncomfortable back seat, Rebecca quickly opened the door, stepped out, and stretched her stiff muscles. Although all she could think of was going inside the dig to see her husband, she forced herself to see to the cargo first.

Her military companions immediately began unloading the large, rectangular box from the back of the jeep. The crate's hefty weight alone made it difficult to move, but when combined with the fact that it was the size of a small desk, it became truly cumbersome. Jumping in to help with a sagging corner, Rebecca and the others began moving their cargo away from the back of the jeep as a group of several technicians and scientists converged on the vehicle. Their excitement was palpable, causing

Rebecca to wonder once again exactly what it was that had accompanied her arrival.

Practically pushing her out of the way, one of the technicians in the front of the group grabbed the side of the box and barked out commands. "Careful! Careful! This crate is extremely important. Watch out on the left. Jonas, take that side. Easy now."

Like a swarm of ants carrying off a prized piece of food from a picnic, the technicians and scientists scurried away toward the northern entrance of the central building, leaving Rebecca and the others from her group to follow in their wake.

"Can I leave my bags in the back temporarily?" she asked the driver as he exited the vehicle.

"Yeah, no problem," he replied casually, "but I can't guarantee their safety."

Since she had nothing of real value among her things, and considering that she was inside a military camp, she decided to chance it. Leaving her suitcase and overnight bag in the back seat, she turned and began walking in the direction the techs had taken. As she reached the double doors leading into the dig site, Rebecca felt her pulse quicken, both from the prospect of seeing Jeffrey again and from the thirst for discovery that ran deep in her veins. Taking a steadying breath, she pushed open the door and entered the complex.

It seemed as if she had stepped into another world. All around, broken and cracked pillars stood like giant sentinels staring down at her. Several crumbling walls jutted out from the fractured flooring, which appeared to be made of a type of marble with swirls of white and tan coloring. *This is definitely no ordinary archaeological find,* she thought as she stared around at the intricate carvings that adorned the marble pillars and walls. Even in its current damaged condition, it was apparent that the beauty of the ancient ruins had once been exquisite. Stepping around a group of technicians deep in conversation, Rebecca walked up to one of the pillars and began to examine the carving of some kind of reptilian beast that resembled a stegosaurus.

"Are you lost, little girl?" asked a voice behind her. A smile creased her face as she turned around to see a bald man in his late fifties standing behind her. Although only half a foot taller than Rebecca, his poise and demeanor magnified his height in her mind. His white, short-sleeved, button-up shirt with khaki pants and brown dress shoes stood out in sharp contrast to the "NASA"-emblazoned uniforms nearly everyone else in the area was wearing.

"Dr. Eisenberg!" Rebecca said as she leaned forward and embraced the man. "It is so good to see you. You look great! You've lost a few pounds since I last saw you. Is there someone new you're trying to impress?" she asked playfully.

The scholar simply pushed up his wire-framed glasses and smiled down at her mischievously. "Only you, Rebecca. Don't you know you have always been the apple of my eye?"

Rebecca grinned back fondly. "So what are you doing with all of your free time now that you're retired? Are you still dabbling in art?"

"Yes, now and again," he said. "Whenever I can find the time."

"That reminds me, I've been meaning to thank you for the beautiful oil painting you sent us last Christmas," Rebecca said. "Was that Mount Saint Helens?"

"Yes. I painted that one when Nathan and I were visiting Washington a couple of years ago," Dr. Eisenberg answered. "I thought you might like it."

"How is Nathan, anyway?"

"Just fine," the older man replied with a fatherly smile. "He is following in his mother's footsteps. He has become quite a good pediatrician, you know. If only Ruth had lived long enough to see the grandchildren," he said as he proudly pulled from his pocket a digital photo card that cycled through several photos of his progeny.

"They're so cute! You must be so proud," Rebecca said, a hint of emotion coloring her voice as she looked at the snapshots. She had wanted to have children for many years, but although she and Jeffrey had tried, they remained childless. And now, at forty years old—and with a struggling marriage—her chance at motherhood seemed all but vanished. Handing back the photo card, she quickly changed the subject.

"This is quite a place you've got here," she said, turning to look around while taking a moment to compose herself.

"Yes, indeed," Dr. Eisenberg said with pride. "The find of a lifetime."

"But why all the security?" Rebecca asked, again facing the professor. "I admit that it's a well-preserved and fascinating discovery, but it just seems like overkill."

"Didn't NASA brief you on what is here?"

"They didn't have time," Rebecca replied. "I had to cash in every favor I had built up during my years with NASA, as well as add a few new IOUs, just to get back on the roster. But that took so much time that I was barely cleared just before the supply shipment left. Dr. Goldsmith pulled a few strings so I could accompany them, and he convinced the higher-ups that you would brief me when we arrived. He said they didn't much like the idea, but were willing to make an exception for you and Dr. Goldsmith."

Dr. Eisenberg was silent for a moment, then his countenance changed and he became much more serious. "Maybe that's for the best. It might be better if you hear about our discovery firsthand. Rebecca, do you know why I requested you specifically? Do you have any idea why I asked you to come here as my assistant?"

Rebecca felt that familiar churning of her stomach that signaled the onset of worry or fear. Something in Dr. Eisenberg's expression and tone of voice made the hairs stand up on the back of her neck. "No," she answered. "But I was extremely grateful for the invitation. Since Jeffrey started on this dig, I've been looking for a way to be with him."

At the mention of Jeffrey's name, Dr. Eisenberg's face darkened noticeably. "Come with me," he said as he put his arm around Rebecca and began directing her towards the southwestern section of the structure. "We have much to discuss."

Rebecca was silent for a few moments as they began walking through the ruins. Finally, she asked, "Why *did* you want me as your assistant, then?"

The professor threw a quick glance at her, then looked around at the bustle of activity. "Not here," he said. "I'll tell you when we get somewhere more private."

The younger woman walked on in silence, her thoughts cycling through the myriad reasons Dr. Eisenberg would need her as an assistant. Giving it up as a fruitless exercise, she decided to change the subject. "So what is this place?" she asked.

"We're not entirely sure," Dr. Eisenberg began. "Jeffrey and Jerome think it may have been some sort of palace. You did know Jerome was here, too, didn't you?" he asked, looking over at her.

"Are you kidding?" she said with a chuckle. "Those two have been nigh inseparable since they studied with you in college. I would've been surprised if he *wasn't* here." More seriously, she added, "Actually, Jeffrey told me a while ago. So, getting back to the subject…what do *you* think it is?"

"It's hard to tell. It *may* be a palace, but it could just as well be a temple, or the foyer to a bathhouse, for all we know," Dr. Eisenberg replied.

"What makes Jeffrey and Jerome think it's a palace, then?" Rebecca asked.

"Well, because of what we found *below*."

"Below?" Rebecca echoed quizzically.

Dr. Eisenberg nodded. "A few years back, during one of the military skirmishes with the terrorists still hiding out in these mountains, one of the explosions exposed part of these ruins. Since Jeffrey and Jerome were working on another dig not too far away, they heard about it and applied to the government for approval to excavate. Once the military rooted out all the terrorists from the area, the government gave it the green light. As they were excavating, they realized the blast did more than just expose the ruins. It also caved in a portion of a wall, which revealed a hidden staircase that led many feet below ground."

As the professor was talking, the pair had been drawing closer to a single structure located in the far southwest section of the ruins. The building was about the size of a small garage with a single door on the front, which was guarded by two Iraqi soldiers with the new Ionian Technology laser rifles slung over their shoulders.

"Here we are," Dr. Eisenberg said as they stepped up to the building. The guards, obviously familiar with the doctor, simply waved him by. He ran his hand under a laser reader while looking into a retinal scanner. After a brief pause, the light on the panel turned green, and was accompanied by a loud click. Grabbing the door handle, Dr. Eisenberg opened the door and gestured for Rebecca to enter.

She found herself looking down at a flight of steps about six feet across. The walls, stairs, and high arched ceiling were made out of the same type of marble as the ruins, and were covered with similar shapes and designs. Although the staircase was well lit with modern lights, Rebecca felt a sinister chill run down her spine, as if some malevolent beast were waiting at the foot of the stairs to devour her.

"You may want to use the hand railing," Dr. Eisenberg stated, misunderstanding the cause of her hesitation. "As you can see, the steps are very large."

Still trying to shrug off the disturbing sense of oppression, Rebecca simply nodded, grabbed the hand rail, and began her descent. At the bottom of the giant steps, Rebecca entered a rectangular room nine feet deep by twelve feet wide. Directly in front of her was a single door as wide as the stairs and over ten feet in height.

As he reached the bottom step, Dr. Eisenberg resumed his narration. "Jeffrey and Jerome ended up here, but they couldn't open the door. They even tried drilling through it and the walls, but everywhere they drilled, they encountered some sort of invisible barrier. That alone would have been more than enough to excite them, but there was more to the discovery than that. This room, which we refer to as the antechamber, was completely empty except for a short table, upon which sat a single book that was written in a language neither of them recognized."

"So, naturally, they called you," Rebecca said with a smile.

"Naturally!" Dr. Eisenberg said in a deep, playful tone as he returned her smile. Removing his glasses, he began cleaning them on his shirt as he continued. "When they showed me the book, I instantly became intrigued. I tell you, Rebecca, I have never seen anything like it." He held up a finger to correct himself, "The book, I mean. It contained diagrams and directions showing how to build a machine. The language in which it was written has similarities to Hebrew. But even though I am fluent in Hebrew, it was beyond my ability to interpret, so we had to bring in a specialist. And boy is he special," he added under his breath as an afterthought.

Lost in her own train of thought, Rebecca didn't even hear the professor's last comment. "But I don't understand," Rebecca said. "How old is this ruin? I was under the impression that it was several thousand years old, at least. How could a book survive all that time without turning to dust?"

"Let me tell you now, Rebecca," her companion said seriously, "you are going to see many things that you will not understand and that don't seem to make any sense. Get used to it. Anyway, the book was made out of a very durable material and was in great condition, considering its age. And as for the dating of the find, that's quite a fascinating story by itself. Based on the numbers of layers of rock above it and the index fossils contained in those layers, and using radiometric dating, we came up with an age that far exceeded even our best guesses."

Rebecca waited several seconds for Dr. Eisenberg to explain further. When it became apparent that he was clearly enjoying the suspense his delay was creating, she decided to humor him and play along. "How old is it? Five thousand years? Surely it couldn't be much older than that?"

Taking a deep breath, Dr. Eisenberg leaned closer and whispered slowly, as if he were afraid the walls might overhear: "Seventy-four *million* years! And that's just the upper ruins. This area below dates at over one hundred twenty-two million years!"

The professor leaned back, his eyes watching Rebecca's face intently as the weight of his words sank into her consciousness. Her brows furrowing in confusion, Rebecca was silent for several seconds as she contemplated his statement. "But that's impossible," she finally responded. "That would put it during the Cretaceous period, which was millions of years before…"

Dr. Eisenberg nodded his head in excitement as he finished her sentence, "…before humans even evolved."

Rebecca seemed frozen to the ground as the implications struck her full force. "Are you implying that aliens built this?"

"We're not *implying* anything. We *know* they did."

The sinister feeling Rebecca had felt before coming down the stairs seemed to engulf her once more. Then, afraid of his answer, she asked Dr. Eisenberg the question burning in her mind. "What do you mean?"

"The book we found contained the instructions for how to build a gravity control device," Dr. Eisenberg explained. "We knew this was bigger than we ever imagined, so we involved the U.S. and Iraqi governments as well as NASA. Our specialist did his best to translate the instructions, but it still took NASA over six months to build a prototype.

"Once it was completed," the professor continued, "our translator also discovered that the book explained how to open this door using the gravity control device." He placed his left hand on the door in front of them for emphasis.

"And what did you find?" Rebecca asked, uncertainty creeping into her voice.

"We found the remains of two of the aliens, as well as another book, and…another machine," Dr. Eisenberg said in hushed excitement.

Could it be true? Rebecca wondered, her mind reeling. *No, it can't be. Aliens can't be real. I know what I believe. Life was created by God, not through evolution. But if that's true, then how do I explain this?* Aloud, she numbly repeated Jeffrey's words, "This discovery will blow all of that religious junk back to the Middle Ages where it belongs!"

The professor, confused by her statement, simply asked, "What did you say?"

Looking up at him, she clarified her thought. "It was just something Jeffrey said to me the last time we spoke."

At the mention of her husband's name, Dr. Eisenberg's face took on a more serious look. "Yes…Jeffrey." Taking Rebecca by the shoulders, he looked at her with concern in his eyes. "Before we go into the main chamber, I…I have to tell you something about Jeffrey. I didn't want to tell you like this, but there's just no time to do it any other way."

The professor's voice and demeanor caused Rebecca to stiffen in concern. "What's wrong? Is he okay?"

"Yes, he's fine. But—"

Before he could finish his sentence, the door in front of them slid open. Standing in the doorway was a woman in her mid-thirties dressed in the typical dark blue jumpsuit with the NASA logo scrawled across the left breast. As soon as the door opened, she looked up from the clipboard in her hand, stared at Rebecca for a second, and then blurted out, "BECKY!"

2

REUNIONS

"LISA?" REBECCA ASKED in astonishment. "Lisa Staley, is that you?"

For a moment, the two women simply stared at each other. Then Rebecca dove forward and embraced her best friend as tears of joy sprang into her eyes. Whether it was due to the shock of seeing her or something else entirely, Lisa became rigid as Rebecca's arms enveloped her. A moment later, she relaxed and weakly returned the hug.

Pulling back from the embrace, Rebecca wiped the tears from her eyes and laughed. "Look at you! You cut your hair and got highlights!" she exclaimed as she pulled gently on the ends of Lisa's hair, which fell just below her ear.

Several seconds passed as Lisa just stared at Rebecca, as if still trying to accept the reality that she was actually there. Finally snapping out of her daze, Lisa glanced at Dr. Eisenberg, then back to Rebecca, her expression a mixture of surprise, confusion, and, oddly enough, something that bordered on discomfort or even fear.

"Oh, that," Lisa said, running her fingers through her hair. "I had that done months ago. I just got tired of taking care of it all of the time."

"Well, you look great!" Rebecca complimented. "And I see you're still keeping in shape. How are the girls? Jenny must be…what, fifteen now?"

"Sixteen, and going on twenty-five," Lisa corrected. "And Amanda becomes a teenager in April—God help me," she added with a forced smile.

Rebecca shook her head in amazement. "I can't believe it has been that long. It seems like just yesterday that we returned from Ka'esch—" she cut herself off, but it was too late. "I mean, 2021 PK."

Just as she had feared, Lisa's face changed slightly. Not much, but Rebecca knew her friend well enough to know that her usage of the name of the planet and not its designation made Lisa uncomfortable. Only a few of her family members and friends knew the truth about what had happened on that life-altering trip almost seven years ago.

And a couple of them, like Lisa and Jeffrey, didn't believe it. They found it easier to believe she had had an "intense dream" during her two-week coma rather than believe it had been a vision given to her by the Creator of the universe. Rebecca unconsciously reached up with her right hand to touch the circular scar that marred her skin beneath the clothing on her left arm, just above the elbow. She was thankful that God had left her with a physical reminder of the vision so she would forever know that what she experienced on Ka'esch had been more than just an "intense dream." Unfortunately, as powerful a reminder as it was to her, it was not enough to convince her husband or her best friend.

Rebecca and Lisa, both lost in their own thoughts brought on by Rebecca's remark, let an awkward silence hang heavily in the room.

Finally, clearing his throat, Dr. Eisenberg spoke up. "So, Mrs. Staley, what brought you into the antechamber?"

Taking a deep breath to shake off the momentary lull in the conversation, Lisa responded. "I came looking for you. I tried calling, but you must've turned off your comm."

Dr. Eisenberg nodded. "Yes, I did. Is something wrong?"

"No, nothing's wrong," she said with an odd note to her voice, as if referring to more than just the doctor's comment. "It's just that the techs said it should take them a couple of hours to install the core, and the brass wants us to run a test this evening at 1900 hours."

"Excellent. Thank you for letting me know," Dr. Eisenberg said. "Now, if you'll excuse us, I was just going to give Rebecca the grand tour," he continued as he put his arm around Rebecca and began to lead her past Lisa and through the doorway.

Before they had taken more than a step, Lisa held up a hand to stop them. "Wait. Doctor, I...I was also going to tell you that Dr. Jennings wants to see you," she said hurriedly. "She has a question about the Egyptian pyramids. Why don't you let me show Becky around? It'll give us a chance to catch up."

Although Rebecca had no idea why, it was obvious that Dr. Eisenberg wasn't at all happy with Lisa's suggestion. After a few seconds of consideration, he nevertheless capitulated. "Fine," he stated, his expression contradicting his words. Turning toward Rebecca, he put a hand on her shoulder. "It was wonderful to see you again, Rebecca, and I'm glad you're here. I'm sorry we didn't get a chance to...visit more. I'll see you later," he said, giving her a gentle kiss on the forehead. "Again, I...I am sorry."

Without waiting for a reply, Dr. Eisenberg glanced at Lisa, then headed back up the giant staircase. Rebecca watched him go, wondering exactly what was going on.

"So," Lisa said, bringing Rebecca's attention back toward her, "I was thinking—"

Rebecca, still puzzled by the previous conversation, interrupted her. "Lisa, first tell me what's going on."

Lisa frowned. "What do you mean?"

"C'mon, Lis. There was some definite tension between you and Dr. Eisenberg," Rebecca said, frustration altering the tone of her voice. "And he mentioned something about Jeffrey. What's wrong with him?"

Lisa's features softened as she looked at Rebecca. "Becky, I...well, the bottom line is... you need to talk to Jeffrey and ask him yourself. I didn't want Dr. Eisenberg to tell you something you should hear straight from Jeffrey."

The blood drained from Rebecca's face. "Tell me one thing: Is Jeffrey sick, or dying?"

Lisa tried to smile, but it was tinged with sadness. "No. It's nothing like that."

"Where is he?" Rebecca asked.

"He went into the city to pick up some supplies. He should be back soon," Lisa said. "Becky, I understand your concern. You know what? I think it might be better if we head back upstairs and wait until Jeffrey gets here. Whattaya say?"

Rebecca turned slowly to stare at the wall as she considered her friend's suggestion. She wondered whether she should just wait for him, and tried to fight off the nagging sense that whatever was going on obviously wasn't something good. Then again, she wanted to know what it was that Jeffrey was so convinced would challenge religion. In fact, it might be better for her to learn what that secret was without him around to complicate things.... At least it would help take her mind off whatever was going on.

But what if Jeffrey gets mad because I didn't wait for him to show me around? she couldn't help but wonder. If he did get angry, it could strain their relationship even further. *Lord help me,* she prayed fervently.

Making up her mind, Rebecca looked back at Lisa and shook her head. "No, I want to see it now, if you don't mind. It will be one less thing Jeffrey will have to worry about," she said, forcing a smile.

Lisa studied her friend's face for several seconds as if trying to read her mind. "Are you sure?" she pressed. "I really think you should wait for Jeffrey. You know how he is."

Rather than deter her, however, Lisa's words had the opposite effect. *She doesn't want me to go in there,* Rebecca suddenly realized. The two women had been friends since they met in the Marines almost twenty years ago. And although they hadn't seen much of each other in the last three years, Rebecca could still read Lisa well enough to know she was hiding something.

"My mind's made up, *Corporal*," Rebecca said, attempting to lighten the mood with a grin.

Clearly not thrilled with her friend's decision, Lisa resigned herself with a sigh. Then, with a grin of her own, she said, "Oh, I see how it is. You didn't have to pull rank on me. Right this way, Gunnery Sergeant, *Sir!*"

Stepping through the doorway, Lisa led Rebecca into the chamber beyond. Scattered throughout the large, rectangular room were numerous work stations, each occupied by NASA employees deeply engrossed in their individual tasks.

"This is what we call the 'workshop,'" Lisa said as they walked. "We call it that not only because this is where we do much of our work now, but because Jeffrey and Jerome believe this was the original workshop of the designer."

"The designer?" Rebecca asked.

Lisa stopped walking and faced Rebecca. "Yes. Weren't you briefed at all?"

Rebecca shook her head. "No. There wasn't time. Dr. Eisenberg was in the process of filling me in."

Lisa frowned. "You must've pulled quite a few strings to get here without having time for briefing. So, are you telling me you don't know what's here?"

"Only what Dr. Eisenberg told me," Rebecca replied. "He said that you found a couple of books and alien corpses. Was there something else?" she asked anxiously.

"Yes. That," she said, pointing to the far end of the room.

Looking past the throng of workers, Rebecca could see into the room beyond the chamber in which she currently stood. At first, her mind couldn't quite make sense of what she was seeing. Squinting her eyes, she began walking closer to get a better view. Suddenly her eyes grew larger and she stopped in her tracks. Turning back to face Lisa, who had followed her across the room, she frowned. "A pyramid? What's a pyramid doing underground inside another building?"

Lisa drew nearer as she answered. "It's more than just a pyramid. It's a spaceship!"

Rebecca sat in stunned silence for several seconds as she processed the news. "*That* is what the aliens flew in to get here? But how? Does it work? Where are the alien bodies now?"

Instead of answering her questions, Lisa placed her left arm around Rebecca's shoulder and steered her toward the right side of the room, which looked more like a laboratory than an archaeological dig. Various kinds of scientific equipment littered the tables and hung from the walls. Lisa led Rebecca to a door that appeared to lead into a storage closet, judging by the dimensions. As they neared the door, Lisa leaned over to one of the workers and whispered something into his ear. The man nodded, then resumed working.

As she placed her hand on the security panel and looked into the retinal scanner, Lisa said, "In here is where we keep the 'designer' and his 'bodyguard,' as we like to call them." She waited a second until she heard the telltale click of the lock, then grabbed the handle and pulled open the door.

Although Rebecca had tried to brace herself for whatever it was she would find inside the room, she was still shaken to the core by the sight of the two giant bodies resting inside the glass cases.

"Dear God!" she exclaimed in hushed awe.

"They are the real thing, Becky. You're looking at two genuine extra-terrestrials."

Rebecca's mind reeled. *Could it be true? But if there really are aliens, then how do they fit in with what I believe about God and the Bible? Were they also created by God? Think, Becky. When you come across something you don't understand, fall back on what you know to be true. I'm convinced that evolution can't be true, so that means they had to be created by God. But how does that fit with the Bible? Did God create some other race of beings on another planet?*

"It messes with your mind, doesn't it?" Lisa said. "I mean, we were always taught that if evolution could create life on earth, then it is statistically probable that evolution could create life on other planets as well. I just never thought I would live to see a real alien, even if it is dead. The funny thing is, they don't look anything like those pictures you see of the gray aliens with the big eyes and large heads."

Rebecca turned to look at her friend. "Lisa, you know I don't believe in evolution anymore."

Lisa returned her gaze. "I know," she said. "But then again, I thought maybe a little evidence like what we've found here might bring you back to the fold. So tell me, then, if evolution isn't true, how do you explain these?" she challenged, pointing at the bodies. "Does this look like the handiwork of God? Look at the teeth and the grotesque, animal-like features. These things don't look like they were created by a loving God, but rather by a mad scientist—or by evolution."

Suddenly, Rebecca remembered the words that Sikaris, the angel from her vision, had written in his last letter to her: "Always remember what you learned during your time on Ka'esch. Keep it in the forefront of your mind so that your faith will not waver during the difficult times that lie ahead." Closing her eyes, Rebecca shook her head to clear her mind and focus her thoughts. *Could this be what Sikaris was referring to?*

Looking back at Lisa, she replied firmly, "You see what you want to see because of what you believe. You believe evolution is true, so you see aliens. I believe we were created by God, and so I believe that, somehow, these creatures must have also been created. That doesn't necessarily mean they were created by God. Perhaps you were right when you said they were the creation of some mad scientist. I don't have the answers right now, but I'm going to rely on what I *know* to be true."

Lisa looked at her with frustration. "How can you hold to such a blind faith in the face of hard evidence?"

"But that's where you are mistaken," Rebecca countered. "It's not the evidence that we are disputing, but the *interpretation* of that evidence. These bodies didn't come with labels attached saying, 'Hi, I evolved.'"

"I hope you'll change your mind after you see their spaceship," Lisa replied sadly.

They stepped out of the storage area and Lisa resealed the door. As they headed back toward the center of the room, Rebecca spotted a familiar face approaching her, smiling as he drew near. Unlike most of the others she had seen, he wasn't wearing anything with a NASA logo or insignia. Instead, the six-foot-two man was dressed in a pair of tan pants and a simple brown polo shirt that matched his brown eyes and complemented his dark complexion and short hair. "Becky, it's good to see you again," he said warmly.

Returning the smile, Rebecca stepped forward to give him a welcoming embrace. "Jerome, how are you? It's been too long. How are Tarshwa and the kids?"

"Tarshwa just finished her second book. Her publisher said it should be out by next fall," Jerome said with pride. "The twins are doing great. They're sophomores now, can you believe it? And...and Joy is almost fully recovered."

Rebecca's expression filled with concern. "Yes, I heard about the accident. I'm glad to hear she pulled through."

"Yeah. It was tough on all of us. Especially Tarshwa. She somewhat blamed herself for letting Joy go to the prom with that jerk. I only wish I had been there instead of here," he said regretfully. "But that's all ancient history. So tell me, how have you been?"

"I've been okay, just working a lot," Rebecca said dryly. Not wanting to go into detail about her research against evolution, she simply changed the subject. "This is quite a place you have here. Lisa was just going to show me the ship."

"Actually...Jerome, would you do me a favor?" Lisa asked. "I've really got to go check on a couple of things. Would you mind showing Becky the ship?" she asked, sounding urgent.

Jerome looked at Lisa for a moment, and it seemed to Rebecca that something unspoken passed between the two others. "Sure, sure," Jerome said, his gaze returning to Rebecca. Then, holding his arm out for her to take, he said, "Right this way, ma'am."

Giving her a final embrace, Rebecca held Lisa at arm's length for a moment and smiled once again at her best friend. "Thanks, Lis. It's been so good to see you again. I'll see you around."

Lisa gave another awkward, halfhearted smile. "Yeah. See you around, Gunny," she replied, using Rebecca's military nickname.

Rebecca turned and followed Jerome as he led her toward the opening leading to the room with the pyramid. As they were about to enter the room, she gave one final glance in Lisa's direction to see her friend wiping away the vestiges of tears from her eyes.

3

THE PYRAMID

"SO WHATTAYA THINK? She's a beauty, huh?" Jerome asked, forcing Rebecca to put her concern for Lisa out of her mind.

"Yes, it is magnificent," she responded in genuine admiration of the fifty-foot pyramid looming before her. Its bulk covered most of the floor space in the room, leaving only fifteen feet on each side between the base of the pyramid and the wall. Ten of those fifteen feet were taken up by a flight of giant-sized steps that led from the five-foot walkway that encircled the room down to the pyramid itself. The size of the steps gave the chamber the overall effect of a square coliseum. Directly in front of her, at the bottom of the two-foot-wide steps, gaped the entrance to the pyramid. Even in the modern illumination, its massive maw seemed to beckon to Rebecca menacingly. A shudder passed down her spine at the mental images of what it would have looked like in the flickering flames from primitive torchlight.

Diverting her thoughts from their current disturbing path, she quizzed her new guide. "So you really think it's a spaceship? I mean, it doesn't seem to make sense to me. Where are the boosters? Are they buried under the floor? And how would it get out? Does the roof open up?"

"Well, we don't know exactly what the designer had in mind regarding the roof," Jerome answered. "The roof doesn't open, so we had a crew dig up the area. Once we have this thing running, which should be sometime this evening if all goes well, then they'll tear up the ceiling so we can get it out.

"As for the boosters," he said with a smile, "that's another thing entirely. They *are* buried in the floor, so to speak. I take it, then, that Lisa didn't tell you about Elmer or the technical journals?"

"Elmer? Who's Elmer?" Rebecca asked.

"Elmer is NASA's new toy. Its real, unimaginative name is 'Multi-Function Utility Droid.' We shortened it to MFUD, which sounds like Elmer Fudd—the character from that old cartoon that aired way back before the new millennium. You know, the one who used to chase that one rabbit—what's his name?"

"Beetles Bunny, wasn't it?" Rebecca offered.

Jerome laughed heartily. "No, not Beetles—Bugs!"

For the first time in recent memory, Rebecca let out a deep laugh that brightened her spirit and chased away her misgivings—at least momentarily.

"Yeah, so anyway, we now just call it Elmer. Come on. Let me give you a tour of the ship and then I'll introduce you to Elmer and show you the technical journals," Jerome said as he led Rebecca down the steps toward the entrance.

No matter how much Rebecca tried to shrug it off and chalk it up to superstition, she couldn't ward off the feeling that grew with each step she took towards the pyramid. A heavy, malevolent presence weighed upon her mind so much that as she stood at the threshold of the pyramid, she was forced to stop.

Jerome, noticing her discomfort, asked with concern, "Becky? Are you okay?"

What's wrong with me? she chastised herself. For a moment, she considered saying something to Jerome, but it was obvious that he didn't feel anything wrong, and it would probably just add fuel to the fire. After all,

Jerome and Jeffrey already thought she had gone a little crazy with her religious beliefs. *Lord, whatever it is, help me and protect me,* she prayed quickly. Although the presence was still there, she could feel it lighten somewhat, as if it had retreated a short distance away, but was still lurking and awaiting the chance to pounce once more.

"Yeah, I'm fine," she reassured him, offering the best smile she could muster. "It's nothing."

Not fully convinced, Jerome nevertheless let it pass, much to Rebecca's relief. Taking a steadying breath, she stepped inside the pyramid.

The entrance hallway extended twelve feet before branching off to the left and right, then continuing around to the back of the pyramid. Jerome led her to the fork, then stopped.

"The pyramid is basically built around this central room," he explained, indicating the wall directly in front of them. "This square room houses the power source for the entire ship—the core that arrived with you. The techs are installing it now, as a matter of fact, so I'll show it to you later. That's what all the noise is coming from around the passage to the right, in case you were wondering. It took us a while to find the entrance to that room. The only way in is through a secret door in the northeast corner. We never would have found it if we hadn't had the blueprints."

"These…aliens…just happened to leave you the blueprints?" Rebecca asked skeptically.

Jerome ran his hand over his cropped hair. "Well, it's not so much that they left them. You saw the bodies. We think the shorter one was in the process of finishing it when he died. Do you wanna see them?"

"The blueprints? Sure. Why not?" Rebecca asked in a mock casual tone.

Jerome took a step into the left passage, then turned to look towards the main entrance. Framing the entrance hallway from the inside were two doors, each facing rooms located in the southern section of the pyramid. "According to the blueprints, this was supposed to be the kitchen," Jerome said, grabbing the handle of the western door.

"The kitchen?" Rebecca asked. "You keep the blueprints in the kitchen?"

"No, this was *supposed* to be the kitchen, based on the original plans. Now, this is the office of the man who is in charge of them. After you," he said as he opened the door for her.

The room's lone occupant was a slightly overweight man in his mid-thirties. His black, greasy hair looked as if it hadn't been washed or combed in decades, and was matched by his wrinkled T-shirt, which sported the logo of some band Rebecca had never heard of. A pair of smudged blue jeans that looked like they might have been older than their current owner perfectly complemented the rest of the man's unkempt appearance. The most curious thing about him, however, was the simple fact that he was dancing and singing in the middle of the room even though Rebecca could hear no music.

"She's got the looks that KILL! Huh!" he grunted as he spun around in a complete circle, his white tennis shoes squeaking on the stone floor. As he finished his spin, he caught sight of Rebecca and Jerome standing in the doorway. Grinning sheepishly over his shoulder, he slowly turned the rest of his body around to face them. "Hi!" he said casually.

"Mack, I'd like you to meet—"

"Wait a second," Mack said abruptly. Reaching with his left index finger, he pressed down gently on his right wrist. Instantly, a blue-tinged holographic image appeared, hovering over his arm. Mack quickly touched a point on the image with his free hand, and then once again pressed the same spot on his arm, causing the image to vanish.

"Sorry about that. Now, with whom do I have the honor of making an acquaintance?" Mack asked cordially, his voice suddenly becoming deeper and more dignified.

"Mack, I'd like you to meet Rebecca," Jerome repeated.

Mack extended his right hand in greeting and gave Rebecca a weak handshake. "It's a pleasure to meet you, Rebecca."

"You too," she replied. "I'm going to be Dr. Eisenberg's new assistant."

"New assistant, huh?" Mack said, raising an eyebrow. "I didn't know he needed one."

Rebecca ignored the comment. "Pardon my asking, but what was that you did a moment ago with the hologram? I've never seen that before."

Jerome looked down at her and grinned. "Mack has made a few... additions to what nature gave him."

"I'd call them improvements, not just additions," Mack countered proudly. "This particular improvement happens to be a Lydian 3 nanoprocessor with holographic display and touchpad." Seeing that Rebecca didn't seem impressed, he assumed it was due to her obvious lack of understanding. Feeling the need to enlighten her, he expounded further. "In essence, I have an entire computer embedded under my skin, with a mini holographic imaging device that projects a computer keyboard and screen I can operate with a simple touch of my fingers."

This time, Mack's explanation produced the desired result. He watched in satisfaction as Rebecca's eyebrows rose in surprise. "That *is* quite an improvement."

"Yeah," Jerome said skeptically, "except that this particular improvement is connected to a set of nanospeakers embedded in his ears. Half the time, Mack's walking around jamming to music only he can hear."

"What can I say?" Mack said, grinning from ear to ear. "I'm a man who marches to the beat of a different drummer."

"That'd be fine if you only did it when you're alone. But it's quite annoying when others have to throw things at you just to get your attention!" Jerome countered.

Ignoring Jerome's tirade, Mack looked at Rebecca and asked, "So, to what do I owe the honor of your visit, Ms. Rebecca?"

"I'd like to show Rebecca the books we found in both the antechamber and the workshop," Jerome said, answering for her.

Mack's eyes lit up with excitement, and Rebecca noticed through the curtain of curly hair that his eyes had an odd, greenish-blue hue to them. *Probably another 'improvement,'* she thought.

"Sure! It would be my pleasure," Mack said as he beckoned them to follow him over to his work desk against the southern wall, which Rebecca guessed to be the outer wall of the pyramid, judging by its inverted slope. The rest of the room, she noticed with interest, contained an odd assortment of books written in several languages piled haphazardly on shelves and tables, mixed with various bits of science fiction and New Age paraphernalia.

Lying open on the desk were two strange-looking tomes, each bound in what looked to be a grayish-colored reptilian skin and measuring about a foot wide and fifteen inches in height. Mack pointed to the one on the left side of the desk as he spoke. "This was the first one Jerome and Jeffrey found in the antechamber. As you can see by the drawings, it describes how to make a gravity control device. Of course, it's written in a language no one has ever seen before. This posed a problem, but nothing too major. Once I realized it had some similarities to ancient Hebrew, the rest was downhill."

"Didn't Dr. Eisenberg recognize that it was similar to Hebrew?" Rebecca asked in an attempt to deflate Mack's bravado.

"Well, yeah," he stammered, "but there was much more to it than that. That was just the beginning. It still took me over three months to translate, and I had to do quite a bit of research."

"Indeed," Jerome said, picking up the story before it became sidetracked further. "Once Mack had the book translated, NASA began working on prototype models for the gravity control device."

"NASA has been trying to develop an anti-gravity device for years," Rebecca said. "I bet they were as excited as kids on Christmas morning."

"They may have been working on it for a while, but this design was completely different," Jerome explained. "It took them in a whole new direction. And even with the instructions and diagrams, and the best minds on the planet, it still took them more than half a year to finish the prototype."

"So it worked?" Rebecca asked excitedly.

"Like a charm," Mack chimed in. "I take it you haven't introduced her to Elmer yet, huh Jerome?"

"No, but that's our next stop," he replied. "Anyway, as it turns out, we couldn't open the door to the main chamber because—"

"Because of the invisible barrier," Rebecca finished for him. "Dr. Eisenberg mentioned that the book also told you how to bring it down."

"That's right. When we entered the main chamber, we found the two bodies Lisa showed you, as well as this second book," Jerome continued, pointing to the book on the right.

"This one took me even longer to translate," Mack said. "Even though I was starting to get the gist of the language, it was just much more complex and, as you can see, it's quite a bit thicker. But it was well worth it; this one tells how to build and operate the Pyramid of the Ancients!"

"The what?" Rebecca asked in confusion.

Jerome pursed his lips in mild annoyance. "'Pyramid of the Ancients' is the name Mack has lovingly given the ship."

"It's a great name, huh?" Mack asked, like a child seeking his parent's approval. "The way I figure it, the ancients are the alien astronauts who left the ship here millions of years ago."

"Anyway, as I started to tell you earlier," Jerome said, taking over the narrative once again, "it turns out that the ship's 'boosters' are four massive gravity control devices housed underneath the pyramid, one under each corner of the base."

"So the core that arrived with me today—" Rebecca began.

"—is the central power supply for the ship," Jerome finished. "NASA has been working on it since we found this book almost exactly two years ago. It's the last piece of the puzzle. Once it's installed, this baby should be ready for action! You arrived at the perfect time."

Rebecca, overwhelmed, simply shook her head in amazement.

"C'mon Becky. I've still got to introduce you to Elmer," Jerome said. "Thanks, Mack. We'll see you at the test run tonight."

"Sure, no problem," Mack replied. "It was a distinct pleasure to meet you, Ms...." Mack's words trailed off as he held his hand out once again towards Rebecca.

Rebecca grasped his hand firmly in her own as she replied. "Mrs. Evans."

Mack froze as if suddenly dropped in a vat of liquid nitrogen, his hand still holding Rebecca's. "Evans? As in—Jeffrey Evans?" he asked, his eyes widening.

"Yes. Jeffrey is my husband," Rebecca confirmed.

Although she didn't think it was possible, Mack's odd, greenish-blue eyes widened even farther, looking as if they were going to fall out of his skull at any second. He glanced at Jerome, then returned his gaze to Rebecca. After several seconds, his consciousness finally returned to reality. Realizing he was still holding Rebecca's hand, he quickly released it and apologized.

"S-sorry 'bout that," he said, obviously embarrassed. "It's just that I...I...you just caught me off guard, that's all."

"Thanks again, Mack," Jerome said quickly. "Becky, let's go, shall we?"

"Sure," Rebecca said numbly, her mind still pondering Mack's odd reaction to her name.

As they left the kitchen and headed toward the back of the pyramid, Rebecca quickly forgot about Mack's response as her attention became focused once more on examining her surroundings. She noticed that every six feet, the inner wall turned toward the outer, western wall for another six feet, then turned back north again to repeat the process. After three of these repetitions, the pattern inverted itself as they passed the center of the pyramid and began approaching the northernmost section of the structure.

Rather than going into one of the doors in front of them, however, Jerome led her up a steep stairway that ran along the outer side of the central room's northern wall. Based on the sounds coming from around the corner as they ascended the stairs, it appeared that the techs were still busy installing the power core.

At the top of the stairway, Rebecca and Jerome entered into a small, square room twenty-four feet on each side. The walls sloped inward towards the center of the room, indicating they were obviously in the apex of the pyramid. Where the four walls should have converged, however, was a six-foot-square gap in the ceiling. Directly below the gap, in the center of the room, was a large, square pedestal made out of a silvery material that shimmered in the fluorescent light. The pedestal was the same width as the gap, and it reached up from the floor to stop several feet shy of the opening.

Running nearly the entire length of the southern wall was a control console containing a myriad of knobs, buttons, levers, and displays, all with labels written in the same strange language as the technical journals she had seen in Mack's office. Due to the unusual height of the console, several bar stools were placed in front of it at various intervals.

All this initially escaped Rebecca's notice as she entered the room. For the moment her foot hit the top step, her attention had been captured by the sight of a tall African woman crouched in front of a cylindrical robot that rested on the floor next to the pedestal. The torso of the machine, which Rebecca guessed to be roughly three feet in diameter and nearly the same in height, rested on a triangular base, with smaller, eight-inch cylinders underneath each point of the triangle. The head of the droid wasn't much more than a black cylinder with a domed top and tiny lights, which seemed to resemble beady eyes. Its vocalizer was nothing but a series of small holes in the vague shape of a mouth located just under the eyes. All in all, it was apparent that the droid was built more for function than aesthetics.

As Rebecca and Jerome approached, the woman acknowledged their arrival with barely a glance in their direction. Stepping closer to the droid, Rebecca noticed one of its front panels was open and the woman was busy adjusting some of the inner circuitry.

"Yes, Jerome? Do you need someting?" she asked in her heavy accent, her eyes never once straying from her work.

"Akwen, I'd like you to meet Rebecca. She's Dr. Eisenberg's new assistant. I'm just showing her around, and I wanted to introduce her to you and Elmer," Jerome said.

Akwen looked up momentarily, judged her with a simple glance, and then summarily dismissed her as unimportant. Out of politeness, however, she replied, "Nice to meet you. As for Elmer, if you want to actually speak to him, you will have to wait a few more moments. In case you cannot tell, he is currently experiencing anoder glitch and I had to shut him down."

Jerome's brows furrowed. "That's the third one this week, isn't it? That can't be good."

"Well, dey don't call it a prototype for noting," she said, seeming annoyed at his comment. "Dere. I tink I got it." Standing to her feet, she brushed off her blue NASA coveralls, removed the tie from her straight, shoulder-length hair, and proceeded to return wayward strands to their original positions. She was a beautiful woman, but her thick bones and nearly six-foot stature left no doubt in Rebecca's mind that this was a woman you wouldn't want to trifle with. Her hair once more firmly secured, Akwen looked down at the droid and said, "Elmer, power on."

Immediately, the lights that served as the droid's photoreceptors lit up and the head began to swivel around in a 360-degree circle, as if carefully analyzing its surroundings. A moment later, the cylinders on the triangular base began to emit a dark blue light accompanied by a gentle hum as the droid rose slowly into the air.

"Greetings, Dr. Nancho. How may I be of service?" it asked in a pleasant tenor voice.

Looking impatiently at Rebecca, she said, "Dis is Elmer. His official title is Multi-Function Utility Droid. He was designed to be able to perform many different tasks. Each of dese compartments around his torso contains a different tool. His entire torso rotates to give him more flexibility when trying to use a tool in tight places. What else would you like to know?"

In an effort to ward off any further ire from Akwen, Jerome decided to continue to the explanation himself. "Elmer also contains one of the first computers to use a set of the new Biomatrix information storage chips."

"Really," Rebecca said, impressed. "I've heard about those. They modeled them after the informational storage capabilities of DNA, right?"

"Yeah, and our pal Elmer here has a complete set of them," Jerome replied. "Hook him up to a terminal and he syncs up his memory with the contents of the *entire* World Wide Web!"

"It's not quick, doh," Akwen corrected. "First you have to get him hooked up correctly, which takes awhile, den you have to leave him dere for ahlmost a week. Now, if you will bot excuse me, I need to take Elmer back to my workshop to run a full systems check. Elmer, let's go."

"Thanks, Akwen," Jerome said as she nodded briefly and began heading towards the stairs, the droid following behind her like an obedient puppy.

"It was nice to meet you," Rebecca called out as Akwen reached the steps. Her only reply was a halfhearted wave of the hand. Once Akwen and Elmer were gone, Rebecca looked over at Jerome and gave him a lopsided grin. "She seems like a real pleasure to have around, huh?"

Her companion chuckled lightly. "Yeah, about as much fun as a root canal. In case you hadn't guessed, she has a slight prejudice against Americans. *Especially* American women. C'mon, I need to check in with the techs to see what the progress is on the installation of the core."

As the two headed down the steps, Rebecca spoke. "Speaking of the core, it seems like the pedestal in the control room is a shaft that leads down into the central core room. Is that right?"

"Yes. We're not exactly sure how it all works, but it seems that the power emitted by the core is concentrated through four conduits in the floor of the central room towards the four gravity control engines, as well as up through the shaft and out through the top gap," Jerome answered as they reached the bottom of the steps. Turning to the right, they made their way around the northern edge of the room housing the core.

"I can understand why it would send power to the engines," Rebecca mused, "but why send energy out the top of the ship?"

"Again, we're not sure, but if all goes well with the test in a few hours, we should find out soon enough," he said, stopping as they rounded the corner of the stairs. As they arrived, the last of the techs who had been installing the core were exiting the central room and closing the door behind him.

Suddenly, Rebecca caught sight of the figure of a man entering the pyramid. Instantly, she felt her face flush and her pulse quicken. It was amazing that after all these years, just the sight of his dark brown, wavy hair and chiseled features was enough to cause her heart to flutter. Although he had gained a few extra pounds over the years, his typical well-worn jeans and tucked-in, solid gray T-shirt still fit him comfortably. He may not have been the most handsome man in the world, but their history together had forged a bond that had deepened her love for him. This time, however, her excitement was mingled with uncertainty. She felt a rush of jumbled emotions crashing over her, leaving her feeling confused and disoriented.

As he rounded the corner, their eyes locked and he stopped in his tracks. Try as she might, Rebecca found it impossible to read his thoughts. His face had become an impenetrable mask, his feelings locked up securely in an emotional vault of his own making.

"Hi, Jeffrey," she said cautiously. "Surprise."

"I was told you were here," he said, his voice inflectionless. "Thanks for showing her around, Jerome. Give me a few minutes here, then we need to meet to discuss a recent development."

"Sure," Jerome nodded, seeming eager to leave them alone. "It was great to see you again, Becky. See ya around." Rebecca's mind was so focused on Jeffrey that later she could only vaguely remember saying goodbye to Jerome.

As he and the last tech were exiting the pyramid, Rebecca reached up and touched the hair on Jeffrey's chin. "I see you're sporting a mustache and goatee now. It looks nice—"

"What are you doing here?" her husband interrupted in a forced whisper, his voice a mixture of frustration and disappointment.

His response only triggered Rebecca's own emotions. "Gee, a simple, 'Hi, how are you?' might be nice. Why do you *think* I'm here? I came to see you. After all, I am still your wife."

A momentary flicker of…something…crossed his face. "Becky, this is the last thing I need to deal with right now. In case you haven't noticed, I'm in the middle of something extremely important. In just a few hours, this thing goes online. I'm sorry, but I just can't drop everything and go out to see a movie with you."

A kind word turns away wrath. The words echoed in her mind, their truth causing the scathing retort she had been about to unleash to catch in her throat. Taking a deep breath, she eventually reeled in her own frustration and anger. "I understand, Jeffrey. I'm not asking you to drop everything right this minute. I just wanted to be near so that when you *do* get a free moment, we can spend some time together. This is obviously an important day for you. I won't get in the way. I don't want to cause you trouble."

As she spoke, Jeffrey's anger began to defuse. Finally, he took a deep breath of his own, and his expression changed to one of worry. "That's good, because I have enough trouble already."

"What do you mean?" she asked, alarmed.

"I just got word that someone sold a copy of the technical specs for the gravity control device on the black market. To make matters worse, it turns out they were purchased by a terrorist organization."

4

TEST AND TRIAL

TRUE TO HER word, Rebecca made herself scarce during the rest of the evening, despite the fact that every fiber of her being wanted to talk to Jeffrey one on one to find out what had Dr. Eisenberg and Lisa bothered and upset. However, she knew that forcing the issue during such a critical time in Jeffrey's work would only drive him farther away. Since Dr. Eisenberg and the others were busy preparing for the testing of the ship, she decided to spend the remaining couple of hours familiarizing herself with the layout of the compound.

As 1900 hours drew closer, she decided it was time to join the rest of the techs, scientists, and military personnel gathered outside the fabricated building covering the dig to watch the progress of the test on monitor screens. Due to the uncertain outcomes that could result from the test, only those directly involved would remain inside the chamber.

Rebecca scanned the crowds standing in front of the various screens set up specifically for the test in search of Jeffrey or Dr. Eisenberg. She finally spotted her husband standing next to Jerome, Lisa, and Akwen at one of the terminals to her left. She was about to head over to the group when she heard Dr. Eisenberg calling her name behind her. She turned to see him standing next to Mack, who signaled for her to join them. For a moment, she was torn as she tried to decide which way to go. She chose to work her way through the crowd to join the doctor. The last thing she wanted was to be a distraction to Jeffrey.

"They are down to the last thirty seconds," Dr. Eisenberg said when she drew within earshot. As the final countdown began, she found herself thinking back to what Jeffrey had said a couple of hours earlier. A digital copy of the technical specs for the gravity control device had been sold to terrorists. Only someone with a fairly high level of clearance would even have access to those documents. She had been allowed to see them only because of her history with NASA and because of her relationship with Jeffrey and Dr. Eisenberg—and even then, she was not allowed access to digital copies.

That meant someone in the inner circle had sold them out.

It was bad, but it wasn't like it was a weapon or even the ship specs… at least, as far as they knew. The military had been able to discover this breach of security, but what if there were others they hadn't caught?

Her thoughts were brought back to the present by a firm, militaristic voice coming through the loudspeaker. "Five…four…three…two… one…initiating power sequence."

A palpable silence fell over the onlookers as they waited…and waited…and waited. Finally, after several minutes, the loudspeaker came to life again. This time, a different voice spilled forth; the words were colored by frustration and disappointment. "Command, the ship is not powering up. We tried the sequence three times, but still nothing. It seems that we may have to go back to the drawing board."

Tendrils of disappointment quickly worked their way through the crowd. So many hours of work, so much effort, and they *still* had nothing to show for it. Rebecca glanced over at Jeffrey and saw that his left hand was resting against his forehead. Next to him, Lisa appeared to be offering words of encouragement while Jerome placed a reassuring hand on his shoulder.

As she stood watching them, trying to decide whether to go over and offer her own consolation, one of the techs came walking up at a brisk pace. "Dr. Eisenberg, Mr. Nielson, Colonel Mellic would like to speak to you immediately."

"Of course," Dr. Eisenberg sighed. "Tell him we are on our way."

Mack's facial expression clearly reflected his puzzlement. "I don't get it, Doc. Did *we* miss something, or do you think it is a tech issue?"

"I don't know, but I'm sure Colonel Mellic wants us pouring over the journals one more time just to make sure." Turning to face Rebecca, the professor said, "I know you have had a rough trip, and it looks like it may be a long night for us. There is a cot set aside for you in tent B8. Why don't you turn in, and we'll talk in the morning?"

A sudden weariness stole over her body as if the doctor's words had somehow caused it to manifest itself. "Thank you, Doc. I appreciate it."

"Good night, Rebecca," he said with a smile.

"Good night, both of you," she said, waving to them as they departed.

Once they had left, Rebecca looked briefly for Jeffrey. But as she expected, he was already long gone. Retrieving her bags from the jeep, she headed off towards B8 and located the tent without any problem. Finding her cot, she dropped her bags unceremoniously onto the floor and lay down wearily on the hard mattress. Despite her tiredness, she found it difficult to sleep. Too much had happened, and too many unanswered questions were still floating around inside her mind. Finally, after trying to sleep—unsuccessfully—for several hours, she got up, put on a pair of jeans and a navy blue T-shirt with a Marines logo on the sleeve, grabbed her black leather jacket, and stepped out into the crisp night air to clear her head.

As she walked, she began to pray softly, her prayers vanishing into the night along with the vapor caused by her warm breath on the cool night air. She passed several guards dutifully patrolling the grounds, as well as several civilians, but for the most part, the camp was quiet. If they were still working to fix the ship, there was no sign of it above ground.

Lord, what am I doing here? Rebecca prayed, her eyes drifting upward to rest on the panorama of stars stretched across the night sky. *Give me wisdom and help me say and do the right things. With all that's going on, how am I going to find a minute to talk with Jeffrey? If only…* Without even realizing it, Rebecca had been walking toward the entrance to the dig site. Much to her surprise, Jeffrey opened the door and began walking down the path to her left.

Without even thinking, she called out softly. "Jeffrey."

He stopped and turned in her direction, squinting to see in the dim night lights of the compound. "Who is it?"

She took a step toward him, allowing one of the area lights to shine on her face. As recognition set in, Jeffrey's head drooped immediately and his shoulders slumped. Letting out a defeated sigh, he spoke, his voice taking on an edge of weariness. "Look, Becky, I…I really don't feel like talking right now. It has been a long, trying day. I just want to go to bed."

What is wrong with him? Am I that much of a burden? Rebecca struggled against the pain and anger that threatened to rise up within her. "I didn't mean to bother you; I was…I am just concerned," she said with uncertainty. "How is everything with the…the ship? Did they find out what the problem was?"

"No. Nobody has a clue," Jeffrey answered, frustration evident in his voice. "Why are you still awake, anyway?"

"I…I couldn't sleep," she said truthfully. "I was…I am worried."

Jeffrey, sensing what was next, tried to cut her off. "Becky, not tonight. I—"

"—Jeffrey, please," she blurted out, losing her inward battle for control as she stepped closer to him. "I need to know what's going on with you."

She half expected him to deny that anything was wrong and ask her what she was talking about. Instead, he just stared at her for a few moments in silence. Then, resigning himself to his fate with a heavy sigh, he said, "What…where do you think those creatures down there came from?"

"Don't try to dodge the issue—"

"I'm not," Jeffrey added quickly. "I just…your answer is important."

She studied his face skeptically, trying to figure out how her answer could possibly have anything to do with their relationship. Finally giving up, she answered him simply. "I don't know what I believe yet. This is all so new, and I need more time to study the evidence."

Jeffrey wasn't satisfied with her answer; his expression told her so as clearly as if he had spoken the words aloud. "Yes, but do you believe they are aliens?"

Rebecca paused to consider how to best phrase her response. "You know I don't believe in evolution," she said. "Therefore, I don't believe that life can evolve on other planets. If they are aliens, then they had to be created by God, and I just don't believe, based on their appearance, that God would create anything so…I don't know…vile."

"If they're not aliens, then how do you explain them and the ship, and the language?" Jeffrey asked.

"I don't know," Rebecca said, beginning to lose her patience at his persistence. "I've been thinking a lot about it, but I need to do some research. It's possible that these are some of the ancestors of the half-human, soulless beings that lived about fifty thousand years ago, before God created Adam and Eve. Their bone structure, particularly their cranial shape, does match those of some of the australopithecine fossils."

Jeffrey stared at her as if she had just gone mad. "Listen to you! I can't believe you really believe that garbage! You talk as if Adam and Eve were real people. They weren't. It's just an old Jewish myth. It's not real history. And why would God make half-humans before Adam? Was He just practicing? The Rebecca I knew would never believe such bunk."

Before she could even think of a defense, he continued, as if an emotional dam had burst. "Look, I don't know what happened to you on that planet, but whatever dream or vision you had, that is no reason to give up on science and logic. I refuse to accept things on blind faith. Unlike you, I can't just check my brain at the door to the church."

Stung by his words, Rebecca initially felt her face flush in shame.

However, something in her spirit rose up, causing her flush to darken further in conviction. "No, you're wrong. Your beliefs are still based on faith, just like mine. This is not a religion-versus-science issue. It is worldview versus worldview, and interpretation versus interpretation. The question is: Which of our faiths is best supported by the facts? Your faith is in men's fallible theories that change all the time. My faith is in a God who never changes, who has been there since before the beginning of time."

Jeffrey remained silent for several seconds, allowing Rebecca's words to hang in the air. "Rebecca...you wanted to know what's 'wrong' with me, but the truth is that it's not something wrong with *me*, but rather what's wrong with *you*. *I* am the same person I've always been since we met. But *you* have changed. How...how can we make a relationship work when we don't have the same beliefs or...? We barely even have anything in common anymore."

The weight of Jeffrey's words crushed Rebecca's spirit. *Oh, God. No. Please don't let it be so.* "Jeffrey...what...what are you saying?" she asked, her voice barely a whisper.

"I'm saying that...that I think maybe it would be best if we just went our separate ways."

The pressure on her chest, although brought about by her mental stress, manifested itself physically by constricting her breathing. Turning away from him, she hugged herself, as much to ward off the chill of the evening air as to hold together the fractured pieces of her heart.

Jeffrey, seeing her distress, ran his hand absentmindedly through his hair as he searched for words. "What kind of life could we really have together?" he asked. "Isn't marriage supposed to be about sharing your dreams and desires? Isn't that what real intimacy is all about? We would never truly be a part of the other person's world because each of our worlds is based on completely different foundations." Uncomfortable with the silence and not knowing what else to do, Jeffrey continued. "This way, we can each find someone who shares our same interests and goals. Someone who could fulfill us...make us whole. Someone who could fill the emptiness in our hearts."

Rebecca shook her head as hot tears slid down her cheeks. Staring at the ground, she said sadly, "No, Jeffrey. No person on this earth can truly fill that emptiness. There's only One who could do that."

"I'm sorry, Rebecca," Jeffrey replied softly. "We've just grown apart. It's time to begin a new chapter of our lives. At least we don't have any children to complicate things."

A soft moan escaped from Rebecca's lips and she sank to the ground. Wrapping her arms tightly around her bent legs, she put her head between her knees and began to weep softly.

"Becky, I...I..." Jeffrey said, realizing his thoughtless words had only driven the knife deeper into her heart. "I didn't mean..."

"Just go away," came her muffled reply. "Please."

Not knowing what else to do or say, Jeffrey simply stood motionless. Finally, repeating to himself over and over that this was for the best, he turned and started walking away. Before he had taken more than half a dozen steps, he felt his phone vibrating in its belt clip. Mechanically, he reached down, unclipped it, and raised it to his ear. "What is it, Mack?" he asked numbly.

Mack's excited voice came through loudly from the phone's speaker. "Jeffrey, we figured it out! We know why the ship didn't power up! It turns out we mistranslated a couple of prepositions, which completely changes the power-up sequence."

Despite the current depressed state of his emotions, a surge of excitement flooded through Jeffrey. "Mack, that is fantastic news. Are you sure that's the problem?"

"Hey, is Yoda green and wrinkled?"

"I'll, uh, take your word for it. Are you still in your office?"

"Yeah. I'm here with Dr. Eisenberg."

"Good," Jeffrey replied, his mind quickly banishing all thoughts of Rebecca. Action. This was exactly what he needed. This was where he felt in control. "I didn't see Lisa or Akwen leave the site, so they're probably still around. Call them and have one of them contact Colonel Mellic. I'll call Jerome and have him—"

His progress back towards to dig site was halted abruptly by a sight that turned his blood to water. Standing inside the outer walls of the compound about two hundred feet away was the frightening visage of two dozen gray-skinned aliens, whose soulless black eyes stared coldly at him with the promise of death.

5

INVASION

WHETHER IT WAS due to some power the aliens held or simply to overwhelming terror, Jeffrey's muscles were unresponsive, completely refusing to obey his mental commands. The invaders stared at him for several more seconds, then began to turn in slow motion, as if in a nightmare.

Suddenly, bright lights flared around him and cries rang out through the night as the soldiers in the guard towers brought their searchlights to bear on the beings who somehow managed to materialize out of thin air. A second later, the deafening sounds of heavy laser fire shook Jeffrey from his lethargic state. The soldiers opened fire, but incredibly, the blue beams from the soldiers' weapons passed straight through the creatures. As soon as the first few shots struck the ground, the aliens moved into action.

Still in shock, Jeffrey could only stare in amazement at the aliens darting across the compound. Guards from the towers fought hard to keep the area lit, but the beings kept leaping around so quickly and moving off in different directions that it became impossible to keep track of them.

A new shout drew Jeffrey's attention to the right as a group of soldiers came running toward the aliens, laser rifles blaring. Oddly enough, although the creatures were being fired at from all directions, they seemed content to simply run, dodge, and leap away from their attackers instead of returning fire or going on the offensive. Some even began to dematerialize in one place, then reappear twenty feet away, further adding to the chaos.

Suddenly a hand grabbed Jeffrey's shoulder, causing him to wheel around in fright. He spun so fast, however, that his feet slipped out from under him and he fell backwards onto the ground. Staring up at him was the ghostly white face of his wife.

"Jeffrey, are you okay?" she asked, her voice trembling.

His eyes wide and his hand clutching his chest, he took in several quick breaths before answering. "Becky...thank...God...it's only you."

Glancing around in fear, she reached down and pulled Jeffrey to his feet. "We've gotta get out of here."

"Yeah," Jeffrey replied, his own gaze fixated on the surrounding confusion. Not more than fifty feet away, a soldier screamed in pain as a beam of green light pierced his side, dropping him to the ground. As Jeffrey watched him fall, he saw two shadowy forms detach themselves from one of the nearby buildings and begin heading rapidly in his direction. They didn't seem to have any physical substance, but appeared to be made of some kind of mist. He could make out a vague humanoid shape and what looked like small horns cresting the heads, but all else was shrouded in shadow as they moved in his direction.

Jeffrey cursed violently, then grabbed Rebecca's hand and began running toward the opening of the dig site as if the very hounds of hell were on their heels. As they reached the entrance, a soldier from the inside opened the right door just enough for them to get through. Jeffrey shoved Rebecca in, then threw one last quick look at the approaching shapes. Staring back at him were two sets of small, blood-red eyes so dark they were almost lost in the blackness of the night. Frozen in horror, Jeffrey stood in the doorway until a hand grabbed him around the arm and pulled him inside just as a blast of green energy hit the wall where his head had been seconds earlier.

The soldier who had just saved Jeffrey's life slammed the door shut. Gasping, Jeffrey looked at the man and swallowed hard. "Thank...thank you," he managed. "There are two...things...like shadows...out there. They're coming toward the door!"

"Go downstairs by the ship. You should be safe there. I'll radio the team below to let them know you're coming," the soldier said as he and the ten other soldiers with him took up positions facing the door.

"C'mon," Rebecca urged, grabbing Jeffrey's hand again. Together they ran full speed toward the entrance to the stairwell. Jeffrey began fumbling with the retinal scanner and laser reader the moment they arrived. Just as the lock clicked open, Rebecca gasped, causing Jeffrey to spin around. Impossibly, another dozen aliens stood in the center of the room behind the guards, who were still facing the door.

"Behind you!" Rebecca screamed, pointing at the aliens. The soldiers whirled around and began firing, causing the aliens to jump out of the way. However, the moment their backs were turned, the entrance doors exploded, sending the soldiers tumbling to the floor. Before they could recover, beams of green light lanced out from the now-open doorway to finish off the men. Despite the fact that there were no more attackers, the aliens continued to leap and dodge back and forth like dancing nymphs as two dark figures came floating through the smoke and debris of the explosion. Spurred into action by their fear, Jeffrey and Rebecca flung open the door and ducked inside, pulling it closed behind them.

"Jeffrey, what are those things?" Rebecca asked as they fled down the stairs.

"I don't know," he said between gasps for air. "I was...going to ask you...the same...question."

They had barely reached the bottom of the steps when the door behind shuddered as something heavy pounded on it, sending tiny showers of dust down upon them. "Do you think it'll hold?" Rebecca asked.

"I don't know, but I'm not waiting around to find out," Jeffrey replied as they stepped through the door and into the workshop. The moment they cleared the opening, several soldiers exited into the antechamber and took up positions on each side of the stairs, weapons pointed at the door above while several others stayed back just inside the open door of the main chamber. The beating from above suddenly ceased, replaced by an eerie silence.

Jeffrey and Rebecca stopped and stared back the way they had come, hoping beyond hope it was over. As they stood there, one of the soldiers approached. "What happened up there?" he whispered.

"Watch your backs, Colonel," Jeffrey replied quickly. "Somehow, the aliens seem to be able to teleport, or something. One minute they were outside the door, and the next second they were standing right behind us. But for some reason, the aliens don't seem to be attacking. There are two shadowy, demon-like things that you need to really worry about, though. They—"

Before Jeffrey could finish his thought, an explosion from the top of the stairs sent shock waves through the entire chamber. Without hesitation, the guards at the bottom of the stairs opened fire.

"Hurry!" the colonel shouted at them. "Get into one of the storage rooms and hide. Here, take these," he added tossing them two handheld laser pistols. Turning back to his men, he commanded, "Michael, Jonas, watch our backs. Make sure none of those—"

Before he could even finish his sentence, another group of twelve aliens materialized directly in front of Rebecca and Jeffrey, surrounding them and the soldiers in a semicircle. Letting out a scream, Rebecca lifted her weapon towards them and prepared to fire.

God help us! she prayed fervently. Just as she was about to pull the trigger, however, something within her caused her to hesitate. The aliens before them appeared…different. Now that she was just a few feet away from them in better lighting, she could tell that something wasn't right about the way they looked. They seemed…fuzzy, as if they weren't real.

Run through them. The thought hit her with such suddenness and with such clarity that she didn't pause to think through her actions. "Jeffrey, run towards them. *Now!*" she yelled as she sprinted straight at the beings.

"What? Becky, *wait!*" Jeffrey called after her.

She braced herself for impact as she barreled toward the creature. However, the collision never occurred. Instead, the moment she should have come into contact with the alien, it disappeared, sending her tumbling off balance onto the floor of the chamber. Jeffrey, seeing what happened, immediately stopped firing his gun and rushed after her. Picking her up off the floor, he glanced back at the soldiers, still busy firing at the nimble aliens.

"What...what happened?" he asked, dumbfounded.

"I don't know," she replied, shaking her head. "Somehow I just knew they wouldn't attack. For some reason they seem to be ignoring us. C'mon, now's our chance. Let's go," she said as she headed toward one of the storage rooms at the end of the chamber.

"No," Jeffrey said, grabbing her arm near the elbow. "Let's get to the ship." Pulling out his comm as they ran, he called out, "Akwen, can you hear me?"

"Yes, I hear you. What is going on out dere?" Akwen replied anxiously.

"We're under attack. I want you to start the power-up sequence immediately. Once you have power, I want you to shut the outer door of the ship—understood?"

"Yes, but—"

"No time for questions!" Jeffrey shouted. "Becky and I are almost inside. Now *DO IT!*" He cut the connection and returned his comm to his pocket as they reached the inner chamber that housed the pyramid. Once they were through the opening, Jeffrey slammed his hand down on the button that closed the wall-sized door separating the two chambers. When the door began to close, he took one last look back into the workshop and saw to his dismay that the battle was nearly over. The last couple of soldiers had begun retreating quickly along the wall of the chamber, but they were quickly cut down by several quick bursts of green light that seemed to emanate from the two dark shapes that had just appeared in the doorway leading into the workshop.

"They're still coming!" Jeffrey cried, panic eroding his calm. Once the door was completely closed, he engaged the locking mechanism, and together he and Rebecca headed down the steps toward the main entrance to the pyramid, where Jerome stood waiting.

"Do you think it will hold them?" Rebecca asked, desperate for Jeffrey's assurance.

"Hold who? What's going on?" Jerome asked.

Jeffrey simply shook his head, his own fear giving way to frustration and anger. "How should I know? I thought the main door leading to the stairwell was supposed to be able to withstand an explosion, yet they blew right through it anyway. Our security measures only seem to slow them down."

As if to punctuate his words, the three heard the unmistakable sound of the locking mechanism on the massive door begin to disengage.

"What? That…that's impossible!" Jerome said, his body rigid with shock.

Ducking down behind the right edge of the doorframe with his laser pistol primed and ready in his right hand, Jeffrey grabbed his comm with his left and flicked it on. "Akwen, we need you to close this door NOW!"

"We are almost ready. Just a few more seconds," she replied curtly.

The wall-sized door slid open, then abruptly stopped after just a few feet. The familiar green beams of energy flew out of the opening and struck several of the light fixtures in the large chamber, sending showers of sparks and broken glass in all directions as they exploded. Immediately, the brightness in that portion of the chamber grew darker, momentarily blinding them as their eyes adjusted to the new light.

"Jerome, you can't do any good here," Jeffrey said as he squeezed off several shots toward the now-open doorway. "Becky and I will try to slow them down. Go see if you can give Akwen a hand."

His voice too weak to even reply, Jerome simply nodded in agreement and headed off into the pyramid toward the stairs leading up to the control room.

"Can you see them?" Rebecca asked her husband as she fired off several shots of her own, her body safely hidden behind the door frame on the left side.

"No. It's too dark to—wait! I just saw movement off to the left. Look out!" Jeffrey shouted as a large projectile hurtled toward them in the dark and exploded just outside the entrance of the pyramid, sending them sprawling across the floor of the entrance hallway.

Barely conscious, Rebecca lifted her head off the floor and looked over to see Jeffrey's unmoving body lying face down several feet to her left. Turning back to face the entrance, the last thing she saw before darkness claimed her were two sets of murderous red eyes moving towards the pyramid…

"Five…four…tree…two…one…*Ignition!*" Akwen called out, her voice a mixture of excitement and trepidation as she moved the final lever in the power-up sequence all the way to maximum. Instantly, the control panels lit up as energy coursed through the circuitry.

"Hah! I knew it!" Mack shouted, slapping the back of his right hand into his open left palm in excitement. In his enthusiasm, he accidentally knocked over the stool he had been sitting on moments earlier, sending it crashing to the floor of the control room. "Now let's get the door shut—"

But even as Mack's finger hovered over the button that would shut the outer door, the light on his display screen switched on its own accord. "What the…?" Mack stammered. "The door just closed by itself," he said in amazement, looking over at Akwen, who stood on his right.

Suddenly, several of the display screens lit up with row upon row of strange numbers and symbols as a low rumble passed through the ship. Lisa jumped back from her control panel as if she had been bitten by a snake. "What was that?" she asked, her voice quavering.

Before anyone could respond, the ship shuddered and rocked, causing each of them to grab on to the control console to keep from falling over. "Akwen, shut it off!" Mack yelled as panic threatened to overwhelm him.

"I'm trying!" she yelled back, her own terror causing her voice to raise an octave. "Noting is responding!"

"What's going on?" Jerome asked from behind them as he reached the top of the steps.

"Elmer!" Akwen called out to the droid that hovered near her right shoulder. "What are dese numbers?"

"They appear to be calculations," the droid replied in its always-calm voice.

"Calculations for what?" Mack asked nervously.

"Oh, my Lord," Dr. Eisenberg whispered softly; the pallor in his face sent chills through each of them.

"What's wrong?" Lisa asked from beside him, giving voice to the concern written on each of their faces.

He lifted his head and regarded each of them in turn, his features frozen in a mask of shock and dismay. "I believe the ship is taking off…"

6

LIFTOFF

"TAKING OFF!" MACK repeated in alarm. "As in 'going up'? But we'll smash into the ceiling of the chamber!"

Akwen shot him a frustrated look. "Tank you for pointeen out da obvious," she said as she shoved him out of the way. Her fingers moved over the controls, frantically trying to find something that would respond to her commands. After several seconds, she slammed her hand down on the edge of the panel and swore vehemently. "Elmer, can you use your computer interface to connect with da ship and shut down de power?" she asked.

"I will try to do so, Dr. Nancho," Elmer said as it floated toward the right side of the control panel that housed the interface. As it moved, its entire torso rotated in a clockwise direction until the arm containing the computer attachment was facing forward. Elmer reached the port and plugged in while the five men and women waited anxiously. Although in reality it only took a few seconds, it seemed to Akwen and the others as if several days had passed. Finally, Elmer's rounded head turned toward Akwen, its small, beady eyes looking at her dispassionately.

"I am sorry, Dr. Nancho," it said. "There appears to be another program built deep into the ship itself that is overriding all systems. There is nothing I can do."

"That's it! Game over, man! Game over!" Mack said in despair; his hands held over his head in surrender.

"So…so what do we do now?" Jerome asked, grasping the back of one of the stools so tightly that his knuckles turned white.

"We pray," Dr. Eisenberg said softly in defeat as he bowed his head.

Akwen snickered in derision. "Of course. When tings turn bad everyone suddenly becomes religious," she mumbled as she continued to work the controls on the console in futility.

All of a sudden, the rumble of the ship's large gravity control engines increased. A moment later, a beam of pure white light exploded out of the top of the central shaft, causing each of them to whirl around in surprise, then immediately shield their eyes from the light.

"What the…" Mack stated in disbelief. Raising his right hand up to touch a tiny control on the bridge of his nose, he activated a small projector embedded in his skin that produced a thin holographic shield in front of his eyes, allowing him to look directly at the light. "The beam is going through the opening in the roof. It's…look at the walls!" he cried out.

As the group stared in awe, the walls and floor began to dissolve until they were translucent, allowing the astonished onlookers to see the vague outline of the chamber beyond. The entire pyramid continued to change until it was almost completely transparent. Only the outline of the walls and floor gave any indication of the pyramid's structure. Even the central pillar, stairs, and control panels faded until they were mere ghosts of their former substances.

Mack's stomach lurched as he stared down at his own feet, which now appeared to be standing on nothing at all. Tentatively, he bent down and touched the floor to assure himself that it was still there. As he did, he noticed Rebecca and Jeffrey were lying on the level below him, seemingly unconscious.

However, before he even had time to be concerned about whether they were still alive, his heart nearly stopped as he noticed his tennis shoes and legs had begun to change. Standing slowly, he raised his right hand in front of his face, fear causing his knees to wobble unsteadily. As he stood rooted to the spot, his hand and arm started to disappear before his eyes.

Letting out a startled cry, Mack stumbled backwards and fell to the floor. As he lay there staring at his arm in panic, his chest begin to tighten and each breath became more and more difficult. Frantically, he groped around in his pocket and withdrew his inhaler. Just as the muscles in his air tubes began to relax, gasps from the others drew his attention away from his own predicament. Akwen, Jerome, Dr. Eisenberg, and Lisa had all become ghost-like. Eyes wide in shock, none of them could do more than stare at their extremities. Even the droid had become confused by the images being received from its optical receptors, and remained still as it ran diagnostic tests in an effort to locate the problem.

The men and women were snapped out of their shock as the outlines of the slanted walls blazed with energy. Four beams of white light identical to the one in the center of the room shot from the floor to join with the central beam, causing them to raise their arms to block the radiance. However, this gesture proved fruitless as the light simply passed through their ghostly appendages and momentarily blinded all of them except Mack, whose holographic lenses were still in place. While they were still trying to recover from the temporary blindness inflicted upon them by the sudden influx of light, the ship began to move upward.

"Oh Jesus, God, Buddha, Mohammad, Confucius, Lords of Kobal...please help!" Mack cried out the words in rapid succession. "I don't wanna die!"

As the others groped around in fear, waiting for their eyes to adjust to the sudden brightness, Mack watched through the transparent walls in horror as the ceiling of the chamber rapidly drew closer. "Aaaahhhh!" he shrieked in panic, the pitch of his voice rising so high that it sounded like that of a sick banshee. Reflexively, Mack raised his arms above his head in a futile effort to ward off the collision that was mere seconds away.

Suddenly, Mack's cry became strangled as he watched in mixed terror and fascination as the ceiling of the chamber passed straight through the ship and his own body as if he were a mere phantom. In less time than it took for his brain to even register the fact that he was still alive, he found himself hurtling through the night sky at breakneck speed in a pyramid that appeared to consist of nothing more than blazing beams of white-hot energy.

"My God," Lisa breathed as she stared around her in wonder. Whether it was due to the fact that their eyes had adjusted to the brightness of the light, the light itself had dimmed, or some other bizarre explanation, she and the others now found that their vision had returned. After a couple of minutes, the ship effortlessly passed through the atmosphere; the panorama of stars suddenly burst forth on all sides as the earth receded below.

As they took in the breathtaking view around them, they felt the inertia of the ship begin to slow, which was further evidenced by the softening of the hum of the anti-gravity engines as they slowed their rotation.

"What's wrong now?" Mack asked, his mind finally calming down enough to form a coherent thought. "Why...why are the engines slowing down? Are we running out of power?"

"How should I know?" Akwen spat back as she scanned the controls. "It was hard enough to read dese displays when dey were not nearly invisible."

"Dr. Nancho," Elmer said, "it appears from the readouts that we have almost reached the predetermined distance set by the program that is running the ship."

Jerome, relaxing his grip on the back of the ghostly stool in front of him, used it to keep himself steady as he walked on the nearly invisible floor. Having finally moved far enough around the stool, he sat down carefully, uncertain whether the virtually transparent object could indeed

support his weight. Once he was fully convinced of its still-solid proper-
ties, he relaxed into it and breathed deeply in an attempt to release his
fear and tension.

Lifting his head from its posture of prayer, Dr. Eisenberg pushed up
his glasses with his left hand and brushed the remnants of several tears
from his eyes with the other. As he finished repositioning his glasses, a
scuffling sound caught everyone's attention. They all looked towards the
source of the sound to see Rebecca and Jeffrey attempting to navigate
their way up the stairs, their own bodies just slightly less transparent
than the steps themselves.

Noticing that Jeffrey and Rebecca were leaning heavily upon each
other as if injured, Dr. Eisenberg and Lisa crossed the small room towards
the stairs. Their task was made more difficult by the movement of the
ever-changing background of celestial objects. Finally reaching the top
of the steps, Lisa reached out to Jeffrey and embraced him, taking some
of his weight off of Rebecca. With Jeffrey's weight gone, Rebecca, herself
weak and bruised, nearly collapsed. Dr. Eisenberg grabbed her around
the waist and supported her long enough for her to regain her strength.

"Jeffrey, thank God," Lisa said in relief. Releasing her embrace, she
shifted her weight around to his left side to help him to walk. "What's
happening to us?"

Still groggy from the explosion that had knocked him unconscious,
Jeffrey merely shook his head slowly and muttered, "I don't know. We…
we certainly didn't expect this."

Jerome, coming to his senses, walked unsteadily over to them and
supported Jeffrey on his right side. Together the five of them managed
to make it back to the stools while Akwen studied the controls and
Mack stared out into space, his fear having been replaced by wonder and
excitement.

At last, after several minutes of flight, the ship halted its forward
momentum and hovered in orbit above the earth. The majesty of the
blue and white orb momentarily washed away all of the terror that had
gripped them from the recent events.

"I had forgotten how beautiful it is," Rebecca breathed softly. "Look, Lisa. There's the *Independence*," she said, pointing towards the space station they had docked at briefly during their voyage to 2021 PK seven years ago.

"Yeah," Lisa said weakly, her body language revealing the aftereffects of her recent adrenaline rush. "And is that the sunlight collector over by the moon? The laser and particle accelerator must be somewhere over there, too. That was quite a ride, wasn't it, Gunny?"

"I hate to break up dis lovely trip down memory lane," Akwen said sarcastically, "but we need to figure out what just happened and what we are going to do now."

"At this point, I think the only thing we can do is speculate," Dr. Eisenberg said. "Do we know anything for certain?"

Before anyone could answer, the transparent walls darkened, blocking out the view of the stars, and the hum of the engines increased. At the same time, everything inside the ship returned to its normal, opaque appearance, much to everyone's relief. Expecting the ship to begin accelerating once again, they braced themselves by grabbing onto the control console and each other. However, although the engines began running again at full speed, they felt no sensation of movement. Eventually, they relaxed enough to resume conversation.

"I dunna know how much more of this aye can take," Mack said in exasperation with a nearly perfect Irish accent.

Ignoring his weak attempt at lightening the mood, Rebecca turned to look at the others. "Are we moving?"

"I don't think so," Jeffrey replied. "It's nearly impossible to tell without any kind of window."

"But if we aren't moving, then why are the engines still running so hard?" Dr. Eisenberg asked in confusion.

"According to my sensors, Mr. Evans is correct: The ship is not moving," Elmer offered. "However, the ship's engines are running at full capacity and I am getting a very unusual output reading from them that I am unable to interpret."

"That's it!" Mack flicked his wrist back and forth rapidly, causing his fingers to create a thumping sound. "We must be traveling through hyperspace or something!"

"What do you mean?" Jeffrey asked.

"It fits!" Mack said exuberantly. "The reason there were no hangar doors in the ceiling of the chamber is because the ship didn't need them! It just…I don't know…phased right through them."

"Phased?" Lisa repeated.

"Yeah. There's this superhero who can walk through walls—" he began.

"—Great. I'm glad we haven't lost touch with reality," Akwen interrupted.

"Wait, Akwen," Jeffrey said, holding up a hand. "Let's hear him out. After all, we aren't exactly dealing in the realm of known physics."

"Anyway," Mack continued, "in the comics they called it 'phasing.' So, the ship has the ability to phase itself and its occupants—that's us"— Akwen rolled her eyes—"and it lifted off into orbit. Then it took a few moments to calculate the jump to hyperspace—because as you know, 'hyperspace ain't like dustin' crops, boy,'" Mack said, doing his best Han Solo imitation. Noting that his Star Wars reference fell on unappreciative ears, he cleared his throat nervously and continued. "Yeah, so, anyway…then the ship switched over to its hyperdrive, or FTL drive, —that stands for 'Faster Than Light,' in case you didn't know—and it darkened the windows so we all wouldn't go crazy from looking into the depths of hyperspace, and *whammo!*" He clapped his hands together for effect. "Off we go to the other side of the galaxy!"

The others exchanged glances as they considered his words. Jerome was the first to speak. "It sounds crazy, but then again, it's about as good an explanation as anything I could have come up with."

"Does anyone else have another theory?" Jeffrey asked. "Akwen? What do you think?"

"I tink you Americans watch way too many crazy movies," she said sharply. "He *may* be right. But it might also be dat da ship just malfunctioned when it reached orbit, so dat the engines are spinning but da drive isn't engaged. We may just be sitting here until we run out of oxygen, or da ship reenters da atmosphere and we burn up."

After a moment of uncomfortable silence, Mack spoke softly with a grimace on his face. "Gee, I definitely vote for my interpretation. At least with mine we don't all die some horrible death."

Sensing Akwen's irritation with the language specialist, Jeffrey quickly stepped in. "Okay, so we at least have a couple of working hypotheses."

"Regarding the ship, yes," Dr. Eisenberg said. "But what happened on the ground, Jeffrey? We only heard confused radio chatter and gunfire."

"Hey, that's right," Mack chimed in. "Did you see any real aliens? What did they look like?"

At the mention of them, a shiver ran down Rebecca's spine as Jeffrey began relating the events that occurred. After a brief summary, he concluded, "I don't know what those demon-looking things were, but they were certainly working with the aliens."

"Maybe they were aliens who were looking for bodies to possess, you know—disembodied aliens," Mack suggested.

"You know, Mack, an hour ago, I would've thought you were completely crazy," Jerome said. "But after what I just witnessed, I think I could believe just about anything."

"Well, whatever they were, I don't think any of us would be standing here right now if you hadn't gotten those doors shut when you did," Jeffrey said. "Those things just about had us."

As the others continued their conversation, Dr. Eisenberg studied Rebecca's face, which seemed riddled with concern. "What is it, Rebecca?" he asked quietly so as not to interrupt the others.

Rebecca shook her head as her eyes stared straight ahead. "Something isn't quite right. I know everyone is convinced that they were real aliens, but…there are a couple of things that just don't fit." She spoke in a low voice to keep her conversation with Dr. Eisenberg private. "For one, something was wrong with the aliens' appearance. They didn't look… real…when I ran towards them. And secondly, why didn't the aliens attack? They just jumped around and…dodged. They didn't have any weapons, and they didn't seem to have a specific objective."

"But Jeffrey said they killed several men with green lasers and were heading towards the ship," the professor countered. "It seems obvious they wanted it."

"No. The *aliens* didn't kill the men. It was the demon things," Rebecca said, turning finally to look at him. "Somehow, I think *they* were the real attackers. And I think they may have been *real* demons."

She expected the doctor to look at her skeptically, but instead he just shrugged. "I hope we never find out. But as for now, I don't think you should express your views to the others. I don't think they share your belief in demons."

"No, you're right," she said with a sigh. Glancing at Jeffrey, she mumbled to herself, "In fact I know they wouldn't."

"…seems to me that the first order of business for us now is to see if we can figure out how to get control back of this ship," Jeffrey was saying. "Akwen, you and Lisa are our ship specialists. You know the inner workings of the controls better than anyone. See if the two of you and Elmer can figure out how to shut down this foreign virus or program. Mack and Dr. Eisenberg, why don't you—"

"Yeah, we know—'go over the technical journals one more time to see if there is anything we missed,'" Mack finished for him.

"Right. See what you can do. Becky, why don't you help them?" he added as an afterthought.

Acknowledging the suggestion with a nod of her head, she followed Mack and Dr. Eisenberg as they carefully walked over to the stairs and began to descend. For the next several hours, they went about their tasks without incident. Rebecca, who really couldn't be of much assistance, was mostly left to her own thoughts. She frequently caught them straying in Jeffrey's direction, replaying in her mind the words he spoke to her before the attack. What would happen to them now? Would they even survive this? Closing her eyes, she offered up several prayers for their safety.

Suddenly, Dr. Eisenberg's comm beeped. "You three may want to get up here," Jeffrey's voice said. "Elmer just informed us that the engines have begun to slow down."

"We're on our way," Dr. Eisenberg replied. They dropped what they were doing and headed out the door. A minute later, they were back in the control room.

"Engine speed reducing to ten percent," Elmer said.

"Were you able to get control of the ship?" Dr. Eisenberg asked as they joined the others at the main control panel.

"Elmer was able to work his way into da system enough dat we may be able to control our lateral movements, but not much else," Akwen reported.

"So what does that mean?" Mack asked.

"It means when we get back to Earth we may not have to land in the same location as before," Jeffrey answered. "Unless, of course, you want to go back to the dig site for a second round with those aliens and demon things."

"Uh...let me think—no thanks," Mack said quickly.

They waited nearly five more minutes before they felt the vibrations of the engines slow drastically, followed by Elmer's report. "The engines have slowed to their previous orbiting speed." For another minute, they waited in tense anticipation, wondering if Akwen might not have been right after all.

Suddenly, the walls lightened until they could once more see through them. A moment later, their bodies and everything else around them became transparent as well. Not knowing what they might see outside the ship, they all let out an instant sigh of relief at what lay before them.

"It's earth!" Lisa cried in joy. "Thank God! We didn't go anywhere."

"All right!" Jeffrey said, raising his fists in triumph. "Now let's just see if we can figure out how to land this thing."

"Wait," Rebecca said, her eyes narrowing. "Where is the *Independence?*"

"We're on the other side of the world," Lisa answered. "Look. There's North America. The *Independence* must be on the other side."

"That could be," Dr. Eisenberg commented thoughtfully. "However, where are all of the satellites that should be in orbit?"

Before anyone could answer, the engines abruptly stopped running. After a few terrifying moments of complete silence, they slowly revved back up.

"Do you hear dat?" Akwen asked, her ears straining. "Da engines sound different."

"You are correct, Dr. Nancho," Elmer confirmed. "They are now running in reverse."

Even as the words left the droid's vocalizer, the ship began to move towards the planet.

"Hold on!" Jeffrey shouted as they drew closer to the atmosphere. Although they braced themselves as best they could, it proved to be unnecessary. Much to their surprise, the reentry turned out to be as smooth and uneventful as their liftoff. Soon, the clouds parted and the ground started rushing towards them.

"Elmer, see if you can land us north of the site, near—"

Jeffrey stopped midsentence as the numerous lights on Elmer's body dimmed and went out. The droid gently sank to the floor as its gravity control units slowed down and stopped. "What the—!" Jeffrey said in surprise.

"Oh no. What a great time for da glitch to kick in," Akwen said, frustration written on her face.

"Glitch?" Mack repeated. "What glitch? No one said anything about a glitch!"

"Akwen, can you move the ship manually?" Jeffrey called out.

"I can try," she said as she grabbed the controls.

The others watched with apprehension as Akwen moved the ship northward even as they drew ever closer to the ground.

"Akwen, what are you doing?" Jeffrey yelled. "We're heading too far south! We need to land in the U.S."

"If you tink you can do a better job at driving, you are welcome to try!" she shouted back as she yanked on the controls.

Within moments, the ship began to slow its descent as individual treetops became visible. "Over there, Akwen," Jeffrey called out. "Try to land in that clearing near the base of that mountain."

The pyramid gave a sudden lurch and moved slowly toward the indicated area. Soon, they were directly over the clearing and the ship decelerated to a crawl until it was resting on the ground. Immediately, the pyramid reverted to its original opaque appearance as the white energy beams dissipated.

"Look!" Jerome said in relief. "We're back to normal."

"Nice landing, Akwen," Jeffrey said with a smile. "By the way, did anyone see what country we ended up in?"

"Central America—somewhere near the Yucatan Peninsula, I believe," Dr. Eisenberg said as he stood. "I believe I saw a small city beyond the forest to the east."

"I don't care where we are or where we go!" Mack said as he headed for the stairs. "I'm just glad to be back on earth."

Akwen suddenly frowned as she worked her hands over the controls several times. Jeffrey, noticing her frustration, asked, "What's wrong?"

"I can't shut off da power. Da switch doesn't seem to be working."

"Well, just leave it on for now. We'll worry about that later. C'mon," he said.

After making sure the main entrance doors were opened, they all headed towards the stairs. As they rounded the corner leading into the entrance hallway, however, they stopped abruptly as fear once more gripped them in its crushing grasp. Side by side in the entranceway stood two shadowy figures with malevolent, blood-red eyes.

7

GOLIATH AND HERCULES

"IF ANY OF you even so much as twitches in a way I don't like, you will die," said a deep voice emanating from one of the figures. The words were not spoken so much as growled, and oddly enough, sounded slightly muffled, as if coming from behind a mask or helmet. Although the voice wasn't what she would have expected from the demonic apparitions in front of her, Rebecca didn't doubt for a second the speaker's sincerity.

"Who…who are you, and what do you want?" Jeffrey managed, his voice trembling.

"Who we are is not important," came a second voice. It resembled the first one in that it was muffled and sounded like an animal's growl, yet it was pitched slightly higher and its timbre was brighter. "As for what we came for, well…" it laughed wickedly, "we are standing in it."

Jeffrey swallowed hard. Summoning his courage, he asked, "And if we refuse to give it to you?"

Rebecca had heard many strange types of laughter in her life, especially those of the alien creatures she met in the vision back on Ka'esch. But the feral, guttural noises produced by these dark, formless beings unnerved her more than anything she had ever heard. Once their mirth was spent, the one blocking the right side of the hallway edged towards them.

At its approach, Jeffrey, Rebecca, and the others, who were already huddled together with their backs to the central room, began inching around the corner towards the stairs. Suddenly, a section of the gray mist that was the creature's body detached itself. The shadowy arm reached up quickly and grabbed Jeffrey around the throat. As it did, an amazing transformation occurred that left them all dumb with shock.

Beginning with the hand that now gripped Jeffrey, and continuing up the right arm and through the rest of its body, the shadowy figure began to coalesce into the form of a man. Where once was thin, shapeless mist, hard steel now shone out in the dim light of the hallway. Within a few seconds, the shadowy form had been completely replaced by an enormous, armor-clad figure. Its face was hidden behind a wide, V-shaped visor attached to the front of a helmet adorned with four wicked-looking horns.

Effortlessly, the nearly eight-foot giant lifted Jeffrey off the ground and slammed him into the wall of the central room, pinning him there. As Jeffrey gasped for air, Lisa let out a strangled cry.

With its left hand, the being reached up and removed its helmet. All the color drained out of Rebecca's face and her stomach threatened to divulge its contents. What stood before them, while resembling a man in posture and basic bone structure, also had the unmistakable features of a wolf. The thing's head was almost completely covered with coarse black hair, except for the portion of the face surrounding the eyes, nose and mouth, which was covered with thick, ash-colored skin. Its eyes, coal black, were definitely human-shaped, yet seemed soulless and wholly devoid of compassion. The hairy, pointed ears and slightly elongated nose twitched nervously as its thick, pinkish-gray lips pulled back in a sneer to reveal a row of dirty, razor-sharp teeth. Its putrid-smelling breath alone was almost enough to cause Jeffrey to lose consciousness.

"Have you ever heard the myth about a little man who faced a giant?" the monstrous thing snarled as it moved its gaping maw to within inches of Jeffrey's face. "Well as it turns out, I am named after that giant, and I can assure you it will take more than some pathetic sling to bring me down. But if you want to take a shot at me, I would love the chance for a little light exercise." Just as Jeffrey's eyes had begun to roll back into his head from lack of oxygen, the creature released its grasp, allowing his body to crumple to the floor.

Rebecca and Lisa knelt to help Jeffrey, who was struggling to draw air through his injured windpipe. As they propped him up against the wall, the second being moved forward to join the first, its form altering with each step to become a near-identical twin to Goliath. However, when it removed its helmet, they could see that the features of each figure were as different as night and day. While Goliath resembled a werewolf, the second giant bore a striking similarity to a gorilla, albeit a very human-looking one. In fact, Rebecca couldn't help but draw a comparison between this creature and illustrations of Neanderthal Man.

"You!" Goliath snapped, pointing at Mack. "Bring me the digital copies of the technical journals as well as the original books." When Mack's fear caused him to hesitate, the creature boomed, "MOVE IT. NOW!"

Mack complied and headed through the door in front of him into his study. "Hercules, watch him," Goliath said. The second giant quickly rounded the corner and moved into the room. Despite the height of these creatures, they still easily cleared the twelve-foot high doorways.

A moment later, Mack returned with two books and a small flash drive in hand. Nervously, he glanced over his shoulder to see Hercules hovering over him, a wicked grin splayed across its features.

"Good," Goliath said smugly. Setting its helmet on the floor, it took the items from Mack. Opening a small pocket on its left arm, the giant dropped the flash drive into it and resealed the pocket. Then, taking the books, it slid them into a sleeve built into the inside of the armor on its back. With the newfound acquisitions safely stored away, the giant turned its attention back to the group.

"Dr. Akwen Nancho from Cameroon, isn't it?" Goliath said mockingly, its gaze focused upon her.

"Yes," Akwen said with fierce pride, refusing to show fear to her enemy.

Goliath nodded with approval and, looking over at Hercules, grinned cruelly. "I like this one. She's got…character." Turning back to Akwen, it commanded, "Let's get our prize here running again. You will take us to the coordinates I give you, where our benefactors await our arrival. I do believe they will be most excited to see us. Hercules, watch the rest of them while I take my new girlfriend upstairs."

Terrified at the prospect of being alone with this monster, Akwen quickly lied, "I cannot run it alone. I need Jeffrey to help with da liftoff."

Goliath narrowed its eyes at her skeptically. "No, you don't need his help. You can run it on your own like you did to get us here."

Akwen's face lit up in surprise. "Yesss," Goliath drew the word out slowly, as if relishing the taste of it. "We were watching you from below, thanks to the wonderful ability of this machine to become transparent."

"But," Jerome said in confusion, "if you could see us, then why…"

The creature, flaunting its position of power over them, cracked a sinister smile. "In case you hadn't noticed, my partner and I have the uncanny ability of making ourselves, shall we say, difficult to observe."

An involuntary shudder passed through Jerome as he thought of these two creatures watching every move they made during the several hours that had passed during their trip into space.

"You must not have been watching very carefully, den," Akwen challenged. "For if you had, you would have noticed dat I frequently needed help with translations and with reading displays from da oder panels. Da ship's controls are written in an alien language dat I cannot read."

"Fine. You can have your help. But not him. This one can help you," it said, grabbing Mack by the neck of his T-shirt and causing a strangled cry to escape from his lips.

Not letting her disappointment show on her face, Akwen set her jaw, turned around abruptly, and headed toward the stairs. Shoving Mack on ahead, Goliath followed.

A minute later, the trio reached the control room. Sitting down at the stool directly in front of the piloting controls, Akwen turned and faced the creature that stood behind her. "In case you didn't notice during our first trip, dere is much we still don't know about dis ship. Dere is some kind of computer virus dat is controlling much of it. If I have any hope of gaining full control, I will need da help of my droid."

Looking down at the inert machine on the floor, the giant nodded. Removing a heavy laser pistol from the holster on its thigh, Goliath pointed it at the droid. "You may activate it. But if it—"

"—Yes, I know," Akwen interrupted. "You don't have to repeat your trets."

Despite her impertinence, Goliath smiled. Akwen got up from her stool, knelt down next to Elmer, and began adjusting a few of the droid's components. Satisfied, she stood and said, "Elmer, power on." After a few moments the tiny white lights that served as eyes lit up as the machine's circular gravity control engines began to whir softly, raising the droid gently into the air. "Greetings, Dr. Nancho. How may I be of service?"

"Plug into da computer, Elmer. We need to see if we can get more control of da ship once we launch," Akwen said as she resumed her seat in front of the controls. Obediently, the droid hovered over to the computer interface and plugged in. "You do realize, of course, dat dere is a definite possibility dat it will take several minutes for Elmer to get me some control, or, it is even possible dat da computer virus might lock him out completely. After all, do you really tink I meant to land us out here in da middle of nowhere?"

"Listen, woman," the giant being growled impatiently. "You may think I look like a mindless beast, but I am much more intelligent than you realize. I watched all of you quite carefully, and I also know you were able to gain some control of the movement as we were about to land. I know your limitations, and I know your strengths. If you give me any less than your full effort, I'll be able to tell. Now, fire it up."

Akwen returned the creature's intimidating stare for a moment, then swallowed hard and turned away. Despite her outward calm, she felt the sweat on the back of her neck accumulate and run down between her shoulder blades. "Okay, Mack. Let's begin da launch sequence."

Akwen poured over the displays and readings, running through the checklist and making sure everything was online. Just as she was about to feed power to the engines, something caught her eye. "Oh no. Dat's not good," she said softly.

"What's the problem?" Goliath asked, leaning closer to her.

"Look here, at dis gauge. Dis line represents da ship's power. It should be up here, but it is not. Mack, what does dis say?" she asked, pointing towards one of the displays.

"Um…it says…ten percent energy and…" he paused for a moment as he studied the readout. "It says we…um…only have ten percent of our power. We can't launch."

Goliath grabbed Mack's face with long, dirty fingers, and stared at him intently, as if trying to read his mind. Terror filled Mack's eyes as the creature studied him. Finally satisfied that the man was telling the truth, it let him go. "How long will it be before the system recharges?" Goliath asked.

"Recharges? I…I don't know if…if it ever will recharge," Mack stuttered.

"It must recharge," Goliath retorted. "No one is foolish enough to make a ship that can only fly once."

"But you must understand, da power core for dis ship is just a prototype," Akwen added quickly. "We didn't even know if it would work at all."

Considering her statement, Goliath turned to look at Elmer. Figuring that the droid's programmers probably hadn't spent the time to teach it to lie, Goliath decided to try a different method of confirmation. "Ask your droid if the ship contains a system for recharging the power core."

Akwen did as she was commanded. They waited for a moment as Elmer communicated with the computer. Finally, the droid turned its head towards Akwen. "Yes, Dr. Nancho. The system is currently in the process of recharging the core. It should be up to full power in four hours."

The giant smiled in satisfaction. "I thought so. Those aliens that built this thing knew what they were doing. So, it looks like we'll be spending some time together. Shut down your droid, then we'll go back downstairs to join the others."

Once more, Akwen did as she was told. After Elmer was disconnected and powered down, she, Mack, and the creature descended the steps and rejoined the others. As they stepped into the hallway, Akwen noticed that during their absence the others had all had their wrists bound securely behind them with rope and had been seated on the floor, their backs to the central wall of the pyramid.

"Sit," the ape-like giant said forcefully, pointing to an empty section of floor next to Dr. Eisenberg. As soon as Akwen and Mack were seated, Hercules proceeded to check them for weapons and bind their wrists as well. Once that was completed, the two giants walked towards the entrance of the pyramid and conversed quietly, all the while keeping a watchful eye on their prisoners.

"Akwen, what happened?" Dr. Eisenberg whispered. "Why didn't we take off? Is something wrong with the ship?"

Akwen related briefly what had happened in the control room. After a moment's pause, Lisa spoke the question haunting each of them. "What are they going to do with us?"

The words hung oppressively in the air like black fumes from burning oil threatening to smother them all in despair. Finally, Akwen whispered so quietly the others had to strain to hear. "We still have Elmer."

Before anyone could comment on Akwen's statement, the two giants ended their conversation and turned their attention back to their captives. Reaching down, Hercules grabbed Jeffrey, Rebecca, and Jerome, and hauled them to their feet. "Move!" it barked, herding them towards the pyramid's entrance.

"Where are you taking them?" Lisa called out, fear stabbing into her heart.

Goliath gave an evil smile. "Don't worry. They're just going for a little walk."

Jeffrey turned and gave Lisa a forced smile, but was quickly shoved from behind by Hercules. They stepped out into the haze of the afternoon sun, which was diffused by several dark clouds blanketing the sky. An oppressive heat washed over them the moment they exited the pyramid.

"So where *are* we going?" Rebecca asked their captor as the group strode across the clearing towards the nearby line of trees that marked the edge of a thick forest. To the north and west, the trees extended to the skirts of a line of snow-capped mountains. Although the view to the south and east was obscured by more trees, they could hear the sound of a large waterfall somewhere nearby. Under other circumstances, Rebecca would have found the place absolutely beautiful. Now, however, all she could think about was survival.

When the giant didn't reply to Rebecca's question, Jeffrey looked over his shoulder. "Do we at least get the courtesy of an answer?"

"Shut up and keep moving," came the gruff response. "You will find out soon enough."

As Jeffrey started to turn back around, he noticed the creature had removed its laser pistol from the holster. His muscles tensed and he began to sweat profusely as his mind frantically searched his surroundings for something that could be used as a weapon. Unfortunately, the creature had taken his and Rebecca's laser pistols. Time was running out, and barring a miracle, there wasn't any way three bound, weaponless prisoners could take out the armed, armored, and well-trained giant.

As they walked, the sound of the waterfall grew louder until they stepped out of the forest and onto the banks of a shallow river. About sixty feet to their left, a majestic cascade of water plunged over a hundred feet to land in a pool lined with large boulders and jagged rocks. To the right, running parallel to the river, an enormous tree lay on its side several dozen feet from the water's edge. The roots of the tree were covered with large chunks of dirt, and fanned out in all directions like the tentacles of some giant sea creature.

"That's far enough," Hercules said, stopping in front of the downed tree. "Stand with your backs to the tree." Silently, the prisoners obeyed the creature's command. As they turned around, they found themselves facing down the barrel of the giant's laser pistol.

"Oh God!" Rebecca said in shock. Closing her eyes, she began praying fervently.

"Before you shoot us, could you at least explain why?" Jeffrey asked, hoping desperately to find something he could use to convince the creature to spare their lives. Next to him, Jerome had started breathing so hard that Jeffrey was afraid he was going to hyperventilate. Furthermore, Jerome's panic was starting to infect Jeffrey himself, causing his own pulse to quicken until he was afraid he was going to collapse.

The giant just shrugged, then said nonchalantly, "It is nothing personal, just business. We were sent to get the technical plans, not bring back prisoners. Since we ended up with the ship itself, we also need people to operate it and who know how to read the language. Everyone else is just dead weight."

Jeffrey's mouth had become so dry he had to try several times just to make a sound. "B…but…you do…you do need us," he managed, his mind working overtime to latch onto something that would save them. "We were the first…we found the ship. We know…the bodies! We have firsthand knowledge of the bodies that were found. We—"

"Nice try," their captor said coldly. "I'm just doing my job. You can turn around if you want. It might make things easier." As it spoke, the creature leveled the gun at Jerome's head. Eyes wide with fear, Jerome was visibly shaking and his breathing had become erratic.

"Pl…pl…please," Jerome pleaded. "I…I have a wife and three children. My…my daughter is in the hospital…I—"

"Spare me," the monster sneered. "There is nothing I hate more than a whiner."

Jeffrey suddenly dove toward the giant just as its finger tightened on the trigger. The creature swung the gun at him as it fired, sending a beam of searing green energy slicing through Jeffrey's gray T-shirt and into the flesh of his left shoulder. Opening her eyes that had been clenched shut in desperate prayer, Rebecca screamed as she saw Jeffrey lying on the ground.

The giant reached down and picked up the wounded archaeologist by his shirt. "That's more like it," Hercules said. "Someone who is willing to go down fighting. Just for that, I'll save you for last." With a mighty heave, the giant tossed Jeffrey to the side, where he landed next to the fallen tree several yards away.

Directing its attention back towards Jerome and Rebecca, Hercules raised its weapon again and pointed it at Jerome. Suddenly, a dark shadow obscured the hazy sun, causing the giant to look up quickly, weapon ready and searching for a target. But searching turned out not to be the problem. Instead, the giant faced the decision of which target to aim at. For diving down towards Hercules and the captives were four large pteranodons.

8

SERPENT-BIRDS

HERCULES, UNNERVED BY the sudden appearance of the winged reptiles, completely forgot about the prisoners. Even though the creatures' black bodies were only about the size of turkeys, their twenty-foot wingspans and razor-sharp beaks made them formidable enemies, even for the nearly eight-foot giant. Backing up quickly, Hercules frantically sent a dozen beams of green energy lancing up at the lead pteranodon, scoring several hits. The creature let out a cry of agony as its black, scaly skin was scorched and seared by the laser.

"Goliath, I'm under attack! I'm by the waterfall. I need help immediat—ugh!" the rest of the giant's message was knocked from its body as the wounded pteranodon crashed into Hercules' chest, knocking both to the ground.

Two of the other winged reptiles aborted their attack dives, choosing instead to land near their wounded comrade in hopes of finishing off their prey. The last pteranodon, however, spotted Rebecca and Jerome standing near the fallen tree and changed the direction of its dive. Letting out an earsplitting squawk, it swooped down to within inches of their heads.

"Jerome, duck!" Rebecca yelled as she dropped to the ground. A split second later, Jerome was beside her, his eyes wide with fear.

Having missed its prey, the creature pulled up sharply and landed several feet from the tree. Turning in their direction, it let out several more agitated squawks as it began crawling awkwardly towards them.

Looking around anxiously for some weapon or hiding place, Rebecca spotted a two-foot gap between the tree trunk and the ground. "Quick, under here!" she cried as she rolled her body into the hole. Thankful for the protection of the leather jacket, she nevertheless received several minor cuts on her face and hands from the sticks and branches protruding from the tree. Following right behind, Jerome's body bumped into hers just as the pteranodon's pointed beak thrust into the ground, narrowly missing them...

"Goliath, I'm under attack! I'm by the waterfall. I need help immediat—ugh!"

Cursing violently, Goliath grabbed its helmet and sprinted toward the opening of the pyramid, leaving the prisoners behind. Before the giant was even out of view, Akwen used the microphone built into her lip and said hurriedly, "Elmer, power up."

In the same instant, Lisa curled her knees up to her chest, moved her bound hands under her legs, and brought them up in front of her. Jumping to her feet, she looked down at Akwen, who was copying her maneuver. "Akwen, do you still have that laser pistol in your workroom?"

Getting to her feet beside her, she nodded. "Yes. I'll get it." Sprinting toward the door at the bottom of the stairs, she flung it open. As she did so, she called to the droid. "Elmer, come downstairs now!"

By the time Akwen had retrieved the weapon and returned to the corridor, the droid was obediently waiting for her at the bottom of the stairs. "Elmer, cut dese ropes," she commanded. Immediately, the droid's torso began to rotate clockwise. Stopping abruptly, a compartment slid open and a small, circular saw began spinning rapidly. As the droid cut through the ropes, Akwen looked at Lisa. "Dis is an old pistol, and the charge is low. Don't waste any shots."

"Man, is there anything Elmer *can't* do?" Mack said. "It has as many gadgets as R2D2!"

"Sometimes life copies art," Dr. Eisenberg said with a worried grin as Akwen and Lisa, newly liberated, rushed past them and headed out the door.

After several attempts to extract its prey from under the tree, the pteranodon gave up and began searching for easier quarry. Rebecca and Jerome breathed a momentary sigh of relief until Rebecca noticed the object of the creature's interest. "Oh no! It's going after Jeffrey!"

Using her feet and shoulders, Rebecca moved past Jerome and crawled out of the hole. Slipping her bound hands under her feet so they were now in front of her, she got into a crouch. Near the water's edge, Hercules was attempting to fend off two of the creatures with its fists, the laser pistol seemingly lost in the river during the melee. Judging by the blood smearing the ape-like giant's face, it seemed to be losing.

To her left, Rebecca saw Jeffrey struggling to get to his feet as the flying reptile crawled towards him using the three-fingered claws on the top of its bat-like wings. In his panic, Jeffrey tripped over the edge of the roots and fell, landing hard on his uninjured shoulder.

Squawking madly, the creature inched ever closer, pointed beak snapping open and closed rapidly. Grabbing a thick tree branch in her bound hands, Rebecca stood and charged the beast just as it neared Jeffrey, who was lying on his back kicking wildly at the creature. Swinging like a baseball all-star, Rebecca let out an anger-filled battle cry as her makeshift club connected solidly with the pteranodon's skull.

As the creature collapsed, Rebecca dropped the branch and bent to assist Jeffrey. A moment later, Jerome appeared, and together they helped him to his feet. Directly in front of them, the last two pteranodons had

Hercules pinned down. Howls of pain could be heard coming from the giant as the creatures tore at his flesh like vultures.

"Hurry, let's get out of here while they're distracted," Rebecca whispered intently. "If we go around the other side of the tree, we might be able to make it back—"

Her words were cut off by sudden movement from the edge of the forest. Sailing through the air towards the flying reptiles was a small, metallic object. As it landed, Rebecca's eyes grew wide. "Grenade!" she yelled, pushing the others to the ground.

They lay still, waiting for the explosion to rip into their bodies. However, instead of the expected blast, the only sounds they heard were the pteranodon's wild screeching and the loud thunderous beating of wings as the creatures took flight, followed by several shots from a laser pistol.

Looking hesitantly towards the location of the metallic object, Rebecca and the others froze in surprise and shock: Jumping about and moving all over the area were a dozen of the same gray aliens that had attacked them at the dig site.

"What the…" Jeffrey said in confusion. "Where did they come from?"

"And what happened to the grenade?" Jerome asked.

Rebecca's face lit up. "That's how they did it! Don't you see? The aliens aren't real! They must be some kind of 3-D projections."

"You mean, like holograms?" Jerome offered.

"Yes! And that grenade must be the source of the images," she continued. "Goliath and Hercules used them to confuse the guards. Then they camouflaged themselves and took them out with their lasers."

"And just now Goliath used it to spook the pterodactyl things," Jerome finished.

"Well, that's one mystery solved," Jeffrey said through clenched teeth as a fresh wave of pain from his injured shoulder lanced through his body. "But the question is: What do we do now? Goliath is still—"

Jeffrey's lips froze in mid-sentence as the giant's large frame came into view. Looking around cautiously, it leapt onto the fallen tree two dozen feet in front of where they lay on the ground. Still keeping an eye on the treetops, it removed its helmet. Jumping off the tree, it set the helmet on the ground and knelt down to examine the body of Hercules. After several seconds, the wolf-like creature stood and quickly spotted them. Still shooting fleeting glances at the sky, the giant casually strode over to where they lay.

"So, I see the three of you managed to dodge death for a little bit longer. Stand up," it commanded. Slowly, the three of them complied. The moment they were fully erect, the giant's left hand snapped out towards Rebecca and grabbed her throat. Throwing her sideways, it slammed her back hard against the fallen tree. Simultaneously, it raised the pistol in its right hand and pointed it directly at Jeffrey's head.

"Now, one of you had better start talking. If I'm satisfied with your answer, you will all live. If not...well, you are smart. I don't think I need to spell it out for you."

"I...I don't understand," Jeffrey stammered. "What is it you want to know?"

"I want to know where you brought us," Goliath snarled. "What kind of game are you playing? This can't be earth. I just watched my partner get killed by creatures that have been extinct for over sixty-five million years!"

Jeffrey paled as he shook his head. It is one thing to be tortured and killed for withholding information, but how do you convince someone that you honestly don't have the answers? "We don't...we don't have any idea what's going on. Please, you have to believe us! We're just as confused as you!"

"You expect me to believe that after years of working on this ship, you have no idea what it does?" Goliath sneered. "That's not a very good answer."

Letting out a cry of despair, Rebecca watched helplessly as the giant mercilessly pulled the trigger...

◆

The sound of the weapon discharging almost caused Lisa to give away her position. Only her military training and the knowledge that she probably had just enough juice for a single shot had kept her from rushing at the wolf-like creature. Since leaving the pyramid, she and Akwen had split up, hoping Akwen might be able to create a distraction long enough for Lisa to get close enough without being noticed.

Afraid of what she would see, Lisa peeked slowly around the tree she had hidden behind. Her heart leapt with relief as she saw that Jeffrey and the others were still alive, albeit shaken badly by the bolt that had just barely missed Jeffrey's head.

She was still more than forty feet away, too far to risk a shot. In addition, the roots of the tree were obscuring her line of sight. The only chance she had for success was to catch Goliath by surprise, and right now she was still in the monster's peripheral vision. If she moved out from her hiding place, it would surely see her. She decided to bide her time, hoping her delay wouldn't cost the lives of one of her friends.

As Lisa watched, the giant turned its attention toward Rebecca, leaving Lisa free to move. "Consider that your one warning shot. Now, would you like to add anything to his pathetic answer?"

"You've been watching us since the ship launched. If you think we planned any of this, then nothing we can say will convince you otherwise," Rebecca said defiantly. As she spoke, Lisa took a deep breath and crept out from behind the tree. Drawing on all of her skills and training, she moved slowly and silently towards them, her weapon poised and ready.

Off to her right, she spotted Akwen crouched behind a tree with a short, sturdy branch in her hand. Suddenly, she stood and heaved it with all her might in the direction opposite Lisa. As the branch crashed to the ground, Goliath turned and fired off several shots in the direction of the sound. Springing into action, Lisa moved towards the group as quickly and quietly as possible.

Unable to detect the source of the sound, Goliath spun around and began scanning the entire area. Seeing Lisa out of the corner of its eye, it dropped Rebecca and turned towards this new enemy. With less than fifteen feet separating them, Lisa dove forward as a laser blast narrowly missed her head. Pausing momentarily to aim, she squeezed the trigger. Grunting in pain as the bolt slammed into its chest, Goliath collapsed to the ground with a heavy thud.

For several seconds, no one moved. Finally, Lisa stood, and together, she and Akwen ran forward to join their friends. As she arrived at the body of Goliath, Lisa quickly reached down and exchanged her depleted laser pistol with the giant's charged one.

"Is it dead?" Jerome asked nervously.

Bending down, Akwen felt its neck for a pulse. "No. It appears dat its armor absorbed much of da impact."

Rebecca and Jeffrey, both nursing their injuries, stood slowly. Still keeping the gun trained on the body of the giant, Lisa moved over to help Jeffrey. "Are you okay? When we heard the gun go off, we thought… thank God you're alive. How's your arm?"

"It's okay," he said, wincing as she lifted an edge of the burned clothing to examine the wound. "The blast just singed the shoulder a little. It stings, but I can still move my arm."

Having finished her examination of Jeffrey, she looked over toward Rebecca, who was leaning back against the tree for support. "How about you, Becky?"

Rebecca let out a deep sigh of relief. "I'm fine. Thanks, Lis. Thanks, Awken. We owe you big time."

"Sure, Gunny," Lisa replied. Her eyes met Rebecca's briefly, and she smiled haphazardly before looking away.

Stepping over to where Jerome stood, Akwen began cutting his bonds. "What do we do with him?" Jerome asked, nodding his head toward Goliath.

"Tie him up and leave him here," Akwen said dispassionately.

"But let's do it quickly before those pteranodons return," Jeffrey commented as he scanned the sky.

Using the rope they had been bound with, they tied Goliath's hands and feet. Just as they were turning to leave, Jerome sucked in a quick breath and placed a restraining hand on Jeffrey's arm, causing him to stop in his tracks. "Don't…move," he said slowly and quietly, his gaze fixed upon something across the river. The others, sensing the urgency in his voice, obeyed instantly. Following his line of sight, their eyes grew wide. Stepping out cautiously from the cover of the trees onto the edge of the river were fourteen primitive-looking men dressed in loincloths and covered with war paint. The warriors were armed with an assortment of spears, bows, clubs, shields, and stone knives—all pointed menacingly in their direction.

9

NATIVES

THE NATIVE WARRIORS inched ever closer to the group, their spear and bow tips never dipping or straying from their targets even a fraction of an inch. As they crossed the shallow river, they began to spread out in a semicircle. Rebecca knew if they waited any longer to act, they would soon be surrounded on all sides. The same thought had obviously occurred to Lisa, because Rebecca felt her tense and saw her raise the laser pistol.

"No!" Jeffrey whispered intently as he shook his head, his eyes wide to emphasize his point. "You might take out one or two, but they would surely kill us all quickly enough. They've probably never seen a gun before, so if you can hide it without drawing too much attention, they may not take it from you."

Heeding Jeffrey's advice, Lisa slowly turned so that Rebecca's body was between the pistol and the warriors, blocking their view of the weapon. Then she slid the gun into the inner pocket of her jumpsuit.

"Of course, if dey decide to attack us, den we go out fighting," Akwen said while nervously watching the advancing natives.

As the warriors circled around them, Rebecca and the others stood back to back in the center, forming a circle of their own. The tension in the air was smothering as each group studied the other distrustfully. Finally, Jeffrey lifted his hands into the air and offered a friendly smile. "Hello," he said. "We are friends."

One of the natives stepped warily inside the circle of warriors, his spear pointed directly at Jeffrey. In his left hand, he held a circular shield adorned with several colorful feathers. His face was painted completely white, giving Jeffrey the disconcerting impression that he was staring at a lifeless zombie or ghoul rather than a living, breathing human. Further adding to the native's bizarre appearance was a bone necklace; its dirty whiteness contrasted sharply with the dark, reddish-brown color of the man's skin.

Stopping several feet away from Jeffrey, the white-faced warrior, whom Jeffrey assumed to be the leader, looked over at Goliath. An angry frown creased the man's face as he studied the giant. Looking back at Jeffrey, he spoke. His words sounded like a jumble of harsh consonants.

"Great," Jeffrey said under his breath as he continued to smile. "Where is Mack when you need him?" The smile froze on his face, however, as the leader stepped closer until the two men were nearly nose to nose. Jeffrey had never in his life been as conscious of his Middle-Eastern heritage as he was now. He could only imagine how odd he must look to a person who had probably never seen anyone from another race.

The leader cautiously walked around the inner circle, studying each of them in turn. Reaching up a hand, he examined the highlights in Lisa's hair, then turned and rubbed the sleeve of Rebecca's leather jacket between his fingers. As he reached Akwen and Jerome, he stopped and stared more intently. For a minute, Jeffrey feared Akwen would punch the man as he touched the dark skin on her arm in curiosity. Stepping back, the leader called out something to the other warriors as he pointed at Akwen and Jerome. Another warrior, whose nose was pierced with a three-inch bone, came up beside the leader and the two talked briefly, all the while staring at the two dark-skinned humans.

A shout arose from one of the warriors who had circled behind, causing the leader to break off his conversation and walk over to join him. The other warrior pointed to the corpses of the two pteranodons, and Jeffrey could hear him speaking rapidly and emphatically, all the while gesturing back and forth between the dead creatures and Jeffrey's group.

Taking advantage of the distraction, Jeffrey whispered, "Akwen, will your microphone implant work this far away?"

"Yes," she replied quietly, her voice giving away none of the excitement his question sparked within her.

"Good," Jeffrey continued. "Can Elmer track you using the mic's radio signal?"

"Yes," she responded once more.

"Then tell Elmer to have Dr. Eisenberg and Mack follow us and be ready to move when we give the signal."

Mumbling so no one else could hear, Akwen passed along the instructions as the leader returned to the head of the outer circle. Jeffrey and the others, knowing their continued existence hinged on what happened next, held their breath as the native began calling out orders to the rest of his hunting party. Once he finished speaking, three of the warriors broke formation and began using their knives to cut lengths of vine, which they used to bind the wrists of their prisoners.

"And I was just getting the circulation flowing again," Jeffrey said wryly. "What do you think they're going to do with Goliath?"

As if the mere mention of the name had roused him, the giant opened his eyes and quickly took in the surroundings. Jeffrey, wishing the natives would kill the creature, was disappointed as the warriors forced him to stand, their spear tips mere inches from the giant's throat. Looking back over his shoulder, Jeffrey hoped Mack and Dr. Eisenberg would be able to follow them and somehow work out a way to get them out of this. Turning back around to face forward, he noticed that while their wrists were being bound, several other warriors had tied up the wings of the two dead pteranodons and strapped the dead animals to the backs of two of the other warriors. Once the warriors were satisfied that everyone was securely bound, they headed out.

The leader of the natives walked in front of the group while the rest of the warriors surrounded the band of prisoners. Much to their discomfort, Jeffrey and the others were forced to walk side by side with the stoic giant. The warriors prodded them forward and forced them to cross the river. The frigid mountain water, which rose up to their knees, soaked their pants and chilled them to the bone. Once on the other side, the wet clothes clung to their bodies and made walking difficult.

"Now I understand why the natives don't wear pants," Jeffrey muttered.

Waiting until the processional had settled into a groove before risking conversation, Jeffrey sidled up to Akwen. "What did the doc and Mack say?" he whispered.

Throwing a glance at the nearest warrior to make sure they weren't going to get speared for talking, Akwen replied, "Dey said dey have an idea, and dey will have Elmer send me regular updates on deir progress."

"What if Elmer experiences a glitch?"

"I have explained to Mack how to reset his system if dat happens," Akwen said.

"Good. Did they give you any idea about what they had planned or how long it would take before they're ready?" Jeffrey asked.

"No, but whatever it is, I hope dey hurry," she answered, a worried expression overshadowing her face. "I may be wrong, but we may have anoder problem."

Not liking the sudden change in Akwen's demeanor, Jeffrey's brow furrowed. "What kind of problem?"

"According to da ship's controls, it will take four hours to recharge da core. It has already been over half an hour. Dat gives us just over tree hours before da core is fully charged."

Confused, Jeffrey asked, "So, where is the problem?"

"When we first powered up da ship, da computer took over and launched automatically," she explained. "Once we landed, da computer would not let us turn off da power..."

"…which means that once the ship has reached full power again, it could launch without us, leaving us stranded here in 'Jurassic Park,'" he finished, his eyes closing momentarily in understanding.

Nodding in affirmation, Akwen continued. "Each minute we walk furder away from da ship will take us an additional minute on da return trip. If Dr. Eisenberg and Mack take more den two hours to find us, it will be almost impossible to make it back to da ship in time."

Rebecca, who had overheard the conversation, walked on in silence as she considered what Akwen had said. *Are we going to be able to escape from these natives? If we do, will we be able to get back to the ship before it takes off? And what will we do if we're stranded here? Where are we, anyway? How can there be pteranodons and primitive indigenous people still living in the middle of the twenty-first century? Are we even on earth? It looks like earth, but nothing seems to make sense. And who is Goliath? Where did he come from?* Try as she might, Rebecca couldn't make the pieces of the puzzle fit together.

She soon lost track of time. As they traveled, her eyes drifted over to where Jeffrey walked between Jerome and Lisa. She studied her husband's face, noting the concern and worry etched there. *Oh Lord,* she prayed quietly, the deep wound in her heart reopening as she watched him. *What am I going to do about him? Is there still any love in his heart for me, or has his logical side pushed away all of his feelings? Why is all of this happening? Is this your way of forcing us to spend time together so we can rekindle our relationship?* Despite her pain, Rebecca laughed inwardly at her own foolishness. *Sure, Becky, God's going to have you attacked by giants, pteranodons, and primitive men so you can spend more time with your estranged husband. They say God works in mysterious ways, but this would certainly be the strangest. I don't know, maybe this is just another vision or a dream. Maybe I'll just wake up and find out I've been in a coma like last time and Jeffrey will still…*

Rebecca's thoughts were suddenly interrupted as Lisa called out softly, "What on earth is that?" Following her gaze, Rebecca could barely make out the shapes of two more natives standing beside a large animal

farther ahead on the trail. As they drew closer to the beast and its care-
takers, Rebecca could see that it was facing away from them and was
hitched to a small wooden trailer. The animal itself had thick, stump-like
legs, and stood approximately six feet tall. It resembled a small elephant,
except its skin was scale-like and dark green with numerous ebony-col-
ored swirling patterns in various places across its hide. In addition, it had
an extremely long, thick tail, similar to that of...

"A triceratops!" Lisa exclaimed in shock as the creature turned its
head to watch the approach of the hunting party.

"Not quite, but darn close," Jeffrey said in awe. "This thing only has
one horn. That would make it a...mono-something. Mono..."

"Monoclonius," Jerome finished. "You never were very good at
remembering names, even in school." The warriors brought them to a
halt several feet behind the trailer. As they stood admiring the animal, the
two warriors who had been carrying the dead pteranodons unstrapped
them from their backs and placed them on the trailer alongside several
other dead animals, prizes from other recent hunts. Goliath, ignoring the
others, took advantage of the delay by sitting down and closing his eyes.

"Amazing, simply amazing," Jeffrey said, ignoring the friendly jab.
"Look at the swirling camouflage patterns on its body."

"Yeah, bones certainly don't tell you anything about the skin. It's a
shame fossilized skin is so rare," Jerome commented.

"This one looks kind of small," Jeffrey said. "I remember studying
these when we were doing our grad work. Remember when we visited
Dr. Sellman at that dinosaur excavation in the North Dakota badlands?
He mentioned that the monoclonius was much smaller than the toro-
saurus he was working on. He said they were usually...twenty feet long,
I think. This one doesn't look to be more than about twelve. Do you
think it's a juvenile?"

Jerome thought for a moment before responding. "I don't think so.
Maybe this one's a runt, or the few other specimens are abnormally large.
Remember one of Dr. Eisenberg's axioms: 'Bones can only tell you so
much.'"

"Jeffrey, look!" Lisa said in astonishment. "The cart the dinosaur is hauling doesn't have wheels! It's just floating in the air."

Jeffrey and the others immediately turned their attention to the trailer containing the dead animals. "Would you look at that?" Jerome commented. "We were so busy studying the monoclonius that we totally missed this."

Although they couldn't get close enough to the trailer for an in-depth examination, they could see traces of bluish light reflecting off the forest floor beneath the cart.

"It looks like some kind of gravity control device, just like what Elmer uses," Akwen stated.

"But how could primitives have such technology?" Jeffrey asked. "Do you think there might be some connection between them and the aliens who built the pyramid?"

Jerome shook his head. "This is just too bizarre. I wish the doc were here. Maybe he would have some sort of clue."

"I wish he were here too," Akwen echoed. "What is taking dem so long? We are running out of time. It has been over an hour since we landed. And, in case you haven't noticed, we have been traveling down-hill da entire time. Dat means we have to head back *uphill* in order to return to da ship. Dat is going to tire us all out pretty quickly."

"Have you tried to communicate with Elmer?" Jeffrey asked.

"Yes, and he has not responded, which worries me even more," Akwen said.

"Don't worry," Jeffrey replied with more confidence than he felt. "Doc won't let us down."

Akwen, clearly not encouraged by Jeffrey's statement, simply rolled her eyes and turned away, ending the conversation.

Once the warriors had the bodies of the pteranodons securely tied to the trailer, the party continued its march. The hazy afternoon sun had begun its lazy descent toward the horizon, causing the shadows around them to stretch and lengthen. The group walked for another twenty minutes without incident, which only increased the tension levels of the prisoners. *Something* should have happened by now. A couple of times, Rebecca had to remind herself not to look behind for signs of Mack or Dr. Eisenberg. If the warriors caught her looking, then they might expect an attack.

The trail wound its way through the forest, at times passing between large hills and mounds. As Jerome and the others rounded one such mound, he jabbed Jeffrey in the ribs with his elbow. "Look!" he whispered as he raised his bound hands to point to a large monolith sitting on the ground off to the left of the trail. The object was a ten-foot-tall, gray boulder made of basalt and sculpted into the likeness of an African head wearing a helmet. The lower jaw of the giant statue rested firmly on the ground, and its eyes were closed as if in meditation.

"What is that?" Rebecca asked.

"It's one of the famous Olmec heads," Jerome answered.

"Who were the Olmecs?" Lisa asked.

"They were a pre-Columbian race of people that lived in south-central Mexico from around 1400 BCE all the way up to the beginning of the Common Era," Jeffrey said. "Many believe they were the parent culture of the Aztecs and Mayans. Their name means 'rubber people' in the language of the Aztecs because they extracted latex from a local tree and used it to make rubber."[1]

Before he could say any more, the white-faced leader of the warriors motioned to two of his warriors, who turned around and grabbed Akwen and Jerome by their arms and pushed them over to stand near the stone head. Fear coursed through Jerome's veins, causing him to trip, and he nearly fell forward onto his face. Finally gaining his footing, he took a deep breath in an effort to calm his nerves.

His fear was unwarranted, however, as the native leader seemed content to simply stare at the two of them and compare their features to those etched into the rock. Two of the other warriors approached their leader, and the three began gesturing and talking rapidly in their language.

"What's going on?" Rebecca whispered to Jeffrey, never once taking her eyes off the situation unfolding before them.

"Well, based on the interest they had in Jerome and Akwen when they first captured us, I would say the only place they've ever seen African facial features before is on this Olmec head," Jeffrey answered.

"Wait a minute," Lisa said. "If the Olmec people lived over three thousand years ago, how would they know what Africans looked like? Africans weren't brought over to Central America until the slave trade began."

"That's one of the great mysteries about the Olmec heads," Jeffrey said. They are considered to be OOPArts."

"A what?" Lisa asked.

"OOPArts stands for 'Out-Of-Place Artifacts,'" Jeffrey replied softly, his attention still focused on watching what the warriors were doing. "It basically means artifacts that don't fit with the accepted historical timeline."

Although Rebecca found Jeffrey's comment interesting, her concern for Jerome and Akwen prevented her from delving further into the subject.

Their curiosity in Jerome and Akwen apparently satisfied, the warriors returned the two dark-skinned companions to the line. Jerome, thankful to still be alive, closed his eyes, bowed his head, and breathed deeply. Coming up beside him, Jeffrey did his best to encourage his longtime friend.

"Hang in there buddy. You'll make it."

Jerome looked up at him, concern etched on his features. "I don't know how much more of this I can take, Jeffrey. I'm an archaeologist, not some street fighter or athlete. I enjoy quiet work, not this. I have to admit, I am scared."

"Hey, man, it's going to be okay," Jeffrey said softly.

"C'mon, don't insult me," Jerome snapped back. "Don't tell me some stupid platitudes. I know we're in serious trouble here. We may not make it back. I may never see my wife or kids again. My daughter is in the hospital and I don't even know if she's okay. We're already up to our necks in hospital bills, and if I don't come back...how will Tarshwa...? Jeffrey, promise me that if anything happens to me—"

"—No," Jeffrey interrupted. "Don't even go there. Let's just focus on making sure we get back. Is that a deal? Focus."

Jerome was silent for a few seconds, then, looking at Jeffrey eye to eye, he nodded slowly, his face resolute. "Yeah. It's a deal."

Jeffrey smiled warmly at his friend. "C'mon, we're going."

A moment later, the warriors prodded the dinosaur forward and they continued their journey. A few minutes farther down the trail, the forest to the east began to slant downward sharply, allowing the group to see over the tops of the trees and down to the plains beyond. The panorama was breathtaking. Far to the east, a vast body of crystal blue water stretched to the horizon. Between the water and the small mountain upon which they stood lay a vast plain covered with lush green vegetation. As breathtaking as the natural vista was, the small group of prisoners found that what was *on* the plain took their breath away far more, but for a completely different reason.

"Oh my Lord!" Lisa whispered in awe. "It's an ancient city!"

"But it's inhabited," Rebecca pointed out. "Those aren't just sightseers."

"Dose look like pyramid temples, like what da Aztecs and Mayans used to build," Akwen added.

Jerome's eyes suddenly grew wide with fear. Doing his best to control his breathing, he leaned over to Jeffrey. "Do you recognize where we are? And this city is *inhabited!* Do you know what this means?"

Staring straight towards the city, his mind still whirring with the implications, Jeffrey nodded slowly. "Yes. I don't understand how it's possible, but we've been captured by real Mayans!"

10

MACK'S ESCAPE PLAN

"WHAT!" LISA EXCLAIMED a little too loudly, causing the warriors nearby to raise their weapons instinctively. Softening her voice, she continued. "You mean, Mayans—as in 'cut-your-still-beating-heart-out-of-your-chest-and-sacrifice-you-on-a-temple-altar' Mayans?"

"Yep," Jeffrey said curtly. "And that's probably what they have in mind for us."

For the first time since their capture, Goliath spoke to them. "So how much longer are you going to wait for your friends to rescue you? I have a means of freeing my wrists, but I can't take on all of these warriors alone. If we work together, at least some of us might be able to make it."

They walked on in silence as each considered the short selection of options. Finally, Jeffrey spoke for all of them. "We'll give them ten more minutes. If they haven't contacted us before then, we'll try to escape on our own."

Time seemed to drag on interminably as they walked, each one counting the minutes and mentally preparing for the inevitable confrontation. As the ten-minute deadline neared, they passed another hill that had risen up on their right. On the other side of it, a strange fog blanketed only a fifty-foot-square area on the right side of the trail, and nothing else. Tendrils of mist floated eerily across the trail, causing the warriors to raise their weapons and look about them nervously, their eyes frantically searching the fog in an attempt to peer into its mysterious depths.

"What's that smell?" Jerome asked, his nose wrinkling as he sampled the air.

"I don't know," Rebecca said. "But it smells like…refrigerant." The warriors were also sniffing the air and talking to each other; their movements were quick and agitated.

A sudden, horrifying wail pierced the air, echoing off the nearby mound. The high-pitched, otherworldly sound froze the blood in their veins. "What…what was that?" Lisa asked, fear seizing her heart.

The Mayan hunters were obviously asking each other the same question. Weapons in hand, the captors momentarily forgot about their prisoners in light of this new, unknown threat.

"Now's our chance!" Goliath whispered intently. "They're not watching us. Be ready to act." Reaching into a sheath hidden inside the armor around his waist, the giant produced a small knife. Flipping it over deftly in his hands, he began to cut away at the ropes tying his wrists. Just as the ropes fell away, the warriors and prisoners alike gasped in dread as an apparition appeared out of the mist and began floating towards them, its cloaked body hovering several feet off the ground.

Another shriek pierced the air, prompting the captives to reflexively reach up to cover their ears. As it approached, the hooded specter raised one of its arms. A blast of yellow energy shot out from the end of its cloaked arm to strike the hindquarters of the dinosaur, causing the creature to sprint forward down the path, howling in pain. Several warriors were nearly trampled as the stampeding animal ran past them, the wooden trailer gliding silently behind it.

The Mayans began backing away hurriedly, a few managing to loose arrows at the specter as they moved. One of the shafts struck the floating figure in the side with a dull, metallic thud. After its initial impact, the shaft began to fall until the tip of the arrow snagged on the fabric of the cloak.

Lisa moved close to Goliath, casting quick glances up at the approaching figure. "Quick, cut my bonds! I have a weapon we can use," she said, afraid to reveal to the giant who the weapon's original owner truly was. The wolf-like creature quickly sliced through the vines tying Lisa's wrists as the cloaked figure shot several more beams of yellow energy at the warriors' weapons, splintering them with impeccable accuracy.

Hands freed, Lisa reached into her inside pocket and began to extract the laser pistol when suddenly Akwen appeared at her side. "Wait!" she shouted in Lisa's ears. Turning her head to look at her, Lisa was caught completely off guard as Akwen started to laugh. Thinking perhaps the Cameroonian woman had lost her mind, Lisa pulled the pistol out of her pocket and raised it toward the floating figure.

Putting her still-bound hands on Lisa's arms, Akwen forced her colleague to lower her weapon. "Don't you see? It is Elmer!"

The others were dumbfounded as they stared at the cloaked form. The Mayan leader shouted something and the warriors began to break off the attack, many of them weaponless due the cloaked figure's precise hits. As they ran off down the trail after the departed dinosaur, two other figures emerged from the mist.

"Ha! I told you it would work, Doc!" Mack said as he and Dr. Eisenberg ran forward to greet them. He stopped abruptly, however, as he noticed that Goliath was no longer bound. Lisa, realizing the threat was now standing beside her, quickly pivoted and raised her weapon. But the giant was faster.

Reaching out with his massive hand, Goliath attempted to grab the gun from Lisa's hand. Reacting at the last second, Lisa slipped the weapon below the giant's outstretched arm. However, since Lisa still hadn't fully recovered her balance from the pivot, the sudden dodge caused her to lose her footing. Falling to the ground, she quickly rolled over and pointed the blaster at the giant, only to have it kicked from her hand by Goliath's large foot.

"Freeze, Goliat'!" Akwen yelled. "If you even so much as twitch in a way I don't like, my droid will fry you where you stand!" she spat angrily, mocking the giant with his own words.

Goliath stood motionless as he sensed the robed figure hovering several feet behind his back.

Rebecca reached down with her bound hands and helped Lisa to her feet as Jeffrey walked over and retrieved the gun. "Let's not waste any more time. Those Mayans could be back any minute now. Doc, Mack, let's get these vines cut. Then we can tie up this thing and get moving."

"Wait!" Goliath said. "You can't leave me here."

"Wanna bet?" Jeffrey's eyes narrowed as he raised the pistol toward the giant. "Just watch us."

"If you leave me, then you and the woman will die," he said, looking over at Rebecca.

"What are you talking about?" Rebecca said as she felt the hairs stand up on the back of her neck.

"Just before the pyramid lifted off, Hercules and I injected miniature explosives into your bodies while you lay unconscious. If you kill me now, those explosives will detonate. Only I can tell you where they are and how to deactivate them."

Rebecca felt a sudden heat course through her body. *Is it true? Could I have a walking time bomb inside of me?* "No," she said in defiance. "I've never heard of such technology. It has to be bluffing."

"But can we risk it?" Jeffrey asked nervously.

Far in the distance, the sound of a hunting horn rang out. The group exchanged rapid glances with each other as Mack began frantically hacking at the vines binding Rebecca's wrists with his knife. "Well, ladies and gents," he said rapidly, imitating a very proper British accent, "might I suggest that we take this bloke with us and postpone this conversation until a more opportune time..." switching over to his regular voice, he finished, "...such as...in orbit?"

"I believe Mack's right," Dr. Eisenberg seconded as he finished cutting the vines off of Jerome's wrists.

"Fine. Akwen, tell Elmer that he is to guard this thing at all times, and if it threatens us in any way, then he is to kill it," Jeffrey instructed. Akwen immediately nodded in affirmation and began commanding the droid. "Now let's get out of here."

The group ran back down the trail for more than ten minutes, frequently glancing over their shoulders for signs of pursuit. The farther they ran, the more each person's physical conditioning, or lack thereof, began to show. Eventually, Jeffrey called a halt to allow time for Mack, Jerome, and Dr. Eisenberg to catch up. Once they had regrouped, Jerome, still panting heavily, asked, "Do you…think they are…still following us?"

Jeffrey shook his head. "I don't know, but I don't want to take any chances."

"I will ask Elmer to continually scan da area for any movement," Akwen suggested as she removed the black blanket that had served as the droid's cloak. "Dat way we don't have to keep looking over our shoulders."

"Good idea," Jeffrey said. "We need to keep moving, though. We're running short on time. If we hold to our current pace, we should be able to get back to the ship before it launches."

"Besides, we need to at least keep walking," Rebecca commented. "After running so long, we shouldn't just stop. We might cramp up."

"Come on, give us a break!" Mack complained. "I'm not used to all this activity. My calves are already burning something fierce with all of this uphill climbin'."

"Oh, quit your whining," Akwen spat in disgust. "We wouldn't be in such a hurry if it hadn't taken you so long to rescue us!"

"Wow, that's gratitude for ya," Mack said sarcastically. "While you guys were enjoying your pleasant afternoon stroll on a nice dirt road, we had to first come up with a plan for rescuing you, then figure out how to make a cloak for the Grim Reaper over here, and then work our way through the jungle to get in front of you guys." He paused to take a breath, which he did very loudly and dramatically. "As it is, if you hadn't stopped to sightsee at those big stone heads, we might not have been able to set our ambush properly. So I'm entitled to a little whining!"

For the first time any of them could remember, Akwen backed down at Mack's monologue and apologized. "Well, you made us worried," she said. "Sorry."

Mack was so stunned by his surprising verbal victory that he just stared straight ahead, his mouth hanging open in shock. The tension that had plagued the group for the past several hours drained away as they all—including Akwen—let out hearty laughs. Goliath, still under the ever-watchful eye of the floating droid, simply ignored them.

"I do have to say, that was quite an ingenious plan you concocted," Jerome said with a grin. "But I have to ask: Where did you come up with that wail? I doubt that sound was in Elmer's original memory banks."

"Actually, because Elmer has nearly the entire World Wide Web stored in his memory, I just got the sound bite from a website. It was from this movie I saw that had these creepy, undead ancient kings who wore cloaks and who were chasing after this short guy who had this special magic ring—"

"—and so we figured since we couldn't fight the warriors, we would play off of their fears and scare them off," Dr. Eisenberg said, interrupting Mack and saving the rest of them from a lengthy explanation.

"Well, we're all in your debt," Rebecca said. "Thank you both."

"Yes, we are very grateful," Akwen said sincerely. "But I still would like to know why I couldn't reach Elmer. Why didn't you contact us to let us know where you were? We had just about given up on you and were ready to try to make our own escape, which probably would have gotten us killed."

"We did try to contact you through Elmer," Dr. Eisenberg explained. "However, each time we tried, Elmer just shut down. We think the glitch he has been experiencing is related somehow to his wireless unit."

"Yeah, it's a good thing you told us how to reset him before he glitched out on us, or we never would've been able to find you," Mack said.

Akwen nodded. "I'll have to check it when we get back to da ship."

As they began walking once more, Rebecca fell in line next to Dr. Eisenberg. "How are you holding up, Doc?" she asked.

The doctor smiled at her as he wiped sweat from his bald head with a pocket handkerchief. "I'm hangin' in there, Rebecca. I'm just glad I decided to join those aerobics classes this past year. Otherwise, I never even would have made it this far."

Rebecca returned his smile. "Just let us know if you need to take a breather."

They made good time, despite the fact that they were walking uphill much of the way. An hour passed with no signs of further pursuit, much to their relief. Before long, they turned off the path and had begun heading straight west toward the shallow river, and their hearts rose as they heard the sounds of the waterfall in the distance. Even more, they still had over twenty minutes before the pyramid would be fully charged, giving them some time to spare.

As they continued to walk, an uneasy feeling began to creep over Rebecca. Although the sensation continued to grow stronger, the source of her anxiety managed to hover just on the edges of her conscious thought.

"Oh, that waterfall sounds great right about now," Mack said. "I think I'm going to stand near the edge of it for a minute or so and let the mist just cool me off."

"The waterfall," Rebecca said softly. That was it. There was something wrong about the waterfall. Suddenly she had it: "Does the waterfall sound louder than it did before?" she asked the others.

They paused for a moment to listen. "Now that you mention it, it does sound a little louder," Jeffrey confirmed.

"Yeah, so what?" Mack said. "Maybe you just didn't notice it as much before because you were *prisoners!*"

"No, she's right," Goliath said. "Something's wrong. The rumble we hear is from more than just the waterfall."

"Elmer, do you—"

Before the words even left her mouth, Elmer suddenly announced, "Dr. Nancho, several animals just left the trail behind us and are heading this way. And there appear to be two or three humans riding each animal."

Without another word, the eight companions took off running as fast as they could. Within a minute, they reached the shallow river and the waterfall. Slowing only slightly, they splashed into the river and waded across. Just as they reached the other side, the unmistakable sounds of animals tramping down the path drowned out the thunder of the waterfall. Turning to look over her shoulder, Rebecca saw a group of eight monoclonius dinosaurs charging toward them, each with two riders seated on their backs.

"They must have gone back to the city for reinforcements!" Lisa shouted.

"Or called for help with those horn blasts," Goliath added, pausing to grab his helmet, which was still lying next to the fallen tree where the giant had placed it before being taken captive.

"Elmer, see if you can slow dem down. Shoot at deir mounts!" Akwen cried out. Dutifully obeying orders, the droid turned back around towards the oncoming warriors and opened fire. Several of the beasts in the front of the line swerved to the side to avoid the yellow laser blasts, causing the riders to nearly lose their balance. Elmer continued to fire as it floated backward, following Akwen and the others in their flight.

Although Elmer's initial shots succeeded in frightening the dinosaurs, it didn't take long for the iron wills of their masters to get the animals heading back in the right direction, in spite of the continued laser fire from Elmer.

"They're getting closer!" Mack yelled. The physical exertion conspired with Mack's burst of fear to cause his lungs to begin to close. Wheezing and struggling to breathe, he slowed down and leaned against a tree while groping in his pocket for his inhaler. Seeing him stop, Rebecca halted her own mad dash and ran over to help him.

"Mack, are you okay?" she asked as she pulled up next to him.

The language specialist removed the inhaler from his mouth and was just about to reply when an arrow slammed into the tree near his head. Looking sideways at the wooden shaft, Mack's eyes widened with the realization that his life had just been spared by mere inches.

"C'mon!" Rebecca yelled as she grabbed him by the arm, shaking him out of his stupor.

Together they ran to catch up with the others, who had just exited the forest and entered the clearing. Through the trees, Rebecca could barely make out the shape of the pyramid still sitting calmly in the center of the clearing. Arrows whizzed around her and Mack as the dinosaurs and their riders drew closer. Rebecca threw a quick glance over her shoulder to see one of the lumbering animals bearing down on her. The second warrior, sitting behind the driver, was preparing to launch his spear at her when suddenly a bright green laser bolt slammed into the thick hide of the animal, causing it to stumble. Both the riders flew from the animal to land in a heap several feet away.

Still running full tilt, Rebecca turned back around and saw Lisa standing in the clearing, Goliath's gun in her hand. "Hurry, Becky!" she shouted as she unleashed several more deadly bolts into the woods toward the Mayan hunters. Next to her, Elmer continued to rain down a steady stream of laser fire as it floated backward in the direction of the pyramid.

As they entered the clearing, Rebecca could hear Mack's breathing become more and more labored as he fought against the respiratory malady that threatened to close down his lungs.

"You can make it, Mack," Rebecca said as she put an arm around him. "We're almost there. Just a few more feet."

An explosion rocked the ground behind them, causing Rebecca and Mack to stumble and fall. Roars of pain bellowed from the dinosaurs, and the unnerving sound mixed with the cries of the Mayan hunters. Looking around in confusion, Rebecca saw Goliath's massive form materialize several feet behind her, another grenade held ready in his right hand.

"Rebecca, are you hurt?" Dr. Eisenberg asked as he came running up to help her and Mack stand.

"I'm fine," she said, throwing a sideways glance at Goliath as he passed her and headed towards the entrance to the pyramid.

"It looks like Goliath's grenade broke up the charge," Lisa said as she hurried up beside them, her body and gun still pointing backward. "Let's hope they're smart enough to know when they're outgunned."

As Rebecca and the others turned toward the entrance to the pyramid, now just twenty feet away, they stopped in alarm as the main door closed with a bang. A moment later, the low rumble of the pyramid's engines filled the clearing.

"It's lifting off!" Mack gasped. "What is Akwen thinking?"

"Hurry, up the side steps!" Rebecca shouted. "We can get in through the hole in the roof!"

Weary as the travelers were, they climbed faster than they thought possible. Goliath, large legs taking the steps two at a time, dropped through the hole as the engines picked up speed. Elmer floated through right behind the giant, weapon still trained on the creature. Based on past experience, Rebecca knew only seconds were left before the ship would begin to phase and the beams of white energy would course through the opening, cutting off their entrance.

Finally, the group arrived at the summit of the pyramid. As they reached the six-foot-wide square opening in the ceiling, they saw Jeffrey and Jerome standing below, beckoning for them to jump. Without hesitation, Rebecca and Lisa helped Mack through the opening. Once he was clear, Rebecca signaled for Lisa to follow him. Nodding quickly, Lisa swung over the edge and disappeared.

"Go, Doc," she said hurriedly as the whine of the engines continued its crescendo.

"No, you go first!" he shouted. "I'll be right behind. There's no time to argue!"

Not wanting to leave him, but afraid to waste any more time, Rebecca grabbed the edge and swung her legs through the hole. Jeffrey and Jerome immediately grabbed her and lowered her gently to the floor. Looking up anxiously, she watched as Dr. Eisenberg gripped the edge and dropped through the hole just as the beam of light shot out from the central pillar, blinding them all.

11

EXPLANATIONS AND THEORIES

"DR. EISENBERG! WHERE'S Doc?" Rebecca called out as she shielded her eyes from the light streaming through the hole in the ceiling. "Did he make it? Doc!"

"I'm here, Rebecca," came a weak voice from somewhere off to her left. "Tired and bruised, but still alive."

"Thank God!" she breathed. Walking carefully on the now-disappearing floor, she crossed over to the professor and hugged him, allowing the fear and anxiety from the recent events to drain out of her.

"What happened?" Lisa asked, her voice tinged with confusion and barely contained anger. Marching over to where Akwen sat on the stool directly in front of the control console, she swore. "Why did you start the liftoff so soon? What's the matter with you—"

"—Stop right dere before you say someting you will really regret!" Akwen commanded as she swung her head around to look at Lisa. "I did not start da liftoff sequence. We underestimated da time it would take for da ship to recharge. I ran up here to get ready to shut da door once everyone was inside, and discovered dat da core was fully charged. I tried to stop da liftoff, but it was too late. Now, if you would be so kind,

I need you to watch dat ting," she said, nodding in Goliath's direction, "so dat Elmer can plug into da computer and help me get control." As Akwen turned back to the piloting station, her body, along with everyone else's, began to phase to match the ship's now-transparent walls.

Lisa, feeling foolish but unwilling to let go of her anger so easily, raised her weapon and pointed it at the giant, who stood silently near the top of the stairs. "You, get away from there. Over to the other corner, now!" Without a word, the giant followed instructions. Reaching the northeast corner of the room, he sat down cross-legged on the floor as the streams of white light shot up from the corners of the room to join with the central beam. A moment later, the pyramid began lifting off the ground.

"Oh…" Mack groaned as he leaned up against the nearly invisible central pillar, his eyes closed in pain. "I think that herd of dinosaurs somehow leapt into my head while we were climbing up the pyramid. I've got a splitting…*Whoa*. Man, that's cool," he said, cutting himself off as he opened his eyes and watched the ascent into orbit through the transparent walls.

Now that the fear of what would happen had worn off, the pyramid's passengers found themselves enjoying the view as they traveled through the different layers of the atmosphere and crossed over into the blackness of space.

"It's almost like flying," Jerome commented softly.

"Yeah, except without the wind in your face," Jeffrey said. Looking at his friend, he grinned and said, "Yah know, it's too bad Tarshwa isn't here to see this."

Jerome laughed. "Are you kidding? She would've had a heart attack before we cleared the tree line!"

Before long, the engines slowed down and the vessel settled into orbit around the planet. Thirty seconds later, the walls darkened, the interior of the ship returned to normal, and the engines revved up once again.

"Well, so far this trip has been exactly like the last one," Jeffrey said, "which means we probably have several hours until we start to descend out of orbit. So, I think we should make good use of that time by putting our heads together to figure out what exactly happened down there.

"But, before we officially bring this 'meeting' to order, we have a little unfinished business to take care of," he said as he walked over to where Goliath sat on the floor. "Lisa, give me the gun."

"What…what are you going to do?" Lisa asked, her voice showing her concern over Jeffrey's request. Handing the weapon over, she watched as he studied it briefly, then pointed it directly at the giant's head.

The others, who had gathered around in a semi-circle, stood in tense silence, waiting to see what Jeffrey had planned.

"Who, or what, are you, and who sent you to attack us?" Jeffrey asked sternly, his hand shaking slightly as he held the pistol.

A sound that was part growl, part laugh escaped from Goliath's lips as he stared unblinkingly back at the archaeologist. "So now you're going to play soldier, is that it, Mr. Evans? Are you sure you can handle that thing without hurting yourself? Maybe you should let your ex-Marine wife hold it for you."

Fighting to control his own temper, Jeffrey took a deep breath before continuing. "You seem to know a lot about us. Who do you work for?"

The giant sat motionless for a moment. Then, apparently deciding to divulge his secrets, he replied. "Hercules and I are cybernetic organisms programmed to guard the secrets of this pyramid."

"Whoa…" Mack said in awe as he ran his hand through his black, unruly hair. "You mean you're a robot? Like the Terminator!"

Ignoring Mack's comment, Jeffrey continued to stare hard at the giant, as if trying to visually locate signs of Goliath's robotic nature. "Who created you and programmed you?"

"We don't know," the giant said, his thin lips lifting in a contemptuous snarl. "It may be difficult to believe for someone with your vast intellect, and I have no proof, but I'm telling you the truth. When Hercules and I awoke, we found ourselves inside of a cave in the middle of Iraq. We already had preprogrammed into our memories your names and details about the layout of your compound and dig site, as well as knowledge on how to operate the weapons and technology we were given."

"If you don't know who programmed you, den who were dese 'bene-factors' you mentioned earlier?" Akwen asked, her eyes narrowing. "You were quite certain dat dey would be happy to see you when you arrived with dis ship."

Goliath answered without hesitation. "We don't know who they are, but our mission was to recover the technical books and any digital copies of them, as well as destroy the pyramid. If they wanted us to recover the books, don't you think they would also give us a location of where to return them?"

"And just how were you going to destroy the ship?" Rebecca asked, her mouth suddenly dry.

"Our bodies are powered by nuclear reactors. Once I escaped with the plans, Hercules was going to detonate his reactor."

"A suicide mission," Lisa breathed. The realization of what would have happened to them had they not launched the pyramid struck them all simultaneously, causing a somber silence to blanket the room.

A moment later, Jeffrey swallowed hard, his hand unsteady on the pistol's grip. "And so what will you do now that Plan A didn't succeed?"

Goliath let out another growled laugh. "If you are wondering if I am going to blow myself up to complete the mission, you can rest at ease. The plans themselves are to be saved if at all possible. They are the first priority. However," he added, his eyes narrowing menacingly, "while we were captured, I set my reactor so that it would explode if I am 'killed,' so I recommend that you think twice about pulling that trigger."

Looking at the gun in his hand, Jeffrey nodded. Deciding to take the giant's advice, he took a moment to consider his options. Making up his mind, he pulled the trigger.

"WHAT ARE YOU DOING!!!" Mack screamed in panic. "Didn't you just hear what it said! Oh my... We're gonna die! We're all gonna die!"

"Relax," Jeffrey said calmly as he handed the weapon back to Lisa.

"I didn't kill it. I lowered the power setting to non-lethal. It'll just be asleep for awhile." Stepping over to the body that was now slumped over on the floor, Jeffrey reached around Goliath's back and located the hidden sleeve where the giant had placed the technical books. Once they were removed, he unzipped the small pocket on Goliath's left arm and removed the flash drive containing the digital copies.

"Do you think it was telling the truth?" Jerome asked.

"It's hard to tell," Jeffrey said as he stood to his feet once more. "As it said, we have no proof that it is telling the truth. However, I do find it a little convenient that we can't 'kill' it without risking blowing ourselves up, just like we couldn't leave it behind because it planted some kind of nano-bomb inside us."

Rebecca shook her head. "I don't find that hard to believe at all. People who are focused only on their own survival take extra precautions."

"One thing's for sure, I don't trust it," Jeffrey said. "Until we have a better idea of what's going on, I don't want us to have to keep someone guarding it at all times. Especially since we don't know what kind of hidden weapons it may still have. We know it has a knife and some grenades stashed somewhere, and who knows what else. And I'm not sure it's a wise idea to go snooping around its armor. Who knows what other kinds of hidden traps it may have to keep people from taking its stuff? So unless anyone has a better idea, I'd just as soon we keep it on ice."

"What do we do now?" Jerome asked.

"Well, for starters, I think we should try to put our heads together and see if we can't figure out what happened down there," Jeffrey suggested.

"It would probably be a good idea to start with a list of what we know for certain," Dr. Eisenberg offered.

"Dat shouldn't take long," Akwen muttered.

"Okay," Jeffrey began. "Correct me if I am wrong. We know we landed on earth in Central America. We also know that we encountered live pteranodons, which have been extinct for over seventy million years."

Jeffrey's statement brought a buried thought to the forefront of Rebecca's consciousness. She nearly interrupted Jeffrey, but then thought better of it. She didn't want to mention it without first getting verification.

"We also saw live monoclonius dinosaurs, which have been extinct for over sixty-five million years, being used as steeds and beasts of burden by humans," Jeffrey continued. "Since we know humans and dinosaurs were separated by millions of years, we have a major discrepancy. We also know the Mayan civilization ended well over a millennium ago, and we know that they didn't have anti-gravity technology, which poses several other problems."

"I think a good place to start would be with the question of whether or not what we experienced was real," Dr. Eisenberg stated. "Could it be that someone, for one reason or another, has decided to play an elaborate hoax on us?"

"Or perhaps we are part of some mind-altering experiment," Jerome offered.

"Or maybe we're all dreaming," Lisa said, looking at Rebecca. Returning her friend's gaze, Rebecca tried to read her expression and the inflection of her voice. Lisa quickly looked away, leaving Rebecca unsure as to whether her comment was meant to be sarcastic or genuine.

"That gunshot from Goliath was real enough," Jeffrey said, rubbing his wounded left shoulder. Suddenly, Rebecca realized his injury was located just a little higher than the wound she herself had received during her trip to Ka'esch. *Is this a coincidence? Could we really be having a mass vision? But if so, to what end?* she wondered.

"And let us not forget dat Hercules was killed by dose pteranodons," Akwen pointed out.

"That's true, but what if Goliath and Hercules are part of the plan to confuse us?" Dr. Eisenberg countered. "Maybe Hercules didn't really die."

"Well, I for one have a hard time believing this is a mass hallucination," Jeffrey stated. "As for being a hoax, I can't think of any logical way anyone could believably create the things we saw."

"But that's what we thought about the aliens that originally attacked us, and they just turned out to be holograms," Jerome replied.

"No, those aliens were different," Rebecca said, shaking her head. "When I saw them up close and in good lighting, I could tell they weren't real. Besides, that pteranodon I hit was solid. If it had been a hologram, then that tree branch I swung would have passed right through it."

"Besides, why would anyone want to go through all of the time, trouble, and expense to create such a wild hoax?" Lisa questioned.

"Could the dinosaurs and pteranodons have been robots?" Dr. Eisenberg suggested.

"No, I don't tink so," Akwen said matter-of-factly. "Robotics has come a long way in da last fifty years, but I don't tink it is possible yet to make a life-sized, self-sustaining, robotic dinosaur."

"But what about our giant friend here?" Jerome said, pointing at Goliath's motionless form. "It seems pretty realistic for a robot."

"If *it* is really a robot," Akwen replied. "As far as I know, Elmer is da most advanced form of artificial intelligence known to mankind. But even he is quite far removed from da complexities of creating a machine capable of doing what Goliath can do."

"So do you think Goliath was created by aliens?" Dr. Eisenberg asked.

"It is possible," Akwen shrugged.

"Maybe Goliath was created by the same beings who created this ship," Jeffrey suggested. "That might explain why they were sent to retrieve the technical journals and destroy it."

"If that was really what they were sent to do," Rebecca offered. "I'm not sure we can trust anything Goliath said. Maybe Goliath and Hercules are not robots at all."

"Do you think there's a way we could find out if it is a cyborg?" Lisa asked

"What about Elmer?" Jerome said with excitement. "Does he have some kind of scanner that could—"

Akwen cut him off before he could finish his sentence. "—No. He is not equipped with anyting like dat."

"Okay, getting back on track, I think we're all agreed we can rule out the theory that this isn't real," Jeffrey concluded. "So, if it is indeed real, how do we explain these discrepancies? Mack, you've been pretty silent through all of this. As our resident sci-fi expert, do you have any theories?"

Still sitting on the floor with his back against the central wall, Mack opened his eyes momentarily to look up at Jeffrey. When he spoke, his voice sounded weak, like he was suffering the aftereffects of a night of partying. "Well, I've given it some thought," he said. "It seems to me the most logical explanation is that this ship we're riding in is not a spaceship at all, but rather a device that can travel to other dimensions."

For a moment, no one said a word. Jeffrey broke the silence. "Would you care to elaborate? What kind of other dimensions? What makes you think that?"

"The only way to make all the evidence fit together is if we're no longer on *our* earth," Mack expounded slowly, his head continuing to throb with each word. "Some scientists have speculated that there may be parallel universes to our own. They're the same in many ways, but events happen differently in each one. Did any of you ever see the remake of *The Planet of the Apes*?" When no one nodded in the affirmative, Mack let out a snort of disgust. "Don't you guys ever watch movies?" His head suddenly pounded heavily, causing him to regret his short outburst.

"Not any of those old, two-dimensional ones anyway," Jerome said.

"Hey, at least those were more than just special-effects extravaganzas," Mack replied. "They had character and depth! Give me a good 2-D flick with a real plot any day over these modern, over-priced, and over-produced 3-D pics."

"Just get to your point," Akwen said.

"Well, at the end of the movie, the human character travels back to earth," Mack continued after throwing Akwen a dirty look. "Only it isn't the earth he left. He lands his spaceship in Washington DC. There's a Lincoln Memorial, but sitting in Lincoln's chair is an ape. On this earth, apes evolved to become the dominant species on the planet, yet it resembled earth exactly, even to the point of having the same monuments and buildings."

"So let me see if I understand you," Jeffrey said, cocking his head slightly as he stared down at Mack. "You're suggesting that we traveled to an earth where dinosaurs never died out and the Mayan civilization survived until the modern era?"

"Precisely," Mack confirmed. "Not only that, but maybe the Mayans conquered the whole world."

"Dat is da stupidest ting I have ever heard," Akwen stated emphatically. "I can't believe you even take him seriously."

"Do you have a better theory to explain what happened?" Jeffrey countered, turning to look at her.

Akwen was silent for once, but the firm set of her jaw and fire in her eyes were clear indications that she was not happy.

"I must say that Mack's theory seems a bit far-fetched," Dr. Eisenberg stated. "I think we are missing something very important here, but I just can't seem to put my finger on it."

"Well, at least we have something to go on," Jeffrey said. "I think we'll need more information before we can come up with a definitive answer. We'll just have to wait and see what happens when we land this time. Until then, I think our immediate priority should be to sleep. Most of us had already worked a full day and then some before this whole trip began. Add to that our recent injuries and stress, and I would say that, despite our concerns for getting home, I don't think any of us will have much trouble sleeping."

"I for one would like to get out of these wet clothes before I turn in," Lisa said. "That last run through the river got me soaked. I don't suppose we have anything on this rig to change into?"

Akwen grunted in exasperation. She started to turn away from the group, then paused. "I may have an extra pair or two of NASA coveralls down in my workroom. Dey will probably be too big for you, but you can use dem, if you must." Turning around fully, she strode purposefully over to the control console and sat down.

"That woman has serious issues," Jerome whispered to the others.

"Well, ladies and gents, if anyone needs me, I'll be groaning and writhing in pain in my room," Mack said as he stood and shuffled toward the stairs, his right hand pressed against his forehead.

Turning toward Dr. Eisenberg, Rebecca asked quietly, "Where do we sleep?"

"Sorry, Rebecca. I forgot that you didn't get the full tour," he replied. "When we discovered the pyramid, we found that the room in the southeast corner has two nine-foot beds in it, and the room in the northeast corner has a massive bed that is twelve feet long and six feet wide. They were too big to move, so we just left them in there. Whoever created this pyramid knew they would be going on a long trip. There's even a bathroom located near the 'master bedroom.'"

"You ladies can have the two smaller beds," Jeffrey said. "We'll take the monster bed. Before we do that, however, we need to do something with Goliath. I think the best place to put it would be in the closet of the master bedroom. If we all do this together, we should be able to move it without too much trouble."

Jeffrey's words proved to be mostly true. After much grunting and frustration, they managed to get the giant's body down the steps, through the door of the bedroom, and into the closet.

"If this thing really is a robot, how do we know the stun blast you hit it with will last long enough?" Jerome asked Jeffrey as they exited the closet.

"Good point. We need some way to keep an eye on it," Jeffrey replied.

"If we can find a camera, I'm sure Akwen can find a way to hook it into Elmer," Lisa said. "That way, if Goliath begins to stir, we'll know."

"Great idea," Jeffrey said with a smile. He immediately contacted Akwen using his commlink, and within two minutes, they had the camera set up and the closet door locked.

"C'mon, Becky. Let's go," Lisa said tiredly once their task was complete. Throwing one last glance at Jeffrey, Rebecca wished in her heart that other sleeping arrangements could be made. Banishing her longings, she followed Lisa out of the room.

As the door closed behind the two women, Jerome plopped down on the bed in exhaustion and let out a huge sigh. "What a day."

Dr. Eisenberg walked over to the corner of the bed and began to sit down when he felt Jeffrey's hand on his shoulder. "Wait, Doc," he said. "I'd like to talk to you for a second, if you don't mind."

Straightening up, he looked at Jeffrey, a puzzled expression on his face. "Sure. What's on your mind?"

Casting a quick glance at Jerome, who already appeared to be asleep, Jeffrey looked back at the professor, his expression sober. "I know why you brought Becky here."

Dr. Eisenberg simply stared unblinkingly back at Jeffrey. "Jeffrey, I love you like a son. But what you're doing to her is wrong."

Jeffrey nodded, accepting the rebuke. "I know, but we just aren't compatible anymore. I was...I was going to tell her in my own time. I don't appreciate you forcing the issue."

"I've grown to love both of you over the years. You're making a huge mistake, Jeffrey," Dr. Eisenberg said sadly. "She's a wonderful woman, and she loves you. You're being a fool."

"I love her too. At least, I love the woman she used to be," Jeffrey said regretfully as he raked his hand through his hair. "She's changed so much since she came back from that trip. Now, her new beliefs have made her into someone I don't even feel I know anymore."

"Surely there's still some common ground that you can focus on," the professor said. "At least give it a try before you run and—"

"—No, Doc," Jeffrey said, raising his hand to cut him off. "I don't want to get into all of this right now. That isn't why I wanted to talk to you. I wanted to let you know that just before the attack, Rebecca and I...talked about our relationship. I told her I didn't think it would work anymore, and I thought it would be better if we ended our marriage."

Dr. Eisenberg's eyes began to fill with tears as Jeffrey continued. "I...I was going to tell her more, but...but it just didn't seem like the right time. She was already hurt enough. And then...and then the attack came." Jeffrey paused before looking directly into his mentor's eyes.

"Listen, Doc. Right now we need to focus on getting back home. Once this is all over, I'll tell Rebecca the rest. But let me be the one to tell her, not you."

"Will you be man enough to do it?" his mentor challenged. "Or will she have to find out about it through the grapevine? At least do her the courtesy of letting her hear it from you."

"I will," Jeffrey said sincerely. "Doc, I never intended things to turn out this way."

"No one ever does. Now, if you will pardon me, I think I'll go check on Mack." With that, Dr. Eisenberg shouldered his way past Jeffrey and exited the room. Slumping down onto the edge of the bed, Jeffrey rested his hands against his head and wondered once again how his life had gotten so far out of control.

12

SEPARATION

"DA ENGINES BEGAN to slow down about twenty minutes ago," Akwen stated as Jeffrey and the others, still shrugging off the aftereffects of sleep, entered the control room. "If everyting works like it did last time, den da walls should become transparent again in da next minute or so."

"Thanks for waking us," Jeffrey said. "And we appreciate that you kept working while we slept. We owe you."

"Yeah, well, someone had to keep an eye on tings," she said with an air of resignation, like one who had been chosen to be the designated driver at a party. "Besides, it also gave me a chance to find Elmer's glitch. Dere were some bad wires connected to his commlink, as Dr. Eisenberg suggested. I also discovered dat dere is a door dat covers da skylight," she said, pointing to the opening in the ceiling. Turning slightly to look at Jeffrey, she raised an eyebrow. "You know, if you really want to tank me, you could find me a big plate of koki beans, rice, and egusi."

Jeffrey laughed lightly. "That all depends on where you land us. You might have to settle for sushi or tacos."

"At dis point, I could eat just about anyting," she replied.

"Well, that'll be our first priority," Jeffrey said. "Any progress on figuring out this machine?"

"A little. We haven't been able to find what is causing da ship to launch automatically, but Elmer was able to locate da area of da computer dat controls da recharging of da core," Akwen explained. "I am not positive, but I tink dat we can now control da ship's ability to recharge. So dis time, once da ship's core is close to full power, we can stop da recharging process until we are ready to leave."

"So no more worrying about getting left behind. That's one more thing to check off the list," Jeffrey said in relief as Jerome came up on his left side. Turning to face his friend, he asked, "How's Mack?"

"You know how he is with those migraines," Jerome replied. "It'll probably be around for another couple of hours. Right now he's going back and forth between sleep and whining like a baby. So what's our next plan?"

"Well, first of all we have to see where we land. Akwen is going to try to put us in friendly territory, but she and Elmer still haven't worked out all the kinks. Hopefully we will arrive back on our earth and we can use our commlinks to call for help. Regardless of where we land, though, we've got to get some food."

"That sounds good to me. The only thing edible on this boat is Mack's stash of junk food," Jerome said with a frown.

"Are you kidding? I've seen some of the stuff he eats. I wouldn't call that edible," Jeffrey quipped, causing Jerome to chuckle.

"Here we go," Akwen announced as the engines slowed to minimal levels. A minute later, exactly on cue, the walls began to become transparent, revealing once more the magnificence of the earth from their current position in orbit.

"Everything looks exactly the same as last time," Dr. Eisenberg commented.

"Including the fact that there are no satellites," Rebecca added, disconcerted.

"Hey, now. Let's try to keep our optimism," Jeffrey said as he scanned the planet, searching for anything out of the ordinary. After another few seconds, the ship's engines began working in reverse and the pyramid began to descend. "It looks like we're going to end up in the eastern hemisphere this time. See if you can shoot for Europe. Great Britain would be nice."

"Anyting else I can get for you while I am at it?" Akwen replied sarcastically as she concentrated on the controls. Just over a minute passed as she fought to bend the ship's will to her own. Jeffrey watched anxiously, noticing uncomfortably that they seemed to be descending faster than they were moving to the northwest. At their current rate, they wouldn't make it to their desired destination. Not by a long shot.

"Um…Akwen, we are—"

"I'm not blind!" she shouted back at him, her frustration boiling over. "It's not as easy as it may look."

"Do you think you can at least make it to Greece?" Jeffrey asked. "I would much rather land there than Turkey."

Akwen paused before responding, her face revealing her genuine concern. "I tink I can get us dere. I just hope we don't land in the Aegean Sea instead."

The others watched in silence as the surface of the water drew ever closer. Holding their breath, they kept their gazes fixed on the outline of the southeastern coast of Greece.

"Can you make it to the mainland, over there to the left?" Jeffrey asked nervously.

"No. We're not approaching at da proper angle," Akwen said through clenched teeth.

"Wait! There's an island. Can you set us down there?"

Shaking her head, Akwen glanced at her controls. "No. We are going too fast. We are going to overshoot it. I tink we can make it to where da mainland crosses in front of us," she said, pointing to a four-mile wide isthmus that lay directly in their path.

Suddenly the engines started to slow down, giving Akwen a few moments of unimpeded control. Guiding the ship in a mostly horizontal direction, she headed straight toward the nearby coast.

They were barely five hundred feet inland when the ship became too low to navigate farther. Picking an open patch of fairly level grass-land, Akwen allowed the ship to take over and finish the landing. After another few moments, the white energy beams dispersed and the walls solidified once again, leaving them all breathless.

"That was close," Jerome said, his voice breaking slightly as the last vestiges of anxiety drained out of him. "No offense, Jeffrey, but next time, let's not push our luck. I'll be happy enough just to land someplace where we can be certain to have dry ground beneath us!"

"Yeah, I tend to agree with you," Jeffrey said apologetically. "Thanks again, Akwen. Have I told you lately how great a job you are doing?"

Akwen, herself still recovering from the tension of the last few minutes, didn't respond with her typical sarcasm. Instead, she simply accepted the compliment with a soft, grunt-like chuckle.

"So where did we land?" Lisa asked as she absentmindedly pushed her short brown hair back behind her ear.

"I believe we're on the Isthmus of Corinth," Dr. Eisenberg said. "I would guess that we're only a few miles east of the city of Corinth."

"Thank God! Civilization at last," Lisa exclaimed in relief.

"We need to decide who's going and who's staying," Jeffrey announced. "But before we do that, I want to make sure we have a secure means of communication in case any of us gets separated. So Lisa and I scrounged up enough commlinks for each of us," he said, as he began passing out the devices.

"Have you tested them?" Rebecca asked.

"Yes," Lisa replied. "They're all working perfectly."

"Now that we've landed, shouldn't we try to use them to contact...?" Jerome began. However, as he studied his commlink, his hope died.

"I thought of that," Jeffrey said. "But as you can see, there's no signal."

"Maybe the pyramid is blocking it," Jerome said.

"That could be, but as we noticed earlier, there are no satellites in orbit," Rebecca countered. "At least we can use the commlinks for two-way communication."

"Once we get outside, we'll check for a signal before heading out," Jeffrey continued. "Maybe we'll get lucky. Now, as for who is going, I think it would be fair to let Akwen get some well-deserved sleep, and it seems that Mack is still down for the count, so that leaves Dr. Eisenberg to be the translator, since my Greek never was very good."

Dr. Eisenberg grinned. "Didn't I tell you that you should've taken your studies more seriously?"

Jeffrey returned the smile. "I'll accept that as a big 'I told you so.' Anyway, I would like to go, and I think we should split up our combat experts."

Rebecca opened her mouth to offer to go with him, but Jeffrey, anticipating what she was about to say, cut her off. "Becky, why don't you stay here and hold down the fort? Lisa, you can join Doc and me."

Not shot down that easily, Rebecca spoke up. "If it's all the same to you, I want to go. Lisa can keep an eye on things here."

Jeffrey looked at Rebecca for a moment, as if trying to discover any hidden motives that might be behind her request. Stepping closer to her, he lowered his voice. "Becky, you have more experience than Lisa. I need you to guard the ship. If something happens to it, then we're stuck here. And if Goliath wakes up…"

Rebecca felt her frustration building. "Oh c'mon, Jeffrey. Stop making excuses. It doesn't take any brains to fire a stun shot into a half-comatose giant. And once the team leaves, we simply shut the doors. If anything, you need my experience out in the field. But the truth is you just don't feel comfortable having me around. Isn't that it?"

"I really don't think this is the right time to discuss this," Jeffrey said, his own frustration manifesting itself in his habit of running his hand through his shoulder-length hair. "Why do you always have to make things so difficult?"

"*I'm* making things difficult?" she shot back, her voice starting to rise. "Why don't you start using your head instead of letting your emotions cloud your judgment? I'm the better qualified person for this job, and you know it. You need me, but you're just too proud to admit it."

"Oh don't give me that 'pride' stuff," Jeffrey said scornfully.

"Forget it," she said louder now as she threw he hands up in the air in anger. Spinning on her heels, she walked away from him and headed for the stairs. "Sorry, everybody. Forget I even brought it up. I'll stay here. Have a great trip."

The rest of them stood in silence until Rebecca's retreating footsteps had faded away entirely.

"Spoiled American princesses," Akwen mumbled under her breath.

Walking up to stand behind him, Lisa placed her left hand on Jeffrey's right shoulder. "She's right. She is more experienced than I am. Maybe I *should* be the one to stay here."

His eyes staring blankly toward the top of the stairs, Jeffrey shook his head. "No. Having her around only fogs my thinking. I need to be ready for whatever we find out there." Turning to look at Jerome, he asked, "So, that just leaves you. Do you want to come with us or would you rather stay here? It's completely up to you."

Conflicting emotions registered on Jerome's face. Finally, looking somewhat embarrassed and ashamed, he replied. "All I can think about is my family. If something happens to me..."

"Hey, it's okay," Jeffrey said in understanding. "You don't have to explain, and I don't want you to feel guilty. Lisa, Doc, and I should have no trouble locating some food. Besides, if anything happens, we have our commlinks. We can always call for backup. In fact, with Akwen sleeping and Mack out of commission, we need someone to keep an eye on things up here in the control room."

Nodding apologetically, Jerome smiled weakly, his eyes briefly meeting each of the others' before looking away.

"Akwen, before you leave, we need you to show Jerome how to close the main door and skylight," Jeffrey said.

"A woman's work is never done," Akwen sighed as she signaled for Jerome to follow her over to the control console.

"Well, I guess we should start getting ready," Jeffrey said to Lisa and the doctor. Avoiding Dr. Eisenberg's gaze, which he knew would not be favorable at this particular moment, Jeffrey began moving around the control room and gathering up any items that might be useful for their trip. "First, we'll try to use our commlinks to see if we can contact someone who can help us," he said. "If that's not possible, our priority will be to find or buy some food. I figure our best bet would be to try the city of Corinth. If it turns out we've landed on another of Mack's alternative earths, then we probably won't be able to buy food using our thumbprint ID accounts, so we need to search the ship for anything we can sell. Grab what you can and meet at the entrance in ten minutes."

Allowing his silence to communicate disapproval of Jeffrey's treatment of Rebecca, Dr. Eisenberg headed off to make his preparations.

"Okay, is dere anyting else you would like me to do, or can I finally go to sleep?" Akwen asked impatiently.

His thoughts still on the recent confrontation with Rebecca and Dr. Eisenberg's silent reaction, Jeffrey was startled by Akwen's question. "No, that's it. Thank you."

"Have a safe trip and hurry back," she said, her kind words contrasting with her sour expression. As she headed for the stairs, she called out, "And make sure you wake me for dinner!"

"Don't worry, we need to take good care of our pilot," Jeffrey said with a lopsided grin as Akwen reached the stairs.

Walking up beside him, Lisa gave Jeffrey's hand a gentle squeeze. "Don't worry," she said, trying to reassure him with a smile. "Everything'll be okay. I'll see you downstairs."

Jeffrey stood still, simply watching her go, his tumultuous thoughts momentarily overwhelming him. *Yeah…everything is going to be fine.* He only wished he could force himself to believe it.

13

CONVERSATIONS AND CONVICTIONS

"THAT MAN DRIVES me crazy!" Rebecca said, speaking her thoughts aloud through clenched teeth. Closing the door to the room that had become a bedroom for the three women, she flopped down angrily onto the nine-foot-long bed closest to the door. Now that she was alone, the weight of her emotions bore down on her, threatening to overwhelm her. *What am I doing here? I should never have come. I was fooling myself to think I could save this marriage. He used to go out of his way to make sure I was with him. Now, he doesn't even want me around.*

Mentally replaying her last conversation with Jeffrey, her disappointment dissolved as the simmering coals of her anger were fanned into an inferno once more. Standing to her feet, she began pacing the room. *And to add insult to injury, he has the gall to lie about it!* "'I need you to guard the ship!'" she said aloud, her voice a mockery of Jeffrey's. "Hah! And of course, *I'm* the one being difficult. UGH!"

Sitting down on the bed once again, she looked around for something to throw or kick. Stretching toward the front of the lengthy mattress, she snatched an unlucky pillow and vented her fury into its stuffing.

Her anger spent, a deep sense of emptiness settled into her spirit. As if in a daze, she stared blankly at her surroundings through a curtain of curly, dark hair that had been released from its bindings by her outburst. A single lamp against the eastern wall illuminated the room, which was nearly eighteen feet square, save for the six-foot-square inverted section of the northwestern corner. The entrance to the room was located on the southern end of the inverted corner. Other than the lampstand, the furnishings consisted of only the two giant beds and a five-foot-square table set against the northern wall next to the closet door. The beds were set in an L shape, one against the south wall, the other against the east.

Sighing heavily, Rebecca hunched over and let her head sink into her hands. *Lord, I need some help,* she prayed. *How can I reach Jeffrey?* Before the thought had even finished flashing through her mind, part of the answer came to her. Letting out a soft chuckle, she said aloud, "Yeah. I suppose it *would* help if I didn't lose my temper. Old habits die hard." *Teach me patience, Lord.*

The door to the room opened suddenly, startling her. Practically jumping off the bed, Rebecca turned toward the door, praying it was her husband. The words of apology died on her lips, however, as Akwen stepped through the doorway.

Without even a word of greeting, Akwen strode over to the bed against the eastern wall, sat down on it, and began taking off her boots. An uncomfortable silence hung in the air as Rebecca considered her options. *Should I say something or just leave quietly? She obviously doesn't seem interested in talking, and she already doesn't seem to like me. But who knows what we're going to face in the future? This might be my best chance to clear the air.* She cracked her knuckles absentmindedly and, as she spoke, took a hesitant step toward the Cameroonian.

"Um…I want to apologize for the way I acted up there. I shouldn't have flown off the handle like that in front of everyone." When Akwen didn't speak or even acknowledge her existence, Rebecca cleared her throat and continued. "Akwen, I think maybe you and I have started off on the wrong foot. If I have done anything to offend you, then I just want you to know—"

"Look," Akwen said as she raised her head to stare at Rebecca, her face marred by thinly masked disdain, "I don't much like Americans. I *really* don't like American women. And, to be blunt, I have no patience whatsoever for anyone who believes in an exclusivist, close-minded, supposedly all-powerful hatemonger of a God. So don't even waste your time trying to apologize to me. As if Lisa weren't bad enough, I got stuck working wit Mack. And now you come along. As far as I'm concerned, just let me do my job and stay out of my way. Now, in case you hadn't noticed, while you all were enjoying some nap time, I was working. So I am very tired, and if you don't mind, I just want to sleep." With that, she lay back on the bed and closed her eyes.

Rebecca stood there in complete shock for several moments. Her emotions and thoughts waged a vicious war within her, each vying for dominance. One part of her wanted to lunge toward the large African woman, knock that smug, relaxed look off her face, and send it flying straight into next week! But the other half struggled to rein in the temper that had so often gone unchecked and been allowed to wreak havoc in her life for so many years.

How dare she! Here I am trying to apologize, and she just cuts me off and throws it back in my face! What a stuck-up, rude, racist... A sudden thought flashed vividly through her mind, ending her tirade: *So much for your prayer. How do you expect to learn patience, Becky, unless you're put in situations that challenge yours?*

The truth of that thought worked its way quickly through her soul, deflating her indignation. She sighed heavily, as if trying to expel the remainders of her anger along with the breath from her lungs. Finally feeling she could open her mouth and trust the words that would come out, she said, "I am truly sorry you feel that way. Whatever past experiences you have had with female Americans, and with Christians in general, I hope I have the opportunity to show you a better example."

When Akwen didn't respond, Rebecca turned around and quietly left the room. Shutting the door behind her, she closed her eyes and leaned against it, blowing out a long breath to release her tension. Coming from the stairwell around the corner, she could hear the sounds of Jeffrey and the others searching for items to take with them. Opening her eyes, she looked blankly at the wall as she tried to decide what to do. *Maybe I should go talk to Jeffrey and try to clear things up before he leaves. But that might just make things worse. C'mon, Becky, use your head. You know he needs more time to cool down. He is focused on the mission right now, and our fight is still too fresh. Don't get in a hurry. Just wait for a more opportune time. Now I just have to figure out where I'm going to go until they leave. Maybe I'll just check on Mack.*

Her mind made up, Rebecca crossed the dozen or so feet from the room she just left to the door that led to Mack's workroom. She tapped softly. Receiving no reply, she knocked a little louder and called out Mack's name. Still hearing nothing, she opened the door quietly, concerned for the eccentric language specialist.

Mack's still form lay sprawled out on a large, gray, memory-foam lounge bag he had shoved into the southeast corner of the room. His eyes were closed, his mouth was open slightly, and his arms hung loosely over the edges of the bag like someone who was either extremely relaxed, passed out, or dead. A navy blue, zippered hoodie was draped backward across his chest, making it difficult for Rebecca to see if he was even still breathing. "Mack?" she called out again as she crossed the room toward him. Finally, reaching his side, she touched his arm.

Mack's eyes popped open like a zombie's from some horror movie, startling Rebecca. Letting out a gasp, she stepped backward and tripped over the leg of the nearby table. Her quick reflexes were the only things that kept her from an embarrassing and potentially painful fall. Reaching out with her right hand, she grabbed the corner of a shelving unit and used it to regain her balance, knocking several books to the floor during the process.

Moaning loudly, Mack closed his eyes in pain. Reaching up with his right hand, he placed it on his forehead, partially covering his right eye. With his left hand, he pressed gently on his right wrist. There was a brief flash of light as a holographic computer screen appeared above his wrist, then winked out again. "You know, you *really* shouldn't sneak up on a guy like that," he said, his voice weak.

Rebecca, still recovering from both her surprise and her near fall, simply stared at him, incredulous. "Sneak up? I knocked on your door and called your name several times!" she replied. "Why didn't you answer? Even if you were asleep, I called loudly enough to wake the dead! Didn't you hear me?"

Mack grimaced faintly as he ran his right hand through his unkempt, wavy hair, then dropped it back into his lap. Opening his eyes slightly, he apologized. "Sorry about that. Whenever I get these headaches, I put on a little music to help me forget about the pain."

Remembering what Jerome had mentioned when she first arrived about having to throw things at Mack to get his attention, she rolled her eyes and smiled. Crossing the room, she grabbed a nearby chair and sat facing him. "And how often do you get these headaches?"

"Oh, usually a few times a month," he responded casually. "A lot depends on my stress, and my asthma. I usually get a headache whenever my asthma kicks in."

Rebecca furrowed her brow. "Have you had any tests done to find out exactly what's causing the headaches?"

"We know what's causing it. The headaches occur because of my technology implants," he said, closing his eyes again. "The more implants I get, the stronger my headaches. But I wouldn't have it any other way. The headaches are a small price to pay for the benefits!"

Rebecca frowned. "Yeah, except that pain is the body's way of telling you something's wrong. If you keep ignoring it, and even making it worse, who knows what permanent damage may occur."

Mack simply shrugged. "The doctors tell me the headaches are nothing to be worried about. As long as I rest when I get them, I'll be fine."

Rebecca wasn't convinced. "Just be careful and don't brush it off. Mankind has a way of messing with nature way too much without first considering the consequences."

Mack chuckled. "Now you're starting to sound like Dr. Eisenberg.

So, did you just stop by to scare me to death and preach to me, or did you have something else on your mind?"

"Actually, I came to see how you were doing," Rebecca said.

"—and to avoid certain other members of our illustrious crew, no doubt," Mack said, reading between the lines. When Rebecca didn't reply, he grinned, interpreting her silence as confirmation. "Frankly, I gotta tell ya, I am surprised you haven't killed Jeffrey already, what with all that's goin' on."

The wording of Mack's comment left Rebecca slightly confused, but before she could ask him to clarify, he jumped in with a question. "By the way, where did we land this time?"

Shrugging off the odd comment, she said, "We're on the Isthmus of Corinth, just a few miles from the city. Jeffrey, Dr. Eisenberg, and Lisa are heading out to see if they can scrounge up some food for us. They should be leaving soon."

"Man, I wish I could go. Then again, if this trip turns out to be anything like our last one, I think I'd rather stay here. How come you're not going?" he asked, looking at her quizzically through half-closed eyelids.

When Rebecca didn't answer immediately, Mack reviewed his question and nodded apologetically. "Oh, sorry. I guess things are awkward enough without…just forget I asked." Desperately searching for a new topic, Mack said quickly, "So, what about Jerome and Akwen? They decided to stay behind also?"

"Yes," Rebecca said, glad for the change of subject. "Jerome is keeping an eye on things in the control room while Akwen is sleeping."

"Did she use a bed this time, or her usual coffin?" Encouraged by Rebecca's smile, Mack grinned. "She sure is a piece of work, huh? I bet you guys are getting along just fine," Mack said sarcastically.

Rebecca let out a halfhearted laugh. "Yeah, you could say that. She seems to have something against Americans, and American women in particular. Do you know anything about her past?"

"Not much," Mack answered. "All I know is that she's from Cameroon, she went to Georgia Tech, and she's married with three kids.

Come to think of it, I remember Dr. Eisenberg saying something about one of her kids, a daughter, dying when she was young. I think she was in her teens. That's about all I know. I don't know exactly why she seems to hate Americans though. It seems kind of odd, considering she went to college in the States."

"Maybe that's *why* she hates Americans," Rebecca pointed out. "After all, college kids wouldn't be my first choice for ambassadors."

"That's true enough," Mack agreed. "Well, if it makes you feel any better, she doesn't like Lisa or me that much either. Actually, she respects Lisa because of her knowledge and training at NASA, and because of her military experience. But she really can't stand me. She thinks I waste too much time watching stupid movies, which may be true. And the remarks she's made about my musical tastes cannot be repeated in polite conversation."

"Maybe she'll change her opinion about you some if your theory about this ship proves correct," Rebecca added hopefully. Mack's only response was a weak chuckle. The conversation lulled for a moment as Rebecca reflected upon her last comment. Finally, she asked, "Do you think there could be another explanation for the existence of the dinosaurs we saw, and for the Mayans' hovering carts?"

"Sure," he replied as he shifted his weight on the memory foam. "The number of explanations is only limited by your imagination. Why do you ask? Do you have another suggestion?"

"I'm not sure," Rebecca added, her mind working overtime in an effort to form a coherent picture out of the pieces of the puzzle. "Years ago, when I was doing some research about evolution, I came across a theory about dinosaurs that just seemed far-fetched to me. But now, I'm not so sure. Judging by your love of science fiction, I'm assuming you believe in evolution, right?"

"Sure. I figure if most of the scientists in the world believe in it, then who am I to challenge conventional wisdom? I just trust the experts," he said casually.

"But which experts do you trust? The scientists who believe in evolution, or the scientists who believe in creation?" she asked. "Both have PhDs. And, I wouldn't quite say that *most* scientists believe in evolution. A majority does, but, it is a slim majority. The more we learn about the complexities of the universe, the slimmer that majority becomes."

"Okay, I'll admit that life is so complex it probably didn't start here. Aliens probably seeded earth with life," Mack conceded.

"I used to think so too. But there's a big problem with that theory."

Mack's left eyebrow raised in curiosity. "Yeah? How so?"

"If life on earth is so complex that it must have been created by aliens, then that would mean the aliens must be even more intelligent than we are, since we still can't make life out of nonliving materials," Rebecca explained. "If that's the case, then where did the aliens come from? Did they evolve from nonliving materials? And how long would it have taken for them to evolve all the way up to being not only smart enough to create life, but smart enough to build a ship that could travel across the stars to plant that life on earth?" The more Rebecca spoke, the more she began to gesture with her hands as her "presentation mode" kicked in. "The idea of aliens putting life on earth doesn't answer the question of where life comes from; it only pushes it back farther and farther."

Mack was quiet for a moment as he considered her argument. "Great," he said. "As if my head weren't hurting enough already, now you want me to think too?" He grimaced and rubbed the back of his head. "That's a good point, though. I never thought of it like that. You've obviously spent more time thinking about this stuff than I have. So let me guess: You believe that God created us."

"Yes, I do," Rebecca said unapologetically.

"Well, no offense, but I have a hard time believing there's an all-loving, all-powerful God out there," Mack said. "There are just too many screwed-up things in this world to convince me that God's in charge of things."

"Have you ever even done any research or looked into any of the arguments that support the model of the supernatural creation of the universe?" Rebecca asked.

"No, not really, but logic and personal experience are all the proof I need," he commented. "Maybe when I get older I'll look into it, but it's something I just don't feel the need to spend time on right now."

Rebecca looked at Mack intently, her face reflecting her convictions. "I wouldn't wait too long, Mack. You never know when your time is up. No one is promised tomorrow. Especially when you're flying around in an ancient artifact facing dinosaurs and savage Mayans," she added lightly.

Brushing off her concern, Mack diverted the conversation. "Speaking of ancient artifacts, if you believe God created us, then who built this pyramid? Isn't this proof that aliens exist?"

"I've been thinking about that," she replied. "I don't have a definite answer just yet, but I have a couple of ideas. I wish I could do some research to clarify and/or support them before I share them with everyone. Otherwise, they might think I'm crazier than you," she teased.

"Ha, ha," Mack replied with sarcasm, yet also with a smile. "You know, if you want to do some research, maybe you could use Elmer's memory to look on the Internet," Mack offered. "If Akwen doesn't have Elmer performing any diagnostic jobs or something, you might be able to get him to allow you to do some searching. It's worth a shot."

Rebecca thought about it for a second, then raised her eyebrows as she warmed up to the idea. "That might just be what I need. Thanks, Mack." Standing to her feet, she put the chair she had been sitting on back to its original location, then turned to leave. "I've bothered you enough. Get some rest."

"Hey, no problem," Mack said. "I've enjoyed the company. The pain seems to be lessening, so hopefully I'll be up and around soon. Good luck with your search."

Opening the door, Rebecca stepped out into the hallway and pulled the door shut behind her, pausing to listen for the telltale sounds of Jeffrey and the others moving around. The stillness in the pyramid left no doubt in her mind that they had already left. Just to be sure, however, Rebecca checked each of the rooms on the lower level, and while she was at it, she made sure Goliath was still unconscious. Satisfied, she mounted the stairs and headed into the control room.

As she set foot into the room, she was greeted by the surprising sound of soft moaning. Turning toward the sound, she saw Jerome sitting on a stool at the main console, his head in his hands and his shoulders slumped forward. Stopping abruptly, she started to head back down the stairs when she saw Jerome turn quickly, obviously startled by the shuffling noise made by her shoes on the stone floor.

Realizing it was only Rebecca, Jerome sighed in relief and turned back around just as quickly, his hands wiping rapidly at his eyes. "Hey... hey Becky," he said. Although he tried to sound casual, the tightness in his voice betrayed his inner turmoil.

Caught between her desire to comfort her friend and her embarrassment at stumbling upon him in a moment of weakness, Rebecca merely stood near the top of the stairs and cracked her knuckles. "Hi, Jerome," she said. "Sorry to bother you.... I just..."

"No, no, that's okay," he reassured her as he wiped his nose with a handkerchief. Somewhat composed, he turned to face her again. His red-rimmed eyes and wet face made it apparent that he had been weeping. "What's up?"

Hesitantly, she walked over to him. Reaching his side, she placed a comforting hand on his left shoulder as she sat on the stool beside him. "I...I just...do you...want to talk about it?"

For the briefest of seconds, something flashed across Jerome's face. Rebecca probably would have simply passed it off as her imagination had Jerome not suddenly stiffened and pulled away from her slightly. "Oh, hey, don't worry about me," he said unconvincingly. "I was just...you know...missing my family. It's hard to think I may never see them again. I mean, what if we never get back? What if we're stuck here?"

Although Rebecca could tell this wasn't the only thing weighing on Jerome's mind, she decided not to press him about it. "I know it's hard to ignore the 'what-ifs,' but you can't focus on them. Remember that time shortly after Tarshwa introduced Jeffrey and me at the Christmas party? Her doctor called and said that they found a lump and wanted to do more tests. That whole week you were worried sick with all of the 'what-ifs,' and yet it turned out to be nothing. You have to keep your mind focused on positive possibilities and not on the negatives. I have to believe everything will be okay," she finished with a smile.

Jerome returned her gaze, but his expression reflected his despair. "I've known you for a long time, and I really appreciate what you're trying to do. But, no offense, I just don't have your faith. Hercules was going to murder me in cold blood. All I could think about was…was that this was the end. There are so many things I still want to do in life. It just makes me realize even more that there is no rhyme or reason to things. There is no master puppeteer pulling the strings. Life is meaningless."

Remembering how she felt when she had sat in the cold, dank cell on Ka'esch, she sympathized with her friend. She knew what it was like to be alone and helpless, facing certain death. Even though her experience had just been a vision, the memories and feelings were still real in her mind. "I understand," she reassured him. "I've been there myself, Jerome. I've had the same thoughts at times. But those thoughts led me to understanding that this *isn't* all there is. Life *isn't* meaningless."

Jerome gave Rebecca a weak smile, as if in pity. "Look, Becky, I'm glad you found religion, but I've tried that, and I can tell you from firsthand experience it isn't real. I don't know if I ever told you, but I was raised in a church. I've seen it all. I saw supposed miracle healings, people falling all over the place because God came on them—you name it. But it's all phony. The church is just full of hypocrites and con artists. My parents were good people, but my father got ousted as a deacon just because of petty church politics. And the guy who took his place was caught taking money from the church to pay for his gambling addiction. My brother was sleeping around with half the girls in the church, including the pastor's daughter, and my sister was doing drugs with the other half."

Seeing that his words were having a profound effect on Rebecca, Jerome immediately apologized. "Look, Becky, I don't want to destroy your faith. It's just that…I've seen too much to believe in God. As much as I would like to believe, I can't. There's no one up there calling the shots. We are on our own."

Struck dumb by her friend's pain, Rebecca just sat studying Jerome's face. An intense wave of sadness and compassion flooded her soul and brought tears to her eyes. "I'm so sorry you've experienced so much pain in your life, Jerome. I can't deny your experiences. However, I urge you not to disbelieve in God just because of the actions of some who claim to follow Him. For every one who screws up, there are many more who *never* fall. We need to—"

Jerome held up a hand, halting her. "Thanks for your concern, Becky. But to be honest, I really don't feel like talking about this right now."

"Oh…okay. Sure." Rebecca said. She could feel the compassion that had been building within her crying out for release, like a pressure valve threatening to burst. She wanted to respond to his comments so badly! *If only Jerome would listen, then…* She let out her feelings with a long sigh.

"So…" Jerome said, "what do you think Jeffrey and the others will find out there? More prehistoric, living fossils?"

Rebecca had a difficult time getting her brain to switch gears so abruptly. Her thoughts and feelings were still too caught up in the previous conversation. With a great deal of effort, she forced herself to answer him honestly. Even then, her response was slow and lackluster. "I…I don't know. I have the beginnings of a theory, but I need to do some research first. I was going to see if Elmer was up and running so I could search through his memory." Looking over at the droid for the first time, she saw that it was completely powered down and resting on the floor. "But," she continued, "it doesn't look like that's going to work. By the way, how long ago did Jeffrey and the others leave?"

Glad his effort to steer the conversation into safer waters had worked, Jerome relaxed and leaned backward, stretching as he spoke. "About ten minutes ago," he answered. "They should be checking in soon. The plan was for them to check in every ten minutes to keep us informed should anything unexpected happen. So are you going to tell me this theory you have or not?"

Rebecca shook her head and smiled faintly at her friend. "No way. Not yet. I could be completely wrong, and I would rather not say anything foolish."

"So what should we do to kill time?" Jerome asked, looking around the room as if searching for inspiration. "I don't suppose you thought to bring along any cards on this trip?

"Nope. Sorry," she replied.

"Hey, I thought you military types were always supposed to be prepared?" Jerome gibed. "You're slackin' off."

"Yeah, well what can I say? It comes from hanging around you civvies so much!" she returned. Jerome chuckled lightly and she continued, "Actually, if you feel up to it, I'd like you to tell me what you know of the control board. I've found through past experience that cross-training can be very important in a crisis."

Jerome shrugged. "Sure, I'll tell you what I know. Obviously, Akwen has been the one in charge of the main programming and setup, so if you want to know all the details, you'd have to ask her. But I can show you the basics." Sitting up straight, he swiveled his stool so it faced the console, indicating to Rebecca to do the same.

For the next few minutes, the two were engrossed in conversation as Jerome explained what each of the various knobs and controls operated. He paused momentarily when Jeffrey checked in, then resumed his instruction. He was nearing the end of his explanations when Rebecca pointed to a numeric counter display off to their right. "What is that for?"

Jerome studied it for a moment, a puzzled look wrinkling his features. "Hmm…if I remember correctly, Mack and Dr. Eisenberg weren't able to find anything in the specs explaining this counter. The funny thing is, the number it shows now is not the original number."

"What do you mean?"

"I mean, it has changed," Jerome said. "When we first found the pyramid, this number was set at 001655."

"What does it read now?" Rebecca asked, her curiosity piqued.

"Um...give me a second—I'm still not used to these strange numbers," Jerome said. After a few anxious seconds, he said, "I think it says 000635. Wait...there's something else that wasn't here before."

"What do you mean? What thing?" Rebecca looked down at the small symbol near Jerome's index finger.

"I don't know what that symbol is. We'll have to ask Mack or Dr. Eisenberg," Jerome said.

"Speaking of Dr. Eisenberg, what time is it?" Rebecca asked, suddenly alarmed.

Jerome looked at the clock nearby, his face immediately registering the import of Rebecca's question. "We lost track of time! It's been over twenty minutes since Jeffrey and the others last checked in!"

14

REBECCA'S THEORY

IT TOOK JEFFREY, Lisa, and Dr. Eisenberg a little longer than Jeffrey's ten-minute window of time to find enough items that were of sufficient value, small enough to carry, and yet not vital to their survival. Nearly half an hour after deciding to leave, the three exited the pyramid and headed off across the hilly countryside, heavy backpacks or satchels slung across their shoulders.

The climate outside the pyramid was cool, but not uncomfortably so. A late morning sun was rising lazily in the east, still several hours from its zenith; the warm rays lifted their spirits and bathed them in a yellowish glow. A gentle breeze wafted across the lush green hills, bringing with it the unmistakable smell of the sea. Although the landscape dipped and rolled, the three travelers found it fairly easy to traverse.

As they walked, Jeffrey frequently studied his commlink, hoping desperately that the symbol indicating a satellite signal would suddenly light up. However, after they had walked for more than twenty minutes, he began to lose hope.

They continued in silence, each left to his or her own thoughts. On two occasions, Lisa attempted light conversation. However, it soon became clear to her that both Dr. Eisenberg and Jeffrey seemed intent on their own musings. Finally, Lisa gave up and an uncomfortable awkwardness filled the void.

Despite his conscious efforts to banish them, Jeffrey found his thoughts returning to Rebecca. *How can a person change so much?* he wondered sadly. *I used to know her: how she thought, what she believed, why she acted the way she did—at least, as much as any man can understand a woman. But what could've happened to change her so much? It's more than just her personality. She even looks different. There's something in her eyes…something in the way she carries herself.*

Looking down at his left hand, he massaged the finger where his wedding ring used to be. When he first took it off a year ago, it had felt so strange. Now, he almost couldn't remember what it felt like to wear it. Suddenly, an intense anger coursed through his veins. *I hate religion. Religion stole my wife from me. It destroyed my marriage. This world would be better off without all religion. Why can't mankind just grow up and put away these stupid, childish beliefs?*

"Hey, Jeffrey. Are you okay?" Lisa asked, concern written across her delicate features.

Burying his emotions deep in the vault of his soul, he pasted a nonchalant look on his face. "Yeah, I'm fine," he lied.

Clearly not convinced, Lisa was about to probe further when Dr. Eisenberg spoke up for the first time since they had landed. "No. It can't be," he said in amazement.

"What?" Jeffrey asked, startled by the tone in the professor's voice.

"Look!"

In front of them lay a sixteen-foot-wide pathway made of hard limestone that extended as far as they could see in both directions. Running down the center of the path ran two parallel grooves set just over five feet apart.

Jeffrey stared in awe as Lisa looked back and forth between the road and her two companions. "I don't get it. What's the big deal? It's just a road."

Running up to the pathway, Dr. Eisenberg knelt down and began examining it. "Jeffrey! Look here, carved into the stone bricks. Do you know what those are?" the professor asked, clearly excited.

After studying the markings for several seconds, Jeffrey looked up at his teacher in shock. "Those are from the old Corinthian alphabet."

"Which confirms it!" Dr. Eisenberg said. "This is the Diolkos."

"What is a Diolkos?" Lisa nearly shouted in frustration. "What's going on?"

Jeffrey turned to look at her, his face a mixture of confusion, excitement, and uncertainty. "The Diolkos was an ancient pathway constructed probably sometime between the end of the seventh century BCE and the beginning of the sixth century." As he continued, he crouched down, grabbed a stick from the ground, and began using it to draw imaginary lines in the grass to illustrate his explanation. "It was used to transport ships from the Ionian Sea—here—in the northwest to the Aegean Sea—over here—in the southeast. We landed on the Isthmus of Corinth, which is a four-mile stretch of land that keeps the two seas from connecting. If they didn't use this road, ancient sailors would have to travel several hundred miles around the Peloponnese peninsula, which was a very dangerous trip."

Dropping the stick, Jeffrey stood up and began gesturing with his hands as his excitement overtook him. "Think of it like an ancient railroad. First, they would unload the cargo, which would travel on a separate road. Then they lifted the boat onto a special cart. The wheels of the cart fit into these two grooves in the center of the road to stabilize it. Once they reached the Aegean Sea, they would set the boat back into the water, load it back up and continue on their way."

"Why didn't they just build a canal?" Lisa asked.

"Several tried, including Nero," Jeffrey said, "but the technology wasn't advanced enough. A full canal wasn't created until the late 1800s."

"So why are you both so shocked?" Lisa asked, still confused.

"Because," Dr. Eisenberg explained, "the Diolkos is very ancient and has been nearly destroyed by the ravages of time."

"But it looks fine to me," Lisa said.

"Exactly the point!" the doctor said. "Hurry. There's something I want to see."

Lisa stood staring at the road, her face revealing concern as Dr. Eisenberg began stepping quickly down the stone path. "C'mon, Lis," Jeffrey said, grabbing her arm and snapping her out of her shock.

They walked at a brisk pace for several more minutes until they reached the crest of a small hill, where they stopped abruptly in their tracks. In unison, the three inhaled sharply, awestruck. Stretched out before them was the city of Corinth. The azure waters of the Gulf of Corinth spread out on the horizon.

"Oh my…" Lisa began.

"Jeffrey, the Corinth Canal is west of the Diolkos," Dr. Eisenberg said, his focus never moving from the sight before them. "But it isn't here. And look at the ships in the harbor and the architecture. Do you know what this means?" he asked, finally tearing his gaze away from the vista to look piercingly at Jeffrey. "We're not looking at mid-twenty-first-century Corinth. We are looking at ancient Corinth. We have journeyed back in time!"

Suddenly, their commlinks chirped, startling them. "Jeffrey? Do you copy? Dr. Eisenberg?" came Jerome's frantic voice.

Thumbing on the device, Jeffrey responded. "Yeah, we're still here, and you're going to wish you were too when I tell you what we are looking at."

From the other side of the line they heard Jerome and Rebecca let out sighs of relief. "We're glad to hear you're okay," Jerome said. "You had us worried for a second. Why didn't you check in?"

"Well, um…we kind of got sidetracked. Sorry," Jeffrey replied.

"Sidetracked? By what?"

"Oh, nothing that important," Jeffrey teased. "Just the ancient city of Corinth standing before us." He smiled as he imagined the look of surprise on Jerome's face.

"Could you...uh...clarify that last statement?"

"What is there to clarify?" Jeffrey continued. "We are looking down at the ancient port city of Corinth—not ruins, or a sketch, or model—we're looking at the real deal! A vibrant, flourishing city. We also found the Diolkos, still in excellent shape, and the Corinth Canal is not here. Somehow, we either landed in an alternate earth where ancient Greece still survived to modern times, or...we went back in time."

When several seconds passed without a reply from the two stunned listeners, Jeffrey spoke. "Hey, are you guys still there?"

"Yeah..." Jerome said slowly. "Man, I knew I shoulda went with you. Do you...do you really think we went back in time?"

"We were just discussing that when you called. It sort of fits. First, we traveled roughly one thousand years into the past and ended up with the Mayans, then we went another thousand and ended up in ancient Greece. The biggest problem with that theory is the existence of the dinosaurs and the small fact that Mayans didn't use gravity control. I still think Mack's alternate earth makes the most sense."

"I wonder what kind of spin Mack would put on this," Jerome said.

"We'll have to ask him later. In the meantime, what are you going to do now?"

"We're going to go ahead with our plan," Jeffrey explained. "We'll try to get our hands on some less conspicuous clothing, then just go into the city and see if we can barter for some food. While we're at it, we'll see what we can learn at the same time. I'll try to check in when I can, but it probably won't be at regular intervals."

"You guys take care of yourselves and watch your backs," Jerome said.

"We should be safe enough," Jeffrey responded. "We'll give you a holler if we need you. Over and out." Shutting off his commlink, Jeffrey looked over at Lisa and Dr. Eisenberg and smiled. "I wish I could've seen the look on his face."

Lisa returned his smile with one of her own. "Yeah, that would've been one for the scrapbook for sure. Then again, based on the looks the two of you had on your faces, I think I have a pretty good idea of what his expression would've looked like."

Grinning at her remark, Jeffrey shifted the weight of the pack on his shoulder. "Well, I think we've wasted enough time here. Whattaya say we do some exploring?"

With that, the three of them headed down the hill toward the city.

Jerome and Rebecca sat in silence for several seconds after the connection had been severed. "So, what do you think?" Rebecca asked, intruding on Jerome's thoughts.

Jerome, still mulling over what Jeffrey had said, simply stared blankly, his eyes unfocused as he responded. "Ancient Greece. I can't believe I didn't go with them!"

Rebecca smiled as she put her arm around Jerome's shoulder. "Don't worry. I'm sure Jeffrey will take some pictures for you." Jerome turned toward her, giving her a wry look. Laughing lightly, Rebecca gave his shoulder a playful squeeze, then dropped her arm back to her side. Letting out a sigh, she became more serious. "At least they don't seem to be in any immediate danger."

"Unless they encounter some more dinosaurs," he commented dryly.

"Yeah…" Rebecca said slowly, her attention suddenly turned inward. "Dinosaurs…"

"So, what did I miss?"

Startled, Jerome and Rebecca turned around quickly to see Mack topping the steps and walking toward them, his hand resting against his forehead. Rebecca noticed he had decided to change out of his faded and hopelessly wrinkled rock band T-shirt, and was now wearing a hopelessly wrinkled, plain white T-shirt underneath the partially zipped-up hoodie he had been using earlier as a blanket.

"Didn't anyone ever teach you that it's impolite to sneak up on people?" Jerome said to Mack, his voice rising slightly in irritation.

"Sure," Mack answered casually, "but politeness is overrated. I find it more fun to watch people jump out of their skins. Besides, I'm just getting Becky back for scaring the bejeebers out of me earlier." Grabbing one of the stools, he set it down just behind Jerome and Rebecca and plopped down onto it. "So, what's goin' on? How's the 'away team' doing? Anything exciting happen? Did they find any more dinosaurs?"

"No dinosaurs, but they did find the ancient city of Corinth, seemingly alive and well," Rebecca said. "If it weren't for the dinosaurs we encountered and the Mayan's usage of gravity control, they would believe we had gone back in time. What do you think?"

Mack was quiet for a few moments as he considered her question. Finally, he simply shrugged. "Beats me. Dinosaurs and humans coexisting and Mayan wagons that hover were certainly not in any history books that I ever read, so unless someone comes up with something better, I would have to still stick with my alternate earth theory."

"How's your head, by the way?" Rebecca asked, noting that Mack still seemed to be nursing his headache.

"Much better. The headache's lingering, but I didn't want to miss any more of the fun. Also, as I was lying there, I thought of a way to help you with your research." Looking over Rebecca's shoulder, he nodded toward the inert form of Elmer.

"Yeah? How's that?" Rebecca asked.

"Well, Elmer is the property of NASA, and any of the NASA scientists could use him. They just had to have clearance," Mack explained. "So, since you're an employee of NASA, it just might be that you've already been given clearance." Lowering his voice to a conspiratorial whisper, Mack glanced from side to side, pretending to search for eavesdroppers. "Besides, if that doesn't work, I can let you in the back door. Akwen doesn't know it, but by utilizing my vast network of connections, I was able to get the code necessary for me to link my internal computer to Elmer's memory. That way I could surf the Net as long as Elmer was somewhere in the vicinity. The drawback, though, is that you'd have to use my computer to do your research."

"Let's hope your first suggestion works," Rebecca said sincerely. "Shall we try?" Standing up from her stool, Rebecca strode over to the resting droid with Mack right behind her. "How do you start him up?"

"Easy. Like dis," Mack said, his voice changing into a near-perfect imitation of Akwen's Camaroonian accent, "Elmer, power on."

Immediately, the droid came to life. After its sensors and systems surveyed and analyzed the area and its occupants, the droid swiveled its head to face Mack. "I am sorry, Mr. Nielson, but as I informed you in our conversation dated Wednesday, October 14th, 2035, and in subsequent conversations, unless a registered NASA employee gives you access to my functions, I cannot assist you."

"Elmer, have I told you recently how much you *really* act like C-3PO sometimes?" Mack asked, shaking his head as he chuckled.

"Actually, Mr. Nielson, you mentioned that fact last week in a conversation dated—"

"Forget it. Sometimes you're *worse* than him," Mack said, rolling his eyes.

Rebecca, her face showing that she clearly didn't understand the reference, looked over at Mack. "I don't get it. Who's C-3PO?"

If Rebecca had suddenly sprouted tentacles and started singing opera, Mack couldn't have been more surprised. Staring at her with an expression of utter shock, Mack placed his right hand against his chest as if having a heart attack. "Becky, say it ain't so! You've never seen *Star Wars*, the most famous science-fiction series of all time?"

"Uh...no. Sorry. Sci-fi has never really been my thing."

"I must say, my opinion of you has been forever scarred. Well, you uncultured swine," he said with a mock British accent, "I'll just have to educate you when we get back by having a full *Star Wars* marathon! All ten movies, plus eight seasons of the TV show! It'll be great! In the meantime, let's just say that C-3PO is an annoying protocol droid who can't take a joke and is always giving out useless facts, much like our 3PO number two over here," he said, waving a hand in Elmer's direction.

Turning his attention back to the hovering robot, Mack said, "As a matter of fact, Elmer, we do have a registered NASA employee here. Check your database for a Mrs. Rebecca Evans."

The droid's black cylindrical head swiveled to face Rebecca; the two tiny optical scanners that served as eyes studied her for several seconds. Finally, it turned back to look at Mack. "My apologies, Mr. Nielson. You are correct. According to my last update, Mrs. Evans is once again on the active roster," it said in its light, tenor voice. Swiveling its head once again, it looked back at Rebecca. "Greetings, Mrs. Evans, how may I be of service?"

A little disconcerted by the prospect of talking to a robot, Rebecca hesitated before responding. "Um, I would...I would like to access your memory and do an Internet search for...research purposes."

"My systems are at your disposal, Mrs. Evans. What is the topic of your search?"

Ignoring the droid's question, Rebecca turned toward Mack. "Thanks for your help."

"No problem," he replied nonchalantly. "Ya know, I was just thinking. If you want, I could help you with your search and it would go much faster. I'll just use my computer and you could use Elmer's portable keyboard and screen."

Rebecca paused, her eyes studying Mack's face as she considered his suggestion. "I don't know," she said. "My theory sounds a little crazy even to me, and frankly, I'm a little embarrassed to mention it. Maybe after I've done some research first..."

"Oh, come on Becky, what're you afraid of?" Mack said lightheartedly. "Do you think I'm gonna make fun of you or something? Besides, I've got nothing better to do. Why not help you on some wild goose chase? What have I got to lose?"

Sighing, Rebecca capitulated. "Sure, why not. It *would* make things go faster, and it'd be nice to have someone else around to bounce ideas off of. Let's go over to the table in the corner and set up there."

After taking a few minutes to get things organized and link Mack's computer to Elmer, they were ready. "So, what is this mysterious theory you have? Does it have anything to do with aliens, I hope?"

"No, Mack. Sorry to disappoint you," Rebecca replied with a grin. "Before I tell you, I have to lay a little groundwork. If I'm going to make a convincing argument to the others, I need to get my own thoughts straight, so please bear with me."

"Sure. Say what you want, but I think you just like keeping me in the dark. You know, build the suspense and all. Anyway, go ahead. I'm all ears."

Rebecca put her head down and closed her eyes as she collected her thoughts. After a moment, she looked up at Mack and began. "You know I believe we were created by God. But let me ask you: Do you think that because I am a creationist, any scientific research I do will inherently be biased, and therefore not to be trusted?"

Mack looked a little uncomfortable. "I...uh...I didn't know you'd put me on trial. Can I plead the Fifth Amendment?"

Rebecca rolled her eyes and gave him an impatient look. "Okay, okay," Mack said, "I'll answer your question. Sorry, but I guess I'd have to say yes. After all, creationists are setting out to prove we were created by God, so that makes them biased. Good scientists, however, are simply supposed to look at the evidence and follow it no matter where it leads, not try to make the evidence fit their preconceived ideas. It's the whole 'science-versus-religion' thing."

"Fair enough," Rebecca said. "If you were to add up all of the knowledge in the known universe, what percentage would you say that you know right now? Ten percent? Five percent?"

Mack laughed. "Elmer's memory, as vast as it is, still probably holds only a small fraction of all of the knowledge in the whole universe, and I know only the tiniest fraction of that."

"Okay, so when you encounter some new piece of information, how do you interpret it?" Rebecca asked.

"Well, my professor always said," Mack's voice suddenly changed to sound like an old professor with a thick British accent, "'When you encounter something new, you interpret it by what you have already been convinced is true.'"

"Exactly," Rebecca stated. "'What you have already been convinced is true' *is* your bias. I admit that creationists are biased. But then again, so are evolutionists. The whole issue of creation and evolution is outside the realm of empirical science. It's inaccessible to the scientific method."[2]

Mack looked skeptical. "I don't know. I'm not a scientist, but I know that science has shown over and over that evolution is true."

"You *know* that, or you've *been taught* that?"

"Okay, yeah, so I've *been taught* that. But evidence doesn't lie, and *the evidence* shows that evolution is true," Mack retorted.

"But evidence is neutral. By its very nature, it *must* be interpreted. This pyramid is raw evidence. It exists. The question of who built it or where it came from falls into the realm of interpretation. When we see something in the present, we have to ask what happened in the unobserved past to make it this way. It falls into the category of a..." Rebecca closed her eyes for a second as she searched for the word, "...historical reconstruction![3] You can use empirical science to understand how the pyramid was constructed and how it works, but the questions about the *origin* of the pyramid are totally different."

Seeing that Mack still looked unconvinced, Rebecca continued. "Let me explain it another way. There are two types of science—Empirical, or Operational Science, and Historical, or Origins Science. The first kind uses the scientific method and is based upon processes that can be repeated in a laboratory. Operational Science has given us computers, spaceships, cell phones, etc. Origins Science, on the other hand, is an attempt to reconstruct a past event by studying the evidence that resulted from it. Forensic science and archaeology fall into this category. Think of a detective trying to piece together a crime scene based on the position of the murder victim and the condition of the room in which the crime occurred. Although Origin Science may use Operational Science to analyze the evidence left behind, it's still based on interpretation. And often, there may be multiple interpretations to explain the same evidence."

Mack began nodding his head. "Yeah, I get it. I remember seeing this old whodunnit movie. It was unique because it actually had three different endings. Throughout the movie, several bits of evidence were presented, and then at the end of the movie, each of the three endings had a different character as the murderer. The evidence didn't change, just the interpretation of it."

"Exactly!" Rebecca said. "So you see, in regards to the issue of creation versus evolution, it isn't science versus religion, but rather one scientific interpretation of the evidence versus another scientific interpretation of the same evidence. It's one bias versus another."

"So the question is, 'Which bias is best?' Right?" Mack asked.

"Right," Rebecca nodded. "Our bias should be based on logic and evidence, but in the end it is really a matter of faith. We have to trust that our bias is correct. Hopefully, if we are open-minded enough, we will continually examine our bias in light of new evidence. 'Real gold fears no fire.'"

"Whoa. You lost me there. What does that mean?" Mack said, looking confused.

"If you know that you have real gold, then you won't be afraid to pass it through fire. The fire will simply purify it. But if you have fake gold, then the fire will reveal it to be a counterfeit. In the same way, if your beliefs are correct, then by questioning them, they will only prove themselves true time and again."

"Okay, so everyone has a bias. Where does that leave us?" Mack asked.

Rebecca raked her hand through her curly black hair and sat back on her stool. "We start with our bias, examine the evidence, apply logic, then come up with an explanation. It's kind of like…a computer," she said, pointing at Elmer, who still hovered patiently next to them. "As a robot, Elmer was programmed with the laws of logic. However, if he is fed flawed data, his results will be flawed. If our initial bias is wrong, then all of the explanations we come up with will be wrong. Scientists create models to explain the evidence. A good model should be relatively simple, and able to make many specific predictions. If it doesn't, then it should be changed or discarded."

"I see where you're going," Mack said suddenly. "You think our belief in evolution, our 'bias,' has caused us to create a wrong interpretation about what's happening to us. Am I right?"

Rebecca nodded. "That's right."

"So what is your theory then?" Mack asked, intrigued.

"Well, since you believe in evolutionary history, you don't believe we've gone back in time," Rebecca explained. "But what if we really *have* gone back in time and it's our theories about the past that are incorrect?"

"Wait a second," Mack said, his eyes growing larger. "Are you saying what I think you're saying?"

Rebecca smiled. "Yes, I am. I know it sounds crazy, but I believe that dinosaurs really did coexist with humans!"

15

RESEARCH

"DINOSAURS AND HUMANS living together throughout our history? Wow. And they say *I* have a wild imagination!" Mack said. "You're going to need some pretty good evidence to convince Jeffrey and the others."

"Look, I told you it was a little crazy," Rebecca shot back, suddenly feeling defensive. "I'm not even sure I believe it myself. That's why I wanted to do research before I told anyone. Now, if you don't want to help me, then that's fine. I'll just do it myself."

"Whoa! Sorry!" Mack said hurriedly, raising his hands in surrender. "I didn't mean to put you down. It's a very interesting idea, it's just—"

"It just seems hard to believe," Rebecca finished. "All my life, I've believed that dinosaurs lived millions of years ago, and now…I'm not so sure. How could so many people be wrong? But then again, I believed the same thing about evolution, and now I'm convinced I was wrong about that too." Rebecca sat in silent contemplation for a second, then looked over at Mack. "Well, we won't get any closer to an answer by just sitting here. So, are you in or out?"

Mack snapped out of his own thoughts. "I'm in! Where do we even start?"

Pressing the keys on the wireless keyboard linked to Elmer, Rebecca watched as a holographic screen appeared directly in front of her, the image being projected from the keyboard itself. As she typed, she said, "The idea that dinosaurs coexisted with humans is not new. Back when I was first researching evolution, I came across several websites that mentioned the possibility. At the time, I thought the people who ran those sites were just wackos who didn't know anything about real science, so I just ignored them."

"And now you're the wacko!" Mack teased.

Without skipping a beat, Rebecca shot him a wry grin and said, "Yeah, and that makes you the wacko's assistant." Just as Mack was about to reply, the information Rebecca had requested appeared on the screen. "I've found it. Just do a search using the keywords 'dinosaurs and humans.'"

Rebecca waited a moment for Mack to get to the same screen, then said, "I'll take the first couple, you skip down a few and check out the others."

"Yesss, Massster," Mack said in an imitation of Igor.

A couple of minutes passed in silence as they scanned the pages in front of them until finally Mack let out a soft "huh," his eyebrows raised in surprise.

"What is it? Did you find something?" Rebecca asked.

"Yeah," Mack said, deep in thought. "This guy says that maybe humans did live with dinosaurs, but they were just called by a different name. Do you happen to know when the term 'dinosaur' was invented?"

Rebecca shrugged her shoulders.

"It wasn't until 1841! It was coined by a man named Sir Richard Owen, who was some famous British anatomist and a big shot at the British Museum. When he saw the bones of *Iguanodon* and *Megalosaurus,* he realized they belonged to a group of reptiles that had not yet been classified. So he came up with the name 'dinosaur.' And, do you know what 'dinosaur' really means?" Mack said with a sudden air of superiority.

"Please enlighten me, oh Wise One," Rebecca said with sarcastic reverence.

"That's better," Mack said smugly. "Flattery will get you far. Anyway, dinosaur actually means 'terrible lizard' in Greek."

"So if they weren't called 'dinosaurs' in the past, then what does he think they were called?" Rebecca asked, in puzzlement.

Mack looked directly at her and paused for dramatic effect. "Dragons!" he said in a deep, raspy voice.

Rebecca sat motionless as her brain processed the idea. "It does kind of make sense, doesn't it? After all, nearly every culture in the world has some kind of legend about dragons or sea monsters. It would make sense that they would be at least somewhat grounded in reality."

"Maybe," Mack said. "But then again, many of those legends involve fire-breathing dragons with wings. Do you think dinosaurs breathed fire too?" Mack said skeptically.

"I don't know about that," Rebecca countered. "Lots of legends start out with truth that eventually gets twisted as time passes. Why don't you stay on this search while I look up 'dragon legends' and see if there is a connection with dinosaurs?"

Again, they worked in silence for several minutes. Suddenly, Rebecca's eyes narrowed, then grew wide as she continued to read, surprise etched on her face. Quickly, she backtracked and found several other pages confirming what she had just read. Finally, she called out to Mack. "This is fascinating! I did a search on dragon legends, and found a page listing numerous examples that could refer to dinosaurs.

"Listen to this one. This is from a chronicle of 1405 about a giant reptile at Bures in Suffolk. 'Close to the town of Bures, near Sudbury, there has lately appeared, to the great hurt of the countryside, a dragon, vast in body, with a crested head, teeth like a saw, and a tail extending to an enormous length. Having slaughtered the shepherd of a flock, it devoured many sheep.'"[4]

Rebecca stopped reading and looked up at Mack, who was uncharacteristically quiet. "Here's another one," she continued. "This one's from a chronicle that is still archived in the Canterbury Cathedral's library. It states that on Friday, September 26, of 1449, in the afternoon, two giant reptiles were fighting on the banks of the River Stour, which marked the English county borders of Suffolk and Essex. It even gives the color of the creatures! One was black, and the other 'reddish and spotted.' Eventually the black dragon lost and the locals called the location Sharpfight Meadow.[5]

"This page contains many more," Rebecca said in excitement. "And from just glancing at them, they're not even written like legends, but rather as eyewitness accounts. Some of them give detailed descriptions of the creatures, as well as specific dates and times. Oh, and look at this!" Rebecca said, pointing to her holographic screen. "Here is a table listing eighty-one locations in the British Isles alone in which dinosaur activity has been reported, and it says there are nearly two hundred such places in Britain!"[6]

Mack was stunned. Finally, he looked at her with a seriousness she had rarely seen. "Yeah, but couldn't all of that just be local superstition or something? That's just one website, after all."

"But it's not!" Rebecca countered. "Before I mentioned it to you, I double-checked on a couple of the stories by searching for them specifically, and I found all sorts of pages that corroborated the accounts. Do your own search if you don't believe me."

With a blank look on his face, Mack nodded. "Yeah, I might just do that. After all, if we're going to convince anyone else, we'll have to make sure we have lots of examples and evidence from different sources."

Nearly bursting with excitement, Rebecca resumed her search. Several more minutes passed. This time, Mack was the one to interrupt. "Hey, Becky, I found another page that lists several more, including *Beowulf*. Did you know that in the poem, Beowulf kills a creature called a 'lyftfloga'—boy, try saying that fast ten times—that matches the description of a pteranodon?[7] And before that, he kills the 'Grendel,' which is described as having large jaws but tiny forearms.[8] You don't think that the Grendel could be a…"

Rebecca merely smiled. "T. rex? Who knows? But it does beg the question: If humans had never seen dinosaurs before, how could they come up with descriptions that match real dinosaurs? Is it just a coincidence?"

Mack shrugged. "I must admit, my skin is beginning to crawl. Sci-fi and fantasy are one thing, but this…" Mack stopped midsentence as he read the page that had just appeared on his screen. Shaking himself as if chilled, he looked at Rebecca with a grin. "You're going to love this. I found an article about pteranodons. It lists several accounts from different parts of the world about flying reptiles that fit the descriptions of pteranodons, such as the thunderbirds from Native American legend, a creature called the 'Piasa' by the Illini Indians, and…" he paused for dramatic effect, "the 'serpent-birds' of the Mayans!"

Rebecca jumped out of her seat so fast she knocked it over. "Let me see!" she practically shouted at Mack as she stood next to him and read the page.

Laughing, Mack pointed to a portion of the page and began to read. "Jose Diaz-Bolio, a Mexican archaeologist, discovered an ancient Mayan relief sculpture in Veracruz, Mexico, of a bird with some features of the Pteranodon. The November 1968 edition of Science Digest published an article on this 'evolutionary oddity' called 'Serpent-bird of the Mayans.' The serpent-bird, says Bolio, 'is not merely the product of Mayan flights of fancy, but a realistic representation of an animal that lived during the period of the ancient Mayans—one thousand to five thousand years ago.' "[9]

Rebecca was left speechless.

"Congratulations!" Mack said, clapping her on the back. "You guys fought off some Mayan serpent-birds! Way to go."

Still stunned by what she had read, Rebecca silently began making her way back to her own stool when Mack stopped her.

"Oh, wait! Before you sit down, there's one more thing I think you would find interesting," Mack said. "Have you ever heard of a creature in the Bible called the behemoth?"

Her brow furrowed in concentration as she searched through her memory. "Yeah, I remember reading something about it. There's a passage in..."

"Job," Mack offered.

"Yeah, Job," Rebecca confirmed. "It was a large creature. If I remember correctly, most commentators believe it was just an elephant or hippo."

"This lady mentions that interpretation," Mack said. "But she says those animals don't fit the description completely. She has the passage printed here. Let me read it to you. This is from Job 40:15–19. 'Look at the behemoth, which I made along with you and which feeds on grass like an ox. What strength he has in his loins, what power in the muscles of his belly! His tail sways like a cedar; the sinews of his thighs are close-knit. His bones are tubes of bronze, his limbs like rods of iron. He ranks first among the works of God...'"(NIV).[10]

Staring blankly ahead as if in a trance, Rebecca repeated the words, "...his tail sways like a cedar." Blinking her eyes, she looked at Mack intently. "A cedar tree was enormous, wasn't it?"

"That's what it says here," Mack replied. "According to this, they were one of the largest trees of the ancient world. Both elephants and hippos have tiny tails. It then says that the passage in Job could have been describing the diplodocus or the apatosaurus. Both were gigantic plant-eaters with thick bones and strong muscles."

Typing rapidly on the keyboard, Rebecca pulled up the passage from Job. Scanning the screen, she shook her head in amazement. "I've read this before, but it just never clicked. Mack, did you keep reading that passage? In chapter 41, it describes another creature called the leviathan. Give me a second, I want to read this."

Curious, Mack found the same text Rebecca was reading. Once she had finished looking it over, she did another search, retrieving several articles discussing the chapter. "This creature sounds as massive as the behemoth, yet it lives in the water. 'Who can penetrate his double layer of armor? Who can open his jaws, surrounded by those terrifying teeth?

His pride is in his rows of scales...Strength resides in his neck...He regards iron as straw, and bronze as rotten wood. No arrow can make him flee; slingstones become like stubble to him...His undersides are jagged potsherds...He has no equal on earth.'[11] This page makes a connection between the leviathan and the Sarcosuchus imperator—boy is that a mouthful," Rebecca said as she stumbled over the words. "It was also called the super croc. Or, the leviathan could have been a liopleurodon, which could be up to eighty-two feet long! A giant sea reptile fits the description better than a regular crocodile, which is what I was always told. And it says there are other places in the Bible that mention sea monsters, or sea dragons. Psalm 74:13 refers to 'the dragons in the waters,' and Isaiah 27:1 reads, 'and he shall slay the dragon that is in the sea.'"

Mack looked doubtful. "Yeah, but the passage in Job 41 also says, 'Flaming torches shoot from his mouth; fiery sparks fly out!' Now we're back to fire-breathing dragons. It sounds like the author is just writing about a mythological creature."

"Maybe," Rebecca said. "But in chapter 39 of Job, it talks about over half a dozen real animals, such as goats, deer, donkeys, and even ostriches. Why would the author list real animals and then switch to fictional animals? Wouldn't that weaken his argument? What if, instead, the idea of fire-breathing dragons came from reality? Hold on," she said as she concentrated once more on her screen. "I'm going to check something out real quick."

Going back to his own search, Mack was soon deeply entrenched in sifting through the many pages of information. Rebecca reached out and grabbed his arm, startling him. "What? What did you find now?" he asked.

"Mack, have you ever heard of the bombardier beetle?" Rebecca asked excitedly.

"No. I don't like creepy things too much, unless they are creepy *alien* things."

Ignoring his comment, Rebecca plunged on. "It says here this little beetle mixes two chemicals in its body to create a hot, gaseous spray that

can be ejected from its body at predators. The spray can reach temperatures of up to 100 degrees centigrade![12] This isn't some fictional animal!
What if some dinosaurs could do the same?"

"I don't know..." Mack said thoughtfully. "Maybe."

"Oh, come on, Mack. This from a guy who believes in aliens?" A
hint of frustration was evident in Rebecca's voice.

"I'm not saying I don't believe it. It's just...amazing to think about.
And I can guarantee you, Jeffrey won't be convinced."

Rebecca sighed. "Yeah, I'm not sure if anything we say will convince
him. He's pretty fixed in his beliefs. He's so sure of himself."

"Whoa..." Mack said suddenly, interrupting her thoughts. "Then
again, this might help."

"What?" Rebecca leaned over to see what Mack was looking at. On
the screen were several photographs of ancient artifacts. "What is this?"

"This website contains photos of more than thirty ancient artifacts
that contain pictures of dinosaur-like creatures! Next to the photos are
pictures and names of the dinosaurs that may be represented on the
artifacts.[13] There are cave paintings, sculptures...look at this!" Mack said
excitedly as he enlarged the picture. "This is from a Mesopotamian cylinder seal that dates back to 3300 BC. It looks just like an apatosaurus."[14]

"Wait!" Rebecca said. "Scroll back up to the pictures of the cave
paintings. Right there."

"Wow," Mack said in awe. "Well I'll be a Hutt's nursemaid. If
that isn't a picture of a plesiosaur, then I don't know what is. It says,
'Elders of the Kuku Yalanji aboriginal tribe of Far North Queensland,
Australia, relate stories of Yarru (or Yarrba), a creature which used to
inhabit rain forest water holes. The painting depicts a creature with features remarkably similar to a plesiosaur. It even shows an outline of the
gastro-intestinal tract, indicating that these animals had been hunted
and butchered.'"[15]

Mack continued to scroll down the page, briefly examining the
various pictures. "Definitely bookmark that page, Mack," Rebecca said,
returning once again to her seat.

"Okay, so, based on what we've found so far, let's assume that dino-saurs *did* live with humans," Mack said, just as Rebecca was preparing to continue her own search. "The question then becomes: What happened to them?"

"I think the answer is pretty obvious," she commented. "They probably just went extinct. I mean, animals are going extinct all the time, which is why we have endangered species programs. Maybe, being so large, they couldn't find enough food. Or maybe environmental con-ditions weeded them out. Add to that the fact that they were obviously hunted by humans. And then again, who knows? Maybe there are even a few left."

"What?" Mack asked, his face showing skepticism. "What do you mean? Like, Bigfoot sightings or something?"

"Not quite. It's just that the earth is a big place, and not all of it has been explored," Rebecca explained. "I remember reading that near the end of the 1900s, scientists near Sydney, Australia, found several pine trees that were thought to have been extinct for over fifty million years. The same thing happened with the coelacanth. In the mid 1900s, they suddenly found these fish off the coast of South Africa, even though they thought they had been extinct for millions of years. Anyway, we don't know but that someday someone might find one hiding out somewhere."

"If you *were* to find one alive in our time, I bet that would convince Jeffrey," Mack said.

Rebecca gave a halfhearted grin. "Don't count on it. He would probably come up with some reason it was fake. You know, aliens built a robot or found some leftover DNA in a freezer and cloned one."

"Hey, that's not bad!" Mack chuckled. "Now you're starting to think like me!"

"Great…" Rebecca said with false enthusiasm while suppressing a grin. Returning her thoughts to the task at hand, she resumed her search-ing. Minutes passed in silence as both were engrossed in their individual work. Deciding to try a different approach, Rebecca began searching images instead of just articles. After a few moments of browsing through pictures of various dinosaurs, she came across one that grabbed her attention and clicked on the link to read the caption.

"Mack!" she called over to him. "There's a picture here of a T. rex leg bone that had not completely fossilized! Inside the leg bone, they found red blood cells! It says here 'the shape and location suggested them, but blood cells are mostly water and couldn't possibly have stayed preserved in the sixty-five-million-year-old tyrannosaur...so far, we think that all of this evidence supports the notion that our slices of T. rex could contain preserved heme and hemoglobin fragments.'[16] It also states that there were several other cases of unfossilized dinosaur bones being found, including some duck-billed dinosaur bones on the North Slope in Alaska.[17] Of course the scientists were baffled! They believed the bones were old. But what if they weren't? What if they were from a dinosaur that died relatively recently?"

"That's a possibility. Add it to the list of possible proofs. We're starting to get quite a collection. This puzzle may yet come together." Mack's expression revealed his genuine interest. "You know, you might just make a believer out of me yet."

Rebecca smiled. "So you think maybe I'm not such a wacko?"

"Well, I wouldn't go that far," Mack replied with a grin. "Anyway, I didn't want to interrupt you before, but since you brought up the subject of unfossilized dino bones, let me read you a paragraph from this very interesting article I found." Bringing up the archived file, Mack scanned it rapidly to find the portion he wanted, then began to read. "The *Geelong Advertiser,* of Victoria, Australia, reported in July 1845 about the finding of unfossilized bone forming part of the knee joint of some gigantic animal. The paper reported showing it to an Aboriginal they regarded as particularly intelligent. He identified it immediately as a 'bunyip' bone, and unhesitatingly drew the picture...When the bone was shown to other Aboriginal people who 'had no opportunity of communicating with each other,' they all instantly recognized the bone and the picture as being of a 'bunyip,' a common word in some

Aboriginal languages for a frightening monster. They gave detailed, consistent accounts of where a few people they knew had been killed by one of these. The creature was said to be amphibious, laid eggs, and from the descriptions, appeared to combine 'the characteristics of a bird and an alligator'—i.e. a bipedal reptile. (Note that no crocodiles or alligators are found in Australia except in its far north—Geelong is deep in the south). One of the Aboriginals, named Mumbowran, showed 'several deep wounds on his breast made by the claws of the animal.'[18]

"The article goes on to list several other examples of possible dinosaur sightings," Mack went on, "including a bunch from the Congo jungles in Africa. Supposedly, explorers and natives have reported sightings of creatures that fit the descriptions of dinosaurs, even into the twenty-first century! The natives even have a name for them. They call them *Mokele-mbembe*. I wonder if Akwen has ever heard of those stories."

Rebecca let out a soft chuckle. "Yeah, well, neither of us is on very good terms with her, so I think we should probably just keep it to ourselves."

"I tink you are right," Mack said, imitating Akwen's accent. Switching back to his normal voice, he cocked his head to the side. "You know, Becky, something just occurred to me. That article mentioned a creature with the characteristics of a bird and an alligator. I thought science had proven that dinosaurs evolved into birds. But if that isn't true, then how do you explain it?"

"Well, I have to tell you, even when I was an evolutionist I didn't believe that," Rebecca said. "Dinosaurs and birds just have way too many differences. Once I became a creationist, I did some studying on the complexities of bird feathers and flight. One time, I listened to an entire hour-long presentation just on the intricacies and microscopic structures of a single feather! Add to that the fact that birds have to have hollow bones, extremely strong breast muscles, many smaller muscles to control each individual feather, a specialized digestive system, and several other things just to fly. There's no way dinosaurs turned into birds."

"But what about all of those supposed half-bird, half-dinosaur fossils they've found?" Mack asked.

"Again, going back to our earlier conversation, it all comes down to interpretation," Rebecca explained. "People see what they want to see. Most of the scientists I've talked with believe they are just fully extinct birds, not some transitional hybrid. Sure, they may have some similarities to dinosaurs, but that doesn't prove they're related. Especially considering that the feathers on those specimens are fully formed and contain all of the complexities of modern birds."[19]

"I'll take your word for it. I never looked into it much," Mack stated. "I kind of liked the idea of it though. And it makes for a good story." Rubbing his temple with his left hand, he turned his attention back to the holographic screen in front of him. Rebecca resumed her own search as well, until soon they were both lost once more in their work. Focused as they were, neither noticed Jerome approach until he was standing directly next to them.

"Hey, you two," he said casually. "It sounds like you guys are really making progress, from the little I can hear."

They looked up from their holographic computer screens nearly simultaneously. "Oh, hey, Jerome," Mack said, sounding a little embarrassed to be helping Rebecca.

"Well, I was just heading downstairs to see if I could find something to drink and wanted to know if one of you would be willing to take a turn playing night guard."

"Yeah, sure," Rebecca said as she leaned back and stretched. "I could use a break anyway."

"Great. Thanks." Jerome said. "So, Becky, did you find what you were looking for?"

"Some, yes. But there's just so much to sift through," she said as she stood up and began walking over to the control panel.

"Well, I'll be expecting a fifty-page thesis on my desk when you're finished," Jerome said, winking at her as he headed down the stairs. Stopping on the second step, he turned back around. "I'll be back in a few. If I can find anything, would you guys like me to bring you some?"

"Yeah, that'd be great," Mack said, glancing at Jerome. "I might have one or two cans of warm energy drinks in my room. If you find them, bring me one, would ya?"

Jerome's hesitation enhanced the undisguised disgust on his face. "Sure. And you, Becky?"

"I'll take some water, thanks," she answered as she sat down in front of the console. After checking the monitor to make sure Goliath was still unconscious, she reviewed what Jerome had told her about the controls. She found herself staring at the dial with the numbers on it and paused to study the strange symbol Jerome had discovered next to the numbers.

"Mack," she called out, "can you come here a second? Can you tell me what this symbol means?"

Standing up, Mack stretched and walked over to join her. He took one look at the symbol and shrugged. "That is a...oh yeah, that's the equivalent of a minus sign. Hey, wait a second, these numbers are different."

"Jerome and I noticed that earlier. I meant to ask you about it."

Mack leaned in closer to study the numbers. "In this case, it wouldn't be a minus sign, but rather a negative sign."

The truth struck Rebecca like a lightning bolt, causing her to gasp. "What was the original number?" she asked with a panicked voice.

Startled by her sudden reaction, Mack blinked rapidly several times as he tried to retrieve the number from his memory. "Uh...001655, I think. Why? What's wrong?"

Ignoring his question, she asked, "And what number does it show now?"

"It shows 000635. Why?"

"Don't you mean, -635?"

"Yeah. Why?"

Rebecca quickly ran the calculation in her head. "Let's see, 2,038 minus 1,655 equals 383. And 635 minus 383 equals... That's it! This is proof that we went back in time."

Mack, completely lost, stared at her as if she had gone insane. "What? Where did you get the number 2,038, and why did you subtract it…"

From the look on Mack's face, Rebecca knew he had reached the same conclusion she had. "Now you get it? These numbers represent years. For whatever reason, when you found the pyramid, the date was set to 1655. We started in 2038. It now reads -635. That means we went back in time 2,290 years, which would put us in the year—"

"In the year 252 BC!"

16

TALES FROM CORINTH

"THEY'RE COMING!" JEROME called out to Rebecca and Mack from where he was sitting at the control console. "Jeffrey just called on the comm and said they were successful. They're bringing back food!"

Rebecca and Mack let out sighs of relief. No one in their group had eaten in nearly half a day, and it had been longer than that for a few of them. At the thought of food, Rebecca could hear her stomach rumble in anticipation.

"I wonder what they're bringing?" Mack asked. "I don't suppose they were able to find any hamburgers."

"They didn't say," Jerome said. "But seeing as how they said they went shopping in the ancient city of Corinth, I highly doubt it."

"Well, beggars can't be choosers, I guess," Mack said. "Now I actually know what that means. Man, knowing my luck, they probably bought some of that stuff that grows on trees and usually has a skin on it."

Rebecca laughed. "What, fruit?"

"Yeah, that's it. I really don't care for that stuff," Mack said, grimacing. "I don't mind fruit-flavored snacks, but the real stuff itself... no thanks." As he finished his thought, Mack's stomach growled loud enough for Jerome—who was on the other side of the room—to hear. "Then again, at this point, I think I could even eat a banana."

"Wow, now there's a stretch," Rebecca said sarcastically. "Mack, you should really change your diet. If you keep eating junk food, you're going to end up overweight, with severe health issues, or finding yourself in an early grave."

"I don't have to worry about the overweight problem," Mack said. "I take those new pills that cause your body to burn all the fat you take in. As for the health issues, well, who wants to live forever?"

"We should probably go wake Akwen," Jerome said, changing the subject. "Any volunteers?"

Rebecca and Mack looked at each other. "No thanks," Mack said, throwing his hands in the air. "I'd just as soon wrestle with an angry Klingon than wake her up. Besides, one of my personal rules is 'Never disturb a sleeping vampire.'"

Jerome waved a hand at Mack in dismissal. "Forget it, I'll do it. Becky, keep an eye on things for me again, would you?"

"Sure," Rebecca replied as she began shutting down the keyboard she had been using to access Elmer's memory. Rebecca and Mack had been surfing through the droid's vast memory banks for the past several hours, taking only a few breaks here and there. She felt confident now that her theory was supported by more than just her imagination. Although at times they found themselves at dead ends or at websites of conspiracy theorists and fringe pseudo-scientists, they had gathered quite an impressive collection of well-documented information. *Now all I have to do is present it to the others in the right way and at the right time,* she thought in frustration. ... *If there is a 'right' time.*

Jeffrey, Lisa, and Dr. Eisenberg returned within the hour with sacks of food slung over their shoulders. Their spirits were high and they were nearly bursting with excitement. As they entered the pyramid, they were immediately set upon by Mack, Jerome, Akwen, and Rebecca, eager for the food they carried and for news of what they had discovered.

"Nice duds! Where did you guys pick up those outfits?" Jerome asked the moment they walked through the entrance.

"There's a souvenir shop just around the corner," Jeffrey joked. "We thought authentic Greek costumes would be perfect for the Alpha Chi Rho reunion."

Grinning widely, Jeffrey, Lisa, and Dr. Eisenberg set their bags on the floor, opened them up, and tossed each of the others some fruit and bread.

"Sorry, Akwen, but they were fresh out of koki beans and egusi, but we did manage to get some rice," Jeffrey said, grinning. "We need to cook it, though."

Flashing him a rare smile, Akwen replied, "No problem. I'll show you Americans how to cook rice. I don't suppose you bought any seasonings?"

"Actually, we did get a few," Jeffrey answered. "We'll show you later."

As he handed Rebecca the food, he looked at her briefly, his face showing no signs of regret or even recognition that anything had occurred between them. Rebecca found her own frustration beginning to grow again. *Typical. Some things never change. We get into a fight, and he pretends it didn't happen. Nothing ever gets resolved. It just festers and builds. Except now it's become a cancer. I would almost prefer that he avoided looking at me. At least then I would know it was still bothering him.* Brushing aside her thoughts, she ate her food and focused on what Lisa was saying.

"It was amazing. You should have seen the clothes these people wore. The colors were so vivid, and the jewelry…simply gorgeous!" Lisa said.

"But let's not get ahead of ourselves," Dr. Eisenberg admonished. "Standing here in the open doorway isn't prudent. Let's get inside and close the door. Then you can eat in peace and we can talk." As he spoke, Rebecca noticed with concern that his eyes scanned the horizon for signs of movement.

"Good idea," Jeffrey commented. "We're not sure, but we may have been followed. We certainly don't want any more unexpected visitors. Speaking of which, how is our stowaway? Still on its extended vacation in cyborg dreamland?"

"Yes," Rebecca said before Jerome could reply. "It started to stir once, but we promptly took care of the situation."

Jeffrey nodded. "Great. Well, let's all move somewhere more comfortable. Akwen, is the core fully charged? Can we leave if we need to?"

"I don't know. I just woke up," Akwen answered. "Considering dat we've been here for more dan four hours, da core should be fully charged. But da question is: Where would we go? We still don't know how to control da ship completely."

"Well, we can discuss that later. At least we know we can leave if anybody comes snooping around. We still need someone to keep an eye on things, but I know no one will want to miss the conversation, so let's head upstairs to the control room. Mack, we'll need to grab a few chairs out of your room."

It took several minutes to get everyone situated and comfortable. They set the extra chairs next to the table on the western wall of the control room. Despite his complaining about the menu, Mack practically inhaled his food and quickly requested more. While they ate, Lisa and Dr. Eisenberg took the rest of their provisions downstairs. After storing them in Akwen's workroom, they put away the few of the unsold metals and changed their clothing. Jeffrey, meanwhile, after quickly removing his Greek clothes, kept an eye on the monitors. When Lisa and the doctor returned, they sat on the stools in front of the control console since there was no room near the table. Finally, when everyone was once again present, Jerome asked the question that had been on all of their minds: "So, what did you see? What was it like?"

Jeffrey was the first to respond. As he spoke, his face lit up like a sports fan who just won tickets to the Super Bowl. "It was…like walking through a history book. Except no book could capture the sounds—"

"—or the smells," Dr. Eisenberg said. "We were hoping to take you there, but as we said earlier, we believe we may have been followed. Maybe we can return here someday."

"Followed?" Mack said. "By whom?"

Jeffrey held up a hand. "Let's start at the beginning. Dr. Eisenberg, since you were the one responsible for getting us out of this jam, why don't you tell it?"

The others looked at the doctor, eager for the story. Dr. Eisenberg cleared his throat loudly before beginning, embarrassed by all of the attention.

"Once we saw that we were indeed looking at the ancient city of Corinth, we knew our first order of business would be to get new clothing," he said. "We also thought that Lisa's hair, with its highlights, might attract unwanted attention. So, we waited near the road until we saw a trader pass by, his cart loaded with clothing. I approached him alone— one old man dressed oddly would not be nearly as strange as *three* people dressed oddly, and I am the only one who speaks fluent Greek. After much negotiating, I was able to convince him to exchange three garments for some of the metals we had brought along. I then returned to where Jeffrey and Lisa were waiting, and we put on our newly acquired clothing."

"It took me forever to figure out how to get my hair covered with that head scarf," Lisa interjected. "I wish we had had a camera."

Taking a drink of water from his glass, Dr. Eisenberg continued, his expression becoming serious. "If only I had paid closer attention, I would have noticed that the trader showed too much interest in the metals we had brought along, and he charged me much more than those three outfits were worth.

"Anyway, we entered the city of Corinth easily, as there were many other travelers and traders entering. We went down to the marketplace that was on the harbor. It was all we could do to keep our minds focused on our task. We were so overwhelmed with it all. We found ourselves going from stall to stall to examine what would be, in our time, priceless artifacts. Statues of all sizes and shapes, representing various gods and goddesses, jewelry, art…and the buildings! The exquisite architecture! And there was music and street dancers and performers of all kinds!

"Finally, after nearly an hour and a half of simply taking in the sights and sounds, we felt it was time to make our purchases. But, unfortunately, as we were heading back toward the food stalls, we were accosted by three men."

At this pronouncement, Rebecca and the others exchanged glances. "Were any of you hurt?" Jerome asked.

"No, but they took all of the metals we had planned to use to trade for food," the doctor replied.

Mack looked down at the half-eaten bread on the table in front of him. "So, how did you get the food, then?"

"After they grabbed our bags, Jeffrey took off running after them," Dr. Eisenberg continued. "He followed them and watched as they met up with the trader who sold us the clothes, and several other ruffians. We were clearly outmatched, and frankly, feeling quite desperate.

"Then, as if by divine providence, a kind man with gentle eyes came along and said he recognized the men who had robbed us. He said this trader and his gang frequently preyed upon unsuspecting visitors. He also directed us to a friendly vendor who would be sympathetic, and who might be able to help us."

Dr. Eisenberg paused and took another long drink of water from his cup. Pushing his glasses back up onto his nose with one finger, he continued. "As it turned out, this particular vendor dealt in items for sailors and merchants. When we arrived at his booth, my eyes were immediately drawn to the many maps he had for sale. There were numerous ones of the surrounding regions, but one map in particular caught my eye." With a dramatic flourish, Dr. Eisenberg placed a rolled piece of parchment about two feet long on the table in front of him.

"This is a map of the entire globe."

Jerome was the first to pick up on the importance of the doctor's statement. His eyes grew wide in amazement and he sat bolt upright on his stool. "Global? But that's impossible. The ancient Greeks didn't have the capability to travel the globe. Let me see!"

"Wait, there's more," Dr. Eisenberg said, holding up a finger. "When I was studying art, I also learned a thing or two about mapmaking. I can tell you from experience that this map is amazingly accurate. Whoever made it had a high degree of technical skill and considerable knowledge of mathematics. In addition, not only does it include North and South America, but it also shows the coasts of Greenland and Antarctica, *without ice.*"

Jerome looked back and forth between Jeffrey and Dr. Eisenberg. Suddenly, he grinned widely. "Okay. Tell me, Doc, how did Jeffrey convince you to go along with this joke?"

Jeffrey laughed and slapped his hand on the console. "What did I tell you, Doc? I told you he wouldn't believe it." Turning to Jerome, he said, "Frankly, I still don't know if *I* believe it. It just seems to add further proof that we're not on our own earth. Maybe we went back in time, but we must have switched into an alternate universe as well."

Jerome nearly leaped out of his seat to grab the parchment still sitting in front of the doctor. As he began carefully unrolling it, Rebecca, Mack, and Akwen gathered around to look over his shoulder.

While the others studied the map, Dr. Eisenberg raised one eyebrow at Jeffrey and continued. "I'm not so sure—at least regarding this map. There've been numerous cases of ancient maps being found that are very accurate. And as for the coast of Antarctica, have any of you heard of the Piri Reis Map?"

Seeing that none of them showed any sign of recognizing the name, the doctor elaborated, the inflection in his voice changing into his "teacher" mode. "In 1513, a famous admiral of the Turkish fleet drew an amazingly accurate map based on source maps from the fourth century BC or earlier. This map also showed the coast of Antarctica, and it was said that the only way to draw a map with that accuracy was to use aerial surveying."[20]

This time, Jerome wasn't the only one who was surprised. "Really?" Jeffrey commented. "I had never heard of that. So that means whoever drew the original maps must have drawn them before ice formed on Antarctica. That would have been over six thousand years ago! How do they explain it then? Who do they think drew the original maps?"

Dr. Eisenberg shrugged. "No one knows. It has always been a mystery. But the point is this: What if we have gone back in time, and this is one of the source maps that he used?"

"That's just too crazy to think about," Jerome said, shaking his head in amazement as he finally looked up. "Do you realize that this would be an amazing find, even in poor condition? Yet this one is pristine! The colors and writing are so vivid! This'd be worth a fortune in our time!"

"If you could convince anyone that it's genuine," Dr. Eisenberg commented dryly. "It's in *too* good shape."

"There were other items that caught our attention besides the map," Jeffrey said, taking up the narrative. "Unfortunately, we weren't able to get any of those. Next to the maps were optical 'lenses' called 'sun-stones' the sailors could use to determine the position of the sun even when it was covered by clouds. [21] And this vendor even had an Antikythera Mechanism!"

Jerome's face lit up in excitement while Rebecca, Mack, and Akwen frowned. "What is an 'anti-catheter mechanism'?" Mack asked. "Whatever it is, it doesn't sound pleasant."

"The Antikythera Mechanism was a device found in 1900 AD on an ancient ship that was sunk in the Aegean Sea," Jerome expounded as he carefully rolled up the ancient map and handed it back to Dr. Eisenberg. "It was discovered near the island of Antikythera, thus the reason for the name. As you can imagine, it was extremely corroded when they first brought it to the surface. What makes it so fascinating is that inside the mechanism were more than thirty high-quality bronze gears. The gears of this device were so complex that they matched the quality of modern gears, which are made using special machines. [22] It has always been a mystery how ancient man could have created such a device."

"But what does it do?" Rebecca asked.

"Several theories were presented," Dr. Eisenberg said. "But it wasn't until scientists used gamma radiography to look beneath the corroded metal case. They then had an engineer construct a working model of the device. It turned out to be a planetarium showing accurately the astronomical positions of not only the sun and moon, but also the planets Mercury, Venus, Mars, Jupiter, and Saturn.[23] The sailors used it to aid them in navigation."

"Man, I wish I could have seen one," Jerome said wistfully.

"Excuse me, but would you tree professors save da lecture for da classroom and get back to da story?" Akwen seemed frustrated. "We can debate da finer points of ancient human intelligence later."

Jeffrey looked over at Dr. Eisenberg and grinned. "Sure. I make a motion to table this discussion until later. All in favor, say 'aye.'"

Ignoring Jeffrey's sad attempt at humor, Akwen turned her attention to Dr. Eisenberg as he continued. "So we talked to the vendor and explained our situation. He said he could give us a little food, but not nearly what we needed. As we were talking, I noticed a drawing on the wall of a strange creature. The sketch was rather poor, but it bore a striking resemblance to a plesiosaurus."

At this, Mack and Rebecca exchanged meaningful glances. Their brief visual communication went unnoticed by the others, whose attention was fixed on Dr. Eisenberg.

"That's odd," Jerome commented. "How would they know what a plesiosaur looked like?"

"That's exactly what we thought," Jeffrey said.

"We asked the vendor how he came to have the picture," Dr. Eisenberg continued. "He said that many years ago when he was a sailor on a ship, they encountered the carcass of one of these sea monsters. He drew the crude picture of it, measured it, and threw it back into the sea. They were afraid it would spoil their catch of fish.

"It was then that the idea struck me. Asking for a sheet of parchment and ink, I sketched a more complete and detailed drawing of the creature based on our modern understanding of bone structure. When the vendor saw the finished drawing, he was astonished," Dr. Eisenberg said.

"So, to make an already long story short," Lisa interjected, "Doc ended up drawing several sketches of various sea monsters, and the vendor gave us plenty of food in exchange. I think he was planning on selling them to other sailors who had seen the creatures."

Mack's faced wrinkled. "I don't get it. Why were you worried that you were followed, then?"

Jeffrey looked at the others. "Well, while we waited for Doc to draw the sketches, I went back to see if I could find the guys who took our stuff. I managed to find two of the ones who robbed us. I jumped them, catching them by surprise. I grabbed one of our bags and took off running. I was able to give them the slip, but we didn't want to take any chances. The vendor was kind enough to help us get out of the city through a more secluded area."

Lisa threw Jeffrey a look of disappointment. "Even so, we think we might have seen someone tailing us as we headed back here."

"Wow, that's quite a story," Jerome said, sitting back and shaking his head.

"So what did all of you bums do while we were risking our necks?" Jeffrey asked.

"Not much," Jerome said. "Akwen slept, I played lookout, and Mack and Rebecca did some research."

"What kind of research?" Jeffrey asked.

Mack looked at Rebecca, who sat momentarily frozen with indecision. *Should I tell them? Is now the right time?* Deciding to take the chance, she cleared her throat. "I have a theory that may help explain some of what you told us as well as what we saw with the Mayans. It may also help us determine what we should do from here. But before I explain it, I want you all to promise that you will hear me out completely and look at the evidence we gathered fairly before making a judgment."

Dr. Eisenberg and Lisa looked at Rebecca with a mixture of confusion and curiosity. Jeffrey and Akwen, however, began to frown. "Look, Becky, if this has anything to do with your creationist beliefs, then I would rather not be a part of this," Jeffrey said. "I know what you believe, and I know you're convinced you're right. Let's just leave it at that."

Rebecca bit her tongue to keep from replying in anger. Although she did her best to appear calm, her frustration manifested in her old habit of cracking her knuckles against her leg. Swallowing hard, she replied, her voice forced and strained.

"This has nothing to do with my beliefs. In fact, what we found actually goes against what I originally thought."

Jeffrey stared at her for another moment before speaking. "Fine. Then I'm all ears."

For the next forty-five minutes, Rebecca laid out all the evidence she and Mack had collected. Once finished, she concluded by saying, "So I believe we have indeed gone back in time, and we're not in an alternate universe. Rather, it seems that our understanding of history has been incorrect."

Rebecca stared at all of them throughout her presentation, searching their faces for signs of their reactions to her theory. What she observed was not encouraging. Dr. Eisenberg seemed sympathetic, but skeptical; Jerome and Lisa simply looked unconvinced; and Akwen seemed bored and even hostile, while Jeffrey sat stoic and unemotional—a bad sign. When she first proposed the idea that dinosaurs may have lived with humans, Rebecca thought Jeffrey was going to get up and leave. He stayed, however, although Rebecca was not certain that was for the best. As someone the others looked to for leadership, his sour mood was clearly infecting everyone else. Once she finished, there was silence for a moment before Jeffrey spoke.

"Even if that were true, Becky, it still doesn't explain anything about the Mayans' hovering carts. How do you explain that?"

She thought for a moment before responding. "I did a little research on that as well while you were gone. Although I didn't find anything specific about gravity-control technology, isn't it true that there is no evidence that Mayans used wheeled carts, even though toys with wheels have been found?"[24]

Jeffrey glanced over at Jerome, then returned his attention to Rebecca. "That is true, but it doesn't really prove anything. There could be numerous explanations for that."

Deciding to try a different approach, she asked, "Dr. Eisenberg, the Piri Reis map is real, right?"

Caught off guard, the doc simply responded, "Yes."

"And the Antikythera Mechanism is another known...what did Jeffrey call them before...Out-of-Time Artifacts?"

"Out-of-Place Artifacts," the doctor corrected. "OOPArts. Yes, they are real."

Her train of thought suddenly reminded her of a previous conversation. "And Jeffrey, when we were captured by the Mayans, you said that one of the mysteries of the Olmec heads was that they were shaped like Africans, right?"

Jeffrey's eyes narrowed, as if trying to figure out where Rebecca was headed with her question. "Yeah. So?"

"I think, based upon all of what we've seen, it seems obvious that ancient humans were much smarter than we originally thought. It makes sense. They had devices and 'sun-stones' to navigate across vast oceans, and they developed maps that were extremely accurate. What if the mystery of the Olmecs isn't really a mystery at all? What if the Olmec people carved African heads because they really *did* see Africans? They carved the heads to resemble real people they had encountered and traded with."

"—And even more," Mack interrupted, "what if they were able to cross these oceans and map out Antarctica before the ice because they had been given the technology to do so from aliens?"

There was a groan from Akwen and Rebecca, but for different reasons.

"Actually, I think Mack may be onto something there," Jeffrey chimed in, his expression turning thoughtful. "After all, it would explain how the makers of the Piri Reis map were able to get information that was only available through aerial surveying, and it would explain how the Mayans were able to get anti-gravity technology. And, it fits with what we've observed with this pyramid. But as for the dinosaurs…sorry, Becky, but I just don't buy it. Evolution is a proven fact, and all the evidence shows that dinosaurs lived millions of years ago. If you want to convince me of a theory, you can't contradict something we all know to be true. Feel free to spend your time on pseudo-science if you want, but I for one don't want to hear about it."

Although Rebecca was not surprised by Jeffrey's reaction, she found herself becoming frustrated. "Less than an hour ago you were wondering how it was that the sailors could have known what plesiosaurs looked like. Well, I've given you an answer. If you don't believe my theory, then how do you explain that?"

Jeffrey's own emotions became riled up by Rebecca's challenge. As a result, his voice took on an icy tone and was filled with unconcealed impatience. "Look, Becky, just because I don't have an answer right this minute doesn't mean I'm going to throw out established science for some…far-fetched creationist theory. For all we know, those sailors might have just caught a big shark, or whale, or some other large sea animal that looked kind of like a plesiosaur, and when the vendor saw Doc's sketch, he decided he could get those gullible sailors to believe it resembled what they saw."

Rebecca looked around at the others and noted with satisfaction that none of them, with the exception of Akwen, seemed to buy into Jeffrey's explanation.

Sensing tensions build, Dr. Eisenberg intervened, hoping to circumvent the inevitable explosion. "I think we've exhausted this topic. The bigger question now is: What are we going to do? I think it's clear to all of us that we've gone back in time. Whether it's in an alternate universe or our own history is irrelevant. How are we going to get back?"

Without hesitation, Akwen spoke up, her statements causing a heavy stillness to settle over the group. "It seems clear to me dat da ones responsible for building dis pyramid have set it to return to dem. If we want to get back to our time, our only choice is to continue on until we find dem...and hope dat dey will be friendly enough to show us how to return."

There was silence in the room for several seconds as the group considered the logic of Akwen's statement. Then, just as Lisa opened her mouth to speak, Jeffrey cut her off.

"Look lively, everyone," he said, swiveling around on his stool to face the control console. "We have visitors."

"I knew they were following us," Dr. Eisenberg said as he rose from his stool to stand beside Jeffrey. "That's them, all right," he said as the faces of the figures on the computer screen became clearer. "And it looks like they brought some friends."

"Do we fight them off?" Lisa asked.

"No, I've got a better idea," Jeffrey said, the beginnings of a grin creeping onto his face. "Let's give them a show they'll never forget." Turning toward Akwen, he smiled broadly. "Well, captain, I think we've overstayed our welcome. What do you say we get going?"

Akwen returned his smile. "Fine wit me," she said, moving over and sitting down on the stool Jeffrey had just vacated. Within moments, they could all feel the rumble of the ship's engines coming online, like the growl of a giant monster awakening from a deep slumber. "Just make sure you get a recording from da camera. I want to see da look on dere faces when we disappear."

They all watched the monitor with interest. The dozen or more men were approaching the pyramid stealthily, when suddenly, unadulterated panic registered on each of their faces as the pure white beam of energy shot through the roof of the pyramid. Jeffrey and the others let out a shared laugh as the men broke and ran for cover. A few moments later, the pyramid was gone. As they ascended, they watched with continued amusement as the men rode away toward Corinth, their horses running at a full gallop.

17

LANDING

"**DA ENGINES ARE** slowing down," Akwen announced. "Da walls should become transparent very soon."

The group had gathered in the control room in excited and nervous anticipation. Although they were now used to the transitions the pyramid experienced during each journey, and although they had now survived four such jumps, they still found themselves nervously clutching panels or table edges in expectation.

Since leaving the Isthmus of Corinth, they had made one more uneventful trip. Landing in a deserted location on the western coast of Florida, they quickly scouted out the area. Finding no civilization, they filled whatever containers they could find with fresh water from a nearby stream, and added to their supply of fruit from the several trees they discovered. However, before they could do more, they were forced to seek shelter inside the pyramid as a large storm with near-hurricane-force winds slammed into the area. Their scouting expedition thwarted, they passed the rest of the time quietly as they waited for the core to recharge.

During that time, Rebecca tried talking to Jeffrey on several occasions, but to no avail. He either avoided her or, when she was successful at cornering him, he merely deflected her questions and stonewalled her. Finally, hurt and confused, she asked Dr. Eisenberg for advice. Although she could tell from the doctor's troubled expression that he knew more than he let on, he refused to help her, merely saying this was between Jeffrey and her.

Giving up on her fruitless attempts to mend her personal situation, she focused instead on trying to convince Dr. Eisenberg of her theory. With more time on their hands, Rebecca was able to go into detail about her research, as well as show him the various documents and websites she had uncovered. After they had been at it for several hours, the doctor removed his glasses and began rubbing at his temples with his fingers.

"Are you okay?" Rebecca asked.

Looking up at her, he smiled. "Yes, I'm fine," he said. "I'm just a bit over-whelmed. I'll admit that I am very intrigued by what you have uncovered."

Rebecca could barely contain her excitement. Noting her expression, Dr. Eisenberg held up his hand. "Hold on a second, Rebecca. You know I love you, so I have to be honest with you. I don't want to give you false hope. I find your arguments compelling, but one doesn't just throw out a lifetime worth of study and research in one afternoon. I need time to think about this."

Her enthusiasm somewhat diminished, Rebecca was nevertheless thrilled at his response. "I understand. But consider this: You don't have to throw out your study or research. The evidence remains the same. The fossils have not changed. It's only how you view that evidence that needs to be changed."

Replacing his glasses, Dr. Eisenberg smiled at her as he considered her words. "*You* have changed, my dear Rebecca. And I like what I see. Jeffrey sees it too, but he's too stubborn to...well, he's just too stubborn," he finished awkwardly.

Rebecca stood silently before her friend, her turbulent emotions revived by his words. However, before either of them could say more, Akwen's voice came over their commlinks, calling them all to the control room.

Giving her a gentle hug, Dr. Eisenberg stepped past her and headed out the door. Pausing for a moment to collect herself, Rebecca turned and followed. As they reached the top of the stairs leading into the control room, they saw Jeffrey leaning over the control panel, studying what they now believed to be the "time indicator."

"Well, 'when' are we this time?" Jeffrey asked.

Mack leaned over to check the numbers along with him. "When we left Florida, it read -1590,which would have put us at 1207 BCE. It now reads -2432, which means we should be arriving at…"—activating his holographic computer, Mack quickly fed the numbers into it—"2049 BCE."

"How much farther do you think we'll have to go back until we find these aliens, or 'ancients,' as Mack calls them?" Lisa asked. "And what if we miss them? What if they're on the other side of the planet, or…"

Jeffrey laid a calming hand on her arm. "Let's not worry about that now. But judging by what we know about the map we found, they would have had to have mapped out Antarctica before there was ice, so that means we need to go to about 4000 BC or so. Akwen and Elmer think they are close to figuring out a way we can use this thing to fly around the planet so we don't have to just stay where we land. With a few more jumps, they should have it down. They've already figured out how to control how far back we go. So, if we think we're getting close, we can make shorter jumps. Right now, at our maximum of roughly one thousand years per jump, it shouldn't be long."

Still unconvinced, Lisa forced a smile at him. "I just want to get home," she said. "It feels like forever since I've seen my girls. And you know how Amanda is. She's such a worrywart. What do you think's happening at home?"

"Nothing," Mack interrupted, his voice casual and relaxed.

"What?" Lisa said, throwing him a sidelong glance.

"Nothing is happening at home. Think about it, we are in a t-i-m-e m-a-c-h-i-n-e," Mack said, drawing out the words. "When we get back, we can arrive at the exact time we left, so although it will have been days for us, no time will have passed for them. The journey for us will seem instantaneous to them!" he said, his voice sounding like Dr. Emmett Brown.

"Wait!" Jerome butted in. "I know this one…wasn't that from that old movie from the 1980s…uh…*Back to the Future*?"

Mack was so stunned that someone actually recognized one of his obscure movie references that he nearly fell over in shock.

"Great. Way to encourage him, Jerome," Jeffrey said sarcastically.

Akwen's voice interrupted, calling them back to the moment. "Here we go. We should be reverting right about…now."

Although Akwen's timing was off slightly, the travelers didn't have to wait more than a few seconds before the walls turned clear, offering a sight that turned their blood to water. Much of the planet that hovered below was obscured by thick layers of swirling, dark clouds. What they could see, however, caused an intense unease to settle over them. From where they floated in orbit, they had a clear view of a massive hurricane in the Western Hemisphere that looked to be roughly the size of Alaska. Peeking through the dense cloud cover in the Northern Hemisphere, they could see large patches of white that seemed to stretch on and on without end. To the south, where the clouds were thinner, they could see the deep blue of the ocean, but oddly mixed with sections of dark brown.

"Wh…wh…what happened? Is…is that earth?" Lisa stammered.

Jeffrey shook his head in confusion. "I don't know. It's hard to tell with all of that cloud cover."

"And that has to be the mother of all hurricanes!" Mack said in awe. "That thing looks like it could swallow half of North America!"

So captivated was she by the sight in front her, Rebecca didn't even look at the others as she asked, "If that's earth, then where did all of the clouds come from?"

Dr. Eisenberg pursed his lips, his brow furrowing in thought at her question. "I'm almost afraid to make a guess. Do you see how those clouds over there look different from the ones directly below us? Do they remind you of anything?"

Akwen spoke up, her voice sounding ominous. "Yes. I have seen clouds like dat before. Dey were from aerial photographs of volcanic eruptions."

"Volcanos?" Lisa said, concern filtering into her voice. "But in order to create that much ash, there would have to be several going off at the same time, or they'd have to be enormous!"

"Hold on," Jerome said. "Can you see that landmass just to the left of those clouds over there? What does that look like to you?"

"That looks like the western edge of Alaska," Jeffrey replied. "Look, there are the Aleutian Islands coming off of the southwestern edge. But," he paused, his forehead wrinkling in confusion, "but it's connected to Russia!"

"There must be some kind of landbridge connecting them," Rebecca added in shock.

"So what do you think all of that brown stuff is in the ocean?" Mack wondered. "And check that out over there," he said, pointing to a section of the planet near the horizon to their right. "What about that gray stuff in the north? It looks like…"

"Ice," Dr. Eisenberg finished. "That was my initial thought. It looks like Greenland, but it's much too far south. There's only one thing I can think of that would produce that much ice so far south. An ice age."

At this pronouncement, they each looked away from the planet for the first time to stare at the doctor in disbelief. Jerome shook his head, rubbing the back of his neck with his right hand as he did so. "This doesn't make any sense. How could we have arrived during an ice age? Every jump takes us back in time about one thousand years, and the time indicator says we should be around the year 2049 BC. That's nowhere *near* being far enough back in time for an ice age. Not to mention the fact that we didn't see any ice during our last jump. There's no way it could've all melted that fast."

"I don't know where or *when* we are, but I don't want to go down there," Lisa said, pointing toward the planet, her calm resolve beginning to crack.

"Well, we don't have any choice," Akwen retorted. "Da engines are reversing. We are about to get a firsthand view of what is going on wheder we like it or not. Here we go."

Each of the pyramid's passengers stood transfixed as the planet drew nearer and nearer; everyone's senses were so focused on observing what was happening around them that no one dared utter a single word. The transparent walls of the spacecraft offered a view that was at once spectacular and frightening. The speed at which they were traveling was such that within moments, they had pierced the atmosphere and were headed directly toward the massive hurricane. Immediately, they plunged into layers of clouds so thick that Rebecca became disoriented. A terrifying sensation of falling or being flung through the air by powerful winds crashed over her, despite the absence of any kind of breeze or sound within the pyramid. In desperation, she groped about in the visual chaos until she suddenly felt a strong hand grab her own.

"I'm right here, Rebecca," came Dr. Eisenberg's voice from beside her. "Close your eyes—it helps immensely."

Following his advice, Rebecca closed her eyes and began to pray. Instantly, she began to feel the vertigo lessen. She kept her eyes closed for several more seconds until Jeffrey's voice shattered the stillness.

"We've hit an opening in the clouds. Quick, look for some sign of land. We've gotta figure out where we're heading."

"It is hard to tell what is land and what isn't!" Akwen stated. "What is all of dat stuff on top of da water?"

Dr. Eisenberg sat bolt upright. "Logs! Those are enormous log mats made of what must be billions of trees!"

"But where and how—" Rebecca began, but her question was cut short by a shout from Lisa, who was pointing toward the horizon far out in front of them.

"Over there! A coastline!"

"It's the western coast of Europe!" Jeffrey breathed in relief. "Akwen, take us down...What's wrong?"

Beads of sweat began trickling down the dark skin of her forehead as Akwen fought what appeared to be a losing battle with the controls of the pyramid. "Da ship is not responding! I have absolutely no control! Elmer, what is going on? I tought we had dis problem fixed?"

There was a moment of tense silence as Elmer communicated with the computer. At last, its head swiveled around to face them. "Dr. Nancho, all systems seem to be functioning normally. The program that controlled our flight on previous occasions is not the cause. I cannot determine the source of this interference."

Jeffrey and Akwen exchanged concerned glances. "That's not good," Jeffrey commented dryly. "Akwen, do what you can to get control. If we land in the water or on a volcano or something—"

"Yes, I know!" Akwen snapped back in irritation as her fingers moved deftly over the control board, desperately searching for anything that would respond.

The others, knowing their fate rested with Akwen's piloting skills, watched helplessly as the pyramid continued its descent. They quickly left the ocean behind and began moving inland when they encountered yet another patch of thick clouds.

"Akwen, are you having any luck?" Jeffrey asked, his voice sounding tight and strained.

Slamming her fist down on the edge of the console, she swore in frustration. "Not a single ting. It is as if someone else has taken control of da ship."

"Dr. Nancho, the ship just changed course by 13 degrees to the southeast and our descent has begun to slow," the droid said, its voice as casual as if it had just read the selections on a restaurant menu.

Suddenly, they broke through the bottom layer of clouds and were welcomed by a vista so magnificent that there was a gasp from nearly everyone in the room. Stretching out below as far as they could see was a colossal sheet of ice that covered the surface of the planet, reflecting the diffused rays of the hazy sun. Dotting the barren landscape were large boulders, trees, and other bits of debris, most of which were either partially or completely encased in layers of ice and snow. To their left, a range of mountains graced the horizon like mighty sentinels, their dark, jagged ridges standing out in sharp contrast to the endless blanket of white.

Jerome's voice broke the stillness with such abruptness it caused Rebecca to start in alarm. "Jeffrey, look! That wall of earth directly ahead of us. Do you see it? I think that might be a terminal moraine!"

A reluctant smile began to spread across Jeffrey's face. "Yeah, I think you're right."

"What's a terminator moraine?" Mack asked. The quiver in his voice and the expression on his face revealed his fear that it would turn out to be some kind of mythical monster.

"A *terminal* moraine is the mound of debris deposited at the end of a glacier," Jeffrey commented offhandedly without even looking at Mack. "Akwen, can you—"

"At dis point, I can't do anyting! So just shut up and hope whatever is controlling dis ting knows how to land it too," Akwen barked.

Akwen's outburst only seemed to add to the heavy presence of tension and fear that had settled in the room. Not wanting to add further to that tension, Jeffrey forced himself to swallow the verbal counter-assault that sprang readily to his lips.

Fortunately, they were already heading in the direction Jeffrey wanted to go. Ahead, just on the other side of the large mound of earth that was being bulldozed by the glacier, patches of bare land became more abundant. The ship, now flying only several hundred feet off the ground, continued forward, leaving the massive sheet of ice behind.

"Thank God," Lisa breathed. "We could've been in serious trouble if we had landed in the middle of that."

"Yeah, well we're not out of dis yet," Akwen said as she tried once again to gain some control over the machine. "Dese mountains still have a lot of snow on dem. If we get buried in an avalanche, den it is all ov—"

She stopped in mid sentence. "I have control again! Whatever was controlling da ship has released it!"

Rebecca looked at the doctor, her eyes brimming with hope. Giving her hand a gentle squeeze of reassurance, Dr. Eisenberg, his own face white and lined with worry, offered her a unconvincing smile. "We're going to make it," he said. "Have faith."

"Akwen, we're getting too low," Jeffrey noted. "Can you gain us any altitude?"

"I don't tink so," Akwen replied, her earlier antagonism having lessened considerably now that she was once more in control. "Da ship's core is almost depleted of energy. We need to land very soon. Do you have any preferences?" she asked.

Considering that they were still in the midst of a snow-covered, heavily mountainous region, Jeffrey didn't like any of their current options. "Just get us as far away from the glacier as possible," he said. "The winds seem to be blowing from that direction. Do you think you could get us to the opposite side of that ridge? That should at least give us protection from the brunt of the wind. By the way, does anyone have any idea if this thing has heat when *not* jumping through time?" he asked, his eyes glancing around the interior of the still nearly invisible pyramid.

Lisa shrugged. "Not that I know of. The general consensus among the techies was that the core somehow would provide heat and oxygen when in space. No one was sure how it operated because they were dealing with too many new variables. That was one of the questions they were going to research once the ship was online. We weren't supposed to take it for a full test drive yet!"

"Well, let's hope for the best," Jeffrey said. He took a deep breath and let it out in a long sigh as Akwen maneuvered the pyramid over the ridge Jeffrey had indicated. On the other side, the mountain sloped sharply downward toward a large, frozen lake nestled in the center of a wide valley surrounded on all sides by cliffs.

"Dis is not good," Akwen said worriedly. "Dere is no place to land!"

"What about over there?" Jeffrey pointed toward a more-or-less flat outcropping on the side of the slope. "That looks big enough. Set it down there."

Not happy with the location, yet seeing no other viable options, Akwen steered the pyramid over to the indicated area and set it down gently. Immediately, the walls returned to their normal appearance as the white energy beams dissipated.

Even before the engines had fully shut down, a blast of arctic air spilled in through the opening in the ceiling, instantly causing the temperature within the pyramid to plummet several degrees. Reacting swiftly, Akwen slammed her hand down upon the switch that closed the hatch. As it slid into place, a low rumble passed through the pyramid.

"Wha…what was that?" Mack whispered, afraid that even his voice might cause a reoccurrence of the disturbing sound.

"I don't know, but let's hope it doesn't—"

A second rumble shook the ship violently.

"Uh…I hate to say it, but I don't think these rocks are entirely stable," Mack said in panic.

"Really? Tanks for stating da obvious!" Akwen said snidely. Grabbing for the controls, she began preparations to start up the engines again. However, as she studied the gauges, she shook her head in futility. "It's no good. Da core is completely drained."

The sound of the howling wind lashing against the pyramid seemed only to add to the chill of Akwen's pronouncement. Then, softly at first, the sound of crumbling rock could be heard as if coming from far off in the distance. Gradually, the noise increased in volume and was accompanied by a third shudder that seemed to come from deep beneath them.

"Grab what you can!" Jeffrey shouted. "We've got to get out of here before—"

The sentence was left unfinished. For at that moment, the rocky shelf they had landed on crumbled under the weight of the pyramid, sending them sliding wildly down the steep incline toward the icy lake below.

18

ICE AND WIND

FOR THOSE FIRST few terrifying seconds, it seemed to Rebecca as if time itself had slowed to a crawl. The pyramid listed dangerously to the left as it began to slide down the side of the mountain, sending its occupants scrambling to grab onto anything that would keep them from tumbling into the slanted wall. Rebecca and Dr. Eisenberg, who had been standing on the left side of the central core shaft, barely had time to throw up their arms to protect their heads before being slammed heavily against the hard stone. The force of the impact knocked both of them from their feet and sent them sprawling toward the triangular crevice where the wall met the floor.

Momentarily stunned, Rebecca stared around her in confusion, her mind unable to make sense of her surroundings. Her curly black hair clung to her face, making her already-blurred vision even worse. Her arms throbbed where they had collided with the wall, and she wondered briefly if at least one of them might be sprained. The roaring sound of the pyramid as it rode the avalanche down the slope nearly deafened her. Yet through the clamorous noise, she could make out the barely audible sound of a familiar voice calling out to her.

Trying once again to get her bearings by relying on her distorted sense of sight, she fought to locate the source of the voice crying out to her so urgently. Finally, her eyes settled on the form of a man who was pointing emphatically toward…something. Suddenly, the fuzzy images in her mind converged, bringing the knowledge of impending danger.

Jeffrey, Lisa, Jerome, and Akwen were clinging desperately to the computer console, which ran the length of the wall directly to Rebecca's left. Next to them, Elmer, still plugged into the computer, had clamped onto the console using one of its many arms. Directly in front of her, Rebecca could see strands of Mack's unruly hair sticking out from the other side of the central core shaft. And on the right side of the core shaft, wedged between it and the railing at the top of the stairs, was the source of the danger. The heavy, wooden table that normally rested upon the opposite wall was now looming over her about twelve feet away, threatening to come crashing down at any moment. Although the floor was tilted at just less than 45 degrees, she knew the weight of the table would be more than adequate to crush her if it became dislodged.

A groan from beneath her reminded her that she had not been standing alone when the avalanche began. Gritting her teeth against the pain in her body, she braced her arm against the wall and pushed herself off the still form of Dr. Eisenberg.

"Doc!" she said as she began shaking him, her eyes darting frantically back and forth between the table and her friend. Turning his head to the side, she noticed a large, ugly gash on his forehead; the blood from the wound was beginning to trickle down the floor. "Jeffrey, he's hurt! Help me!" she cried in panic.

Before the words had left her lips, however, the entire pyramid shook violently as it came to a sudden halt. The crash jarred the table loose, sending it sliding directly toward Rebecca and the doctor. Screaming, Rebecca threw herself on top of him in a futile attempt to shield him from the crushing weight.

However, because of the height of the table and the slant of the wall, the edges of the tabletop collided with the stone first, stopping its descent mere feet before it reached them.

No one stirred for nearly a minute, each afraid the slightest movement might cause the avalanche to begin anew. Outside, they could still hear the sounds of rocks striking the sides of the pyramid as the mountain continued to vent its anger against them. Eventually, even these sounds ceased as the remnants of the rock slide came to rest. At last, Jeffrey lifted his head to look around at the others. Still afraid to move, he simply called out, "Is everyone okay?"

"Jeffrey, Doc's hurt!" Rebecca yelled, her own pain momentarily drowned out by her concern for her friend. "Hurry!"

Using the computer console to control his descent, Jeffrey moved cautiously down the sloping floor until his boots were able to reach the wall. Moving over to join Rebecca, Jeffrey helped her get out from under the table that had nearly pinned them to the wall. Still dazed, Rebecca sat down on the floor, her back leaning up against the wall as Jeffrey bent to examine his mentor.

"Doc!" Jeffrey called out softly. "Stay with us. C'mon, Doc!"

The older man's eyes fluttered open weakly, accompanied by a pain-filled moan. "That's it, Doc. Try to focus on my voice." Ripping off a small section of his shirt, Jeffrey began carefully cleaning the blood away from the wound.

"I don't think the cut is life-threatening, but we need to stop the bleeding and get him bandaged up," Jeffrey said to the others, who were still hanging on to the side of the computer, afraid to move.

"What do we do now?" Mack asked, his voice laced with fear and uncertainty.

"The pyramid must have become wedged against something as it slid down the slope," Jeffrey began, his mind working rapidly. "We have to get out of here as soon as possible in case it breaks free again and plummets into the lake. I'll go check the front entrance and find out if we can get out that way. In the meantime, we need to patch up the doc and see to Becky's injuries. Lisa, you've probably got the best medical training, so why don't you handle that? Mack and Jerome, grab as much food and survival equipment as you can and stuff it into carry bags. Akwen, see what cold-weather gear you can find—jackets, blankets…whatever. Work as fast as you can, everyone—but be careful."

Akwen, Jerome, and Mack nodded their assent and worked their way up the inclined floor toward the stairs. Jeffrey, turning toward Rebecca, stared deeply into her eyes. Startled by the conflict of emotion reflected in those deep brown pools, Rebecca felt her own buried hurt and pain at Jeffrey's rejection resurface—as well as her love. For the briefest instant, Jeffrey appeared about to speak, then changed his mind. Giving her shoulder a gentle squeeze, he quickly stood and made his way to the stairs.

"Hey, Gunny. Is anything broken?" came Lisa's familiar voice next to her.

Still lost in the aftershocks of that moment of near vulnerability, Rebecca took several seconds to respond. "No. I…I think I just bruised my arms when I hit the wall. I'll be okay," she said, offering her friend a pained smile. "See to Doc first."

Weakly returning the smile, Lisa nodded and began examining Dr. Eisenberg's wound. "It doesn't look too bad, Doc. The frames of your glasses are pretty bent out of shape, but other than that, I think we should have you back on your feet in no time," she said, calming her patient, who was beginning to come around. "Becky, I'm going to go grab the med kit. Stay with him and try to keep him talking. Hopefully he doesn't have a concussion."

With the help of Elmer, which had floated down to hover near them, Lisa worked her way up the slope to the other side of the room. Wincing in pain from the soreness that was already beginning to set in, Rebecca moved over to where the doctor lay and cradled his head in her lap. Within moments, Lisa had returned and began cleaning and bandaging his wound, her hands shaking. Abruptly, the pyramid shuddered and groaned around them, causing the three to freeze, their eyes widening in fear.

From below, Rebecca could hear Jeffrey curse loudly in frustration. A moment later, he appeared at the top of the slanted stairs, his normally handsome features lined with worry and alarm. "The front entrance is completely blocked. Our only hope is to try to go out through the opening in the roof," he said as he slid down the sloping floor toward them.

"But what if it's covered?" Lisa said, her voice shaking slightly. "If we open it, then all that snow and debris will fall down on top of us!"

Jeffrey reached out and grabbed her shoulders to reassure her, his own quivering hands betraying his confidence. "We'll all climb to the other side of the room so that if that does happen, we'll still be able to go down the stairs. Besides, it's our only chance." Hoping to change the subject, Jeffrey looked down at Dr. Eisenberg and smiled. "Welcome back, Doc. You gave us quite a scare."

"I'm glad to still be with you," he said with a weak voice. "It sounds as if we are in a bit of a bind. What happened?"

"The shelf we landed on gave way. We appear to be wedged against something halfway down the slope," Jeffrey said. "We need to move you to the other side of the room. If you hold on to Elmer, he should be able to carry you there. Do you think you're up for that?"

Easing into a sitting position, Dr. Eisenberg stared back at them with determination. "Yes, I think so."

"Jeffrey, maybe you should go behind him, in case he passes out, or falls off," Rebecca suggested.

"Yeah, good idea," Jeffrey agreed. "Let's get moving. The others should be just about finished. The sooner we get out of here, the better. We still don't know if this thing is stable."

As if in response to his words, another rumble passed through the ship. Once again, fear rendered them immobile for several seconds as they waited to see if their downward plunge would continue. When it had passed, they began moving in earnest, eager to escape from this possible death trap.

Dr. Eisenberg was barely situated with his arms around Elmer when

Akwen arrived back at the top of the stairs, her arms laden with several jackets and pairs of gloves. "Jeffrey, I found enough jackets for everyone, but no heavy coats. I also found several pairs of work gloves. Dey are not thick, but dey are better dan noting. And if we use blankets on top of da jackets, we should stay warm enough. Da blankets are at da bottom of da stairs. I'll be back wit dem in a minute."

"What about Mack and Jerome?" Jeffrey asked as Akwen turned to leave. "Are they almost finished?"

"Yeah, right here," Jerome called from below. "We stuffed as much food and equipment as we could into five different backpacks and carry bags. Give us just a few seconds to get it all to the top."

Akwen shook her head. "We should open da hatch first. Let's not waste time if we don't need to. But pass me da blankets. We need dose now."

Complying with Akwen's wishes, Jerome and Mack handed the blankets up to the others, then, leaving the bags at the bottom of the stairs, they joined the rest. A few moments later, they were all huddled together along the side of the central core shaft as high up the sloping floor as they could get, each wearing a jacket, gloves and wrapped in a blanket. "Okay, Elmer, open da hatch."

Had they not already been holding their breath in anticipation, the blast of arctic air that streamed in through the hatch once it was open would surely have caused them to suck in a quick breath. Along with the wind, large chucks of ice and snow poured through the opening, cascading down to accumulate along the bottom of the sloping floor. As the freezing slush rained in, they could hear the rest of the debris above them shift, causing another shudder to wrack the pyramid.

"Shut it, NOW!" Jeffrey yelled as the snow began rising toward the edge of the stairs.

However, just as Akwen was about to give the command to Elmer, the stream of snow ceased and the light shining in through the hole darkened drastically. A large object had become wedged in the opening, allowing only thin slivers of light to shine through.

"What…what happened?" Mack said, his voice quivering both from the cold and frayed nerves.

Placing his feet onto the side of the tilted central shaft, Jeffrey climbed precariously to its top to get a better look at what it was that blocked the aperture. "A boulder," he said in defeat. "And a big one, from the looks of it."

"So…so you mean we're trapped in here?" Mack asked, panic beginning to cloud his reason. "That's it! There's no way out! The only thing to do now is wait until we freeze or until this thing shakes itself loose and we wind up in the lake!"

"MACK!" Jeffrey yelled, hoping to stem the rising tide of fear. "Don't give up just yet. The good news is that light is still visible around all of the edges. That means there's nothing else but this boulder blocking the hole. If we can figure out how to move it, we can still get out of here."

His words had the desired effect. Gradually, Mack calmed down, his once-rapid breathing returning to its normal rate with the help of his inhaler. "Yeah…okay. So…so maybe we could, like, blast it with the laser or something. Maybe blow it up!"

Lisa shook her head. "No, we can't do that. The explosion would probably set off another avalanche."

"Well then, what about Elmer?" Jerome suggested. "Couldn't he just float up there and push it out?"

"No. His gravity control units are not strong enough to lift it by himself dat far off of da ground," Akwen stated.

"What if we all get up there and push, then?" Mack offered, his panic threatening to return.

Jeffrey stood fully erect and placed both gloved hands against the hard stone. However, the wound in his shoulder from Hercules' laser blast caused him to wince as he tried to put weight on the muscle. "I don't know. It doesn't look impossible. The problem is, there isn't much room up here. We could probably only fit two people together, and unless one of you has been pumping steroids recently, I don't think there are any two of us who are strong enough to…"

His voice trailed off suddenly, even as his eyes grew wide with inspiration. Following his train of thought, Rebecca shouted out in excitement, "Goliath!"

The others quickly grasped the meaning of her statement, their own faces mirroring Rebecca's enthusiasm.

"That's it!" Mack gasped, relief flooding over him.

Cautiously making his way down the side of the central shaft, Jeffrey looked at each of the others in turn. "Jerome, you and I will go wake up our cyborg friend. Mack, Lisa, and Akwen, bring the food up here so that we can be ready to move. C'mon, let's go." Shuddering from the cold, Jeffrey wrapped his blanket around himself tighter and headed down the stairs, followed immediately by an apprehensive Jerome.

"Jeffrey, are you sure this is such a good idea? I mean, what happens *after* we get his help moving the boulder? Isn't there some other way to move it?"

"None that I can think of, and we're quickly running out of time... Hold on. It's starting to come around now."

Jeffrey, blaster leveled at the large being, stepped back as Goliath began to stir. Rolling over, the giant opened his eyes and peered groggily at his captors.

"Goliath, listen, we don't have much time," Jeffrey explained. "We're all in danger, and we need your help. I don't have time to explain everything, but we need to get out of the ship. The front entrance is blocked, and we need your help to move a boulder that's wedged in the top opening. If you help us, we'll let you go free."

Goliath narrowed his eyes at them, suspicious. "Why...why is it so cold? And why are we leaning to the side?" he managed, his consciousness beginning to return to its normal functioning. Before Jeffrey could answer, a short rumble passed through the pyramid, and they felt the floor beneath them shift slightly.

"There's no time," Jeffrey urged. "We're all going to die if we don't get out soon!"

Rising uncertainly to his feet on the sloping floor, Goliath stared hard at them both, his eyes probing their faces for signs of deception. Seeing nothing but trepidation and anxiety, he nodded. "If I'm going to help you, then the first thing you need to do is put away the gun. If we are truly all in danger, then it sounds like we'll need to work together just to survive. I can't focus on survival if I have to constantly be watching over my shoulder to see if you're going to shoot me in the back."

"Fair enough," Jeffrey said. "But before I lower the gun and undo your bindings, I want you to know that we're stuck high up on a snow-covered mountain, and the ship may be damaged. If you attack us now, you'll have no way to get home."

"Understood," Goliath replied, his voice deep and resonant.

Lowering the gun, Jeffrey tucked it into his belt and cut the giant's bindings with his pocket knife.

"Where's my helmet?" Goliath asked.

"Here," Jeffrey said, as he picked it up off of the floor and handed it to him. Then, turning around, he led the way out of the makeshift prison and back upstairs to where the others waited. Wasting no time, Goliath surveyed the area, placed his helmet on his head, and climbed atop the core shaft.

"Jerome, you're going to need to help him," Jeffrey said.

"Me? But you're probably stronger," Jerome replied.

"That may be true, but my shoulder is still sore from that shot I received from Hercules. I can't put too much strain on it," he said.

Reluctantly, Jerome climbed up next to Goliath, his eyes reflecting his discomfort at the proximity of the giant. Bracing themselves, the two pushed against the boulder, their muscles straining against the resistance. Immediately, the rock shifted, sending small showers of powdery snow down upon their backs. As carefully as possible, so as not to start another avalanche, they pushed the boulder off to the side opposite the slope.

Grabbing the edges, Goliath heaved himself up and through the opening. A second later, his massive arm reached back inside, took hold of Jerome's outstretched arm, and pulled him through as well. Looking around, Jerome nearly lost his balance as the precariousness of their position fully struck him.

The pyramid rested against the side of a small cliff that jutted out from the slope. The bottom corner of the pyramid seemed to be wedged between the cliff itself and several large boulders—but only barely. It wouldn't take much to break it free and send them sliding once more down the slope toward the frozen lake that now lay less than fifty feet below them.

"Look over there," Goliath said, pointing with his right hand. Although the sun was mostly obscured by a mass of gray clouds, the sunlight that did make it through reflected off the snow around them. Shielding his eyes from the diffused light, Jerome followed his gaze and saw what had caught the giant's attention. The mouth of a large cave lay just above them and off to their left. "If we head down the pyramid to where it meets the cliff, we should be able to cross over and climb up to the top," Goliath pointed out. "The cliff isn't too steep, and it looks like it contains numerous hand and foot holds. The climb shouldn't be too difficult, provided the snow and ice don't cause us to slip," he added casually, although to Jerome it seemed that the giant was taking perverse pleasure in poisoning him with seeds of doubt.

Leaning his head back through the open hatch, Jerome explained to the others their current situation and plan. As quickly as they dared, Jeffrey and Lisa passed the backpacks and carry bags full of food up to Jerome and Goliath. Once that was accomplished, Jerome pulled Jeffrey through, with the help of Lisa from below. Then, stepping back from the hatch, they watched as Elmer hovered up through the opening with Dr. Eisenberg in tow.

However, as soon as they made it through, the droid began to falter, causing it to tip dangerously to the side. Letting out a cry of terror, Dr. Eisenberg lost his grip on the droid and fell onto the pyramid. Reacting quickly, Jeffrey and Jerome reached out and grabbed Dr. Eisenberg as he began to slide.

"Watch out!" they heard Goliath shout. Turning around, they watched in horror as Elmer drifted out of control into the boulder that had been blocking the hatch. Jarred by the impact, the boulder tilted to the side and began tumbling down the side of the pyramid, missing Jeffrey and the others by inches.

Suddenly, the pyramid began to shake and shift as it adjusted to the effects of the boulder's departure, forcing everyone to reach out frantically for something to hold on to. For several tense seconds, Jeffrey, Jerome, and the doctor lay unmoving while the cold wind continued to blow mercilessly around them.

Once the pyramid had stabilized, Goliath turned his helmeted head toward Elmer. "Stupid droid. Get that thing back inside before it kills us all!"

Still wobbling, Elmer made its way back into the interior of the ship.

Poking his head back through the opening, Jeffrey called down to the others. "Akwen, what was that all about? Another glitch?"

"No. Elmer says dat his systems were not designed for cold weather," Akwen stated, sadness coloring her words. "It looks like...like we are going to have to leave him behind."

"So what?" Goliath stated coldly. "It's just a robot. If you want to stick around and have a funeral, then be my guest."

Jeffrey threw the giant a disgusted look. "That's an awfully interesting statement coming from someone who is half robot!"

Ignoring the comment, Goliath grabbed a backpack and a carry bag, slung them over his shoulders, and began heading quickly, but carefully, down the pyramid toward the cliff.

"I'm sorry, Akwen. But there's nothing we can do now. We have to go," Jeffrey said sincerely, his tone betraying his sense of urgency. "C'mon, Lisa. You next."

After a hasty goodbye to Elmer, Akwen and the others scurried through the hatch. Grabbing the food and equipment, they cautiously worked their way down to where Goliath had already crossed over to the cliff.

The sight of the majestic, snow-covered mountains surrounding them and dipping down into the icy blue of the lake below filled Rebecca with an odd mixture of wonder and terror. While the white-crested rocks were beautiful, she knew they were also horribly sharp and unyielding. And the lake, while its vast size and shimmering glaze of ice inspired awe, contained cold waters that waited to carry the unwary to a quick death. Returning her concentration to the task of watching her footing on the slick stone of the pyramid, Rebecca moved down the last few feet to the place where the pyramid met the side of the cliff. Several feet above them, on a mostly flat ridge of the cliff, Goliath squatted down, his long arms outstretched.

"Quickly! Pass me the carry bags!"

Just as Jerome was about to hand the bag he was carrying up to Goliath, Jeffrey stopped him. "Wait. Jerome, did you guys by chance grab any rope?"

"Yeah, it's right here," he said, reaching into the bag in his hand and removing a coiled length of thick rope.

Taking the rope, he turned towards Dr. Eisenberg and began securing the rope around the older man's waist. He was about to protest when Jeffrey held up a hand. "It's just a precaution because of your recent injury. We don't have time to argue."

Turning back around, Jeffrey noticed that the two carry bags of equipment and food were already sitting on the rocky ledge next to Goliath, who was even now helping a very nervous and shaken Jerome as he climbed off of the pyramid.

"Here," Jeffrey said, holding out the laser pistol to Rebecca as she stopped next to him. "Why don't you take this? That way you can watch our backs while I help the doc." Nodding in agreement, Rebecca took the weapon and stuck it inside her jacket.

Once Jerome was safely on the ledge, Jeffrey assisted Dr. Eisenberg from below while Jerome held the rope from above. As each of the others climbed off of the pyramid and onto the safety of the cliff, Jeffrey's fear began to lessen. *We're going to make it! We're not out of the woods by any stretch of the imagination, but at least we're out of immediate danger.*

As he pulled himself up to the small ledge, they all let out a sigh of relief. For a full minute, no one moved; they simply stared at the sloping pyramid, each lost in his or her own disturbing thoughts about their uncertain future. Finally, Akwen broke the silence.

"Elmer, shut da hatch," she said, using the microphone embedded in her lip to communicate with the droid. Immediately, the hatch closed, shutting them out and leaving them feeling abandoned.

Without speaking, they turned and followed Goliath as he climbed farther up the cliff, which more or less followed the gradual slope of the mountain. Jerome, having tied the rope tethered to Dr. Eisenberg around his own waist, climbed after the giant, followed closely by the doctor, Mack, Akwen, Rebecca, Lisa, and Jeffrey. On several occasions they were forced to travel more horizontally than vertically, but their sure-footed guide kept them always moving up and to the left towards where they spotted the cave.

Rebecca, her arms still aching from her collision with the stone wall of the pyramid, found the climb excruciating. However, her concern for Dr. Eisenberg, combined with the ever-present threat of falling, kept her mind diverted from her physical pain. She knew her concern for Doc was not unwarranted, because she could tell that every foot of progress he made up the cliff was achieved with extreme effort and determination.

She was thankful, therefore, that the cliff itself was relatively easy to climb—at least it would have been under normal circumstances. The ice and snow, however, plus the cold numbness that had overtaken her fingers and toes, made the journey treacherous. Each of the travelers slipped more than once, and they all received several new cuts and bruises on their bodies from the sharp rocks.

Pausing for a moment, Rebecca caught sight of Goliath in the front of the group. He had stopped moving and appeared to be scanning the area around him carefully. Although she couldn't see his face due to his helmet, his posture gave her the distinct impression that he sensed something she couldn't, something hidden.... A moment later, she was caught off guard as his body suddenly shifted and shrank slightly! Where the hairy, beast-like giant once stood clutching the side of the cliff was now a dark-skinned man of Middle-Eastern descent.

His armor! It contains a cloaking device! I almost forgot, Rebecca thought. *I didn't know it could change into human shapes. Why did it feel the need to change shape now? Did it see something? I wonder what else that armor can do that we don't know about. Could it change shape to look like one of us?* Shuddering at the thought, she shook her head and continued her climb, her body once more complaining at the strain. *Come on, Becky. Hang in there,* she thought, trying to buck up her flagging courage. *Only a couple more minutes and we should—*

A cry from Dr. Eisenberg interrupted her mid thought. Looking up quickly, she watched in terror as the doctor's foot slipped, causing him to slide downward, his frozen fingertips desperately scrambling for purchase on the slippery rock. Jerome, hearing the cry, wrapped his arms around a large rock next to where he had been climbing and held on tightly. A second later, the rope connecting him to Dr. Eisenberg went taut, arresting the doctor's fall. However, during his brief slip, he had bumped into Mack, causing him to lose his grip as well.

"MACK!" Lisa screamed, watching helplessly as their friend fell down the cliff toward the slope below. His body landed hard on the snow, tumbled several times, and then began sliding slowly toward the lake far below.

"Oh, God, no!" Rebecca found herself crying out in a strangled voice. She watched helplessly as Mack's unconscious body moved farther and farther down the slope.

Jeffrey, last in line and thus the closest to Mack, called out frantically to the others. "Rope! I need some rope quick, before he slides..." he choked out. His voice trailed off in futility because he knew Mack would be too far gone before he could ever get the rope ready. Tears misting his eyes, Jeffrey slammed his gloved fist into the side of the cliff and swore in grief and anger. Above him, he could hear Lisa sobbing quietly.

Then, seemingly from out of nowhere, a rough-hewn net attached to a long rope flew through the air and wrapped itself around Mack's body. Immediately, the rope tightened and Mack's body ceased its downward progress. Following the rope to its source, Rebecca's jaw dropped. Staring down at them from the top of the cliff stood seven large, fur-covered warriors.

19

CAVEMEN

ALL ANYONE COULD do for several long moments was stare at the mysterious figures looking down at them. Finally, Goliath—who still looked like a normal, albeit extremely tall, dark-complexioned man—proceeded to climb cautiously toward the warriors, his eyes practically boring holes into them with the intensity of his scrutiny. The others, having finally recovered their wits, also resumed their climb.

Rebecca, relieved at Mack's rescue and frightened by the appearance of the fur-covered hunters, found it difficult to focus her thoughts. Dozens of questions flashed through her mind like lightning strikes. During the time it took her and the others to reach the path that led to the cave, the warriors didn't appear to move at all, almost as if they were wax figures in some museum.

Had it not been for their strange observers, they all would have collapsed in exhaustion as they finally reached the end of their climb. Instead, they forced themselves to stand, with the exception of Dr. Eisenberg, who merely sat with his back propped against a small boulder.

Rebecca couldn't determine any of the features of the warriors because they were covered nearly head to toe with heavy furs and animal hides. Thick hoods were pulled down low, and scarves were tied tightly around their heads to protect their skin from the biting winds. Only their eyes were left uncovered.

Each of the hunters held long, wicked-looking spears in gloved hands. Judging by the practiced ease with which they held the deadly shafts, Rebecca guessed they could raise them to attack position at a moment's notice, if necessary. The warriors made their way towards where Rebecca and the others stood. As they moved, Rebecca was surprised to notice that their legs were somewhat bowed, causing them to move with a waddle-like motion. In addition, she saw that four were carrying two inert forms between them. One was stiff and unmoving, its face completely covered with furs. The other hung limp between them and was covered with netting.

"MACK!" Rebecca called out as his mop of black curls came into view. She started to move toward him, but the sudden wariness she could sense in the eyes of the hunters arrested her motion.

Jeffrey, never taking his eyes off of the fur-clad figures, reached out a restraining hand and grabbed her shoulder. "Hold on, Becky. Let them make the first move," he said cautiously. Casting sidelong glances at the others, he whispered, his teeth chattering from the cold. "There are only seven of them, and four are busy holding Mack and the other body. We can take them if we move quickly. Be ready to act if things begin to turn ugly."

As he finished speaking, one of the warriors standing in the front closed the gap between the two groups. Stopping within a few feet of Jeffrey and Goliath, he stared at each of them in turn, his eyes reflecting surprise and curiosity. After finishing his initial perusal, he spoke. The scarf wrapped around his mouth caused the strange language to sound even more bizarre.

Jeffrey exchanged quick glances with Dr. Eisenberg and Jerome, wondering if either of them had understood. Receiving only puzzled looks in response to his nonverbal questioning, Jeffrey turned back to face the hunter. Shrugging his shoulders, he replied in English, "We don't understand you." When his words elicited no response, he tried again in German, Latin, Italian, and Spanish, all to no avail.

Giving up on verbal communication, the warrior raised his spear toward the cave and gestured invitingly. Then, signaling to the others of his group, he headed off in the direction of the cave, followed immediately by the four who were carrying Mack and the other body. The remaining two hunters waited expectantly for Jeffrey and the others to move.

"Do we follow them?" Lisa asked nervously, her gloved hands gripping the blanket draped around her shoulders.

"I don't see that we have much of a choice," Jeffrey replied. "They have Mack, they have weapons, and we're freezing out here. Besides, if they wanted to kill us, why did they rescue Mack? They seem friendly enough. So unless anyone objects, I say we follow them."

The others didn't seem inclined to argue, largely due to their weariness, Jeffrey suspected. Reaching down to help Dr. Eisenberg to his feet, he grabbed the professor's arm to offer his support. Jerome took up the position on the other side of the doctor, and together they began the short trek up the path toward the cave, followed close behind by Rebecca, Akwen, and Lisa. Taking his place last in line, Goliath eyed the two warriors with distrust. The fur-covered men responded in kind to the giant's expression by tightening their grip on their spears.

Before long, they found themselves entering the mouth of a cave set into the side of the mountain slope. The opening was just over ten feet wide and at least that tall, with billows of smoke escaping from the mouth of the cave along the ceiling. The moment they stepped over the threshold, they felt the bite of the wind subside, bringing relief to their stinging faces. In addition, not more than twenty feet into the interior of the cave stood the source of the smoke: Burning brightly in the center of the cave was a large fire, its dancing flames beckoning to the weary group with promises of warmth and comfort.

Their relief from the wind and excitement at the prospect of sitting near the blaze was tempered, however, by the unnerving sight of a group of four more fur-clad figures standing near the entrance with large torches in one hand and spears in the other. Standing at their sides, two ferocious, wolf-like dogs barked angrily, the hackles on their backs raised in challenge. As if the mere presence of the men was not disturbing enough, the sight of their features caused Rebecca and the others to gasp in astonishment and mild disgust. Unlike the warriors who had met them outside the cave, these had their hoods thrown back and scarves removed, revealing their faces.

It seemed to Rebecca as if she had stumbled into a scene from a documentary about the origin of humans. Although the men were not much taller than her own five-foot, four-inch height, their bodies were thick and stocky. Their arms and legs, though hidden underneath layers of animal hides, appeared to be strong and powerful, the obvious result of hard labor. Their faces, which wore surprised expressions mirroring Rebecca's own, were overshadowed by large, prominent brow ridges and framed by manes of long, reddish-gold hair.

"Jeffrey!" Jerome called out. Despite the low volume of his voice, his excitement was unmistakable. "They look just like—"

"—Neanderthals," Jeffrey finished for him, his own voice tinged with amazement. "Only I think these guys are a lot more intelligent."

As they stood in the entrance to the cave attempting to restore warmth to their frozen extremities, the warrior who had led them there removed his own hood, scarf, and gloves, and held a brief conversation with the four guards. The other warriors removed theirs as well, all the while keeping wary eyes trained on Goliath.

Before long, their guide beckoned them forward as two of the other men calmed and restrained the snarling dogs. Their party proceeded into the cave and passed, single file, around the edges of the fire. Once on the other side, their guide paused and allowed them a few minutes to sit and revive their strength. The weary travelers, thankful for the rest, nearly collapsed in relief. And although the warriors remained standing, Rebecca could tell that they, too, were grateful to once again be in the comfort of a warm cave.

The two men who had carried Mack laid him down gently near Rebecca and Lisa. Immediately, both women began searching for wounds. Finding nothing more serious than a few cuts and bruises, they simply did their best to make him comfortable by using their backpacks as pillows for his head and legs.

As they sat huddled around the fire, each group studied the members of the other with intense curiosity. Moving his massive bulk closer to Jeffrey, Goliath leaned over and spoke in a hushed whisper, his eyes never ceasing to study the cavemen. "In case you hadn't noticed, our number of captors has increased. Three of the cave entrance guards followed us past the fire. Also, the two men carrying the corpse have disappeared. More than likely, they have gone to dispose of the body as well as sound the alarm. If we're going to act, we need to do so now."

Jeffrey shot a sidelong glance at the giant, his face reflecting his annoyance. "And what would you have us do? Attack five armed warriors, not counting the one on the other side of the fire with the two wolves? And what would we do even if we did manage to overpower them? Leave the cave? Where would we go? And what about Mack? We'd have to carry him."

Goliath nearly snarled, but held it in check for fear of showing signs of aggression to their hosts. "Do I look like a fool?" he hissed. "I am well aware of the difficulties of the situation. One of you has the laser pistol which you have been using to keep me unconscious. These things have never seen such technology. You could take out two or three before they ever knew what hit them. If I change my shape, it would undoubtedly shock them long enough for me to remove them from the fight. Once we have subdued them, we could hold them hostage, requiring their friends to give us supplies. If we hold out long enough, we can recover our strength and give Mack time to get back on his feet. And if not, then we may have to make some hard choices. I for one do not want to stay here and trust these primitives. If you won't help me, then I'll take matters into my own hands."

Jeffrey paused to consider the idea. *Maybe Goliath is right*, he thought.

222   KEITH A. ROBINSON

It could work. These warriors look about ready to collapse from exhaustion themselves. If we time it right... Then, just as he was about to reply to Goliath, his eyes fell upon Dr. Eisenberg and the others. "No," he said with quiet resolve, his own exhaustion pushing its way to the surface. "We'd never make it. Dr. Eisenberg is wounded, and the rest of us barely have the strength to move. I'm afraid we need to trust these cavemen. After all, they did rescue Mack—and all of us, for that matter."

Clearly unhappy with Jeffrey's decision, Goliath grunted as he sat up straight once more, legs crossed and posture alert. Jeffrey watched the giant's reaction with concern. *I sure hope it doesn't do anything stupid. Who knows what's going on it that cyborg brain. Hopefully it'll remember that it needs us to pilot the ship and get us back home. But if it decides to stay here and take its chances on its own in this world...*

As Jeffrey's thoughts trailed off, he noticed that light was coming from what looked to be a bend in the cave not more than forty-five feet beyond where they sat. In addition, he could see that the trail of smoke from the bonfire was joined by smoke coming from around the corner before it headed out the mouth of the cave, indicating other fires were burning farther in.

Finally, just as the warmth was beginning to seep through their sodden garments and warm their bones, another cave dweller came around the corner. After spending a few seconds staring unabashed at the strangers, he strode as quickly as his bowlegged stride would allow up to their guide, delivered a brief message, then disappeared around the corner once again.

With an apologetic look on his brutish features, the guide signaled for them to follow him. Immediately, the two hunters who had been carrying Mack bent down once again and lifted him up, ready to move out. Jeffrey and the others rose unsteadily to their feet with extreme effort, once more assisting Dr. Eisenberg—who, Rebecca noted with concern, still seemed unnaturally pale. The guide, seeing that they were at last ready, led the large party of hunters and strangers around the bend.

The new area into which they stepped was clearly the living quarters of these people. Several small fires cast flickering shadows onto the family-sized tents that lined the walls. Each of the nearly fifteen-foot-long, triangular shelters consisted of layered animal skins covering a wooden frame. Two ten-foot-tall, vertical poles were set into holes dug into the cave floor at the front and rear of the tent, with a top horizontal ridge pole hung between them. Several other, thinner, poles leaned against the horizontal one and were tied in place with what looked to be either plant or leather strips. The animal skins that covered the shelters hung in overlapping layers, like shingles on a roof. Where the skins met the cave floor, large rocks had been placed on top of them, probably both to prevent drafts and to anchor the hides to the ground, Rebecca surmised.

Many other curious items could be seen inside the shelters and haphazardly littering the floor around them, as if set down in relative haste. Rebecca could see that it was only with extreme effort that Jeffrey, Jerome, and Dr. Eisenberg—who had perked up noticeably at the sight of the artifacts—kept from reaching down and examining the veritable treasure trove of bone tools, clothing, bowls, children's toys, and other objects.

As they continued walking, they passed a recessed alcove that contained bundles of wood, a long, paddle-like stick, and, curiously enough, a pile of flat stones set in a circle about three feet in diameter. Before she could even guess their purpose, Rebecca overheard Dr. Eisenberg speaking to Jeffrey and Jerome; the professor was once more lost in the enjoyment of lecturing to two of his students. "Do you see those flat stones?" he was saying. "That's a hearth! They use the wood over there to heat up the stones, then they use that paddle to scrape the coals off to the side once the stones are hot enough. Then they can cook their meals. This is identical to what was discovered in Pech de l' Aze in southern France!"[25]

"Do you think they have storage pits dug nearby too?" Jerome asked.

"Most likely," Dr. Eisenberg replied. "They'd have to have some place cold to keep their meat and other foods. If they dig a pit and cover it with rocks, it would keep for a long time, as well as protect it from predators."

If the professor had wanted to say more on the subject, Rebecca never found out. At that moment, their guide led them into another area of the cave that left them all speechless. Scores of cave paintings filled the walls, the images vivid and colorful, unlike the long faded vestiges that the archaeologists were used to studying. Rebecca longed to stop and examine the wonderful depictions of hunts and ceremonies that commemorated important events of these people. She knew that if her own desires were piqued by these drawings, then it must be excruciating for the three archaeologists in front of her to pass them by.

But pass them by they did, because their hosts continued to urge them on deeper into the cave. After leaving the paintings behind, the cave branched into three passages. The first one was narrow and split off to the right. The other two were wider and situated farther down from the first. It was into the leftmost passage that their guide led them.

They walked on for another minute and, after passing a handful of other openings, Rebecca could sense the members of the group, particularly the giant, growing more and more uneasy. Rebecca was hopelessly lost in the maze of tunnels, and she wondered if any of the others could find their way back to the entrance if they were forced to try to escape. She fought against her own fears that began to well up. The dank, musty smell of the cave combined with their slow trek through the dull blackness with just minimal light reminded her of another time and place... Mental images of mutated creatures lurking just out of the reach of the torchlight caused her pulse to quicken.

C'mon, Becky! she told herself. *Don't think about that. Those creatures on Ka'esch were just part of a vision. This is real. Focus.* In an effort to fend off her unwelcome thoughts, she tried to concentrate on her immediate surroundings. A soft moan coming from beside her drew her attention. Looking over, she saw that Lisa was struggling with fears of her own. A look of panic was setting into her features, and her hands were clasping and unclasping seemingly of their own volition. Her eyes darted back and forth, frantically scanning the walls and ceiling.

"Lis, are you okay?" Rebecca asked her friend.

At the sound of her voice, Lisa's body gave a startled jerk. "What? I...I..." she began, swallowing hard. "I...I've got to get outta here. I don't like caves or...enclosed places."

Rebecca, having had her own bout with claustrophobia, nodded in understanding. Reaching out, she placed her left arm around Lisa's shoulder in a comforting gesture. As her arm touched Lisa, she felt her friend stiffen. Lisa looked at Rebecca with an intensity that shocked her. For a moment, Rebecca wondered if Lisa's response had more to it than just her fear of caves. Then Lisa relaxed and laid her head on Rebecca's shoulder as they walked. "Where are they taking us?"

"I don't know," Rebecca replied. "I was wondering the same thing myself." *And where are the women and children?* she wondered. *If we don't stop soon, Dr. Eisenberg may not be able to go on. He's looking so pale, and we're all so tired...*

Then, even as her last thought trailed off, her ears picked up the faint sound of a voice speaking off in the distance. Due to the echo produced by the cave walls, it was impossible to ascertain how far away it was. A few moments later, the volume increased even as several strands of flickering firelight became visible as they were reflected off the walls. Wherever they were going, it appeared they were about to arrive.

Sure enough, within moments the weary travelers found themselves rounding a gentle bend in the cave and entering a large cavern approximately two hundred feet in diameter and thirty feet in height. Standing among the numerous stalagmites and other cave formations were the rest of the cave dwellers. The fifty or sixty people gathered in the underground chamber consisted of all age groups, including a handful of elderly people and at least a dozen or more children.

As the group stepped into the room, those standing nearest the entrance moved to the side to give them space. At the sight of Goliath, several women pulled their young children close and headed toward the outer walls quickly, their expressions an odd mixture of grief, fear, and curiosity. As they did so, Rebecca was surprised to notice that quite a few did not exhibit the same traits as the majority—namely, the large brows and reddish hair. In fact, some looked strikingly similar to modern humans.

Their guide led the party into the center of the cavern and eventually stopped in front of a rock formation that seemed to serve these people as a natural stage. Sitting calmly in a sturdy wooden chair set upon the platform was an elderly man. Although his face was weathered and lined with age, Rebecca could sense a strength and power in him, leaving no doubt in her mind that she was standing before a leader. His frame was old, yet muscular, and he was dressed in similar fashion to the others in the room. However, in addition to his animal-skin clothing, he wore a heavy cloak of deep blue draped around his shoulders, the woven material a sharp contrast to the rest of this people's mostly animal-skin arraignment. His ancient brow was less pronounced than the brow bones of many of the others, and his head was crowned with thin strands of shoulder-length, graying hair gathered into a ponytail near the base of his neck. A full, silvery beard spread over his chest and ended just above his sternum, where it was bound together as a complement to the ponytail. Although he had the common elderly traits of enlarged ears and a thick nose, his eyes appeared sharp and intelligent. In fact, as Rebecca studied the man, she was struck by the wisdom and discernment that emanated from him. Only one other time in her life had she ever encountered a being that exuded that kind of authority…and that being had turned out to be an angel. So who was this man?

As Rebecca's group came to a halt, a hushed silence fell over the assemblage. Each of the cave dwellers studied the strangers in awe. Their gazes dwelled particularly on Goliath, who looked extremely unhappy at the sudden attention. Whispers from the observers were amplified by the natural acoustics of the cavern, creating an eerie ambiance. Finally, the elderly man stood and raised his hand, causing the chatter to cease.

A moment later, he inclined his head toward their guide, who promptly began to speak. After a brief conversation, the leader of the cavemen rose, stepped off the stone platform and walked over to stand directly in front of Jeffrey, Jerome, and Dr. Eisenberg.

For several long seconds, he stared into each of their eyes as if searching for something. He halted to examine Dr. Eisenberg's head wound before moving on. Without fear for his personal safety, he walked around the edge of the group until he was standing before Goliath. Although the giant was nearly three feet taller and his appearance was that of a very powerfully built man, it seemed to Rebecca as if it were Goliath who was the weaker of the two. In fact, for the briefest of instances, she thought she saw fear register on the holographic image that represented the giant's face. Without a word or even a hint of emotion, the leader continued his assessment of their party, all the while leaving the rest of the occupants of the room to simply watch in patient expectation.

He paused as he studied Akwen's and Lisa's features. However, when he approached Rebecca, he stopped completely, his eyes widening slightly. For what seemed like an eternity, Rebecca stood rooted to the spot under the intense gaze of the elderly man. Finally, he nodded his head in affirmation of some unknown question and spoke a few words in his strange language. Placing a firm hand on her arm, he smiled and then turned to head back toward the platform. As he moved away from her, she swallowed nervously and looked at the others, who all wore the same questioning expressions as her own.

Halfway to the platform, the leader stopped as the two hunters who had been carrying Mack stepped forward and gently lowered their burden to the ground. After another brief examination, the elderly man called out to a middle-aged woman who had been standing nearby, and he waved her over. They exchanged a few short words and immediately the woman called out to several other women who disappeared. Before the leader had resumed his seat on the platform, however, the other women reappeared with cloths and water. As everyone watched, two of the women walked up to Dr. Eisenberg and gestured for him to sit. In short order, they had his wound cleaned and dressed. At the same time, three others ministered to Mack.

"What are they doing to Mack? I can't tell," Lisa whispered to Rebecca.

"I can't see very well either, especially in this light," she replied. "But it looks like they're having him drink something. He—"

A sputtering sound interrupted her sentence as Mack coughed several times. Slowly, he opened his eyes and stared around him in confusion; his brain clearly wasn't comprehending the images sent to it from his eyes. Stepping forward, Rebecca pushed her way between the women and knelt down beside Mack. Cupping his head with her hands, she turned it to face her own. "Mack, it's me—Becky. Are you okay?"

After several seconds of looking at her, Mack blinked and nodded. "Ye-yeah. Hi, Becky. Where…where are we?" Looking up at their cave surroundings and noticing the large brows of the women leaning over him, Mack's eyes grew wide with recognition. "Whoa! Who are they? How did we wind up in *Clan of the Cave Bear*?"

Rebecca smiled at him. "I'm glad to see you're back to normal," she said. "You had us worried for a while. As for where we are, well, the short version is that you were rescued by some Neanderthal-like humans and we are currently…guests in their cave."

Mack shot her a quizzical look, but before he could verbalize a question, the elderly leader spoke briefly. Immediately, the women withdrew to join the rest of the crowd. Moving forward, Jeffrey crouched down next to them, his eyes still watching the warriors and their leader warily. "Mack, we're glad to have you back. Do you think you can stand? I have a feeling we're going to need your interpretation skills."

"Uh, sure," Mack replied weakly. "If it's a language I recognize."

Slowly, Jeffrey and Rebecca helped Mack stand. Once he had regained his footing, the leader began to speak. As he spoke, Rebecca and the others watched Mack expectantly, hoping beyond hope that he would be able to understand the language. After a few moments, the leader paused, his brows raised as if awaiting an answer.

"Well, do you understand him?" Jerome asked impatiently.

"Gee, give a guy a break," Mack said curtly. "I just woke up, and I have a splitting headache from that joyride I took down the slope." Turning towards Dr. Eisenberg, he said, "Doc, what do you think? Have you heard anything like this before?"

The doctor frowned, concentrating. "It almost sounds like Hebrew, but the dialect is very different."

"Yeah, that's what I thought, too," Mack replied. "I need to hear more. Maybe I'll try some Hebrew and see if he can recognize any of our words. What should I say?" he asked, looking at Jeffrey.

"I don't know. Start with the basics I guess. Tell them your name and assure them that we mean them no harm," Jeffrey said.

Facing forward once more, Mack began speaking. At first it appeared that the elderly leader did not understand anything he was saying. They took turns speaking, with their guide interjecting comments from time to time. After several minutes, a smile slowly spread across Mack's face. "Aha, now we're getting somewhere. They have a strange way of pronouncing the words, but I think I am starting to piece together a few things. If I'm correct, the elderly man is called 'Father,' or something like that."

"No, not 'Father,'" chimed in Dr. Eisenberg, "but 'Patriarch.' That was about the *only* thing I understood."

"Okay, so what else?" Jeffrey asked.

"Well, this guy standing here is named Terah, and I guess he's the one who found us, right?"

"Right. So what else?" Jeffrey asked again impatiently.

"It seems Terah and some of the other men were returning from some sort of hunting trip or something when they saw our pyramid descend from the sky. So, naturally, they want to know who we are and where we come from," Mack continued. "What should I tell them?"

They were silent for a few moments as they considered how to respond, when suddenly Goliath spoke, his low, gravelly voice laced with pent-up frustration. "Tell them I am a god and you are my servants."

The others turned to stare at him. Jeffrey was the first to recover his ability to speak. "I'm not sure that would be wise," he said. "These people may look like brutish Neanderthals, but they sure aren't as primitive."

"Then what do you suggest we tell them?" Goliath said with a sneer. "We don't even know what the truth is ourselves. Should we tell them we are from another dimension? Or should we say we are aliens? These *are* primitive people. They wouldn't understand what an alien was even if Mack could figure out what word to use. The *only* explanation that would make any sense to them is that we are gods who descended from heaven."

"And what do we do if they don't buy it?" Jeffrey said slowly. Although not happy with Goliath's conclusion, he grudgingly accepted his logic.

"Then we could give them a demonstration of our power. I could change shape and you could use the laser pistol on one of them," Goliath finished, his last words punctuated by a wicked-looking smile.

"Well, whatever we are going to say, we had better decide quickly," Akwen stated as she stared nervously at the crowd surrounding them.

"I don't like it, but I don't think we have much of a choice," Dr. Eisenberg said softly.

Mack grinned, "Okay, I'll tell them. And if they don't buy it, I'll just say that Goliath will grow angry and use his magic!" Turning back to face the Patriarch, Mack began speaking. Initially, the old man's facial expression was unchanged. Then, after asking several clarifying questions, the Patriarch's countenance darkened. Nearby, they saw the warriors tense, and the crowd began moving away from them.

Leaning toward Jeffrey, Jerome whispered nervously. "Something tells me that, um, that he isn't going for it. Now what do we do?"

Before Jeffrey could answer, chaos erupted around them. The warriors closest to them dropped into protective crouches, spears pointed in their direction. Loud gasps of fear and panic erupted from the crowd. In what felt like slow motion, Jeffrey turned around to see that Goliath had reverted to his normal, armor-clad form. Taking off his helmet, Goliath let out a bellow of rage intended to frighten the warriors; the flickering torchlight enhanced the vicious appearance of his wolf-like features.

But the sudden change in the giant's looks had the exact opposite effect. The moment he removed his helmet, the Patriarch rose to his feet and shouted something. Instantly the warriors sprang into action. Goliath, caught off guard by his failed surprise attack, barely managed to dodge the first spear thrust. With lightning-quick reflexes, he spun around, grabbed the spear from the nearest warrior, and landed a kick in his chest, sending him sprawling onto the cave floor. Spinning the weapon in his hands, he struck the nearest warrior with the back end of the spear, then reversed the thrust and prepared to plunge the point into Terah.

However, before he could complete his attack, several strands of thick netting enveloped him from behind. Thrown off balance, the giant tumbled to the ground and lost his hold on the spear. Immediately the warriors set upon him and rendered him unconscious within seconds. Then, just as Terah prepared to land a killing blow, the Patriarch called out once more, halting him.

Leaving the platform, the leader of the cave dwellers strode up to them once more, his expression showing anger and betrayal. Stopping in front of Rebecca, he stared hard at her, his gaze changing to one of confusion. Then, with a quick motion of his hand and a few words of command to Terah and the warriors, he turned around and walked away.

Without hesitation, the warriors ushered them out of the cavern. This time, however, they were not treated as guests, but as prisoners.

20

PRISONERS

"THIS IS GREAT! Just great!" Mack blurted out in exasperation. "Now what are we gonna do?"

"Well, your pacing certainly isn't helping!" Jerome shot back, his own frustration fuelling his anger.

"Stop it, both of you!" Rebecca yelled, standing to her feet. Putting a hand on each of their shoulders, she pulled them over to the far side of the small, dead-end cave that served as their prison cell. This portion of the cave was just over a dozen feet below the main floor. The group's captors had forced them to climb down a wooden ladder into the dank hole. Once in place, the cave dwellers removed the ladder and posted two guards at the top to keep an eye on the prisoners. Rebecca and the others were now left in the cold darkness; a single torch hanging on the wall near the guards served as the only source of light.

"Don't you see that Lisa is about to lose it?" Rebecca chided in a forced whisper. "Her claustrophobia is pushing her emotions to the edge. Your fighting is only making it worse. Now either calmly help us figure out what we're going to do, or do us all a favor and shut up!" Letting go of the two men, she turned and walked back over to where

Lisa lay curled in a ball next to Jeffrey, who held her as one might hold a frightened child.

Feeling like scolded children, Jerome and Mack resituated themselves next to the others on the cold, damp, stone floor. After a few moments of heavy silence, Jerome cleared his throat. "So, uh, do you think that Goliath is even still alive? Or do you think they…"

"It has to still be alive," Mack said softly as he absentmindedly ran his fingers through his mass of curly black locks. "I mean, didn't it say that if it died, the reactor that powers its body would explode?"

"If it—or should I say he, was even telling the truth—" Dr. Eisenberg commented.

"What?" Jeffrey said as he lifted his head, his interest in the conversation suddenly piqued. Lisa, who had finally drifted off to sleep next to him, shifted her weight to rest against him as he spoke.

Dr. Eisenberg shrugged. "Don't you find it slightly odd that the stun gun worked on Goliath at all? Why would a gun designed to stun humans bother a machine, even one that is part human? And you said yourself his story is a little too convenient. We can't kill him because he will explode. Hah! Most likely he just made that up so we'd be forced to keep him alive. In fact, I think he was probably lying about almost everything, even the fact that he put some sort of nano-bomb inside you and Rebecca."

"Well, even if we think it's lying, that's not a risk I want to take," Jeffrey said, "at least until we get back to civilization and have our bodies scanned."

"So if you don't tink it is a cyborg, den what *do* you tink it is?" Akwen asked.

The professor shifted his weight and leaned back against the stone wall in a vain attempt to get comfortable. "That, my dear, is the fifty-million-dollar question. For one thing, I don't believe he's a cyborg. That was most likely a cover story to keep up from guessing his real identity."

"Which is…?" Mack asked, his science-fiction-loving mind engrossed in the conversation.

"Back in the cavern, when Goliath removed his helmet, the Patriarch stood and yelled something, just before his warriors attacked," Dr. Eisenberg continued. "Mack, did you catch what he said?"

Mack's brow wrinkled as he fought to reclaim the memory. Then, after a few seconds, his face brightened a little. "Yeah, I think so, but I thought he just yelled out a word similar to the word for 'giant.'"

Dr. Eisenberg's expression became more serious. "Yes, he did. But not just any word for giant. The word he used was *naphil.*"

A sense of foreboding settled over them, causing the darkened cave to take on a ghostly life of its own. Knowing she had heard that word before, Rebecca wracked her brain in an attempt to locate the source. But before she could figure it out, Jeffrey spoke, his tone taking on an edge of disappointment and even a hint of anger.

"C'mon, Doc. You can't possibly be suggesting that Goliath is one of the Nephilim. I know we've seen some strange things on this trip, but that doesn't mean we should start confusing things even more by throwing fairy tales into the mix."

"I don't understand," Akwen said. "What exactly is a Naphil, or a Nephilim?"

"Well, that all depends on who you ask," Jeffrey said. "A Naphil is singular, and Nephilim is the plural. They're mentioned in the Hebrew Bible, in Genesis chapter 6 to be exact. They were supposed to be the children of the 'sons of God' and the 'daughters of men.' According to the Bible, they were 'mighty men which were of old, men of renown.' Other non-canonical Jewish writings, such as the Book of Enoch and the Book of Jubilees, also support this interpretation. Most scholars simply believe the book of Genesis and the other extra-biblical sources are merely legend and myth, which means that it's useless to even try to figure out who they were because they didn't really exist. Or if they did exist, they were probably just local heroes who were elevated to the status of 'sons of God,' or due to exaggeration, became 'giants.'"

Dr. Eisenberg frowned. "Don't be so quick to discard any ancient text, Jeffrey, even if you don't believe its content. I know I taught you better than that. You can ridicule it if you want, but the fact of the matter is, there is a record of Nephilim in the Bible as well as the other two books, and we just encountered a man who used the term to refer to Goliath."

"But maybe he just used the term as a general reference to Goliath's size," Jerome offered.

"I don't think so," Dr. Eisenberg countered. "Remember, the Patriarch didn't use the word until *after* Goliath removed his helmet."

"So what does that mean?" Rebecca asked in confusion.

"Nothing, for sure," the doctor said. "Only that our giant friend may not be who he says he is, and that these people have some knowledge of ancient biblical stories, which makes sense with the fact that they speak a form of Hebrew."

"Which brings us around to the main questions: Who are these people? And more importantly, what are we going to do?" Jeffrey said.

Jerome chuckled lightly, "I think it's safe to say that our theory about alternate realities is true. I mean, these people look like Neanderthals, but they're certainly smarter. And according to the pyramid, we've only gone back in time about four thousand years, not forty thousand!"

"Unless the pyramid dial is wrong," stated Jeffrey matter of factly.

"Well, it proved accurate for da first couple of jumps," Akwen said in defense. "I don't tink we should start doubting it now. We have enough variables to work wit."

"I agree," said the doctor. "So let's assume for now that it is working correctly. That means either we have entered another reality, or our understanding of our own history is grossly incorrect," he finished, throwing Rebecca a sidelong look.

Grateful that Dr. Eisenberg even offered her theory as a possibility bolstered Rebecca's courage.

"It doesn't really make much difference either way," Jeffrey said. "Right now, we just have to figure out what we're going to do. We can debate our theories later. I think our first item of business is to figure out if we're permanently stuck here. Akwen, can you contact Elmer? If so, find out if he's had a chance to look over the ship, provided it's still stuck on the cliff and not sitting at the bottom of the lake."

Akwen nodded and began speaking, the tiny microphone embedded in her lip transmitting her voice over the airwaves. "Elmer, do you copy?"

The African woman sat in silence for several seconds listening, her eyes staring without focus. Finally, she smiled and looked around at the others. "He is still fully functional. Da ship has not moved, and he is wondering when we will return."

Rebecca felt a lump rise in her throat as tears came unbidden to her eyes. *We still have a chance to make it home! Thank you, Lord!* As she looked around at the others, she could see they were having similar reactions to the news. It suddenly struck her how much harder this whole ordeal must be for the rest of them. At least she and Lisa had military training, and this particular journey was nothing compared to the fear and stress she went through on her trip to Ka'esch. And this time, even if they couldn't get back home, she was at least surrounded by friends.

"Elmer," Akwen continued, interrupting Rebecca's thoughts, "have you been able to examine da ship yet?" This time, Akwen listened for nearly a minute to Elmer's reply while the others waited impatiently for her to relay the droid's answer.

"So…what is he saying?" Mack whispered, eager for a response.

Akwen shot him a dirty look and waved a hand at him in annoyance, her concentration still focused on listening to Elmer. Finally, after what seemed like an eternity to the others, she spoke. "According to Elmer, da ship looks okay enough to fly. However, he says dat da core was damaged when da ship slid down da slope. He tinks he might be able to fix it so dat it will hold small amounts of juice—probably enough for a few short jumps."

At this pronouncement, despair struck at their hearts, like a sledgehammer smashing their fledgling hope into oblivion just as it had begun to take root. Mack was the first to give voice to his emotions. "Wait! You…you mean all we can do is go a little farther *backwards* in time, and then we're stuck? No...no...there's...there's gotta be something we can do. We need to get back to the ship. Maybe we could figure out—"

"Mack," Jeffrey said calmly, his own face reflecting the gravity of the situation, "take it easy. We'll see what we can do. It may not be much, but at least it's something. Akwen, tell Elmer to do what he can and keep us informed on his progress. In the meantime, we have to figure out a plan of escape. Becky, you still have the gun, right?"

"Yes," she replied without inflection. "But don't you think that we should try talking to them first? Goliath already tried force, with disastrous results. Maybe we can convince them that we're not friends with Goliath."

"Good luck with that one," Jerome said sarcastically.

"Fine. We can try talking to them. In the meantime, we should work on a plan to—"

Before Jeffrey could say more, the light in the room brightened as three other cave dwellers entered, one bearing a torch. The prisoners watched the brief exchange between the five men in anxious anticipation. After a few seconds, one of the guards reached over and lowered the wooden ladder down in front of the captives. They were so shocked by this sudden change of events that for a moment, no one moved. Then, just as Jeffrey began getting to his feet, one of the men said something in a commanding voice, his finger pointed directly at Rebecca.

She looked around at the others in uncertainty. "Me? What do they want with me?"

Mack placed a hand on her arm. "He says the Patriarch wants to see you."

She relaxed slightly, her fear turning to hope. This was exactly the chance they were hoping for. "Mack, you have to come with me to interpret," she said. "Explain that to them."

"Yeah, I figured as much," he said with a grimace. "I don't know, Becky. It probably won't do any good. But, if you need my help, then I guess I'll have to go along." Despite his reticence, Mack relayed her message to their captors. With a nod, the guard waved for them to climb the ladder.

"Good luck, Rebecca," Dr. Eisenberg said as she turned to leave. "You can do this. Earn their trust. Our thoughts will be with you."

Squeezing the professor's arm lightly, Rebecca looked at each of her companions in turn, her gaze lingering on her husband. Stepping closer to him, she quickly reached out and embraced him. "Here, take the gun," she whispered into his ear. "I don't want them to find it on me." Slipping him the weapon, she kissed him on the cheek and turned to leave. As she turned, Jeffrey reached out and grabbed her arm, halting her progression.

"Becky…be careful," he said, his features reflecting his conflicting emotions. Rebecca smiled back at him calmly, then turned around and climbed the ladder.

Mack stepped forward and prepared to follow Rebecca up the ladder. As he placed his foot on the bottom rung, he cast a lopsided grin at Jeffrey. "Don't worry, I'll be careful too." Without another word, he began to climb.

Once they reached the top of the ladder, the guards lifted it once more. The newcomers led Rebecca and Mack back through the underground maze. As they walked, Rebecca noticed Mack was fiddling with something on his right wrist. Leaning over to him, she whispered, "What are you doing?"

Glancing out of the corner of his eye to make sure the two guards behind them weren't paying attention, he replied, "I'm activating my digital camera."

Rebecca frowned. "Digital camera?"

"Yeah," Mack said, a wide grin splitting his roguish features. "You didn't think I would have a computer embedded into my skin without a camera and microphone to go with it, did you?"

Rebecca smiled wryly back at him. "You are just full of surprises, aren't you? So, where is it located?"

"Actually, I have two of them. One is located on my left index finger so I can take pictures of myself or anything else I choose to point at—very useful, I might add. The other one is located on my left temple so that I can record whatever it is I'm looking at. That's the one I'm currently using. I've got some great footage of our trip. I started recording back when we encountered the dinosaurs. If we ever get back home, I'll sell it and make a fortune. Anyway, as for right now, I figure if we need to find our way out of here, we can consult the recording."

At this, Rebecca's smile grew even wider. "Pretty slick, Slick."

"Thanks. I got the idea from this movie I saw once where this guy..."

The rest of the journey through the cave seemed to drag on forever as Rebecca listened patiently to Mack's lengthy movie review. Finally, much to her relief, they reached their destination. They found themselves once more in the wide cavern containing the stone platform, and, as with their previous experience, the room was filled with what looked to be the entire population of this people. This time, however, the mood in the room was noticeably different. Rather than curiosity or fear, an intense sadness and gravity permeated the air.

In addition, Rebecca and Mack discovered they were no longer the center of attention. As soon as they entered the cavern, their guides ushered them quietly into one of the farthest corners of the area. The reason for this quickly became apparent: They had been brought here to be observers, not participants.

Standing on the stone platform was the Patriarch, his face solemn and yet peaceful. Before him lay the body of a warrior whom Rebecca assumed to be the same one the hunters had been carrying when she and the others had been rescued. Although Rebecca couldn't understand what was being said, and Mack either chose not to translate or was too wrapped up in the drama to remember to do so, she was filled with an overpowering sense of peace and...joy. Then, as a culmination to the ceremony, a woman stepped forward and lifted a bone flute to her lips and began to play. As the first strains of the melody rose from the instrument, the entire congregation lifted their voices in a hauntingly beautiful song that brought to Rebecca's mind images of both sorrow and a promise of future rest. Tears welled up in her eyes and fell freely down her cheeks. Regardless of what the others believed about these people, and despite their somewhat brutish appearance, Rebecca now knew they were a complex and intensely spiritual people.

As the last notes of the song reverberated through the cavern, four men stepped forward and lifted the litter upon which the body lay, and carried it slowly into a side passage that branched off from the main area. After a few minutes, the men returned, the empty litter hanging sideways between them. The ceremony concluded, the crowd began to disperse. As they filed out, they spoke to one another in gentle tones, the soft whispers mixing with the muffled weeping of several women.

Beside Rebecca, Mack began to stir, as if awakening from a deep sleep. "Wow. I've never been to a funeral like that. I mean, wasn't that amazing how he…Oh man—I forgot! You didn't understand what was being said! Sorry, I…I…"

"Don't worry about it," Rebecca assured him. "It was still beautiful. But I would like to know: Who was he? Did they say how he was killed?"

"His name was Abimael," Mack said. "They didn't say anything specific about him other than the usual. You know—he was a great father, husband, hunter, et cetera. From what I gather, the team that rescued us was out hunting mammoths—can you believe it, real mammoths!—when they were attacked by another group of hunters. They were able to drive them off, but Abimael was killed in the skirmish. I will say one thing I found interesting was that there were lots of references to God. I didn't know Neanderthals were religious."

"They may not all be, just as not all humans from our time can be lumped into one spiritual category," Rebecca replied. "But we should still ask Dr. Eisenberg about it later. What I would like to know is why we were brought here to observe this."

Mack didn't have an answer, and the conversation lapsed into silence

as he and Rebecca watched the last few stragglers make their way out of
the cavern. Once nearly everyone had left, the guards led Rebecca and
Mack through several other narrower passages until they came upon a
curtain made of animal skins that were stretched from one wall to the
other. One of the guards announced their arrival, and a voice on the
other side of the curtain beckoned for them to enter. Pulling the curtain
aside, the guard gestured for Rebecca and Mack to step inside.

They walked into a dry section of the cave that was about the size of
a large study hall or office, which is exactly what it appeared to be. Several
pieces of crude, wooden furniture were set up in a semicircle facing a
small desk and table, which sat along the far wall. Several shelves had been
erected near the desk, each full of scrolls of various shapes and sizes. Next
to the shelves, the backpacks and carry bags full of food and other items
that they had brought from the pyramid sat piled close together. All of
this escaped Rebecca's notice, however, because as soon as she entered the
room, her attention was immediately fixed upon the disturbing sight of
two large cat's eyes glaring at her from the floor of the cave. The eyes were
attached to an enormous head of a saber-tooth tiger whose mouth was
open as if ready to devour any who dared to enter its lair.

So startled was she by the sightless eyes of the animal that it took
Rebecca several seconds to realize that it was the carcass of a beast that
now served as a rug. As Mack stepped in beside her, he blanched and
took a step back at the snarling visage. "Yikes! I would hate to run into
one of those in the wild. That thing is huge!"

Suddenly, a voice spoke from behind them, causing Mack to nearly
leap out of his skin in fright. Stepping into the room was the Patriarch,
followed by three men and a woman. The woman appeared to be about
the same age as the Patriarch, but despite her age, both Rebecca and
Mack were struck by her beauty. Her hair, though streaked through with
silver, must once have been luxurious, and black as night. To complement her hair, her skin was deep brown and matched her eyes, which
were vibrant and full of life.

The three men varied greatly in age: One looked to be in his late twenties, the other was middle-aged, and the other appeared to be just slightly younger than the Patriarch himself. They moved with the steadiness of skilled hunters, and, judging by their hardened muscles, Rebecca had no doubt that was exactly what they were. However, as she looked into their eyes, she could tell they were also highly educated.

The elderly leader walked over to the desk and sat. As he did, the eldest of the men pulled up a chair next to him for the woman to sit on. Once she was seated, the three men stood off to her right, their expressions firm, yet gentle. Once they were in place, the Patriarch indicated that Rebecca and Mack were to sit in the chairs in front of the desk.

Stepping forward, Rebecca bowed to the small group and took her seat, followed by Mack, who attempted his own awkward bow. Once everyone was in place, the Patriarch repeated his question. Immediately, Mack offered the translation.

"Do you like my rug?"

"Yes, very much," Rebecca said honestly. "I've never seen a cat that large. It is quite a magnificent beast."

"Yes, they are," the Patriarch replied. "And not easy to kill. This one was a prize brought to us by my son, Nahor," he said, indicating the youngest man standing next to the woman.

"Son?" Rebecca asked Mack. "Are you sure you translated that correctly?"

"Well," Mack said, "the term 'son' can actually mean 'grandson' or even 'descendant.' More than likely, he is his great grandson."

Rebecca nodded and continued, now addressing the Patriarch. "Sir, I would like to begin by apologizing for the actions of our…companion. We are not his companions by choice."

As soon as Mack had finished translating her sentence, the elderly man held up his hand, his head nodding in understanding. "I discerned as much. For how else could it be that one who has the Spirit of the Living God be in the company of a Naphil?"

Rebecca and Mack were dumbfounded by his reply, and sat motionless for several seconds. Finally, Rebecca found her voice and replied;

her words were infused with awe and amazement. "The...the Spirit? How...how do you know?"

The old man smiled warmly at her. "I do not know who you are or where you have come from, but one who has spoken to the Lord can recognize another in whom the Spirit resides. But come, first let us introduce ourselves. I am called the Patriarch by my people, as I am their father. This is my wife, and these are my sons, Arphaxad, the eldest, is the son of my son Shem. This is Peleg, and the youngest is Nahor, the father of Terah, who rescued you on the mountain."

Rebecca smiled politely at the introductions. "My name is Rebecca, and this is my friend, Mack. We are—" The words suddenly stuck in her throat, nearly causing her to choke. *Terah, Nahor, Peleg, and Arphaxad, the son of...Shem!* The realization hit her with such force that she swooned, nearly falling out of her chair. Mack reached out and steadied her, concern etched on his face. "Becky, are you okay? What's wrong?"

Coming to her senses, she turned and gazed into Mack's eyes. "Mack, don't you realize who this is we're talking to?"

When Mack just stared at her blankly, she breathed deeply, excitement and wonder coursing through her. "We are in the presence of Noah, *the* Patriarch of all mankind!"

21

THE PATRIARCH

MACK'S JAW DROPPED open at Rebecca's statement, his shock rendering him inert. Finally, after several seconds, he blinked and recovered his speaking ability. "Y...you mean *the* Noah? As in Noah's Ark?"

Rebecca nodded numbly, her own mind still reeling from the revelation. Mack turned his head slowly to regard the elderly man seated before him with renewed interest. As the two prisoners stared in amazement at the man, his face became full of puzzlement.

The Patriarch asked a question, but it took Mack a few moments and a prod from Rebecca to bring him back to his senses. "He wants to know how it is that we know his name. He says our faces look familiar, and wants to know if we have met before." As soon as he had finished translating, Mack stared at Rebecca in concern. "What do we tell him?" he asked worriedly.

Rebecca paused to consider their options. "These people have seen Goliath and the pyramid. We've lied to them once. I think our only choice is to tell them the truth."

"But what is the truth?" Mack asked. "We're not even sure ourselves. Is this an alternate universe, did we go back in time, or...or is it something else?"

Suddenly, Rebecca felt a peace settle over her that was so powerful she simply closed her eyes and felt her worry fade away. Slowly opening them once again, she smiled at Mack. "No, we *do* know the truth, even though most of the others choose not to accept it. We *have* gone back in time, Mack. It's just that our understanding of history is so wrong that we didn't recognize it."

Sensing that the others in the room were growing troubled by her hesitation to answer the question, Rebecca turned and spoke directly to them, her voice strong and confident. "Great Patriarch, forgive us for our hesitation and for our previous attempt at deception," she said. "We made a grave mistake by assuming you would not be able to comprehend the truth. We see now that you are wise and great in knowledge, and that your people are honest and good.

"My name is Rebecca Evans, and this is my friend, Mack Nielson. The truth is that we are travelers from the future. In fact, we are *unwilling* travelers, and we are not even sure how to return. The pyramid that brought us here was discovered buried beneath the ground." Rebecca paused, waiting for Mack's translation to catch up with her. "We figured out how to make it work, but we do not fully understand how it operates. It brought us here, and we were forced to land on the side of the mountain. Unfortunately, the ridge we landed on gave way, sending us sliding down the slope. Our only desire is to get back to the pyramid and return home. We never intended harm."

The Patriarch and the others were silent as Mack translated Rebecca's words. When he finished, Mack expected them to become angry in disbelief, laugh at the preposterous story, or dismiss him and Rebecca as insane. What he was not prepared for was calm acceptance and belief in their story.

"So is the Naphil from your own time, or did you meet him during one of your travels?" Arphaxad, the oldest of the three men, asked.

"He is from our time," Rebecca replied. "He and another giant tried to take the pyramid by force, and when the vessel was activated, they traveled with us. The other giant was killed during one of our stops, and we captured this one. However, we were forced to free him when we arrived here because we needed his strength to help us get out of the pyramid.

"Actually, we're not even sure he is a Naphil," she continued. "We don't know anything about him. What exactly is a Naphil?"

The elderly leader's face suddenly darkened, as if merely discussing the topic might conjure up a spirit of evil. "What do you know of the time before the Cataclysm?"

Mack and Rebecca exchanged glances after he finished translating the question. "Do you think he means the Flood?" Mack asked her.

"Probably. Ask him to make sure," Rebecca replied.

After Mack had done so, the old man nodded in affirmation. "Yes. What do you know of the world that existed before the Great Flood?"

"Not very much, Mighty Patriarch," Rebecca said. "The time we come from is over four thousand years after your time, and although there are many legends, only one main account has survived. And most people—including many of my companions—do not even believe that account is true."

A great heaviness seemed to bear down upon the Patriarch at Rebecca's words. Lowering his head in sadness, he was still for several moments. His wife gently laid a comforting hand upon his back and whispered soothing words to him.

Rebecca and Mack, caught off guard by the sudden emotion exhibited by their host, watched in silence. Finally, the elderly man raised his head, his eyes rimmed with tears. "Family," he said, his head turning toward the three men, "this is why we must always teach the young ones about the past. We must teach them the importance of knowing their place in history. For if we do not, then the evil one will cause us to forget the truth. Although it requires great effort, we must write our words down as a witness to future generations, and we must guard those words with our very lives, lest the evil one deceive our children."

Rebecca was struck by the truth of the words. In her mind, she thought back to her college days when she had been taught the theory of evolution by her professors. *I often wondered how such intelligent men and women could be so wrong about the origin of life. But it is simply because they bought into the wrong history. Because they believe the history of evolution, they've become blinded to the evidence of God's existence and handiwork. They've become brainwashed, even as I myself had become brainwashed. They can no longer view the world around them with open minds. He who controls history controls people's minds and beliefs, and thus their very lives.*

As this last idea lingered in her thoughts, she watched the Patriarch stand and cross the room to the shelf containing the many scrolls. "These scrolls are our greatest treasures, for they contain the true history of mankind as given to my forefathers by the Creator of life, blessed be His name." Like a parent picking up a slumbering infant, he lifted a large scroll from its resting place and gingerly brought it back to the desk. "And here is the account of my family, written by my own hand. It is a record of the way in which the Almighty One, blessed be His name, in His inexhaustible wisdom, has chosen to reveal Himself to my family, and to me. It is here that I have written about the Nephilim, that all mankind might remember the evil that was brought upon the race of man."

With deliberate care, the old man unrolled the scroll. Unable to contain their curiosity, Rebecca and Mack stood and leaned over the desk to examine the ancient document. As they did so, the Patriarch began to speak. The elderly leader's eyes lost their focus and his face filled with an intense grief as he became lost in the memory of the past.

"When I was young, my father, Lamech, taught me the history of the earth. He told me how he had spent many days of his youth learning from the true Patriarch, Adam. He passed on to me the truth of how the Lord of all created the earth and the heavens, of how He put the sun, moon, and stars in their place.

"However, this was not what most of those around us believed. At that time, belief in the one true God had dwindled, until only a small number remained." The elderly man's expression abruptly darkened. As he resumed speaking, his voice took on an edge of righteous anger. "Most had been deceived by the evil one and his followers. The Fallen Ones set themselves up as gods and taught that each person could become a god himself after death. Their religion of fleshly pleasures appealed to the masses, enticing them to leave the truth and embrace the lie.

"Eventually, the false gods even began seducing the daughters of men and producing horrible offspring. These were the Nephilim." The Patriarch's lips curled inward, as if the name itself left a putrid taste in his mouth. "They are giants—wicked and vile. Thus it was that the Mighty Lord of Hosts chose to destroy that world and its sinful people by sending a flood to cover all the highest mountains."

"But then surely Goliath can't be a Naphil," Rebecca said in confusion, "unless these demons have returned and begun breeding with human women again after four thousand years." The very thought sent chills running madly down Rebecca's spine.

"Of that, I do not know," the Patriarch replied. "And I will admit that your companion is not as tall as a normal Nephilim, nor does he have the same look about him. Regardless, whatever he is, he is an abomination. The mighty Creator did not create the likes of him. He must be put to death."

Rebecca did not argue the point, especially since they wouldn't be sorry to be rid of the creature. Yet a nagging doubt remained. If Goliath had indeed been telling the truth about the explosives planted in her and Jeffrey's bodies...

Mack spoke to the Patriarch, breaking into Rebecca's contemplations. The elderly leader nodded, and Mack gently grabbed Rebecca's arm and led her over to stand near the bookshelves. "Becky, what are we going to do?" he whispered. "I mean, this guy is clearly loonier than the Joker on heroin! He really seems to believe that he is *the* Noah, and his family is just playing along. You don't actually *buy into* any of this stuff, do you? I might be willing to believe that dinosaurs lived with humans and were called 'dragons,' but Neanderthals living in the Ice Age believing they are Noah and his descendents? That's completely nuts! And half-human, half-demon giants? I don't even think George Lucas or Steven Spielberg could come up with a movie plot that unbelievable."

Rebecca's facial expression was the only answer Mack needed. "You *do* believe this stuff, don't you?" he asked in disbelief. When she didn't respond, Mack shook his head in disappointment. "Becky, look, I don't even believe half of the wacky stuff I say I believe, but this…this is beyond crazy."

"Is it, Mack?" Rebecca replied. "Everything he has said fits perfectly with what's in the Bible. I'm not saying I believe everything, but I don't want to dismiss it so quickly, either. Say what you want about the Bible, but you can't deny that it's a historical document. And it contains some amazing accounts in the book of Genesis."

"Which is why most people believe it's just a myth!" Mack countered. "You don't really believe Noah fit all the animals in the world on a boat, do you? It just doesn't make sense."

Rebecca shook her head as if trying to shake off her own confusion and nagging doubts. "I don't know," she said. "This is all new to me too. I've always believed that God created the earth millions of years ago, and that dinosaurs lived before humans. I always thought the days of creation were not literal days, but long periods of time. I believed that Noah's Flood was probably just a local event. But now, I'm not so sure. What if dinosaurs really *did* live with humans? And what if there *was* a real, worldwide flood?"

Mack grimaced and shook his head, causing his course, black hair to wave about wildly. "I don't know. It just seems too crazy. I mean, out of all of the places in the world, what do you think the chances are that we would crash land right on *the* Noah's doorstep? If you factor in the probability of landing here *during this exact time period,* then it becomes ridiculously impossible."

"Listen, I'm not asking you to believe right this second. I'm still not sure what I believe either. But I want to at least leave the possibility open. I know that statistically it seems impossible, but then again, we still haven't figured out what took control of the pyramid. Maybe someone *wanted* us to meet him and guided us here. Whatever the case, we must assume right now that the Patriarch is not lying, especially if we have any hope of finding a way out of this jam. If we offend him, we're dead. Even if you don't believe him, pretend you do."

"Okay. Yeah. That makes sense," he said, taking in a deep breath to calm himself.

Turning around, Rebecca and Mack headed back over to rejoin the others. Once there, Rebecca bowed slightly and said, "Please forgive us for our discourtesy. So much of what you have said is new to us, and we are still very confused. We would like to learn more about your history. How long ago did the Great Cataclysm occur?"

The Patriarch nodded in acceptance of her apology, then answered her question. Even before she heard the translation, she could tell by the look on Mack's face that the response would be unbelievable. "This year marks the three hundredth anniversary of the Cataclysm."

Rebecca, who was much more familiar with the ages of the biblical patriarchs, was not nearly as surprised as her companion. "Great Patriarch, please do not be offended by my question, but we would be very interested in knowing how old you are. In our time, most humans do not live past their one hundredth year. How old are you?"

The elderly leader's bushy eyebrows rose at Rebecca's statement. "One hundred years is indeed a short lifespan," he said, looking over at his grandchildren. "Surely this must be due to the drastic change in environment after the Flood. I suspected as much. It causes me great sadness to think that my grandchildren will not get to live the long, full lives that their forefathers enjoyed." Looking back toward Rebecca and Mack, he answered their question. "This year marks my nine hundredth cycle."

Mack shot Rebecca a look of disbelief. "Wow!" he said. "This guy's as old as Yoda! I remember hearing somewhere that many of the early characters in the Bible supposedly lived really long lives, but nine hundred years? Surely that's an exaggeration. Maybe he's counting seasons or something. Maybe it's a translation error."

Rebecca shook her head. "No. I don't think so. According to the Bible, all of the patriarchs before the Flood lived to be over nine hundred years, with a couple of exceptions. Didn't you ever do any Bible trivia? A common question is 'Who was the oldest man who ever lived?'"

Mack's face brightened. "Oh yeah! It was some guy with a strange name. I remembered it by coming up with something that rhymed... Me-threw-the-law, I think."

Rebecca smiled. "That's close. Methuselah. He lived to be nine hundred and sixty-nine years old. In fact, I would guess that the other men in this room are around one hundred, two hundred, and three hundred years old."

"But even the oldest doesn't look much over forty!" Mack said, incredulous. "Of course, that's assuming they're telling us the truth."

Ignoring this last comment, Rebecca turned back to face their hosts. "We would be interested in knowing more about what happened after the Flood. If it has been three hundred years since then, why do you still live in caves? Surely there are other, more comfortable climates to live in."

Noah's face darkened yet again. "Therein lies yet another sad tale. After the Mighty Lord—may His magnificent name forever be exalted—brought His judgment upon wicked mankind, I did my best to teach my children and grandchildren to obey His laws. But the sin in men's hearts could not be conquered so easily. The Lord commanded us to be fruitful and multiply, and to spread out and fill the earth once again. However, many of my children did not listen to me. Instead, they turned away from the one true God and began worshiping the created things, such as the sun, moon, and stars. They even began to build a mighty tower, which would serve as a temple of worship as well as a doorway to reach the heavens. To prevent the rest of my family from being enticed by their evil, we fled to the colder, northern regions.

"But our isolation has come at a price," he continued. "The sky in this portion of the land is often filled with dark clouds of ash from the nearby fire mountains, sometimes blocking the sun for days. I believe this has caused some of our people to become sick, and our bones to become bent. But we would rather risk physical injury than lose our souls or our children to the vile gods of those who built the tower."

Walking over to the shelves once again, the elderly man retrieved a different scroll. Bringing it back to the desk, he searched through it. Finding the section he was looking for, he turned it around to face Rebecca and Mack. Leaning over the ancient manuscript, they were shocked by the image drawn there.

"Is this a picture of the tower?" Mack asked the Patriarch in astonishment.

"Yes. You recognize something familiar about the design, do you not?" he asked, his eyes narrowing knowingly.

Mack looked at Rebecca, then back at the elderly leader. "Yes. The shape of the entrance and the overall design have similarities to...to the pyramid that brought us here!" Looking over at Rebecca, Mack could tell she had reached the same conclusion. "Do you think the aliens that built our pyramid also helped build this tower?" he asked her.

"I don't want to be too quick to jump to conclusions. There's so much we still need to learn," she replied, her expression guarded. "Right now, we need to ask questions and listen. We can form our opinions later."

Several hours passed as Rebecca and Mack talked with the Patriarch, each taking turns asking questions and sharing information. During their interview, the Patriarch's wife left the room and returned with bread, cheese, and meat. Once they had eaten, the elderly leader dismissed his wife and the two youngest men, who promptly left the room. Arphaxad, the eldest, sat down on the chair vacated by his grandmother.

Mack, eager to study the scrolls, tried to be patient in his role as translator while the Patriarch asked Rebecca about the world to come. After nearly an hour of answering his questions, Rebecca in turn asked further questions about the time before the Flood. Finally, Mack turned the conversation to the scrolls, at which time Rebecca sat back and let the men speak unhindered by the need for Mack to translate for her.

Left to herself, she began mulling over the enormous amount of information she had garnered from their conversations. How long she sat in contemplation, she couldn't be sure. Lost in her musings, she was startled when Mack placed his hand on her arm. She looked up at him and was taken aback by the look of excitement on his face.

"Becky! I think I've found a way to fix the ship! We just need to—"

Before he could say anything more, he was cut off by the sound of shouts echoing through the cave. Arphaxad leapt to his feet and ran over to the entrance. Pulling back the curtain of animal skins, he was abruptly greeted by a man who was panting heavily, his face lined with worry and fear. Rebecca listened to the brief exchange of words, wishing desperately that she could speak the language. Turning towards Mack, she noticed that his face had turned pale.

"Mack, what is it? What's going on?" she asked.

After a short pause, he turned toward her; his face was ashen. "We're under attack!"

22

FLEEING THE ICE AGE

"WHAT DO YOU mean, 'We're under attack'?" Rebecca exclaimed. "Under attack by who?"

"From what I can gather, it's the same tribe that attacked the warriors on the mammoth hunt," Mack replied nervously. "It seems they're coming into the cave from a second entrance."

Before Mack could say anything further, the Patriarch spoke rapidly to Arphaxad, then urged Rebecca and Mack to follow him. Without arguing, they left the room at a brisk pace, the light from Arphaxad's torch lighting the way.

"Where are we going?" Rebecca asked Mack as they walked.

"The Patriarch asked him to take us back to the holding area, for our safety," he replied.

They hurried down the passage for several minutes. On a couple of occasions, they passed several men armed with spears heading in the opposite direction. Before long, they were back in the holding area. One of the guards on duty began to question Arphaxad about what was happening while the other lowered the ladder and gestured for Rebecca and Mack to descend. Rebecca grabbed the edge of the ladder and had started climbing down when several beams of light flashed past her. At the same time, she was startled by a loud crack echoing off the nearby cave walls. She looked up just in time to see Arphaxad and the two guards collapse onto the ground. Whipping her head in the opposite direction, she saw Jeffrey put the laser pistol back into concealment beneath his T-shirt.

"What're you doing?" Rebecca scolded, angry and shocked. "They're friendly. Mack and I just spent several hours earning their trust, and now you go and pull a stunt like this!"

"Save the lecture," Jeffrey said curtly as he began helping Lisa climb the ladder. "I only stunned them. By the time they wake up, we'll be long gone."

"What?" Mack asked in bewilderment as he tore his gaze away from the unconscious cave dwellers.

"Where will we go?" Rebecca asked, her anger still fermenting.

By this time, Lisa had reached the top, with Jeffrey following close behind. As he reached the ledge, he stood up, grabbed a torch from a nearby sconce with his left hand, and glanced down the passageway to make sure no one else had seen them.

"In case you forgot, Elmer has repaired da ship enough so dat we can at least make a small jump," Akwen said as she topped the ladder.

Rebecca's frown increased at the Cameroonian's condescending tone. "But there was no need to shoot them. I think the Patriarch would have let us go."

"We can't take that chance," Jeffrey said quickly. "And when we heard the cave was under attack, we felt it would be much easier for us to escape in the confusion."

"But...but," Rebecca stammered, "how did you know the cave was under attack?"

"Mack left his comm open so that we could listen in on your conversation," Jeffrey shot back; his patience was clearly beginning to wear thin.

Rebecca had been about to respond, but thought better of it.

Glancing over at Mack, she shot him a glare indicating she felt betrayed. "Why didn't you tell me?" she demanded.

Looking like a child caught with his hand in the cookie jar, Mack looked at Rebecca sheepishly, then turned away. "I don't know. I guess it just didn't seem important."

Rebecca took a deep breath to calm herself. *What's done is done. We're committed now. I only hope they forgive us.*

Once Dr. Eisenberg and Jerome had reached the top of the ladder, Jeffrey turned to Mack. "Okay, lead the way."

"Wait a second!" Rebecca called out. "What about Goliath? If we don't take him with us, then those explosives he planted inside of us will detonate!"

"If they even exist," Jeffrey commented. "Look, we have this one chance to escape and I say we should use it. Even if we wanted to rescue him, we don't know where he's being held. Besides, I believe he just made up that story to keep us from killing him or leaving him stranded somewhere."

"Are you willing to bet our lives on your beliefs?" Rebecca asked.

"I don't think we have much of a choice," Jeffrey said. "All right Mack; let's get this show on the road."

Still feeling less than reassured, Rebecca followed the others as they headed off down the tunnel as quickly as they dared. After only a few moments, Mack stopped the group a few feet shy of an intersection. "There are two men around this bend," Mack whispered. "I don't think we can sneak by without them spotting us, so we may have to take them out as well."

Jeffrey nodded without a word and then peered around the corner, his laser pistol leading the way. A moment later, there were two loud cracks and bright flashes as the weapon discharged. "Okay," he said. "That should take care of that. Now where?"

Mack rewound the images collected from his camera and played them on the small holographic display screen in his wrist. As the group traveled, they could hear distant shouts and sounds of battle coming from somewhere ahead of them, elevating their already-frazzled nerves. In the middle of the group, Rebecca did her best to help Lisa, who was still fighting against her claustrophobia.

After several minutes, they found themselves at another juncture. Mack halted and spoke rapidly to Jeffrey while the others waited. A moment later, Jeffrey turned to the rest of the group. "Mack says our equipment is being held in the Patriarch's study, which is just up the way a little bit. When we get there, Mack and Jerome will go in and grab the stuff while the rest of us wait outside. Then we'll double back to this intersection. Let's go."

Several tense seconds passed as they walked carefully, yet quickly, down the passage. Once they determined that the coast was clear, Jerome and Mack slipped quietly behind the curtain of animal skins. After what seemed like an eternity, they reappeared with the backpacks and carry bags.

"What took you so long?" Akwen whispered harshly. "Dey are going to find us any second and raise da alarm!"

Jeffrey laid a restraining hand on her arm. "Not here. We'll explain later."

Akwen gave him a questioning look, but said nothing further. Turning quickly on their heels, they headed out once again.

The dark, moist cave air combined with the sudden physical activity caused each of them to breathe heavily. In addition, fear of discovery caused their already-heightened nerves to be even more on edge.

As each second passed, however, Rebecca found her hopes beginning to rise. So far, other than the initial two men they encountered near their cell, it seemed like all the others had been called to the battle, leaving the passageways deserted. As for the women and children, Rebecca guessed they had taken shelter somewhere deeper inside the caves so it would be more difficult for the intruders to locate them. Furthermore, Mack's recording served as a perfect guide through the maze of tunnels, so that within a few minutes they were back in the cave with the paintings.

Jeffrey held up a hand, signaling for them to stop. "I expect that there'll probably be a few guards stationed at the entrance to the cave, so when we get into the living area in the next section of the cave, I want everyone to wait there until I take out the guards. Get bundled up again and—"

He never finished his sentence, because at that second, an ear-splitting scream rent the air. "That came from around the corner in the living area," Jerome whispered. "It sounded like...like a young girl."

From up ahead, Jeffrey could begin to make out the faint flickering of torchlight. Passing his own torch to Mack, he held the pistol at the ready and headed forward. "Be ready," he whispered urgently.

As he reached the end of the tunnel, Jeffrey could hear the sounds of a struggle coming from around the bend. Peering around the edge, he could see into the living area containing the tent-like shelters. In the center of the room, two men had wrestled a young girl of about twelve years of age to the ground. Her mouth was gagged with a leather strip, and the men were in the process of binding her hands behind her back. Six other men, all armed with spears, clubs, and knives, were moving across the room and heading directly for him.

Only these men were not from the Patriarch's tribe. These men had darker hair and skin, and stood taller than their mostly red-headed, Neanderthal-like cousins.

Leaping out from concealment, Jeffrey opened fire and caught the first two squarely in the chest with a blast of energy before they could even so much as raise their spears. The sound of the weapon's discharge and the sudden flash of light caused the remaining men to jump back in terror. Taking advantage of their fear, Jeffrey yelled loudly and charged forward, firing as he went.

Two more of the attackers fell at the onslaught. The rest quickly turned tail and fled back around the corner and into the main entrance to the cave. As soon as the warriors were out of sight, Jeffrey reached a hand out to the terrified girl. However, despite his attempts at reassurance, the girl kicked out at him and scooted toward one of the shelters, her eyes wide in panic. Before he could do anything more, Rebecca ran into the area, knelt by the girl, and embraced her. After several seconds of stroking her hair, the girl finally took her eyes off of her rescuer and began to calm down.

Sprinting toward the corner around which the attackers had fled, Jeffrey glanced into the next room, his gun ready once more. However, the only thing that moved in the entranceway was the protective fire, which still burned brightly in the center of the cave. Turning back around, he noticed that the others had already followed him into the room. "It looks like they're gone. Let's get moving before they decide to return."

"Wait a second!" Jerome called out. Reaching down next to the cooking area, he grabbed one of the hand-held, primitive, stone-cutting tools and shoved it into a pocket. Seeing Rebecca's disapproving look, he said defensively, "It's just a little souvenir. I consider it payment for being locked in a hole for hours with very little food."

Disgusted by his weak argument, Rebecca simply looked away and proceeded to free the girl from her bindings. Unable to loosen the ropes, however, she turned back toward Jerome. "At least put your new 'souvenir' to good use. Come here and cut her free."

Without argument, Jerome quickly did as Rebecca requested. As soon as the girl was free, she scrambled to her feet, stared at them in fear, and disappeared around the corner that led back into the portion of the cave with the wall paintings.

"Gee, not even so much as a 'thank you,'" Mack joked.

Taking the lead once more, Jeffrey made his way into the main entrance of the cave. Moving cautiously around the fire, he came upon the bodies of two of the Neanderthal-like cave dwellers and their two wolf-like pets. The animals were clearly dead, as testified to by the gaping spear holes in their pelts. The crushed skull of one of the two men left no doubt that he had been killed as well. The second man, however, appeared to still be breathing despite the large gash on his head, which continued to bleed profusely.

"Doc, help me!" Rebecca called out as she rushed over to the injured man and began tearing a strip of clothing from her shirt to use to clean the wound.

"Becky, we don't have time for this! Those hunters could be back at any second," Jeffrey whispered harshly in exasperation, even as Dr. Eisenberg knelt down next to Rebecca.

"But if we leave him, he'll die!" she retorted.

"Fine. We'll start heading for the pyramid while you two fix him up. But hurry—"

Even as the words left his mouth, Jeffrey caught movement out of the corner of his eye, coming from outside the cave. Just in time, Jeffrey reflexively moved to his left, causing the flying spear to miss him by mere inches. Regaining his balance, Jeffrey lifted his pistol and fired a quick shot as another attacker was releasing his spear. The bolt of energy caught the warrior off guard, causing his throw to miss its mark.

"Back! Back inside the cave!" Jeffrey yelled as he continued firing. But before anyone could react, a heavy weight slammed into Jeffrey's back, causing him to lose his balance as well as his grip on the laser pistol. Crashing hard onto the cave floor, Jeffrey fought to maintain his grip on consciousness. Somewhere off in the distance, he thought he heard someone calling his name.

"Jeffrey, behind you!" came Lisa's voice.

Shaking his head to clear his mind, he turned and saw a dozen or more of the invaders sprinting toward the mouth of the cave, spears and clubs lifted high in the air. Then, at the last second, Jeffrey caught sight of the attacker who had knocked him to the floor bearing down on him once more, a wicked-looking club raised in his hands. Too disoriented to fight back, Jeffrey merely held up his arms in front of him to ward off the attack.

A sudden vicious howl of rage rent the air, causing attacker and defender alike to freeze in alarm. A moment later, the enormous form of a minotaur leapt over the fire and into the fray. The creature's claws slashed out at the warriors, catching them completely by surprise. Several tried to raise their weapons in defense, but the half-human beast merely batted them aside as if they were toys.

Within moments, the warriors still standing fled back down the path away from the cave, leaving their companions to their fate. Jeffrey and the others, still stunned by the sudden appearance of the mythical beast, could only watch in awe as it drove off the attackers. Once all of the attackers were gone, the beast turned around and immediately picked up the laser pistol. It was only after the creature pointed the weapon at Jeffrey and spoke that their brains finally caught up with their senses.

"Well now," the minotaur said, "you weren't planning on leaving without me, were you? How far do you think you would've gotten before the explosives planted inside of you went off? Or did you forget about those little beauties?"

"We…we…" Jeffrey stammered. But before he could say more, they heard the drumming of feet coming from deeper inside the cave.

"It appears we don't have time for our little chat. Our recent captors must've discovered our escape—due no doubt to that slip of a girl who ran screaming down a side passage after she spotted me."

Lowering the laser pistol, Goliath pressed a button on his wrist and his form reverted to his normal helmeted and armored appearance. "Let's let bygones be bygones. You stunned the two men guarding me, thus allowing me to escape, for which I'm grateful. And I just saved your lives, so we're even. Now, I propose a truce. It's clear that none of us wants to get stuck here, or in any other strange location. So until we figure out how to get back to our own world, I suggest we work together."

Picking himself up off the floor, Jeffrey nodded. "Fine. It's a deal. But I recommend we discuss the finer points of this bargain once we're back inside the pyramid."

"Agreed." Without another word, Goliath left the cave at a brisk trot and headed down the path toward the craft.

"What are we going to do?" Mack asked, even as he finished wrapping a borrowed scarf around his head. "We can't trust that thing!"

"I know that, but then again, we don't have any choice," Jeffrey shot back. "Now unless you want to end your days as a caveman, I suggest you get moving! Becky, Doc, are you almost done?"

"Give us another second or two," Becky said as she frantically worked to finish binding the wounded man's head injury. "There, that oughtta do it. Let's go."

Grabbing the doctor's arm, Rebecca lowered her head and the two of them exited the cave into the biting wind and headed off to join the others, now several yards in front of them. Rebecca and Dr. Eisenberg caught up with the rest of the group just as they were stepping off the path leading from the cave. It took several minutes of intense climbing to once more reach the area where they could cross over to the pyramid. Although the downhill climb was much easier than the journey up the mountain had been, Rebecca could tell Dr. Eisenberg was beginning to tire again from the exertion. On occasion, she saw him pause and reach up toward the wound on his head.

We're so vulnerable out here, she thought in concern. *If they attack us now, we're done for.* Casting quick glances over her shoulder every few seconds, she fully expected to see the Patriarch's warriors bearing down on them. But to her relief, it appeared that their pursuers had given up the chase. The others, having arrived at the same conclusion, slowed their pace slightly.

They made it back to the pyramid unchallenged, except by the pervading wind and ice. Within moments, Akwen, Dr. Eisenberg, Mack, and Lisa had entered the vessel through the opening in the ceiling. As Rebecca waited outside the opening for Jerome to climb in, she looked up toward the cave, searching one last time for any signs of pursuit. It was then that she spotted two lone figures standing on the mountain pass near the cave entrance, staring in their direction.

Reaching out, she grabbed Jeffrey's arm. "Look," she said, pointing toward the figures.

"Yes," Goliath said from behind them. "They're watching us. They must have realized we weren't worth the effort, or the risk."

"No," Rebecca said softly in sudden realization. "They're letting us go."

Suddenly, the figure on the right lifted a hand. Without thinking, Rebecca raised her own, bidding the Patriarch a final farewell.

"C'mon, Becky," Jeffrey said beside her.

Lowering her arm, she grabbed the edge of the opening and slipped through, where Elmer waited to lower her to the floor.

"But Father, how can we just let them go? They took the sacred scrolls!"

The Patriarch turned to look at young Terah standing beside him. "But they did not take all of them, my son. The sacred writings of my fathers are still safe with us. They only took my personal writings. And, since I am still alive, they can be replaced."

"But it could take you years to write them again. And do you remember everything they contained? Do you remember all of the lists, and the numbers?"

"My memory is fading, yes," he said with a sigh. "But I still remember the most important points. In fact, I am beginning to believe that it was the Lord's will, blessed be His name, that the detailed account of my journey not be preserved. Perhaps they need it more than we do. I believe that a more concise account will suffice."

"But still, they are thieves and murderers! Justice must be served!"

"Actually, my son, they may be thieves, but they are also heroes," the old man said. "For they not only saved your sister from being taken, but they also saved us all from death or enslavement."

Terah regarded his elder with astonishment. "Pardon my questioning, Patriarch, but why do you say this?"

"Because the Hamite attack at the front entrance was just a diversion so that the second group of attackers could enter through the back and take us by surprise. But fortunately for us, the Almighty Lord, blessed be His name, used the strangers to preserve us, whether they realized it or not. For according to your sister's testimony, it was *they* who fought off the second group. So you see, poor Nadar was killed and Maskooka was wounded not by the strangers, but by the Hamites."

The younger man stood silently next to his elder, contemplating his words as they watched the last of the strangers slip inside the structure. "But how will seeking shelter in there help them?"

"You will see, my son."

They watched for another minute in silence when the pyramid erupted in white light. Terah nearly fell over in astonishment, while the Patriarch seemed unfazed by the strange sight. Then, just as suddenly as it had appeared, the ghostly vessel lifted off the ground and disappeared into the sky.

"Father, were they...were they some of the angelic Watchers that you have mentioned?"

"No, my son. They were merely travelers from far away."

"Forgive me if my questioning wearies you, but how is it that you know?" Terah asked.

"That is a story for another time. For now, let me just say that I have met them before. Now, let us go. We have much work to do," Noah said as he turned back toward the entrance to the cave.

"And what of the Hamites? What if they return?" Terah asked, his eyes scanning the mountain pass for any signs of the intruders.

"Then we must be ready for them. But alas, I believe it is time for us to leave this place. The Ice Wall is moving farther every year, and the weather is getting worse. It is time for us to return to warmer climates, even if it means we have to fight against our own blood. I was wrong to try to hide in these caves. We must take word of the True God back to the rest of the world, lest they perish," he said, his face grave.

Then, as if throwing off a thick blanket, he smiled and put his arm around the younger man. "Perhaps we will move back near your grandfather Shem and his people. I'm sure your new wife will like it there. After all, wouldn't it be better to have your future children born where the sun shines most of the year? It may be a little early yet, but have you begun to think what name you will give your firstborn son when the time comes?"

"Yes. We were thinking of the name Abram…"

23

THE SACRED SCROLLS

"HOW COULD YOU?!?" Rebecca yelled. "How could you steal their most sacred and prized possessions from them? The Patriarch trusted us, and you repaid him by…by…stabbing him in the back! It was bad enough that we deceived them and escaped by force, but this—" Rebecca had fanned the flames of her anger into such a consuming blaze that her mind could no longer think clearly enough to even finish a sentence.

Stepping in between her and Mack, Jeffrey grabbed Rebecca by the shoulders in an attempt to calm her down. "Listen, Becky…"

Whipping her arms up, she knocked Jeffrey's hands off her shoulders. "Don't you 'listen, Becky' me. You put him up to it, didn't you?"

Jeffrey, feeling his own patience dissolve in the face of Rebecca's accusation, frowned darkly. "Yes, it was my idea. When Mack told me the scrolls could tell us how to fix the ship, I knew that if we were going to have a chance at getting home, we'd have to take them along. I knew you wouldn't agree, so I had Mack and Jerome put them in one of the carry bags while the rest of us stayed in the hallway. It was for the best. Maybe if we can get the pyramid working properly, we can go back and return them."

Still fuming, Rebecca spoke, her voice low and deliberate. "We should've just asked them for help. They trusted us, and we betrayed them."

"Oh c'mon! Get off of your moral high horse!" Jeffrey retorted. "We did what we had to do. Besides, what's done is done. We can't return the scrolls until we get this thing fixed. And the longer we argue, the longer it's going to take. So, if you don't mind, some of us have work to do in order to figure out how to get us home."

Rebecca shot daggers through her husband with her baleful glare. Then, without another word, she spun on her heels and headed down the stairs and out of the control room. After she had departed, Dr. Eisenberg looked at Jeffrey with disapproval. "I know you did what you felt you had to do, Jeffrey, but that doesn't make it right."

For a split second, the muscles in Jeffrey's face twitched, as if he was fighting some inner battle for control. Then, as quickly as it appeared, the emotional turmoil was over and Jeffrey's face hardened once more. "I'm trying to get us home. If there was some other surefire way, I would have chosen it."

Unconvinced, Dr. Eisenberg nodded in disappointment, then turned and headed off down the stairs after Rebecca.

Even before Dr. Eisenberg was out of earshot, Goliath let out a short laugh of twisted amusement. "Morality is such a hindrance. I'm surprised that evolution hasn't totally eradicated it yet. They may be throwing morality in your face now, but they'll change their minds once we get the ship fixed."

Jeffrey threw the giant a dark look. "Thanks, Goliath. But somehow your approval of my actions isn't making me feel any better."

Goliath grinned and leaned against the wall, clearly enjoying the other's discomfort.

"Well, I for one am glad dat you took dem," Akwen stated. "And you are right. What's done is done. Now, what is so important about dese scrolls anyway?"

Turning his attention toward Mack, Jeffrey asked, "Why don't you fill us in on what the Patriarch showed you?"

Still struggling with his own feelings of guilt over the theft, Mack shrugged unenthusiastically. "Okay. Well, when the Patriarch showed us a drawing of this tower that these people had tried to build, I recognized similarities to our own pyramid. In fact, I got the feeling that he showed us the picture because he somehow guessed that this tower and our pyramid were made by the same people."

"What? But that's impossible," Jerome stated emphatically. "How could some caveman know anything about our pyramid?"

"Beats me," Mack said. "Maybe the aliens who built the ship visited these people and gave them the blueprints to build their own. Except these guys were planning on making it into more of a square tower that gradually narrowed as it got higher. Judging by what I've seen so far in the scrolls, it would've been bigger than the Giza pyramid."

"But how does that help us fix our ship?" Lisa asked.

"Well, that's the exciting part," Mack said, warming up to the subject. "As it turns out, this tower is more than just a building. I haven't had time to study it enough yet to know exactly what it's supposed to do, but when I looked at the Patriarch's scroll, I immediately recognized that at the center of this tower is a core, just like the one we use to power our pyramid!"

"Are you sure?" Jeffrey asked in shock.

"As sure as Boomer is a Cylon!" Mack said confidently. Unfortunately, since everyone else was unschooled in science fiction lore, their expressions showed that they remained unconvinced. Growling in frustration at their lack of movie trivia knowledge, Mack said, "Yes, I'm sure!"

"Okay, so then what's the plan?" Jerome asked.

"Well, it seems pretty straightforward to me," Mack said coolly. "We just land near this tower, sneak in, grab the core, and sneak out."

Goliath let out a grunt; his lip curled back in a sneer. "And just how do you plan on sneaking in? And have you thought about how we're going to carry the core? From what I know of this pyramid, the core is three feet in diameter and weighs over one hundred pounds. I may be strong, but I wouldn't be able to carry it any great distance. And somehow I don't think they're just going to let us walk right out with such a huge object. Not to mention the fact that since it's at the heart of this massive building, it must be pretty important to them. I wouldn't be surprised if they had some kind of guards or something to protect it."

"Then we'll just have to rely on you to come up with a plan for getting us in and out, since you're the military expert," Jeffrey said, his voice laced with sarcasm.

Goliath brushed aside the implied insult and grinned back at them. "I certainly wouldn't trust any plan that *you* all come up with. Fine. I accept the job. So, where is this tower?"

"It's located east of the Mediterranean Sea in Mesopotamia," Mack said. "I think we should start looking by following either the Tigris or Euphrates rivers. It's probably located near one of them."

"Mack, that's *still* a pretty big area to search. It could take us quite some time to find it," Jeffrey pointed out.

"Well, it shouldn't be too hard now that Akwen has more control of the ship," Mack stated. "We just need to fly around the area between the two rivers until we find a massive construction project. It would be pretty hard to miss, what with the convoy of heavy blocks and stuff that will be leading toward it."

"Good point. Wait a second," Jeffrey said, his face suddenly taking on an expression of suspicion, "did the Patriarch happen to tell you the name of this tower?"

Mack hesitated. "Actually he did. You remember that the Patriarch told us he was *the* Noah, as in Noah's Ark. Well, it turns out that he said the tower wasn't completed because God became angry with the people and confused their languages. Therefore, the tower was called 'Babel.'"

"What?" Jerome demanded in anger and frustration. "Do you mean to tell me that we're going to search for *the* Tower of Babel? And here I was, beginning to think we could actually find a way to fix this thing.

Now you tell me our only hope is to find some mythological tower from the Bible?"

"Take it easy. It may not be as bad as you think," Jeffrey said, trying to put more reassurance into his voice than he felt. "This Patriarch might be a Noah wannabe, but we can't deny the fact that he had in his possession a scroll that had a drawing of the core to this ship and a building that resembles it. Therefore, it stands to reason that what he says is true. Maybe he was familiar with the myths of Noah's Ark and the Tower of Babel and decided to use those names for his own twisted purposes. But we can't let that cloud the truth. Whatever this tower is, it has to be real."

Jerome, seeing the logic in Jeffrey's reasoning, began to calm down. "Okay, so then, how do we find it?"

"First, we need to know when they abandoned the tower," Jeffrey said. "Mack, did you happen to find that out from the Patriarch?"

"Yeah, he said it happened just over two hundred years ago."

Akwen, sitting at the control console, turned to look at the time dial and the core readout. "I tink we should have enough power to make it dat far and still have enough power to search for da tower."

"Hold on a moment," Lisa interrupted. "Why don't we just find the abandoned tower and take the core? It would certainly be easier than trying to infiltrate a guarded construction site."

Jeffrey shook his head. "I don't think that would work. If the core is that important, they would probably take it with them when they abandoned the project."

"But that also means if we arrive at the tower too *early* in its construction, then the core may not have been put into place yet," Jerome pointed out.

"She does have a point, though," Goliath added. "Maybe we could make a short jump and do a reconnaissance of the abandoned tower. That would allow us to get firsthand knowledge of the tower entrances and specific layout. It would be a huge strategic advantage."

Akwen shook her head at the idea. "I don't tink we can do dat.

Da core is unstable right now. Da more jumps we make, da greater da chance dat it will stop working altogedah. I don't tink we should take dat risk."

"I agree," Jeffrey said. "We'll just have to wing it. All right, so we have our immediate plan. Mack, is there anything else you found out from the scrolls?"

"Well, let me reiterate that I still haven't had a chance to go over them completely. But, when I was with the Patriarch, I recognized a couple of symbols on the scrolls that looked very familiar. He then informed me that these symbols were from a language he called the 'Language of Eden.'"

"'Language of Eden'? What's that supposed to mean?" Jerome asked.

"Oh, you guys are going to love this," Mack said, deliberately building the suspense. "The Patriarch then brought out another scroll that happened to contain the same text, but written in this 'Language of Eden.' Well, guess what?"

"Stop screwing around and just get to the point!" Goliath growled.

Mack's enthusiasm deflated. "Sure, okay. Don't be hasty. Anyway, so you can imagine my surprise when lo and behold, the language was the same one used to write the blueprints for our pyramid!"

For several seconds, they all stood completely dumbfounded, including the usually unshakable giant.

"So what exactly does dat mean?" Akwen asked at last.

"It's probably just more confirmation that this pyramid and the tower are connected," Jeffrey said. "Perhaps the aliens who built this thing wrote down the instructions in their language so mankind could copy their technology.

"Whatever the case may be, we need to use the time before we reach the tower wisely," Jeffrey continued. "I'm sure we could all use some food and rest. Mack, grab a quick bite to eat and a short nap. I want you, and hopefully Dr. Eisenberg as well, pouring over those scrolls as much as you can. Akwen, Lisa, and I will take turns at the helm during the jump. Goliath—"

"I know what I need to do," he sneered. "I'm not yours to command."

"Actually, that brings up one more unresolved issue," Jeffrey said, not backing down. "Back in the cave, you offered a truce. I think I speak for all of us when I say we could use your help to get through this. You have skills that are invaluable to us, and you have weapons and technology that we need right now.

"On the other hand, you know that you can't pilot this ship without us, or repair it, and you need our language skills to interact with the locals. So we need you, and you need us. Therefore, I suggest that until we get the ship fixed and learn how to travel back to our time, we have to trust each other."

"And what do we do when it is finally time to return home?" Goliath asked, his voice low and menacing. "Are you going to pilot the ship into some American military base, leaving me at their mercy?"

"Or are you going to try to take us hostage again?" Jeffrey returned the giant's glare.

After a few tense seconds, Goliath leaned back and smiled. "With some training, you would have made a decent soldier, Jeffrey Evans. I offer the following suggestion: When the machine is fixed, I'll give you the laser pistol so that you know I will not attack you. However, if you try to kill me or go back on your word and try to land in some location that will, shall we say, not be a pleasant location for me, then I will detonate the explosives within your body."

Jeffrey thought it over for a moment, then nodded. "Fair enough, as long as you give us the detonator once we have arrived safely in a neutral location."

"Agreed."

Stretching out his hairy, claw-like hand, Goliath grasped Jeffrey's and shook it, sealing their agreement. Then, turning toward Mack, he said, "Now, I need to see the plans for this tower we are going to infiltrate. I need to know as much about it as you can tell me."

Uncomfortable with the prospect of being alone with this beast,

Mack looked around at the others for help. Finally, accepting his fate, he swallowed and nodded. "Sure, right this way. But before we get started, I need to find Dr. Eisenberg."

After they had left, Jerome turned to look at Jeffrey, his face reflecting his uncertainty. "Do you really think we can find it? I mean, what if we miss it and arrive before it was built? Then what?"

"I don't want to lie to you," Jeffrey answered. "We have no assurances that this'll work, but I feel better about our chances than I did a few hours ago. We'll get through this. I'll do everything in my power to make sure you see your family again. Right now, we need to keep our heads clear and focus on finding this tower."

Worry still etched on his face, Jerome nodded reluctantly and followed his friend out of the room, his thoughts dwelling on the family he had left behind.

24

THE PUZZLE OF ANCIENT MAN

REBECCA STARED AT the holographic computer display provided by Elmer with conflicting emotions of excitement, incredulity, and trepidation. *Could it all really be true? It makes sense, but...what will the others think? There's no way they'll believe me. Maybe Dr. Eisenberg...I've got to at least share it with him.*

Jumping up from her seat in the makeshift bedroom, she grabbed the portable keyboard, opened the door, and headed toward Mack's workroom. As she entered, Mack and Dr. Eisenberg looked up from the document they were studying. Mack, still feeling guilty over stealing the scrolls, offered a brief greeting, then buried his head in the manuscript once again. The doctor, however, seeing the look of enthusiasm on her face, turned and gave her his full attention.

"Rebecca, what is it? Have you discovered something from your research?"

"Yes, I have! Doc, it is...it all fits together," she said, nearly bursting with exhilaration. "It's like the pieces of a giant puzzle are starting to fall into place. And the picture it creates is absolutely phenomenal!"

"Show me," he said without pause. "Mack, I'll—"

"Whoa, wait a second," Mack interrupted, "I want to hear this too. Becky always comes up with the most amazing theories! Besides, I think we've learned about all we're going to about the tower at this point. And Akwen estimates it'll be at least another half an hour before we arrive, so we have some time."

Rebecca nodded, pleased at Mack's decision to hear her out. Placing Elmer's keyboard interface gently on the worktable, she activated the holographic screen. "I've been thinking a lot about what the Patriarch said and about what we've encountered on this trip," she said, "and I'm now convinced we've missed the truth about so much because of our misconceptions and preconceived ideas. Yet when I started to do some digging, I was amazed to find that all the scientific and historical support for my new theory was right there in Elmer's memory banks.

"Remember when we first encountered the Mayans and the dinosaurs?" Rebecca continued as she unconsciously brushed a loose lock of curly black hair out of her face. "We assumed that we entered another dimension because we believed dinosaurs didn't live with humans. Then, after doing some research, it seems our assumptions might have been wrong. Well, it now appears that the same is true for the Ice Age and cavemen as well."

"Don't you mean 'ice ages'?" Dr. Eisenberg asked.

"Actually, no I don't," Rebecca responded. "I know I won't be able to convince you in the brief time I have, but you need to read some of the articles I've found. I would like to start by asking you a question. Doc, what conditions are required for an ice age?"

The professor thought for a moment before answering. "Let's see, for one thing, you would need the temperature to drop considerably over large landmasses of the mid and high latitudes. Second, an ice age would require huge amounts of precipitation, which would mean warm oceans."

"Okay, and what is the traditional, uniformitarian explanation for the ice ages?" Rebecca asked.

"Well, it appears that over the past eight hundred thousand years, there was a repeated cycle of one ice age every hundred thousand years.[26] The glacial phase probably dominated for ninety thousand years, while the interglacial phase lasted only about ten thousand years,"[27] Dr. Eisenberg said, his voice taking on its characteristic lecturing tone. "But no one really knows what would have triggered such an enormous change in climate and caused it to last for thousands of years."

"Exactly. But the reason no one has been able to come up with a plausible explanation is that they've been ruling out one major historical event.

"Noah's Flood."

Mack's expression turned skeptical. "But that wasn't real. I mean, that whole story of Noah taking all of those animals on a tiny boat for forty days and nights is just nonsense. We've already been over this."

Not fazed by his doubt, Rebecca stared at him firmly, her convictions remaining strong. "I haven't had time to research the account of Noah's Flood too deeply, but I can tell you it was no small boat. But, let's assume for a second that it *was* a real event: How would a global flood have affected the climate of the earth?

"Think about it. First of all, it would've caused the earth's crust to experience tremendous changes, including earthquakes and volcanism. This, of course, would have a huge impact on the environment and climate," Rebecca explained. "When a volcano erupts, it spews volcanic dust and other particles into the air, which reflects sunlight back into space…"

"Thus causing cooler summers," Dr. Eisenberg finished, his facial features becoming thoughtful.

"Right!" Rebecca said. "And this upheaval would have continued for many years afterward. In fact, the Ice Age portions of the ice cores from Greenland and Antarctic ice sheets show large amounts of volcanic particles and acids.[28]

"As for precipitation, the Bible explains that the 'fountains of the great deep' burst forth during the Flood. Listen to this," she said, scrolling through the article on the computer display. Finding the section she was looking for, she began to read.

> "Crustal movements would have released hot water from the earth's crust along with volcanism and large underwater lava flows, which would have added heat to the ocean. Earth movement and rapid Flood currents would have then mixed the warm water, so that after the Flood the oceans would be warm from pole to pole. There would be no sea ice. A warm ocean would have had much higher evaporation than the present cool ocean surface. Most of this evaporation would have occurred at mid and high latitudes, close to the developing ice sheets, dropping the moisture on the cold continent. This is a recipe for powerful and continuous snowstorms that can be estimated using basic meteorology."[29]

"Would that also cause the huge hurricane we saw when we first arrived?" Mack asked.

"Yes! In fact, that's exactly what these scientists predicted would happen if you had warm oceans and cool landmasses,"[30] Rebecca confirmed.

Judging by the reaction of the two men, Rebecca could tell her argument was beginning to take hold. Emboldened, she continued. "This article then goes on to say, 'Numerical simulations of precipitation in the polar regions using conventional climate models with warm sea surface temperatures have demonstrated that ice sheets thousands of feet thick could have accumulated in less than five hundred years.'"[31]

"Five hundred years?" Mack repeated, incredulous. "That's a far cry from one hundred thousand."

"But it is plausible," Dr. Eisenberg said. "In fact, it is quite believable. One of the problems with the standard understanding of ice ages is that there is no good explanation as to how it would begin and how it would end. Once you have an ice age, it would seem to continually sustain itself because the white surface of the earth would reflect the sun. But the idea that it was caused by a catastrophe explains much."

"—Because once the Flood was over, the oceans would eventually cool, causing less precipitation, thus causing warmer land temperatures, which would melt the ice," Rebecca said, picking up were the doctor left off. "Those scientists who believe in this model of the Ice Age have estimated that from start to finish, it could've occurred in about seven hundred years!"

"—which would make sense based on what the Patriarch told us!" Mack said, suddenly excited. "Do you remember he said that the Flood occurred three hundred years ago? That means we arrived during the beginning of the Ice Age. And that's also why we didn't see any glaciations on our prior jump, which would've been about six hundred years after it had finished."

Dr. Eisenberg shook his head in wonder. "It certainly makes sense. But I still have a hard time believing in a worldwide flood. If there was indeed such a catastrophic event, it would alter the entire face of the planet, thus changing everything we believe about the fossil record and the history of the earth itself."

"But don't you see?" Rebecca pointed out, "That's exactly the point! It *did* change everything, which is why our understanding of history was so wrong. Scientists, in their attempts to reduce variables to conduct their research, eliminated catastrophes from their equations. They assume that the processes we see happening in our time have been continuing at the same rates forever. But this is just an assumption.

"I mean, I'm all for uniformitarianism, unless we have a good reason to doubt it," she continued. "In this case, we *do* have a reason to doubt it. For one thing, we have historical records of a worldwide flood, both from the Bible and numerous flood legends from all over the world. Second, the catastrophic model explains the evidence much better."

"So how would your model explain evidence such as the Greenland ice cores?" Dr. Eisenberg asked.

Rebecca nodded, not the least thrown by the question. "I did come across something about that during my research," she said. "The ice cores *do* contain horizontal bands that may represent annual winter/summer patterns. However, if the weather patterns of the world were in a massive upheaval, as would be the case after the Flood, it's very possible that those supposed 'annual' rings were really pseudo-winter/summer patterns. The frequent storms could cause many rings per year.[32] Once again, this is an example of how the evidence is interpreted differently based on our starting biases."

"Okay, so if your theory is true, then how do the cavemen fit in?" Mack asked.

Rebecca smiled. "That's another exciting part of the puzzle. But let me lead into that answer by asking you another question: What would happen in our time if suddenly all of the technology ceased to function?"

Mack dramatically placed his hand on his heart, his face feigning shock and horror. "What? No Internet? No computer? No music? No video games? No MOVIES? I'd die of boredom within twenty-four hours!"

Rebecca grinned patiently. "Seriously though: What would happen to society?"

Ending his act, Mack shrugged. "Chaos, probably. Massive looting and fighting."

Rebecca nodded. "Okay, now imagine you and your family were the only ones left alive."

At this statement, Mack sobered and his expression darkened. Realizing her words had touched some personal nerve, Rebecca tried to come up with a different approach even as she wondered what had happened in Mack's past to warrant such a response. "Um…what if we were somehow marooned on a different planet that was similar to earth, but had no intelligent life, just animals? How would we survive? Where would we find food and shelter?"

"I think I'm beginning to see where you are leading," Dr. Eisenberg said. "If the entire surface of the earth were altered due to a global flood, those on the ark would have to struggle just to survive. They would be forced to live in huts, tents, or caves as they followed the animal herds."

"Right! And even though they were highly intelligent people, they were still forced to live primitively due to the environment," Rebecca said. "Dr. Eisenberg, correct me if I'm wrong, but doesn't the fossil record show that Neanderthals had *larger* brain cases than modern humans?"

The professor nodded in agreement. "Yes. They were larger by about two hundred cc's, although it's not a fact most scientists publicize."

"So you think they were just regular humans?" Mack sounded skeptical. "I don't know. They looked pretty ape-like, especially the way they walked."

"I'm glad you mentioned their appearance," Rebecca said. "Do you remember when the Patriarch told us that by living in this colder climate, it caused some of his people to become sick and their 'bones became bent'? Well, I found this website that talked about the fact that many scientists believe some Neanderthals may have suffered from the disease called rickets."

"Rickets?" Mack's brows furrowed in confusion.

"Yes. It's a disease that results from a Vitamin D deficiency," Rebecca explained. "It usually affects children. Vitamin D helps with the absorption of calcium from the food we eat. Those who suffer from this disease have soft bones, which cause them to have swollen joints and distorted limbs. This can also result in them becoming extremely bowlegged, and, in more extreme cases, they're completely crippled and unable to walk.

"And get this," Rebecca said excitedly, "although Vitamin D is found in fish oils, milk, and dairy products, it's also made in the skin when the skin is exposed to *sunlight!*"[33]

Dr. Eisenberg smiled at Rebecca in admiration. "I was wondering if you had uncovered that little-known fact in your research. Some of the Neanderthals also suffered from arthritis."

"You always taught Jeffrey to be thorough," Rebecca said, returning his smile. "I guess I picked that up from you as well." Looking back toward Mack, she continued. "And Mack, it's even a well established fact that Neanderthals took care of their sick, buried their dead, used tools, and played musical instruments—and there is even evidence of a form of writing!"

Mack looked stunned. "You found all of this on websites from Elmer's memory?"

Rebecca nodded. "So you see, what we've experienced actually fits with what we know about this culture from research conducted in *our own time period!*"

Although he seemed intrigued, Rebecca could tell Dr. Eisenberg wasn't completely convinced. "Let's not jump to conclusions just yet, Rebecca," he said. "There are still many, many unanswered questions. I mean, if you're right, then how old do you think the earth really is?"

Rebecca, knowing this question would be raised eventually, was prepared. "From the evidence I've gathered, and based upon the genealogies from the Bible, I believe the earth is probably between six thousand and ten thousand years old."

Mack's expression spoke volumes. "But that goes against everything geology has proven in the past two hundred years! And you can't possibly believe all those ancient patriarchs in the genealogies were real people. Those stories are just myths."

"Actually, I *do* believe they were real people and real accounts," Rebecca said with conviction. "Let me ask you, Mack, do you believe King David was real?"

Knowing how Rebecca had used questions in the past to trap him in his thinking, he hesitated before answering. "Yeah, sure. There's plenty of archaeological evidence supporting the existence of King David."

"What about Abraham?"

"Sure. There's evidence for him, too," Mack stated.

"Would you say that all of the names listed between Abraham and David were real men?"

"Yeah."

"So, as you read backward through the genealogy, we have—'this real man was the son of that real man, who was the son of this real man, who was the son of…this *fictional* man'? How does that make sense?" Rebecca asked.

Dr. Eisenberg chuckled lightly at the cornered expression on Mack's face. Stepping in to his rescue, the professor looked questioningly at Rebecca. "Point made. But even still, we can't just discount all of the dating methods that show the earth is indeed billions of years old."

"You mean radiometric dating methods, right?" Rebecca asked.

"Yes, of course."

Rebecca cocked her head to one side as she narrowed her eyes at the professor. "Doc, you know as well as I do there are a lot of assumptions that go into dating a rock. Don't forget I'm married to an archaeologist. You also know that most of the dates that are chosen are based on an evolutionary timescale."

Mack, looking back and forth between the two, finally interrupted. "Do you mind letting me in on your private conversation? Becky, you make it sound as if radiometric dates are flawed. But that's not right, is it Doc?"

After a few seconds of silence, Dr. Eisenberg nodded his head. "I wouldn't necessarily say 'flawed,' per se. But it is true that they're not as clearly determined as most of the published literature suggests."

"How so?"

"Well, to determine the age of a fossil, for example, a scientist would follow several steps," Dr. Eisenberg said with the familiarity of one who had taught the subject for many years. "First, he would observe the present state of the fossil. Then, he would measure the rate of decay of the elements contained within it or the surrounding rock. After that, he would calculate how long it would take for that process of decay to produce the amount of elements currently contained in the sample."[34]

"That seems straightforward enough," Mack said. "So what's the problem?"

"The problem is that several assumptions have to be made," Rebecca interjected. "The best way to illustrate this is with an analogy." Looking around Mack's office, she located a large pitcher currently being used as a pencil holder. Dumping out the handful of pencils and pens onto the table, Rebecca held the pitcher up for Mack to see.

"Now, imagine that this pitcher is a five-gallon bucket. You found it sitting in your backyard and you want to figure out how long it had been there. It currently has two gallons in it. But, you notice there is a small hole in the bottom. You measure the rate at which the water is leaking out of the bucket to be one gallon per week. So, how long has the bucket been sitting there?"

Mack grimaced. "I hated word problems in math class. Couldn't you just write the equation down?"

After receiving a scathing look from Rebecca, Mack held up his hands in surrender. "Okay, okay. Let me see…five gallons, with two gallons left, one gallon per week leak…it should be three weeks. Right?"

Rebecca nodded. "That *would* be correct, but only if you make several assumptions."

"Like what?" Mack asked, genuinely curious.

"First of all, you're assuming that the bucket originally contained five gallons," Rebecca said. "What if it was placed there with less than that? Secondly, you're assuming that no water has been added or lost during the time it has been sitting there."

Mack's face brightened. "Right, I get it: Rain! If it rained, it would mess up the dating."

"Or, what if some of the water evaporated due to extreme temperatures?" Rebecca added. "And third, you're assuming the rate of the leak has always been the same. All you really know is how fast the water is leaking out *now*. What if the water was leaking out quickly at first, but then some dirt clogged the hole, making it leak slower? Or, what if it was a small hole initially, but the hole gradually got bigger due to vandalism, or corrosion?"

"So what you're saying is that with radiometric dating, the scientists are making the same kinds of assumptions," Mack concluded. "But, if these assumptions are incorrect, then the ages they arrive at would be false. Is that right?"

"Exactly."

"But surely their dating methods can't be *that* far off, can they?" Mack asked.

Rebecca turned toward the doctor. "Do you want to answer that one?"

Giving her a slight frown, Dr. Eisenberg said, "Not really. But since you've put me on the spot, I guess I'll oblige." Turning to look at Mack, he continued. "What usually happens is that several methods of testing are used on the same sample. Then, once all of the results come in, we compare all of the dates and choose which date we think most closely matches the age of the surrounding rock."

"And the dates that *don't* get chosen don't get published. Only the accepted date is promoted. By the way, tell him how they usually determine the age of the rock, Doc," Rebecca prodded.

Casting her a look of minor irritation, he continued. "The age of the rock is determined by matching the index fossils found in the surrounding rock layers to the evolutionary timescale, then finding out which method of radiometric dating supports that age."

The expression on Mack's face resembled that of a child who has just learned there is no Santa Claus. "Wait, wait, wait. Let me see if I understand this correctly. First, scientists use a method of measuring radiometric decay that requires them to make assumptions that could potentially undermine their results. Second, they use different types of radiometric dating on the rock layers surrounding the fossil, then they *choose* the method that produces an age closest to what they *think* the fossil to be? And, to add insult to injury, they turn around and use the fossils as indicators to determine the age of the rocks! But isn't that circular reasoning?"

"When I believed in evolution, Jeffrey used to joke that this was one of paleontology's 'dirty little secrets,'" Rebecca said with a smirk.

"The dating methods are based upon evolutionary and uniformitarian assumptions. But if evolution isn't true, and if things have *not* always continued at the same rates that we measure now..."

"...then the dating methods are unreliable," Mack finished.

"And what's more," Rebecca continued, "some scientists began to question the validity of the dating methods, so they decided to try them on rocks of *known* ages, with some interesting results. In the early 1980s, Mt. St. Helens in Washington erupted. The eruption created tons of new rocks. When the rocks were dated using various radiometric dating methods, the results came back with ages ranging from 340,000 to 2.8 *million* years old![35] And this was not an isolated example. Scientists did the same thing to rocks formed from volcanic eruptions in Hawaii and got similar results. There was even one set of rocks that were two hundred years old, yet they yielded ages up to 3.3 *billion!*[36] If we can't trust the methods to accurately date rocks of *known* ages, then why should we trust them to date rocks of *unknown* age?"

When neither of the men responded to Rebecca's rhetorical question, she continued. "Furthermore, *carbon* dating can only date samples up to about sixty thousand years. Yet when they use that method to date samples that are supposedly millions of years old, they still found traces of C-14 in them! If they were truly that ancient, there would be no C-14 left.[37]

"So to get back to my original point, science has not *proven* that the earth is *billions* of years old. In fact, I found some very interesting scientific arguments that indicate the earth *cannot* be billions, or even *millions* of years old. If the two of you aren't completely sick of me by now, I would like to share some of those with you briefly."

Dr. Eisenberg, although not happy about Rebecca telling one of his profession's trade secrets, was curious to hear her out. "Go ahead and show us. But you may want to make it quick. We should be arriving at our destination shortly."

"Okay, I'll be brief, and I won't list all of them." Placing the pitcher she had been using for a prop back on the table, she leaned over Elmer's portable keyboard and cycled through the information until she found the page she was looking for. "Here it is. There are several measurements of change that, when extrapolated backward in time, indicate that these processes could *not* have continued at the same rate as we observe in our time. In other words, the uniformitarian model does *not* make accurate predictions in each of these instances. Only a recent creation with catastrophe fits the evidence.

"First, the earth's magnetic field has been decaying over the last 150 years. Using modern equipment, we can accurately measure the rate of decay. If the intensity of the earth's magnetic field was twice as strong every fourteen hundred years, then one hundred thousand years ago, the magnetic field would have been incredibly strong—comparable to that of a neutron star—making it impossible for life to thrive.[38]

"Secondly, the moon is slowly moving away from the earth," Rebecca continued. "If we take the rate at which it is receding and extrapolate back in time, it would be touching the earth's surface in less than 1.2 billion years. And way before that, it would cause such huge tidal waves that no life could exist.[39]

"A third example is the amount of salt in the ocean. Every year the oceans are getting saltier as rivers dump dissolved salts from the continents into the ocean. At the current rate, and assuming no salt in the oceans to begin with, the oceans would reach their current levels of saltiness in just thirty-two *million* years![40]

"These three examples are just the tip of the iceberg," she stated passionately. "There are many more, including the amount of helium in the atmosphere, the existence of comets, the shrinking of the sun, coral reef growth, and the erosion of the continents—just to name a few.

"So you see, when those who believe in uniformitarianism look at the fossil record, they say we should assume that the same processes and rates of change we observe today were the same in the past. But when it comes to these other areas, then they try to come up with some explanation as to why, in this case, things were *different* in the past."

Dr. Eisenberg, while not completely persuaded, was definitely impressed. Mack, on the other hand, appeared completely amazed.

"How come I've never heard any of this stuff before? No offense, Becky, but it almost sounds as if you made up this stuff just to prove your point."

"Well, then I think you should read it for yourself," she replied matter of factly. "Better yet, I challenge you to do your *own* research, and see what you come up with."

"I may just do that," he stated. "So if you're right, then we haven't entered into an alternate universe, but we *have* gone back in time. Not only that, but the earth is less than ten thousand years old, there really was a worldwide flood, there was one short Ice Age that lasted less than a thousand years, and Neanderthals were intelligent humans who had diseases that deformed their bones. Did I leave anything out?"

"Nope. That about sums it up," Rebecca said.

"And if you're right, then this tower we're looking for is the *real* tower of Babel?"

Rebecca nodded in affirmation.

Mack was silent for several more seconds as he considered all they had discussed. Finally, he asked one more question. "But if all you say is true, then how do you explain this pyramid? Where does it fit in?"

"I'm not exactly sure about that myself," she replied honestly. "Maybe—"

Before she could finish her thought, they were interrupted by Jeffrey's voice erupting from their commlinks. "The engines are slowing down. Do you guys want to stay down there for the show, or join us here in the control room?"

Dr. Eisenberg reached down and activated his comm. "We'll be right there." Placing his hands on Rebecca's shoulders, he looked deeply into her eyes and smiled. "My dear Rebecca, I must say that you've given me a great deal to think about. When we get some more time, I would love to look over all of the information you've gathered and finish our discussion." With that, he gave her a fatherly embrace. "But for now, I think it would be best to join the others."

As the doctor reached over and opened the door, Mack said, "You know, even if your theory is *not* correct, it's at least as fascinating as any of the explanations I've come up with. You gave me chicken-skin a couple of times there."

Content in knowing Mack and the doctor had at least taken her information seriously, Rebecca left the room with them and headed up the stairs toward the control room. Yet, in the back of her mind, Mack's last question continued to nag at her. *If my theory is correct, then who indeed was the builder of the pyramid...?*

25

GOLIATH'S PLAN

REBECCA, DR. EISENBERG, and Mack entered the control room just as the pyramid walls began to fade. Within moments, their bodies became nearly transparent as well. Below them, as usual, was the orb of the earth.

Jeffrey, sitting just to the right of Akwen, was the first to speak. "Look, the ice sheets are nearly gone, meaning we must be arriving right when they first began to form."

"But the cloud cover and giant storms look almost bigger," Lisa noted. "It's a good thing the area where the tower is located is mostly protected from that nasty weather."

"Yeah, I definitely don't want to deal with any more ice," Jerome added. "Good Lord, would you look at that! There are almost no deserts in Africa!"

"What?" Lisa said. "How can that be?"

"Desertification," Dr. Eisenberg announced. Seeing Lisa's confused expression, he explained. "Each year the hot winds from the desert blow onto the land bordering it, causing that area to eventually become part of the desert. Therefore, since the deserts grow each year, then if we go back in time, they would shrink."

"But I don't remember seeing a smaller desert on our last jump," Rebecca commented.

"That could've been due to the fact that we were focused on the ice, the massive hurricane, or the large amount of cloud cover," Jeffrey suggested. "In fact, it may have been the cloud cover that prevented us from seeing the size of the desert to begin with."

Looking down at Akwen, he was surprised to see an expression of longing on her face. "Akwen, are you okay?"

For once, the usually unemotional woman let just the slightest hint of her feelings slip through her stony façade. "Yes, I am fine. I was just imagining what my country must look like on dis earth. Look at it, so lush and green. It must be beautiful. I do miss my country."

"Maybe when this is all over, we can come back for a more enjoyable visit," Jeffrey replied.

Her expression serious once more, she turned and regarded Jeffrey skeptically. "Yeah. When dis is all over. Sure. I'm not going to hold my breat."

Leaning over the control console, Dr. Eisenberg glanced down at the time dial, his ghostly form studying the display intently.

"What does it read?" Rebecca asked.

"It reads -2634. That would put us at the year…2251 BC, 202 years since we left the Ice Age," the doctor said. "Right on target."

Suddenly, the engines began to reverse, indicating they were about to descend. "Okay, everyone. Here we go," Akwen called out.

As before, the ship descended through the atmosphere unimpeded. Within a minute, they began to be able to make out features on the land below them.

"Akwen, you're getting pretty good at this," Jeffrey said as they crossed the continent and drew nearer to the northeastern corner of Africa.

Despite her intense concentration on piloting the craft, she cracked a smile. "Practice makes perfect."

"There's the Euphrates," Dr. Eisenberg announced.

Jeffrey nodded as his eyes began scanning the horizon. "All right, everyone. Keep your eyes peeled. Akwen, keep the river on our left and follow it north."

Several minutes passed as they searched for any sign of the structure. Then at last, Goliath pointed emphatically. "Over there!"

Following his gaze toward the horizon, the others could see what looked like a massive square rock surrounded by smaller buildings on all sides, sitting about a mile inland from the river. Beyond the edge of the city, grassy plains surrounded the area on the north, east, and south and eventually turned into rolling hills populated by copses of trees. To the west, a large caravan could be seen moving up from the river, through the city, and ending at the tower. A similar caravan could be seen heading towards the construction site from the wooded area to the east.

"Akwen, slow down and keep it low—WHAT THE?"

Even as Jeffrey's surprise halted him mid-sentence, Goliath called out to Akwen. "LAND! Quickly, before they see us!"

Her eyes suddenly locating the source of the others' alarm, Akwen immediately complied with Goliath's command and dropped the pyramid below the tree line. Within seconds, she located a large enough clearing and set the ship down. A few moments later, the white beams of energy subsided and the ship and its contents returned to their normal appearance.

"What happened?" Mack asked. "How come we landed so abruptly? What did you guys see?"

"I'm not exactly sure myself," Jeffrey said. "All I know is some kind of floating platform was hovering several hundred feet above the ground. It was pretty close to the tower, so I don't think they saw us from this distance. I thought I saw two figures standing on it."

"They were undoubtedly lookouts," Goliath added. "Even though the pyramid was transparent, the light beams would be at least somewhat visible against the sky. Fortunately, there are enough clouds out there that if we are lucky, we may not have been seen."

"So now what?" Mack asked.

"Well, since the tower is in the center of a plain, we'll need to park here and walk the rest of the way. Otherwise we're sure to be spotted," Jeffrey stated. Turning toward the giant, Jeffrey asked, "Have you put together a plan for infiltrating this place yet?"

Goliath appeared pensive as he considered this turn of events. "The presence of a lookout will make things more difficult, that's for sure. Based on the sketches in the scrolls, I know which entrance I want to use and what route we'll take to get to the core. However, without knowing the exact layout of things as they now stand, there's no way I can make a proper plan of action. I need to know where their guards are and how they're positioned, as well as the overall organization of the construction workers, cranes, et cetera. In short, I need information."

"That sounds logical," Jeffrey said. "Since you can basically turn invisible, why don't you scout ahead, then report back and let us know the plan?"

Grabbing his helmet from the table next to him, he placed it over his head as he spoke. "That was my suggestion also. I should be back within the hour. Be ready to move."

Once he had left the pyramid, Akwen closed the front door. Facing the others, Jeffrey took a deep breath, then let it out quickly. "Here we go. Everyone grab some gear—rope, pocket tools, lighters, flashlights, and anything else you can think of that we might need. I want to be ready to go when Goliath returns."

"Shouldn't we place our own lookout?" Dr. Eisenberg suggested.

"Good idea," Jeffrey agreed. "We certainly don't want anyone sneaking up on us. Doc, are you volunteering?"

The professor shrugged his shoulders. "Sure." As he settled himself into the stool facing the external camera monitor, the others left the room to complete their tasks. By the time Goliath returned, the team members had assembled all the equipment they could find that might be useful and placed them in two of the backpacks.

"There are some interesting and challenging obstacles before us, but it shouldn't be anything we can't overcome," Goliath explained to the others as they stood around the table in the control room, staring down at the drawing of the tower. "I think the best plan is for us to approach the tower from the road that leads from the forest—here, on the east side. The trees grow close enough to the road that we should be able to blend in with the construction traffic without drawing any unwanted attention. You will all need disguises, which I'll get for you."

"How?" Jeffrey asked.

The giant smirked. "The less you know, the better. That way, your delicate consciences won't be unduly burdened. As I said, I will provide the disguises. Then, you'll join the traffic in groups of two. If you all travel together, you'll be too conspicuous."

"Wait a second," Mack said, his voice taking on an edge of mistrust. "You keep saying 'you.' Where will *you* be?"

"*I* will be invisible, so I'll already be inside the construction site and working out the next part of the plan," he said with a sneer. "Now, if there aren't any more stupid questions, I'll continue."

Feeling foolish, Mack simply stared at his shoes and looked apologetic.

"Once *you* reach the construction site, you'll make your way toward this entrance here," Goliath said, his hairy, claw-like finger pointing toward a small entrance on the eastern side. "From what Mack and the doctor have been able to determine from the scroll, this should lead to a room set aside for priests to prepare the sacrifices. There's a passage that goes from this room around the back and into the central chamber of the tower. The core rests in the middle of a raised platform."

"Do we even know if this core is the same size as the one that powers our ship?" Jerome asked. "What if it's proportional to the size of the building?"

"I don't think so," Dr. Eisenberg replied. "All indications from the scroll lead me to believe it's not the size that is important, but the power contained within."

"Even still, our core is pretty large. Have we figured out how we are going to move it?" Jeffrey asked Goliath.

"Yes. There are several large…carts that we can procure," the giant said with a grin.

"Okay, so assuming all else goes as planned, how do we get the core back to the pyramid?" Jeffrey asked. "I don't think they're going to let us quietly walk all the way across the plains with their prized possession."

"Once we have the core, I'll create a distraction," Goliath said.

"What kind of distraction?" Rebecca was almost afraid to hear the answer to her question.

"Let's just say the construction project is going to have a little setback."

Jeffrey slowly looked at each of them. "We have surprise and technology on our side, but this isn't going to be easy. There's no guarantee that any of us will survive this. I can't force you to go, but I must say that I don't think we can succeed unless we all work together. With that being said, I think it would be a good idea for at least one of us to stay behind with the pyramid, just in case. And since Akwen is our only pilot, I think she should remain here. Does anyone else want to stay?"

There were several seconds of silence as each one wrestled with his or her own conscience. Dr. Eisenberg was the first to speak. "I think it's pretty clear that Mack and I need to go. We're the only ones who understand this Language of Eden at all."

"Great, thanks for volunteering me, Doc," Mack said nervously. "But, you're right. I guess I don't have much of a choice. I'm in."

Lisa and Rebecca both chimed in with their willingness to go, causing all eyes to turn toward Jerome. Setting his jaw resolutely, he looked at the others and spoke, his voice shaky, but filled with determination. "You've all risked your lives for me on this trip while I sat on the sidelines. But not this time. I'm goin'."

Clapping Jerome on the shoulder, Jeffrey smiled. "It's settled then. Let's get moving."

Once they had grabbed their equipment and bid farewell to Akwen, Goliath led the group out of the pyramid and into the forest. They were immediately struck by the thick layer of humidity that clung to their skin and penetrated their lungs. The moisture and heat made breathing difficult. Before long, Rebecca saw Mack produce his inhaler and take several puffs in an effort to ease his lungs. *What are we going to do if we have to run in these conditions? Mack will never make it,* she thought worriedly. As they walked, Rebecca's lips moved silently as she offered up prayers for the well being of her friends.

The small group hiked through the woods for nearly ten minutes without incident. As they traveled, they could hear a cacophony of sounds coming from somewhere in front and to the left of them. Hammer falls, stones grinding together, ropes creaking, and a plethora of other noises, including human shouts, grunts, and cries of pain, filled the air. Finally, Goliath held up a hand, halting their procession. "This is far enough. Stay here and wait for me to return."

As they settled in to wait, Goliath activated the camouflage on his armor. Within seconds, he disappeared almost completely as his suit bent the rays of sunlight that filtered through the canopy of leaves and branches. Only the slightest shape of his form could be seen as he moved, and then only if one knew where to look. Before long, the others lost sight of him altogether.

Knowing it wouldn't be wise to risk any conversation, they sat quietly in a small huddle, eyes fixed on their surroundings. They waited for nearly half an hour for Goliath to return. Then, just as they were beginning to wonder what may have happened to him, he materialized directly in front of them.

Mack, who had been leaning up against a tree and mopping his forehead with his T-shirt, nearly leapt out of his skin at the sudden appearance of the giant. Once he had recovered the ability to speak, he whispered harshly, "What are you trying to do—give us heart attacks or something? I nearly soiled my jeans!"

The giant merely grinned wickedly. "I was able to get enough outer garments for all of you, but I didn't want to risk bringing them here. I thought the sight of clothing floating through the air might just be a little out of the ordinary. So I stashed them near the road. Follow me."

Goliath led them deeper into the woods until they could just begin to see hints of movements ahead. Stopping at the base of a tree, he reached down and grabbed several pieces of white clothing. "Here. Wrap these around you and make sure they cover your heads. Especially you," he said as he handed the cloth to Lisa. Reaching out, he gently lifted several strands of her hair and let them slip through his coarse fingers. Lisa recoiled from the touch and shot the giant a look of intense anger. Goliath laughed, taking perverse pleasure at her reaction. "I don't think these people have ever seen highlights in a woman's hair," he continued. "So, as I said, make sure you keep your head covered." Turning away from him in frustration, Lisa took the cloth and began to wrap it around her, all the while casting baleful glances in the giant's direction.

Once they were ready, Goliath grabbed a couple of other items from the ground and passed them out. "These are water containers," he said. "When you enter the construction site, work your way toward the tower, giving out drinks to anyone who asks. This should allow you to move freely. You still have your commlinks, so if anyone gets in trouble, set it to channel one and click three times.

"I'm going to move up near the road and watch the traffic. When there's a break in the convoy, I'll call you on the commlink. Move up as quickly as you can to that spot," Goliath said, pointing to where two trees had grown next to each other, creating enough room for all of them to hide close to the road. "From there, you should be able to move onto the road when another opportunity presents itself. Be ready when I give the signal."

After he had finished speaking, Goliath once more activated his armor and disappeared into the trees. When he had gone, Jeffrey looked around at the others. "I think it would be best if we split up the ladies. So Becky, you go with Doc, Lisa can go with Mack, and Jerome and I will go last." They each nodded their assent and settled in to wait once again for Goliath's signal.

Before long, their commlinks chirped. "Go now," came Goliath's voice. Without a word, they all jumped to their feet and ran as quietly as they could through the woods until they reached the indicated spot.

Her heart thudding in her chest, Rebecca nervously peered around the edge of the tree, searching for any sign of movement. Suddenly, her comm chirped once again. "Team one, GO!" came the muted sound of Goliath's voice. Grabbing Dr. Eisenberg's arm in one hand and her water container in the other, Rebecca stepped out from behind the tree and onto the dirt road.

As their feet touched the packed earth, Rebecca glanced behind her to see the forms of several men coming around a bend in the road. However, it quickly became clear that these men were slaves. The only clothing they wore was a bit of material wrapped around their waists in such a way as to barely cover their nakedness. Their skin was bronzed from long days spent in the sun, and their muscles were hard from intense physical labor. Rebecca's fear of discovery subsided as she realized these men all had their heads down in either humble deference to their masters or plain exhaustion. Each one held a bag over his right shoulder that, judging by the sweat on their brows and their bent posture, was clearly very heavy.

Walking behind the dozen or so men carrying the heavy bags was another man. Rebecca turned around to face forward in fear that he would see her, for it was instantly apparent that this man was one of the slave masters. Fighting against the desire to glance behind her to see if the man was approaching, she continued moving.

About eighty feet ahead of her and Dr. Eisenberg, another group of men trudged up the path. The ones in back appeared to be pushing some kind of cart, although their bodies blocked her view so that she was unable to determine what was contained within.

Before long, Rebecca's fear subsided as it became obvious that she and the others had not been discovered. After another few minutes of walking, the trees on each side of the thirty-foot-wide road began to thin. Finally, the last of the trees gave way, revealing a panorama that stopped Dr. Eisenberg and Rebecca in their tracks. Before them, in the center of a circular city that was spread out over the wide, grassy plain, stood the Tower of Babel.

26

THE TOWER

THE VISTA THAT stretched out before Rebecca and Dr. Eisenberg took their breath. The surrounding city was dwarfed by the magnificence of the tower. Its base, roughly fourteen acres in size, rose nearly three hundred feet from the ground. On top of that, a second layer had been completed, which was neither as wide nor as high. Set approximately twenty feet from the edge of the first, it created a path that wound around the entire edge of the tower. In height, it reached perhaps half the size of the base. And judging by what she could see of the partially completed third level, it would be the same height as the second, yet once again leaving a walkway around the edge. All in all, it gave Rebecca the impression of boxes stacked upon each other, each slightly smaller than the first.

On the southern side of the tower, three long staircases led up to a square entranceway topped with a crystal-like dome. Two of the staircases were built flush against the southern wall; one led to the entrance from the east, the other led to the entrance from the west. The third, central, staircase extended out onto the southern plain, forming a triangle with the other two. On each side of the middle staircase, two rectangular structures were erected, each about half the height of the tower's base, and a quarter of its length.

Although the top two levels were brownish in color, the base of the tower had been covered with highly polished white casing stones, causing Rebecca to be thankful for the cloudy skies. On a clear day, she knew the sun's rays would be blinding when reflected off the shiny surface.

Rebecca was so overwhelmed by the plethora of sensory stimuli that she was startled when Dr. Eisenberg grabbed her arm and began urging her forward. "We must not dawdle," he said. "If we do, we will draw attention to ourselves. Keep moving."

They passed quickly through the city, noticing as they went that in addition to the tower, many of the buildings were also under construction. Within minutes, they left the last of the city behind and found themselves entering the tower grounds.

Surrounding the huge structure on all sides were stacks of building materials. A continuous line of slaves was methodically making piles of wood and logs, even while others were taking the wood for use in the construction. Similar processes were in effect with regards to the massive stone blocks that formed the majority of the tower.

Rebecca was amazed at the sheer size of the blocks. She guessed that each of the rectangular stones was about five feet high, eight feet wide, and twelve feet deep. Due to their massive size, she knew the weight must be well over thirty tons each. Just as she was wondering how such gigantic stones could be moved, let alone lifted, Dr. Eisenberg pointed toward their right. Immediately, Rebecca felt a shudder pass through her body at the incredible sight.

Coming around the northeast corner of the tower lumbered a mighty sauropod. Swirls of yellow were etched on a sea of pale green scales, as if drawn by an imaginative artist. The creature's shoulders stood roughly fifteen feet above the ground, although its head, which rested upon a twenty-foot long neck, could have reached much higher. Oddly enough, Rebecca noted that the magnificent beast wore a metallic collar around its neck. At the base of its skull, an eight-foot long sword-like object extended out from the collar and rested atop the dinosaur's head.

Before she could even begin to guess the purpose of the object, the answer became apparent. Walking next to the creature, just in front of its torso, was a man carrying a rod in his right hand. As they walked, the man suddenly turned the rod to the right. Immediately the dinosaur altered its course and turned, now moving parallel to the eastern wall.

Trailing behind the giant animal was a massive cart that looked to be made of some kind of thick, gray stone or metal; Rebecca couldn't tell which. It was as wide as the beast that pulled it, and nearly as long as the animal's eighteen-foot tail. The cart was laden with a dozen of the massive blocks. As the sauropod completed the turn, Rebecca could at last see that the cart was not a cart at all, but a floating platform. Beneath it, she could see the telltale blue glow of the anti-gravity repulsors.

As Rebecca and the doctor watched, the man holding the rod stopped and pulled the device back toward himself, causing the apatosaurus to follow suit. Immediately, several slaves stepped toward the cart. Within moments, the beast and its burden had been separated. Once the floating platform was disconnected, the dinosaur master turned the huge animal, and they headed back around the corner.

The wheel-less cart, which now hovered next to the tower, suddenly began to rise. Less than a minute later, the platform reached the edge of the tower base. More slaves, who had been waiting patiently for the platform, attached ropes to it and pulled it toward them. From there, they removed the ropes, pushed the platform to the wall of the second tier, and repeated the process until the platform finally rested on the topmost section of the tower.

As they walked farther into the construction site, Rebecca continued to take in her surroundings, her awe increasing exponentially. Finally, she recovered her voice and whispered excitedly to her companion. "Doc, did you see that? I mean, dinosaurs and hovering carts! It's…it's just…unbelievable."

Looking at the doctor, she could see from the look on his face that he was also amazed at what he had witnessed, yet he also seemed somewhat troubled. But before she could ask him what it was that bothered him, she heard a voice yelling something in a strange language. Turning toward the voice, she saw one of the taskmasters calling out to her and waving for her to come closer.

Her pulse skyrocketed and her hands began to shake, threatening to spill the contents of her water pail. *The water pail! He probably just wants water. Stay calm.* "Doc, I'll be right back," she whispered quickly. Walking over toward the man, she tried to study him while keeping her head and eyes down, as would be proper for a slave. The man was bald, but wore a thin headband made of two rows of light blue squares with gold trim. Beneath his matching light blue tunic, she could see that, like most of the other men she had observed thus far, he was powerfully built and slightly taller than average.

Once she reached him, he grabbed the ladle from her container and began to drink; the water dribbled down his short, carefully trimmed beard. After taking several draws of the liquid, he eyed her with curiosity. Using the end of the coiled whip, which he held in his right hand, he lifted Rebecca's chin, forcing her to look at him.

Humiliation and anger rose within her at the man's perusal. Yet, despite the fact that she would like nothing more than to wipe the leering expression off of his smug face, she knew the mission took first priority. But if he touched her…

Suddenly, another man called to her, requesting a drink. With a frustrated look and an expression that promised further investigation, the man with the whip let her go. As she walked toward her next patron, she could feel the eyes of the first boring into her back. Sending up a quick prayer for protection, she continued to move through the area, doling out water to any who asked.

Before long, she realized she had completely lost track of Dr. Eisenberg. Unconsciously cracking her knuckles, she fought against growing panic. *Hang on, Becky. You still have your commlink. If you don't find the others soon, you can use it to learn their whereabouts. You're not alone. Keep your focus and stay calm. Fortunately, it looks like there are many other hooded women serving water. That's interesting. Most of them are wearing their scarves like veils as well. Maybe that's why that man took so much interest in me. Maybe they keep the women hooded and veiled so the men will focus on their work. Well, whatever the reason, it works to our advantage.*

Watching the other women work, Rebecca noticed they were refilling their containers from several large clay cylinders near the wall. Wrapping the loose end of her disguise around her face like a scarf, she headed over to refill her own. Still scanning the area for sign of the others, she was startled when a hand suddenly touched her arm. Whirling around in surprise, she was relieved to discover it was Dr. Eisenberg. "Doc! Thank God it's you! You scared me half to de—"

"That's how they did it, Rebecca!" the professor exclaimed.

"How they did what?" she asked as she looked around to make sure no one was paying any undue attention to them.

"How they built the great pyramids and ziggurats!" he continued. "They used gravity-control technology." Trying hard to contain his enthusiasm, Dr. Eisenberg began speaking; his words came out rapidly in a forced whisper.

"One of the classes I teach is on ancient structures from around the world. It's a fascinating topic, in large part because so much of it is a mystery. Numerous theories have been proposed as to how the giant stones used in constructing the pyramids and ziggurats could have been moved. Even more, we have never figured out how the Egyptians and other civilizations could have fit these massive stones into place with such precision that even after thousands of years, with our modern technology, we would be hard pressed to duplicate it. It's such a mystery that some have even proposed that the pyramids were built by aliens! But now we know. Look!"

Following his gaze, Rebecca watched as a group of slaves working up on the third tier huddled around a stack of the massive stones. Each carried a pair of strange devices. Two of the men split off from the group and moved to stand on each side of the colossal slabs. Both proceeded to hold their arms out in front of them, the tips of the strange devices pointed directly at the spot where the upper block rested against the lower. Suddenly, a bluish flash emanated from the tips of the devices, causing the stone to rise slightly. While the men held their positions, three other men pushed against the rock, causing it to shift sideways. After about a minute of maneuvering, an overseer standing off to the side signaled that he was satisfied with the positioning. The two men holding the gravity control devices powered them down, causing the stone to slowly come to rest.

"Do you see?" Dr. Eisenberg asked. "One of the great mysteries of the pyramids is that although many of the blocks only weighed two and a half tons, some weighed between seventy and two hundred tons![41] How could ancient man, with primitive technology, be able to lift such heavy stones—and more so, place them with the precision of just a few millimeters?[42] Many have proposed the use of ramps, but those ramps would have to be made out of material at least as hard as the limestone the pyramids were made out of. Therefore, the ramps would have to be as large as the pyramid itself! And then there is the fact that no materials left over from the ramps have ever been found."[43]

Before the doctor could say more, he and Rebecca were forced to move out of the way as several workers trudged by carrying armfuls of straw. Once the workers were out of earshot, Dr. Eisenberg picked up the conversation as if there had been no interruption. "Another mystery is that the great pyramid was built in just twenty years. How could these primitive men build such a massive structure consisting of *millions* of blocks, each weighing more than two and a half tons in twenty years?"

Worried they would be discovered, Rebecca kept them moving while the doctor continued. "And in addition to all of that, the four sides of the pyramid are oriented almost exactly with the four cardinal points.[44] How is it that these supposedly primitive people just happened to have built this incredible structure? How could they have such advanced knowledge?

"But we had it all wrong! Because of evolution, we *assumed* they were primitive. But they're clearly *not* as primitive as we believed. With this technology, it wouldn't be difficult to get the blocks lined up per-

fectly, and they wouldn't need even a fraction of the workforce that has
been suggested."

Rebecca shook her head. Despite the ever-present danger that they
might be discovered, she found herself being caught up in the doctor's
enthusiasm.

"And did you know there are many legends from around the world
about levitation?" he continued. "Some are specifically about Egyptians.
I never took them seriously, but now that I have seen this…it all makes
sense. There are also structures all over the world that are made up of
massive stones. Think of Stonehenge, Tiahuanaco, Sacsahuaman."

"I've heard of Stonehenge. But what are those other two?" Rebecca
asked.

"Tiahuanaco is an ancient Incan city located in Bolivia," he explained.
"In it, there's a large piece of rock in the shape of a doorway, known as
the 'Gateway to the Sun.' Not only is it massive, but there are no scratch
marks on the stones. And, even more amazing, the city is at an altitude
of 12,500 feet![45] You need oxygen masks to be up that high.

"Sacsahuaman is another ancient Incan city located in Peru. The
stones used to build this city were carved several miles away, hauled down
and across a swamp, and then placed in their final positions.[46] Many of
the stones are larger than the ones at Tiahuanaco. There is even one that
is estimated to weigh as much as *twenty thousand tons!*" Dr. Eisenberg
said, enunciating each of the last three words for emphasis. "No combi-
nation of machinery today could move so much weight, much less move
it into a specific position.[47]

"All of this begs the question: Why did they use such gigantic blocks
of stone to build these structures? Why not use smaller bricks that were
much easier to transport? Could it be because the gigantic blocks were
not that difficult to move? With this technology, it would be possible for
a single person to move enormous amounts of weight."

A memory emerged from Rebecca's consciousness, causing goose
bumps to travel up her arms. "Doc," she said excitedly, "have you ever
heard of the Coral Castle in Florida?"

Seeing no recognition in his face, she explained further. "My parents live in Florida, and one time they took me to visit it. Sometime between the 1920s and 1950s, an immigrant to the U.S. by the name of Ed… something-or-other *single-handedly* built a structure made of huge stones up to thirty tons each. He called it the Coral Castle. No one knows for sure how he did it, but he was very interested in electricity and magnetism. He even claimed he had discovered the secret of how the pyramids were built! No one saw him do it, and he took his secrets to the grave. And what's more, after it was built, he moved the entire structure to a different location!"[48]

"Fascinating," Dr. Eisenberg stated, his face shrouded in wonder. "And if gravity control wasn't amazing enough, have you seen some of the tools these people are using? As I've been dishing out water, I've been working my way around the construction site. Look over there," he said, nodding toward several workmen to their right. "They're using theodolites!"

"What are those?" Rebecca asked.

"They are surveying instruments. They incorporate small telescopes used for sighting," Dr. Eisenberg explained.

"Telescopes? But I didn't think…" she said, stopping herself mid-thought.

"You didn't think ancient people *had* telescopes," Dr. Eisenberg finished for her. "It seems even *you* are having a difficult time rewiring your own thinking according to your new theory. Even more than that, they are also using iron tools, not just copper,[49] and machine-powered tools!"

"What?" Rebecca responded in shock. "How could they be using machine-powered tools without…"

"Without electricity?" Dr. Eisenberg responded. "Well, it appears they've even developed batteries. From what I was able to see, they're using copper and iron as electrodes instead of carbon and zinc."[50]

As he finished his sentence, one of the construction foremen called him over to give the workers drinks. When he had finished, he caught up with Rebecca, who had her free left hand resting on her forehead.

"There's so much to take in, Doc. Some of it even goes *against* my theory. If these ancient civilizations had all this technology, then why don't we find evidence of it from our time? What happened to it all?"

Dr. Eisenberg smiled. "Actually, Rebecca dear, you have already given us part of the answer to that." Seeing her confused expression, he explained further. "By believing in evolution, scientists have already ruled out the possibility of ancient people being intelligent. Therefore, when they find evidence of advanced technology, they reinterpret it or ignore it."

"Ignore it, like the…what did you call them earlier…Out-of-Place Artifacts. The OOPArts, right?" Rebecca replied.

"That's exactly right. Part of the enjoyment of studying ancient artifacts is the mystery behind some of them. But now we've solved the mystery. For example, I've known for years that Sir William Flinders Petrie, the first modern man to really examine the pyramids, found what appeared to be saw marks on the granite coffer in the King's Chamber of the Great Pyramid, as well as on other stones that had been cut. And I'm not talking about just the soft limestone objects, but also on the extremely hard diorite, granite, and basalt materials used on its construction.[51] But I just disregarded the evidence because I *knew* there was no way the builders of the pyramids could have used electric saws.

"And there are more examples like that," Dr. Eisenberg continued. "Now that I see things differently, I can make sense of them. There's evidence that Egyptians not only used tubular drills, but that their drills could actually penetrate five hundred times faster per revolution than modern drills![52] Do you now see why some people actually believe the pyramids were created by aliens? It's because, to them, since they 'know' that humans were more primitive in the past, and they find evidence of advanced technology, then it logically follows that the advanced technology must belong to someone else."

A look of confusion suddenly appeared on the professor's face. "The only thing that still puzzles me is that if ancient man had such advanced technology, then what caused him to eventually lose it?"

Rebecca considered the question for several seconds before the answer struck her like a bolt of lightning. However, before she could share her insight with Dr. Eisenberg, their commlinks clicked, abruptly ending their conversation. Looking around again to make sure no one was paying them any unwanted attention, they opened the channel.

Although the voice on the other end was barely audible, there was no mistaking Goliath's deep, gravelly voice. "Everyone be ready. Jeffrey and Jerome have one of the floating platforms, and I'm just about finished burning through the outer lock on the door. As soon as I'm done here, I'll create a small distraction north of the door, near the corner. Once everyone's attention is diverted, you'll have just a few seconds to slip through. Be in place in two minutes."

Rebecca and Dr. Eisenberg exchanged glances. "It looks like it's time to get moving," the doctor said even as he began working his way toward the door. Rebecca immediately fell into step next to him. As they approached, they saw several other cloaked figures milling about the area, which they assumed to be their friends. Their identities were confirmed a moment later when Rebecca caught sight of a pair of bluish-green eyes and dark, curly hair under one of the hoods.

The commlinks chirped again. "I see that you're all ready. Here we go."

Just then, the apatosaurus they had seen earlier roared in pain and began thrashing its tail around, knocking men and equipment over indiscriminately. Immediately, all attention on that side of the tower was directed at the howling animal, leaving the way clear for Rebecca and the others. Within seconds, Jeffrey had the door open. Lisa and Mack ducked through the entryway, followed at once by Rebecca and Dr. Eisenberg. A few seconds later, Jerome had the hovering platform through and Jeffrey jumped inside, closing the door behind them and sealing them inside the tower.

27

THE LIBRARY

FOR NEARLY A minute, the entire group sat in complete silence. Outside the heavy wooden door, the roaring of the apatosaurus could still be heard. Then, just as their heart rates were beginning to return to normal, the door opened. Expecting to see an army of workmen waiting to charge at them, they were completely thrown off guard when the door closed as quickly as it had opened.

"What the…?" Before Mack could finish, Goliath's massive frame materialized in front of them. As before, Mack fell backward and nearly knocked over a small table in fright. "Doggone it, Goliath! I wish you'd cut that out! You must really take some sort of perverse pleasure in—"

"Silence!" Goliath whispered harshly. Startled by the giant's serious demeanor, he instantly complied. Rooted to the spot, the giant gazed slowly about the room, searching for any strategic possibilities.

They stood in a relatively small room that was a mere twenty feet wide and thirty feet long. Two wooden tables sat against the north wall, upon which rested several rolls of parchment and a handful of writing utensils. The room was dimly lit by tiny glowing orbs mounted at even intervals along the solid stone walls. After being out in the stifling afternoon humidity, the cool dampness of the tower was a welcome relief.

Making his way quietly toward the room's only exit, Goliath paused and listened intently for any trace of movement beyond the door. Hearing none, he turned and regarded the others, his eyes full of intensity, as if the recent action had invigorated him.

"I don't think we were discovered, but we must move quickly," he said. "Every second that passes makes it that much more likely that they'll discover the melted lock on the outer door."

"What did you do to that dinosaur?" Lisa asked.

"The same thing I did to the lock," he replied with a twisted grin, "I put a generous portion of very potent acid on its hindquarters. Needless to say, it didn't seem to like it very much."

"Okay, so what now?" Jeffrey asked. In the dim light, Rebecca studied her husband's handsome features and saw an expression she had never seen on his face before. *It almost looks like he is...distressed or...afraid. But it's more than fear...it's something much deeper.* Puzzled and disturbed by his countenance, Rebecca could only pray that whatever it was, it wouldn't be too serious.

"I'll take point. With my camouflage, I'll be able to move about freely without risk of being seen. Once I've made certain the way is clear, I'll click the comm. That'll be your signal to move. It shouldn't take us long to—"

Goliath froze, his helmeted head turning slightly as he listened. "Someone is coming! Wait here. I'll take care of this."

Activating his armor's cloaking device, the giant soon disappeared. A moment later, the door leading into the next room opened seemingly of its own volition, then shut once again. Rebecca and the others waited nervously for what seemed like an eternity. Far off in the distance, they could hear the sounds of two voices conversing. As the seconds passed, the voices grew louder until it became clear that those speaking had entered the room on the opposite side of the wall.

"Doc," Mack whispered excitedly, "they're speaking in the Language of Eden!"

"Can you tell what they're saying?" Jeffrey asked, his voice barely audible.

"No. I only had enough time with the Patriarch for a crash course in pronunciation. I know how to read and write it because of studying the blueprints for the pyramid, but to actually speak it…that's a different story. I need to *hear* the language a little more to get the gist of it."

Suddenly, muffled cries came from the other room, followed by two dull thuds. A moment later, the commlinks crackled to life. "Come into the next room. I've found some new clothes for a couple of you."

Exchanging confused glances with Jerome, Jeffrey walked over to the door and slowly opened it. He stepped into the adjoining room, followed close behind by the rest of the group. Before long, they were all gathered around the unconscious bodies of two well-fed men dressed in fine, violet robes decorated with intricate patterns of silver woven into the black fabric of the trim.

"These two priests became a little too nosy for their own good," Goliath said. "Too bad for them, but good for us. Jeffrey and Jerome, put on their robes. In the event that we're seen, two priests and four servants walking around would be much less conspicuous. But make it quick. We don't want anyone to miss these two just yet."

As Jeffrey and Jerome put on their new disguises, Rebecca stared around at the room in which they now stood. It was more than three times the size of the other one, and filled with a dozen identical, six-foot-long tables arranged in three rows of four. From the light of the glowing orbs, which were much brighter in this room, she could see that each of the wooden tabletops was stained dark red with dried blood. Hanging along the walls were various knives and other tools she didn't care t to identify. She suddenly remembered what Goliath had said when he was explaining his plan: *"This should lead to a room set aside for priests to prepare the sacrifices."* A shudder of revulsion passed through her at the unwanted images that invaded her mind. *Even though the tower isn't fin-ished, it seems that they couldn't wait to begin using it,* she thought.

"The door behind me leads into a hallway," Goliath said as Jeffrey and Jerome dressed. "Once I make certain it's unoccupied, I'll give the signal. Head to your right and follow it, then take a left at the next junc-ture. That should lead us directly to the central chamber." After finishing his instructions, the giant became invisible once again, opened the door on the eastern wall, and quickly moved out into the hall, quietly closing the door behind him.

"Man, look at this thing!" Jerome said, frustrated. "I am swimming in this robe. This guy definitely needs to cut back on the late-night munchies."

Despite the humor in Jerome's statement, the tremble in his voice made it apparent that he was waging an ongoing battle for control of his fear. And, if his shaking hands were any indication, it was a battle he seemed to be losing. Mack appeared to be doing little better. At the rate he was using his inhaler, Rebecca feared he would soon run out of the life-saving medicine.

They didn't have to wait long this time. Goliath had barely been gone for more than a minute when the commlinks chirped. Taking a deep breath, Jeffrey smiled nervously at the others. "Here we go again." Opening the door, he led them out into the hallway. They exited the room in groups of two: Jeffrey and Jerome in the front, Mack and Dr. Eisenberg in the middle pushing the hovering cart, and Lisa and Rebecca last.

Although to their fear-wracked minds the corridor seemed to stretch on interminably, in reality, it was less than two hundred feet long. The walls on each side, only a dozen feet or so apart at the base, slanted inward slightly, leaving Rebecca with the uncomfortable feeling that the walls were closing in. More heavy wooden doors that were curved at the tops were spaced along both sides of the hallway at uneven intervals. As they walked, they anxiously watched the ominous portals, fearful one of them would open at any second.

Catching sight of Mack looking over his shoulder frequently, Rebecca reached forward and laid a calming hand on his arm. "Don't," she said. "I know you want to, but fight the urge to look back. Just concentrate on looking ahead. If someone does happen to stumble upon us from behind, they'll probably say something to us first. But if we keep looking behind us, we'll give ourselves away." With a small nod, Mack acknowledged that he understood.

They continued walking in silence down the cold stone hallway. Above them, they could hear the discordant sounds of the construction as it continued unabated. The sheer weight of stone over their heads seemed to be squeezing the air and compressing it in their lungs. The dim lighting and oppressive silence only added to their sense of claustrophobia.

Looking over at Lisa, Rebecca saw her friend's eyes darting from place to place like those of a trapped animal. "Hang in there, Lis," Rebecca whispered. "We're almost there."

Turning to regard Rebecca, Lisa began to cry softly. "I thought I had this conquered. I mean, I went for months being closed up on the *Vanguard* on the trip to 2021 PK, yet I was fine. But there's something about being under rock that just...just..."

As Rebecca reached out to comfort her, she watched Lisa's expression change. In addition to fear, there was also emotional pain, as if some deep scar on her soul had been reopened. Shrinking from Rebecca's touch, Lisa began to cry even harder. "Becky, I'm so sorry..."

Sorry? Sorry for what? Confused by the sudden change in her friend, she simply said the first thing that came to her mind. "It's okay, Lisa. It will—"

The sound of a door opening behind them froze the words on her lips. Everyone in the group tensed. Mack's hooded head began to turn, but abruptly stopped, as if he had just remembered Rebecca's previous warning.

Rebecca's own heart beat painfully against her chest like a frightened bird trapped in a tiny cage.

"Don't turn around," Goliath's muffled voice whispered from ahead. "Just keep walking. They're heading the other direction."

After a few more seconds of overwhelming tension, the group finally reached the end of the passage. Although the hallway widened and continued on to the right and left, Goliath went straight to the door just off to their right. While the others waited anxiously, the giant melted the lock on the door and opened it quickly. Satisfied the room was unoccupied, he ushered the others inside.

Once Lisa and Rebecca had cleared the doorway, Goliath closed the door and switched off his armor's cloaking unit.

"Man, I thought we were toast," Mack said. "When I heard that door open, it felt like some Sith Lord had squeezed my heart in a force grip!"

"It seems like they're all too busy working on the tower to notice us," Goliath commented. "A priest came out of the door with a dozen slaves who were carrying all sorts of tables and large wooden chairs."

"Actually, I'm surprised we haven't seen more people walking around in here," Jeffrey stated.

"Most likely, since this floor is finished, the rest of the priests are probably overseeing the completion of the second and third tiers," Dr. Eisenberg surmised. "Or, they could just be off in another part of the tower."

"Hopefully our luck will hold," Goliath said. "We're now in the room that leads directly onto the platform in the central chamber of the tower. The core should be housed on a raised pedestal in the middle of the chamber. Give me a few seconds to scout ahead, then we'll get moving." Heading over to the set of double doors set into the wall to their left, Goliath cloaked himself and exited.

While they waited, Lisa slid down into one of the plush chairs and reined in her turbulent emotions, her fear subsiding now that they were out of the oppressive hallways. Rebecca and the others, however, began studying the room in which they now stood. Its two longest walls were nearly one hundred feet in length, while the opposite walls were only sixty. The room was elegantly furnished with plush chairs and finely crafted wooden tables. Taking up the majority of the space in the room were the bookshelves. Row upon row of shelves were neatly filled with scrolls and parchments of various shapes and sizes.

To the three archaeologists and the language specialist, it was a treasure of incalculable wealth.

"Just…just look at all of them!" Jerome stuttered. "This discovery would make the Dead Sea Scrolls look like children's books. I mean, texts written over four thousand years ago from a culture that has advanced technology? Think of the historical insights…"

Mack walked over to the closest shelf and unrolled one of the scrolls. "It's written in the Language of Eden. The title says, *The Prophecies of Enoch.*" Replacing that one, he strolled over to another shelf and grabbed another. "Becky, listen to this one: *A Complete List of Land Dwelling Dragon Kinds.* And this one reads, *Understanding the Movements of the Celestial Bodies.*"

While the four men examined the books, Rebecca's attention was captured by the work of another group of ancient artists. Lining the walls of the room were tapestries depicting images of various half-human, half-animal creatures. Although the artistry was exquisite and the color usage dazzling, the subject matter caused a coldness to seep into her bones and steal the warmth from her body.

Observing Rebecca's interest in the images, Dr. Eisenberg walked over to stand next to her. "Judging by their clothing and weapons, I'd say those paintings are depictions of many of the ancient gods," he explained. "That one looks like Zeus. Over there is Baal. That one is probably Odin. How strange. It's almost like they just collected gods from all over the world."

"I don't care who they are. We need to get out of here," Rebecca said with a shudder. "This place is just…evil."

The door opened again and Goliath appeared before them. "It looks like it's there, all right."

"What do you mean, 'looks like'?" Jerome asked in alarm as he returned the scroll he had been examining to its shelf.

"There's a pedestal in the center of the room that's the right size to hold the core. Sitting atop it is a large stone covering. The core is probably beneath the covering," Goliath explained.

Jerome relaxed noticeably. "Will we be able to move it?"

"Probably not without a pair of those levitation devices," Goliath said. "Look around. These priests might have a set lying around here for just that purpose."

Tearing their gazes away from the treasures around them, they began rifling through the various compartments and wooden storage containers set against the wall closest to the double doors. Before long, they stumbled upon a pair of the levitation devices.

"Great. Now how do we work these things?" Jeffrey asked as he studied the strange items.

"Judging by the circular grooves in the grip, it would appear that you are supposed to place your fingers there," Dr. Eisenberg suggested.

While Jeffrey and Jerome attempted to activate the devices, Goliath wedged a chair against the door leading into the hallway to prevent anyone from walking in on them. Finally, after several failed attempts, Jeffrey and Jerome managed to get the tools to work.

"Now, we have one other slight problem that I had not taken into consideration," Goliath said. "The reason the core has a covering over it is probably to protect it from any construction accidents."

"What do you mean?" Jeffrey asked.

"It appears that the central chamber is going to extend up through the entire tower," the giant continued. "But since only a third of the tower has been completed, much of the ceiling is still open to the sky."

"But…but that means they'll be able to look down upon us!" Mack said, fear once more seizing him.

"Which is why Jeffrey and Jerome are going to go alone with me," Goliath said. "Hopefully, the workers will be so busy that no one will even notice us. But if they do, they may not give it a second thought if they see two priests."

"But will just the three of you be strong enough to lift…" Mack began. Then, seeing the devices held in Jeffrey's hands, he smiled weakly. "Oh, yeah. I forgot."

"Everyone else, be on your guard," Goliath said. "Stand near the doors and watch for any signs that we have been discovered."

Having finished his prep talk, the giant activated his armor's invisibility, then opened the door. Jeffrey and Jerome gave one last look to each of their friends, put the hoods from their robes over their heads, then pushed the hovering cart through the open door and entered into the central chamber of the tower.

28

GUARDIANS OF THE TOWER

ALTHOUGH THEY HAD encountered many other fascinating and wondrous sights so far on their journey in the pyramid, Jeffrey and Jerome instantly knew this one would be the most memorable by far. The central chamber of the tower was about a third of the size of the structure as a whole. However, while the tower itself was mostly square, the chamber walls sloped inward, creating what would eventually be a pyramid shape once the construction was completed. The size of the room made the two men feel insignificant. And the statues of gargoyle-like, winged monstrosities that hung on the sloping walls filled them with an uncomfortable feeling of foreboding—as if the stone creatures might come alive and swoop down on them at any second.

The double doors through which they had entered led out onto the left side of a semi-circular raised platform, or stage, that rested against the northern wall. On the other side of the stage, directly opposite where they now stood, was a duplicate set of doors. In the front, center portion of the platform was a large, horned altar nearly eight feet wide and four feet deep. The image of the wooden altar stained with dried blood sent a shudder of revulsion down the spines of the two intruders.

"You don't think they use that thing for anything other than animals, do you?" Jerome asked nervously.

"I don't know," Jeffrey replied, his own voice quavering. "But I'd rather not find out." Looking up, Jeffrey briefly searched through the uncompleted ceiling to see if anyone was taking an interest in them. Although he could make out the silhouettes of several workers standing near the edge, none appeared to be looking in his direction—at least, as far as he could tell due to the backlighting from the diffused sunlight.

Moving down the steps of the platform, the pair made their way toward the middle of the chamber. Just as Goliath had described, a heavy stone slab rested upon a five-foot octagonal pedestal. A short set of four steps surrounded the six-foot high pedestal. As they drew nearer, Jeffrey could begin to make out drawings, symbols, and writings carved into the sides. On the far wall of the chamber, they could see two oversized doors that were obviously the main entrance for the worshipers.

Jeffrey glanced behind him towards the others and saw they had one of the double doors ajar and were watching him intently. Comforted by the knowledge of their presence, he and Jerome climbed the steps toward the pedestal.

"The workers above don't appear to have taken an interest in them," Lisa stated, relieved.

Neither Mack, Rebecca, nor Dr. Eisenberg responded; they merely continued to watch in heightened anticipation as Jeffrey and Jerome crossed the platform and headed toward the stairs.

"I don't like this," Mack said, his head shaking from side to side in apprehension.

"What? What don't you like?" Rebecca asked.

"Don't you think it a little odd that they would leave this very important energy core just sitting out there for anyone to take?" he asked.

"Well, I don't know that I would say just *anybody* could take it," Dr. Eisenberg said. "After all, the doors were locked, it's covered by a heavy stone, and the roof is open. Besides, who would steal it? As far as they know, everyone in the area is either part of their group or a slave. They probably couldn't conceive of any enemy trying to just walk out with it right under their noses."

Unconvinced, Mack continued to scan the room carefully, his eyes probing every dark corner and crevasse. "It still seems kind of odd to me. All I know is that in just about every movie I've seen, there's always some monster or something guarding the treasure."

Rebecca grinned. "Fortunately, this is reality, not some fictional story."

Suddenly, Dr. Eisenberg let out a small gasp, interrupting their conversation. Turning to look at him in concern, Rebecca whispered urgently, "What is it? What's wrong?"

As he turned and met her gaze, Rebecca relaxed somewhat as she read on his face not an expression of fear, but one of revelation. "I've just figured out another piece of the puzzle," he stated.

"What puzzle?" she asked.

"According to the Bible, the builders of the Tower of Babel wanted to build a structure 'whose top may reach unto heaven,'" Dr. Eisenberg explained. "But from what we've seen here of the construction, when it is complete it will not be much more than five hundred feet in height. Furthermore, one of the reasons I had always discounted the story of Babel is because there is no way a building made of stone, or even of *any* material for that matter, could reach up to the sky. It would collapse under its own weight.

"But I just realized my error. The phrase in the original Hebrew has a meaning similar to what we would say when talking about a bigger telescope being built. We say that it will be able to reach farther out into space. We're not referring to *literally* touching the stars, but rather being able to see them more clearly.[53] With the altar, the tapestries in the library, and the structure of the tower, it seems that it's designed partially as a temple of worship to the gods, and to the sun, the moon, and the stars."

As Dr. Eisenberg continued, his expression became more serious. "And what's more, do you notice the similarity between this chamber and our pyramid? It seems obvious, especially considering that they both use the same core, that the technology used in both would be similar. Therefore, it stands to reason that—"

"—that if the pyramid can travel through time and other dimensions, then it may be possible for the tower to do the same!" Mack finished in shock as the implications worked their way through his mind.

"It might not be able to actually fly into space like our pyramid, but what if it could open a kind of space-time portal?" Dr. Eisenberg hypothesized.

"Could it be true?" Rebecca asked, her own mind reeling. Suddenly the biblical account of the event took on new meaning. "If they had completed the tower, then who knows what they might have been able to do?"

"They've reached the pedestal," Lisa said, abruptly ending their conversation and drawing their attention back to Jeffrey and Jerome.

"See, Mack," Dr. Eisenberg said casually, "nothing has attacked them."

"Yeah," Mack said, still skeptical. "Yet…"

Once they had reached the pedestal, Jeffrey worked his way around to the other side while Jerome stayed on the end nearest the stage. Next to him, the hovering platform they had brought with them waited at the bottom of the steps. Although the sound of the workers drifted down from above, a profound stillness seemed to fill the chamber.

As soon as Jeffrey reached the other side, they heard Goliath's voice whisper beside them. "The workers still give no indication that they've seen you."

"That's good news," Jerome said as he licked his lips nervously.

"All right, I'm ready," Jeffrey said. Lifting their arms, the two men held them apart with the levitation devices pointed directly at the base of the cover stone. "On three. *One…two…three!*"

Simultaneously activating the devices, they watched in satisfaction as a field of blue energy appeared and lifted the stone a fraction of an inch off its stand. Although the pedestal was six feet tall, the stairs made it so that the stone floated just above waist level. Raising their arms slowly in unison, the men lifted the cover off of its base. For the briefest of seconds, it appeared to Jeffrey as if the area underneath it was completely empty. His hands began to shake with panic when suddenly, the outline of the energy core appeared. The multi-faceted, spherical object seemed to pulse with a dim, inner light, as if it were alive but dormant.

Across from him, Jerome let out a nervous laugh as the prize came into view. Once the cover had cleared the top of the core, they two men carefully stepped to the side, arms stretched out completely over their heads. Because of the awkward posture, Jeffrey overstepped slightly, causing his foot to slip over the edge of the top step. He regained his balance quickly, but the unexpected movement caused Jerome to over-compensate. As if in slow motion, they watched helplessly as the massive stone slid toward the end of their levitation field, then crashed onto the pedestal stairs with a heavy thud that reverberated throughout the chamber.

"You fools!" Goliath hissed from somewhere near them. "Several of the workers have stopped what they were doing and are now staring down at us! Quick! Grab the core and let's…"

Berating himself for his clumsiness, Jeffrey swore and stepped back toward the core, ready to begin lifting it.

"Stop," the giant hissed, the tension in his voice instantly immobilizing them.

"What…what is it?" Jeffrey whispered, the words sticking in his throat.

"There's something here, in the chamber," Goliath said warily. "I can hear it…"

Slowly, Jeffrey and Jerome turned, their eyes darting anxiously around the room. A clicking sound echoed off the walls, making it impossible to determine the source. A moment later, more clicks joined the first, causing Jerome and Jeffrey to place their backs against the pedestal as their eyes searched desperately for any sign of movement.

"Grab the core and get ready to run," Goliath instructed. "We need to—"

Before he could finish his sentence, they attacked.

From out of the darkness of a deep alcove sprang six dinosaurs. The creatures reached a height of five feet and were just over ten feet long from the tips of their short snouts to the ends of their whip-like tails. The upper half of their bodies was gray, while their bellies were a sickly yellow. Shrieks of rage spewed from their powerful jaws as they charged toward the three intruders. As they ran, their two powerful hind legs pumped hard against the stone beneath them, causing their wicked-looking claws to create the clicking sound that had signaled their presence.

Jeffrey and Jerome, overcome with fear, watched in horror as the creatures closed the gap. Suddenly, a flash of blue streaked through the air and struck the animal that was in the lead, sending it crashing to the floor and tripping up one of the others. The sound and flash of Goliath's weapon broke the spell of fear that had been binding Jerome and Jeffrey. Frantically searching the area for inspiration, Jeffrey's eyes fell upon the floating platform. "Jerome, jump onto the platform!" he yelled as he dropped his levitation devices onto the steps.

Taking in a shuddering breath in an attempt to steady his out-of-control heart rate, Jerome followed Jeffrey's instructions and leapt, his own devices falling forgotten from his grasp. The men landed on the platform at nearly the same instant. Their momentum caused the device to slide sideways just as two of the remaining four animals reached them. As the platform glided away from the pedestal, the creatures snapped out at them, their jaws coming within inches of Jerome's legs, which were still dangling slightly over the edge. Skidding on the stone floor, the dinosaurs quickly changed direction and headed toward their escaping prey.

Meanwhile, Goliath, who had taken out the first dinosaur with his laser pistol, switched targets and sent several shots toward another one of the creatures. After missing twice, his third blast connected and the beast fell forward, sliding to a halt just feet in front of him. The last dinosaur, somehow sensing the presence of the giant, turned and headed straight for him. Immediately, he dove to his right, narrowly avoiding the razor-sharp claws of the charging beast.

Goliath turned his dive into a roll and rose up on one knee just as the animal lunged toward him. Firing his weapon, he wounded it in the shoulder. It howled in pain but pressed the attack, jaws snapping wildly. Raising his arm to ward off the blow, the armored giant brought his weapon around and prepared to pull the trigger at point blank.

However, just as he was about to fire, one of the creature's flailing front limbs connected with his right arm. The force of the contact sent the gun flying from his hand. Searing pain shot through his left forearm, nearly rendering him unconscious. To his horror, his armor's cloaking unit malfunctioned, causing him to become visible. The animal's large, green eye stared at him viciously, its reptilian face inches from his own as it once again clamped its jaws down firmly on his left forearm.

At the appearance of the dinosaurs, Rebecca, Dr. Eisenberg, Mack, and Lisa jumped in fear and surprise. "I knew it! Oh, why did I have to be right this time!" Mack said, mostly to himself as he retreated away from the double doors and back into the library.

"Oh, Lord," Dr. Eisenberg said softly, his voice revealing his dread. "Those are deinonychus* dinosaurs. They'll tear Jeffrey and Jerome apart!"

"The crashing of the stone must have awakened them. We have to figure out a way to help," Lisa said, her mind searching frantically for

---

* Pronunciation: \ die-NON-ick-us

a solution even as her eyes looked around for something to use as a weapon.

As Rebecca watched the first dinosaur fall to the ground and trip up the second, an idea sprang into her mind. Without fully thinking through her plan, she pushed open the door and sprinted into the central chamber. So focused was she on her target that her mind barely registered Dr. Eisenberg's voice calling her. Reaching the stage, she began waving her arms and yelling at the dinosaurs. However, she failed to capture the attention of any of the charging creatures, causing her heart to fill with despair. "No…no…!" she cried out softly as the animals drew closer to Jeffrey and Jerome.

Then, as the two men jumped to safety on the floating platform, renewed hope surged within her. Suddenly, movement off to her left drew her back to the precariousness of her own situation. The deinonychus that had tripped over the fallen leader had risen once again to its feet and had begun eyeing Rebecca hungrily. Backing away slowly, she fought for control of her shaking limbs. *C'mon, you blasted lizard. I've got a surprise for you!* she thought angrily as she reached the back wall of the platform.

The dinosaur's head tracked her every movement as it edged closer. Reaching the bottom of the stairs, it leapt up to the platform and began charging straight toward her. Gauging the distance between her and her attacker, she waited until it was fully committed to its charge. Then, in one swift movement, Rebecca grabbed the thick curtain that hung at the back of the stage and yanked on it with all of her might. The rod holding it in place slipped out of its bracket and crashed down. As it fell, Rebecca reversed direction and dove to her right just as the ferocious animal ran headlong into the fabric. Unable to slow its pace, the beast crashed heavily into the back wall. Wounded by the impact, the frustrated animal swung its claws wildly in an attempt to snag its prey. As she crawled out from under the edge of the curtain, Rebecca let out a cry as razor-sharp talons slashed across her left leg.

The disoriented creature flailed about as it tried to extricate itself from the inhibiting material. Just feet from the enraged dinosaur, Rebecca began dragging herself across the floor as quickly as possible, her leg leaving a trail of blood on the stones. As she inched away from the deadly beast, panic threatened to engulf her as she watched the creature slash the curtain to shreds and extricate itself from the remaining ribbons. Turning its head in her direction, its reptilian tongue flicked in and out rapidly in anticipation of the kill.

Suddenly, a figure rose up behind the animal. Letting out a cry born of adrenaline and fear, Lisa swung at the deinonychus with all her strength, the horns from the altar gripped firmly in her hands. The three-inch-long horns pierced the side of the beast's head, sending it crashing to the floor. Raising her makeshift weapon again, she quickly followed her first stroke with several more until the creature lay unmoving before her.

"Jeffrey, they're coming right at us!" Jerome yelled.

"We need more altitude!" Jeffrey said as he frantically began searching the edges of the anti-gravity platform for the control panel. Finding it, he hurriedly pressed the button for ascent and the platform began to rise. Seeing their prey escaping, the two dinosaurs leapt toward them. The first animal merely scraped the edge with its wicked claws. The second, however, managed to momentarily catch the corner of the platform, causing it to tilt precariously. Jerome fell flat on his stomach and managed to grab onto the edge. However, due to his position near the controls, Jeffrey lost his balance and nearly fell off of the platform. At the last second, he managed to stop his fall by grabbing onto Jerome's ankle. Below, the hungry creatures continued to leap up at them, nearly snagging Jeffrey's legs, which now dangled over the edge.

As quickly as he dared, Jeffrey pulled himself back onto the platform. Breathing heavily, the two men lay still for several seconds without moving. Then, from above, they heard several shouts and commands. Looking up, their hearts constricted inside their chests.

"Uh-oh," Jerome said, his resolve beginning to erode. "It looks like the gig is up. They've seen us. Now what do we do?"

Looking back down at the floor, now twenty feet below them, Jeffrey grabbed Jerome's shoulder. "We have to get to Goliath's gun."

"But how? It's too far away," Jerome pointed out.

"Wait! I've got an idea," Jeffrey said as inspiration struck. Grabbing the controls, he pressed the button once again, causing the platform to rise. As the slanted ceiling drew rapidly closer, a look of uncertainty crossed Jerome's features.

"Uh…Jeffrey, what are you doing?"

"We need to get back over toward the pedestal," he replied. "Get ready to push off from the wall. Wait…wait…NOW!"

Together, they shoved against the wall, causing the platform to begin sliding back toward the center of the chamber. Grabbing the controls, Jeffrey pressed the opposite button. A second later, the platform plummeted toward the floor.

Goliath howled in rage as the dinosaur's teeth dug deeply into the flesh of his arm. Then, to his surprise, the creature let go. But before the giant could recover, one of its massive legs shoved him down onto his back, knocking the wind out of him. In an instant, the creature pounced on top him, its 170-pound bulk pinning him to the floor.

Using its lengthy tail as a counterweight, the deinonychus balanced on one leg and began slashing at Goliath's chest with the five-inch claw that protruded from the animal's second toe. Knowing his armor wouldn't protect him from the claw for long, Goliath extended the knife-sized blade hidden inside a sheath in the armor on his right arm. Reaching up, he plunged the blade deep into balancing leg of the beast and twisted his body to the side. The animal wailed and fell to the ground with a thud. Jumping to his feet, Goliath attacked the creature as it tried to recover. With several quick thrusts of his knife, he ended its life.

Letting out a feral howl of victory, Goliath scanned the area to assess the situation. The two dinosaurs pursuing Jeffrey and Jerome lost interest in their out-of-reach quarry and turned their attention toward him. Seeing his gun lying a dozen feet away, he sprinted toward it as the animals began their charge. Realizing he wouldn't reach the weapon in time, he changed course and headed straight towards the creatures, a battle cry bursting from his lips as he raised his blade in challenge. The giant collided with the foremost of the two dinosaurs with a bone-shattering crunch. Had Goliath been a normal human, he may never have survived the encounter. However, because of his armor and size, he was merely stunned momentarily. His foe, on the other hand, lay dead at his feet, both from the impact and from the six-inch knife wound in its neck.

As Goliath began to rise after the collision, he was thrown face first back down on the ground by the last deinonychus. Weak and helpless, he shrieked in frustration and pain as the animal's claw tore through the armor on his back and dug into the soft flesh beneath.

A bluish light flared above him and the weight of the creature eased. Turning over, Goliath stared in amazement as Jerome and Jeffrey stood on each side of him. In their hands they held the levitation devices, which they had used to lift the dinosaur. Raising one hand, they tipped the blue force field to the side, causing the animal to lose its balance and crash to the floor.

"Goliath, head towards the laser pistol. We'll walk with you and hold it off," Jeffrey said.

"Hold…it off?" Goliath said in confusion and pain as it yanked off the now-dented helmet. "How?"

Even as the words fell from his lips, the creature lunged at them. Jeffrey and Jerome turned the levitation devices so they were perpendicular to the floor, effectively creating a force field. Climbing to his feet as quickly as his torn and bruised body would allow, Goliath and the two others walked slowly toward the weapon while the enraged animal slashed impotently against the bluish field. Finally retrieving the weapon, Goliath picked it up and ended the creature's life with a single, well-placed shot.

"Hurry; we've got no time to lose!" Jeffrey said even before the animal's body hit the ground. "The builders of the tower have seen us." As he finished his sentence, he noticed the deep gashes in Goliath's left arm that had gone all the way down to the bone. *Bone!* Staring up at Goliath's half-human, half-wolf features, Jeffrey wondered once again what kind of being he was working with. Putting aside his questions for a more appropriate time, he turned back to his friend. "C'mon, Jerome. Let's get this core loaded."

Sprinting over to the pedestal, they quickly reactivated the levitation devices. Within seconds, the core was resting gently on the floating platform. Powering down the levitation field, they placed the devices next to the core and began pushing the platform as fast as they dared. Goliath scooped up his discarded helmet and threw it onto the platform next to the other items as they crossed the floor. Behind them, they could hear the sounds of booted feet approaching the other side of the oversized doors.

Upon reaching the stage area, they found Lisa assisting Rebecca as she tried to walk back toward the double doors being held open by Dr. Eisenberg and Mack. Seeing the gashes on her leg, Jeffrey grabbed Rebecca around the waist and hoisted her onto the floating platform alongside the core. At the same time, Goliath tore the armor off of his wounded left forearm, then used several pieces of the shredded curtain as a bandage. Within moments, the group was back inside the library.

As Dr. Eisenberg and Mack closed the double doors behind them, they saw the main entrance doors on the other side of the chamber begin to open. Spurred on by the nearness of their pursuers, they quickly fled out of the library and into the hall.

"They must not know what entrance we came in through," Goliath stated as they ran down the hall. "If we can get out fast enough, we may yet make it. Is there any way Akwen can fly over here to pick us up?"

Before Jeffrey could answer, a door to the right opened up. Goliath's backhand sent the startled priest who emerged from the door into the wall before he even knew what hit him. As they arrived at the entrance to the sacrifice preparation room, they could hear more and more cries coming from the passage behind them. Several doors in the hallway opened as curious bystanders sought the cause of all of the commotion. As their eyes fell upon the intruders, the doors were slammed immediately and even more shouts were raised.

Flinging open the door leading into the preparation room, Jeffrey waited while the others rushed inside, their hearts pounding wildly from adrenaline and terror. Shutting the door behind them, he responded to Goliath's question as they crossed into the outermost room. "No. If Akwen starts up the pyramid, it'll jump automatically. We have to find a way to—"

The words never made it out of Jeffrey's mouth. At that moment, Goliath opened the door leading out of the tower. Awaiting them were at least fifty heavily armed men deployed in a semi-circle around the door, their eyes reflecting clearly their murderous intent.

29

NIMROD

"QUICKLY, BACK THE other way!" Jeffrey called out once he had recovered his ability to speak.

"No," Goliath said as he grabbed his arm. "They'll have all the exits blocked by now. We may have lost, but I for one will not go down without a fight."

Striding boldly through the entrance, the giant glared at each of the warriors surrounding him, daring them to attack. Standing in the doorway, Jeffrey and the others could see that the sight of the wolf-like giant caused the warriors to shift uneasily where they stood. Stopping in the center of the semi-circle, Goliath assumed a battle-ready posture and snarled a challenge. "Who is man enough to fight me?"

Although the warriors couldn't understand his words, the meaning was clear. Several of the men exchanged glances, but none broke rank to enter the circle.

As Rebecca and the others watched the drama unfold, they began hearing the sounds of other warriors moving ever closer to the room in which they stood.

Glancing over his shoulder, Jeffrey said, "They'll be on us shortly.

Let's get out of here. I'd rather have the tower at my back than armed men."

Swallowing hard, the others reluctantly agreed. Moving through the doorway, they left the room. Keeping their backs to the outer wall, they formed a line with the floating platform in the center. Before long, several warriors appeared at the door they had just vacated. Trapped, the companions could do nothing but watch as Goliath turned slowly in circles, daring someone to challenge him.

Suddenly, a shadow fell upon the grassy plain where Jeffrey and the others were standing. Looking up, they watched as a circular platform similar to the one upon which the core now rested floated down toward the ground, near the apex of the half-circle of warriors. Unlike the other floating platforms, however, this one was much larger, and could move horizontally. Standing on the hovering disk and holding onto the railing were two tall men. Based on the flowing purple robe he wore, the one in back appeared to be a priest of some sort. The other, however, was clearly a warrior.

As they watched the second man leap over the edge of the platform and drop the remaining five feet to the ground, it was evident that this was no ordinary warrior. Rising to his full, seven-foot height, he began walking fearlessly toward the giant. Encircling his thick, lower body was a blood-red skirt trimmed in gold that fell to just above his knees. His broad, bare chest rippled with finely toned muscles, and his skin was bronze. A beautiful crystal medallion, nearly four inches in diameter, hung from a necklace of highly polished silver; its multiple facets gleamed in spite of the ever-darkening sky. The face that glared menacingly at the would-be thieves seemed as if it had been chiseled out of granite. A dark, well-trimmed mustache and beard complemented the hard, black eyes. His head was completely shaved except for a long tail of jet-black hair that fell from the back of his scalp down to the middle of his back. Wrist gauntlets and earrings of gold stood out in sharp contrast to the flowing white cape draped over his left shoulder.

At the sight of their champion, the warriors surrounding the intruders stood erect, their faces reflecting a mixture of pride and fear. Stopping not more than ten feet from Goliath, the mighty warrior's left hand rested comfortably on the jewel-encrusted pommel of a four-foot sword strapped to his side.

Although he was nearly a head taller than the man, Goliath was nevertheless impressed by the confidence exuded by the challenger. Here indeed was a foe that could possibly best him. The thought was exhilarating.

Smiling in anticipation of the coming duel, the champion barked out a command to one of the nearby warriors. Immediately, the warrior tossed his sword toward Goliath. As the giant retrieved the offered weapon, the burly man drew his own magnificent sword.

Under other circumstances, Goliath would have welcomed the fight. However, he knew his skill at sword fighting would be no match for this obviously seasoned warrior. Deciding that cheating was better than death, he quickly switched the sword into his left hand, drew his laser pistol, and fired.

Although surprised by the beam of energy that shot out of the weapon, the warrior still managed to dodge swiftly to the left, causing the beam to sail past him and strike one of the warriors behind him. Recovering quickly, he pointed the tip of his sword toward Goliath. Laughing inwardly at the man's apparent stupidity, Goliath prepared to fire again.

But before his finger could pull the trigger, the champion's thumb pressed against a small indentation on the hilt of the sword. A bolt of energy flashed across the sword blade and struck Goliath full force in the chest. For a split second, the giant wobbled unsteadily on his feet as he fought to maintain his balance. Then, losing his battle to remain conscious, he pitched forward, face first onto the ground.

Rebecca and Lisa gasped as Goliath fell. Next to them, Mack began to weep noiselessly, his fear of what fate would befall them finally overtaking his emotions. Placing his sword back in its sheath, the mighty leader motioned for the warriors nearest the tower to bring the prisoners to him. Forcing Rebecca to stand, they took the hovering platform containing the core and pushed it over toward their leader. Realizing that resistance would be futile, the prisoners allowed the men to lead them forward. Seconds later, they found themselves standing single file facing the enormous man. Behind them, warriors stood with swords at the ready, waiting to cut them down should they attempt to escape.

Moving down the line, the mighty warrior studied each of them in turn. Lowering her head, Rebecca began to pray quietly, hot tears spilling down her cheeks and falling onto the soft grass. As he neared Dr. Eisenberg, the leader stopped. Looking down intently at the older man, the giant warrior's expression changed to one of confusion as he spoke.

Not understanding his words, Dr. Eisenberg looked nervously at Mack, who was still crying softly. "Mack, what did he say? Please, don't give up on us. We need you. What did he say?"

Raising his head, he responded. "I…I think he asked something about…about your age. 'How old are you?' I think."

Puzzled by the question, Dr. Eisenberg looked back at the man, whose own expression of confusion had increased as they conversed. "Tell him that I'm fifty-eight years old, and make sure you refer to him as 'Mighty One' or 'Great One' to show deference."

Mack nodded nervously. "I'll…I'll try, but what if I mess it up? I'm still very new at this language."

"Just do your best, Mack," Rebecca said, forcing a smile. "We know you can do it."

Struggling to form the unfamiliar words, Mack relayed the message. Anger flared in the man's eyes. Grabbing Dr. Eisenberg by the collar, he lifted him off of the ground. Staring at the frightened doctor, he asked another question, the words sounding harsh and commanding.

Startled by the man's reaction, Mack paused before translating. "He…he wants to know why you are…playing games by speaking in code. He says, 'The Mighty Nimrod commands you to speak to him personally.'"

"Tell him you're the only one who can speak his language," Jeffrey said rapidly.

His mouth having gone dry, Mack's voice was weak and scratchy. As soon as he finished speaking, Nimrod dropped Dr. Eisenberg back to the ground and walked over to stand in front of Mack. Shrinking back from the man's intense gaze, Mack began to shake uncontrollably. Looking up at the warriors standing behind them, Nimrod called out another command. Suddenly, Jeffrey and the others felt rough hands grabbing them from behind and hauling them toward the tower. A moment later, their hands were tied behind them and they were forced to kneel with their backs to the wall. Next to them, several warriors propped the still-comatose form of Goliath against the tower as well. Satisfied the prisoners were securely bound, the rest of Nimrod's warriors backed away to reform the semi-circle.

"What…what did you say to him?" Jerome asked, panic causing the pitch of his voice to rise an octave higher than normal. Off in the distance, the rumble of thunder could be heard as dark clouds continued to roll over the horizon.

Rebecca's head snapped up. "Don't you get it? This is Nimrod, the builder of the mighty Tower of Babel. Only we've arrived *before* God confused their speech. At this time, the whole world still has the same language! They don't even understand the *concept* of other languages."

Now that she had begun speaking, the words continued to tumble out as more and more pieces fell into place. "And look around you. No one here appears over the age of forty. That's because they were all born after Noah's Flood. The oldest one is less than one hundred years old. But the average lifespan at this time was still in the multiple hundreds of years. Noah and his three sons would be the only men alive at this time who would appear as old as Doc."

Shaking his head in denial, Jeffrey replied, "That can't be true. The Tower of Babel is just a myth!"

Incredulous, Rebecca stared back her husband. Beside her, Lisa began to weep. "Jeffrey, when are you going to wake up and accept the truth?" Rebecca asked in frustration. "The Bible's history is true. You are living in it right now!"

Nimrod, who had been watching their conversation with interest, suddenly grew tired of waiting. Grabbing Mack, he hauled him to his feet. Rebecca and the others ceased talking and focused instead on Nimrod, knowing their very lives hung in the balance. For several minutes, Nimrod interrogated Mack. The language specialist grew increasingly frantic with each passing second. At last, Nimrod backhanded him and sent him sprawling into the grass, causing Lisa and Rebecca to gasp.

As Nimrod picked Mack up off of the ground, Jeffrey felt Goliath begin to stir next to him. Just as the giant opened his eyes, several of Nimrod's warriors were forcing all of them to stand and face the wall of the tower.

"Jeffrey, what's going on?" Lisa said through her tears. "Oh God, I don't want to die!"

"It'll be okay, Lisa," Jeffrey said, the quavering in his voice making a mockery of his attempt at reassurance. "It'll be over soon."

"No, it won't," Rebecca said softly. "It will just begin." Turning toward her friend, Rebecca felt unexplainable peace wash over her. "Lisa, listen to me. Death is not the end. We will all live on after this life. The only question is: Where will you spend that eternity?"

"NO! Please!" they heard Mack yell. Glancing over their shoulders, they saw Nimrod smile sadistically as he turned his back on them.

"Mack, are you okay? What's going on?" Jeffrey called out.

Then they heard Nimrod calling out orders to his men. A moment later, the warriors began jostling Rebecca and the others around—rearranging the order in which they stood.

"Nimrod keeps asking me why we tried to steal the core," Mack cried in anguish. "I told him the truth, but he doesn't believe me! He...he says that if I don't tell him where we came from, he...he will...randomly kill one of you every minute. Oh Jeffrey, Doc, I'm sorry! I tried...I tried..." Sobbing, Mack fell to the ground.

Behind them, they could hear Nimrod yelling at Mack in his strange language. After a few moments of pleading from Mack, they heard the unmistakable sound of a sword being drawn from its sheath.

"Lisa, Jeffrey—all of you—please listen," Rebecca said, her voice filled with urgency. "God sent His Son to die for all of us. All we have to do is believe in Him, and we will be forgiven."

In a barely audible whisper, she heard Jeffrey say, "Not me. He couldn't forgive me. Not after what I've done."

A solitary tear slid down Rebecca's cheek as her heart broke for her husband. What had Jeffrey done that was so terrible he felt he could never be forgiven? "Believe in Jesus now, and you'll be guaranteed eternal li—"

Her words were cut off by the sound of metal striking stone. Afraid of what they would see, yet unable to keep from looking, they turned toward the source of the sound. With a perverse sense of pleasure, Nimrod had walked up and down the line of prisoners, stopped at random, and thrust his sword behind him. The blade struck the stone inches from Lisa's head, causing her to cry out.

Pulling the sword back in front of him, Nimrod walked the line once more. As he neared Dr. Eisenberg, the warrior stopped and yelled toward Mack. Fearing for the doctor, Rebecca turned to look at him. As she stared into his eyes, he smiled back at her, his face full of peace. "My dear Rebecca, I believe." Suddenly, the professor's eyes grew wide with pain as the sword bit deep into his flesh.

30

BABEL

"NOOOO!" REBECCA SCREAMED as Dr. Eisenberg's body slumped against the wall.

Letting out a cruel laugh, Nimrod pulled the sword free and looked with satisfaction at the blood-stained blade. Rebecca tried to kneel down next to the doctor, but was dragged back to her feet by two of the warriors. Through a cloud of tears, she looked over toward the others. Jerome swooned, and appeared about to collapse. Next to him, Lisa wept uncontrollably while Jeffrey stood rigid, his anger twisting his features until he was barely recognizable.

Judging by the sounds behind her, it appeared that Nimrod had given up on interrogating his captive. Large raindrops began to fall around them, quickly soaking their clothing. Thunder echoed loudly off of the tower walls as lightning flashed across the sky. Frustrated that his warped game would be cut short by the worsening weather conditions, Nimrod simply turned to face the thieves. Walking over to stand behind Goliath, he lifted his sword and prepared to mete out justice.

Suddenly, a bolt of lightning struck the tower, sending debris and workers flying in every direction. The warriors standing nearby stared nervously at the black clouds above them as the winds began to pick up.

Then, slowly at first, like a train building up momentum, the cries began. For the rest of her life, Rebecca would never forget the sheer terror and dread carried in those voices. A great cacophony of noise began to grow louder as men called out to one another. At first, Rebecca could not understand the source of their distress. Then, with a force that nearly knocked her off of her feet, the answer hit her: "Listen! They're all speaking in different languages!"

The warriors, hearing the strange sounds coming from the mouths of the workers, began calling out to one another. Within moments, confusion and panic spread throughout the construction site as the torrential rains continued to pour down. In an attempt to restore order, Nimrod began calling out orders to the warriors closest to him. However, at the sound of the words coming out of his own mouth, fear seized his heart.

The moment Nimrod turned away, Goliath sliced through the ropes binding his hands with his hidden knife. Turning toward Jeffrey, he freed him with a swift slash of his blade. Handing the knife to Jeffrey, he said, "Free the others, then grab the core. GO!"

Letting out a snarl of rage, Goliath charged at Nimrod and tackled him to the ground. Caught completely off guard, Nimrod lost his hold on the sword as he fell face down onto the rain-soaked earth.

Grabbing Jerome's wrists, Jeffrey cut his bonds. "Find the cart with the core while I see to the others."

Turning around, Jerome nodded, then ran off into the rain.

"Jeffrey, hurry!" Lisa cried out and she looked over her shoulder at him. She caught sight of three figures running toward them, daggers raised. "Look out behind you!" Lisa screamed.

Spinning around, Jeffrey barely had time to dive out of the way as three of the tower priests charged at him. Startled by the sudden attack,

Jeffrey rolled onto his back just as one of the men leapt down at him. Grabbing the priest's arms to stop the killing thrust, Jeffrey wrestled for control of the dagger.

As they fought, Jeffrey could hear Lisa and Rebecca scream. He knew he had to end this confrontation quickly or he might be too late to save them. Keeping the dagger at bay with his right arm, Jeffrey reached out with his left and grabbed a small piece of the tower that had broken free from the lightning strike. With all the strength he could muster, he slammed the rock into the priest's temple, rendering him unconscious.

Shoving the body off of him, Jeffrey jumped to his feet. Looking toward where the two women had been moments before, he felt his heart sink. Both Rebecca and Lisa were being dragged away in opposite directions by the two priests: Rebecca to the south, and Lisa to the north.

Struggling against the priest, yet fearful of the cold blade being pressed against her throat, Rebecca watched with excitement as Jeffrey defeated the third priest. However, as he leapt to his feet, her world seemed to slow down as her heart shattered and died. After his brief moment of indecision, Jeffrey turned away from her and ran to rescue Lisa.

With a dreadful certainty, Rebecca understood. She understood why Lisa had reacted so oddly when Rebecca had first arrived at the dig site. She understood why Lisa seemed to avoid looking her in the eye. She understood why Lisa had apologized as they walked in the hallway of the tower. She understood why Jeffrey wanted a divorce. It was so that *they* could be together.

The will to live sucked out of her, Rebecca ceased struggling against the priest. A paralyzing numbness set in to the point that she didn't even realize what was happening around her. She wouldn't have been surprised to see a trail of blood flow from the emotional wound in her heart down onto the ground to mix with the rain. The shock was so severe it didn't even register in her mind that the priest had released her, or that Mack was standing next to her, a bloody brick in his hand.

To her, the intensity of the betrayal had opened up a bottomless chasm that was pulling her down...

Fury and rage fueled Goliath's already considerable strength as he pounded Nimrod's face into the soggy earth. Grabbing the warrior's mane of hair, Goliath wrapped it around his neck and began to pull, causing the man's neck to twist awkwardly to the side as his back arched painfully.

Goliath felt the sting of a knife burying itself in his left calf. Letting out a howl of pain and anger, he turned to see that Nimrod had pulled a small dagger out of his leg sheath and was preparing to jab it once again into Goliath's body. Reaching out with his injured left arm, the giant grabbed the hand with the dagger. However, the maneuver caused his weight to shift slightly toward that side. Taking advantage of the momentary imbalance, Nimrod pushed on the ground and sent Goliath tumbling off of his back.

The combatants jumped to their feet and faced off, each one's features reflecting both rage and admiration for his opponent. With light-ning-quick reflexes, Nimrod slashed out with the dagger, striking the edge of the armor plating that covered Goliath's torso. Thankful once again for the protective suit, Goliath counter-attacked. Punching at the hand holding the knife, his fist connected solidly, causing Nimrod to lose his hold on the weapon. Lightning reflected off of the whirling metal as the blade went flying into the rain.

Now weaponless, Nimrod unleashed a series of blows with his pow-erful fists. Backpedaling, Goliath went on the defensive. However, with his wounded left arm, he was forced to use his right to deflect the blows, leaving him no opportunity for attack. Then, without warning, Nimrod

crouched down and swept his left leg out in front of him, knocking
Goliath off of his feet.

Although the giant was taken by surprise, he recovered quickly.
Before the warrior could carry out a follow-up attack, Goliath rolled
to the side, removing himself from Nimrod's reach. Climbing to his
feet, the giant spotted one of the slave master's whips lying in the grass.
Snatching it up, he cracked it several times at the approaching warrior,
sending him reeling back in pain.

Wounded, Nimrod stumbled into a pile of bricks. Grabbing one
in each hand, he began hurling them at his attacker with all of his considerable strength. Goliath dodged the deadly projectiles as his mind
frantically searched for a means to end the confrontation. Eyes locking
onto one of the small, hovering platforms near the bricks, he smiled
wickedly.

Using his protected right arm as a shield for his head, Goliath
charged. Nimrod, abandoning the bricks, sidestepped the attack and
kicked out with his leg. Anticipating the move, Goliath deflected it with
his right arm while throwing a punch with his left. The blow landed
squarely on the warrior's face, shattering his nose. Ignoring the pain and
blood, Nimrod feigned a punch with his right hand, then brought his
left around and dealt a glancing blow to Goliath's temple.

His own face now bloodied and battered, Goliath snarled viciously.
Summoning all of his strength, he backhanded the warrior, the dented
armor on his right arm digging deeply into Nimrod's chin. Dazed,
Nimrod fell back onto the pile of construction materials. Snatching up
one of the bricks, Goliath landed another blow on the man's head, further rendering him senseless. Using the whip, Goliath wrapped one end
around his opponent's throat, then rapidly tied the other end to the
handle of the levitating cart. Just as Nimrod began to recover, Goliath
grinned cruelly and pressed the button on the controls. Nimrod's face
contorted in rage as the device began to rise. Clutching at the whip
around his throat, his body lifted off of the ground and into the air.

◆

"Becky! I need you to snap out of it! Please, Becky!" Mack said frantically. Getting no response, he forced Rebecca to look at him. "Listen to me. Doc is still alive, but he needs help. We have to get him out of here, but I can't do it myself."

Mack's words gradually penetrated the numbness and despair that gripped her soul. Slowly, the light came back into her eyes. "Doc? Where...where is he?"

Thankful she was beginning to come around, Mack pulled her arm around his shoulder and helped her to her feet. Rebecca winced as the injury in her left leg throbbed once again. Finding another abandoned hover cart, Mack grabbed it and brought it over to where Rebecca stood. Helping her onto it, he pushed it over to the wall where Dr. Eisenberg's body still lay slumped over. Although she felt as if her mind were lost in a fog, Rebecca's concern for her mentor and friend called her back to action. Sliding off of the cart, she knelt by the professor and began searching for the wound.

"Rebecca," he said weakly, his face ashen. "You were right. You were right about everything."

"Shhhh. Don't try to talk," she said as she pulled back the torn clothing. "You've lost a lot of blood, and need to save your strength."

"How bad is it?" Mack asked worriedly.

Dear Jesus, please save him! Rebecca pleaded silently. Turning to Mack, she shook her head. "It's too hard to tell in this darkness. The blade caught him in the side. If we can get him some medical attention right away, he might still make it. Help me get him onto the cart."

Just as they were about to begin lifting, Jeffrey and Lisa came running up. The fresh wound in Rebecca's heart began bleeding anew. "Help...Doc," she choked out as she turned away from them.

Without saying a word, Jeffrey and Lisa reached down and helped Mack lift the doctor onto the cart. Standing weakly to her feet, Rebecca grabbed the edge of the platform and sat down next him, stroking his face as they began to move.

The five companions made their way through the continued chaos around them. By this time, those who had been inside the tower and in the city had left the buildings, and were searching frantically for anyone who could understand them. Gradually, groups began to form as people found others who spoke the same language. Fear of further retribution from God caused many to flee into the surrounding area, leaving the intruders unchallenged.

Several minutes later, they spotted Jerome standing near two hovering items: the circular hovercraft in which Nimrod had been riding, and the cart containing the core. "I thought we could use this to get back to the pyramid," Jerome said, indicating Nimrod's platform. Seeing Dr. Eisenberg's still body, Jerome swallowed hard. "Is…is he…?"

"He's still alive," Jeffrey said numbly. "Help me get him into the vehicle."

As they transferred the doctor into the hovering craft, Goliath limped up to them, Nimrod's sword held firmly in his bloody knuckles. "I took care of Nimrod temporarily. However, it probably won't take him too long to free himself and come after us."

"All the more reason to get out of here as fast as we can," Jeffrey replied.

Using the levitation devices, he and Jerome quickly but carefully lifted the core and placed it next to Dr. Eisenberg while Goliath watched for any sign of trouble. A few seconds later, they had all climbed aboard and were ready to leave. Activating the machine, they moved rapidly over the city and the surrounding grassy plains toward the pyramid. A heavy silence fell upon the group as they traveled; each was lost in his or her own conflicted emotions and thoughts of uncertainty about the future.

31

DOC'S CONCLUSIONS

ONCE THEY LEFT the construction site, Jeffrey contacted Akwen with his commlink and brought her up to speed on the situation. By the time they arrived back at the pyramid, she had the medical kit, water, and clean rags ready and waiting in the room the women had been using as a bedroom. The moment they landed, Jeffrey and Jerome jumped out of the floating platform and activated the levitation devices. Goliath and Mack then carefully lifted the doctor and laid him onto the blue force field. Since Lisa had the most medical training, and since she was uninjured herself, the group had decided she would be the one to clean and dress Doc's wound while Mack assisted her. So as the others worked, Lisa and Mack ran into the pyramid to clean up in preparation to receive their patient.

With Dr. Eisenberg secured on the makeshift gurney, Jeffrey and Jerome headed as quickly as they dared into the pyramid. After settling the doctor onto one of the beds, the two men returned to the circular platform to retrieve the core. Within minutes, the core was loaded safely into the vessel.

Rebecca, left by herself, hobbled into the pyramid. Finding a med kit, she made her way into Mack's room and began to bandage her wounded leg. As she worked in solitude, the weight of recent events began to crush her. Tears started to fall, slowly at first. Then, as if a dam had burst within her, she sobbed uncontrollably; her shoulders heaved as she cried out to God.

"All right, Akwen. We're ready to go. Let's get out of here," Jeffrey said as he reached the top step and entered the control room, wet clothes clinging uncomfortably to his body.

"Shouldn't we install da new core first?" she asked.

Jeffrey shook his head. "There's no time," he said. "Nimrod could decide to chase us. If he attacks while we're switching the cores, we'll have no way to run. Let's just make another short jump with the core we have, and then land someplace safe where we can switch them. Another two hundred years back should do it."

Adjusting the controls, Akwen fired up the engines. Before long, they were in orbit around the earth and the walls of the pyramid returned to normal, indicating they were once again on their way.

"Now go change, den come back and tell me what happened," Akwen said.

"Yeah, that sounds like a plan," Jeffrey said. "I'll be right back."

Several minutes later, he returned, dressed in a dark red T-shirt and another pair of blue jeans. Settling onto a stool next to Akwen, Jeffrey filled her in on the details of their trip. Just as he was finishing, Lisa entered the room, her face lined with weariness and concern. She no longer wore her own coveralls, but had changed once again into the oversized pair loaned to her by Akwen after their encounter with the Mayans.

Dropping into a chair, Lisa faced Jeffrey. "I did everything I could," she said. "He needs a real doctor. Mack and...and Becky are with him now. Jeffrey, I…I don't know if he's going to make it. He's lost so much blood."

Wrapping his arms around her, Jeffrey kissed Lisa's forehead and pulled her to his chest. Secure in his arms, Lisa let all the pent-up emotions and anxiety drain out of her. As she wept, Jeffrey felt his own eyes well up with tears. Akwen, patting Jeffrey gently on the shoulder, left the room, giving the other two the privacy she felt they needed to try to come to terms with recent events.

A few moments after Rebecca arrived in the makeshift hospital room, Mack excused himself and left to change his clothes, leaving her alone to stand vigil over the doctor. For Rebecca, time had no meaning. Between her concern for the doctor and her grief over Jeffrey's betrayal, she couldn't think, she could only feel. And the pain she felt forced her to direct her anger at one person. *God, why? Why are you doing this to me? I thought that once I turned my life over to you, you would make things better for me, not worse. Yet it's because of my belief in you that Jeffrey has turned his back on me. Now I've lost my husband, my best friend, and now it looks like I'll even lose a man who has been like a second father to me. Have I displeased you in some way?*

As her frustration welled up within her, Rebecca's doubts grew. *Maybe I've been deceived this whole time. Maybe there isn't a God. Maybe we did just evolve. I just want things to go back to being the way they used to be. If I tell Jeffrey I was wrong about there being a God, maybe he will…will…*

A slight pressure on her arm roused her from her prayer. Looking down, she saw Dr. Eisenberg's hand resting on her own. A moment later, his eyes fluttered open.

Forcing a smile, she wiped away the tears from her red-rimmed eyes and leaned closer to him. "Hey, Doc. How're you feeling?"

Smiling weakly, he said, "I think it would be safe to say that I have felt better."

Rebecca chuckled lightly before her face reverted to its previous expression of worry. "—Which is why you should rest and not talk."

Dr. Eisenberg shook his head slowly. "If my time on this earth is nearing its end, I don't want to waste it sleeping." Seeing tears form in her eyes, he smiled again. "Don't cry, my dear Rebecca. Not for me. I've lived a long, full life. And I look forward to seeing my sweet Ruth again."

Despite his words, Rebecca couldn't stop the tears that began to fall. "But you're going to make it, Doc," she said. "Please don't give up. The wound isn't that bad. Others have recovered from worse injuries."

The professor's expression transformed into mock indignation. "Don't go picking out flowers for the funeral just yet. I don't plan on simply rolling over and dying. However, if it *is* my time to go, I want you to know that I'm ready. Especially now, thanks to you."

When Rebecca didn't respond, he continued. "You were right, you know. Now that my belief in God is real, so many mysteries of the past are beginning to make sense. I never could find a plausible theory about how all of the ancient civilizations just happened to spring into existence at nearly the same time. Or how it was that the ancient languages were the most complex. Or why later pyramids were inferior to the older ones. Or why there were pyramids or ziggurats all over the world. Or why the Mayans had such an advanced system of measuring time. But now I know."

Placing a finger on his lips, Rebecca leaned closer. "Shhh. Don't talk. You need to rest."

"No, Rebecca. I need to tell you this," he replied stubbornly. "You need to know your faith is not in vain. Never doubt what you have seen. Hold strong, despite the ridicule of others."

Closing his eyes for a moment, the doctor took a deep breath and winced in pain. Opening his eyes once again, he continued. "For too long I believed that we humans evolved slowly over millions of years. But if so, then we would be gradually increasing in intelligence as time progressed. Yet in all the years of my studying, time and again I would find examples of the opposite being true.

"But if we were indeed created by God, then it would make sense that the first humans were *extremely* intelligent. Even after you suggested it, I had a hard time making it fit. After all, if humans were so smart in the past, then why did they lose their technology over time?"

Still greatly concerned for the well-being of the doctor, Rebecca answered simply, hoping he would finish what he wanted to say quickly and go back to sleep. "I don't know."

"Don't you see, Rebecca? The tower explains it."

"I'm sorry, Doc, but I don't follow you," she said, honestly puzzled.

"When God confused the people at Babel, they split into various groups based on the language they spoke. Thus divided, each group headed off into different directions: Some went to Europe, others to Africa, and others to Asia. In fact, if I remember correctly, doesn't the Bible state that the original reason they built the tower is because they didn't want to obey God's command to go abroad into the earth?"

"I believe so, yes," Rebecca replied softly.

After a brief fit of coughing, Dr. Eisenberg continued, his eyes burning with passion despite his weakened condition. "But when they left, they took with them different pieces of knowledge and lore. And initially, they used their knowledge to build the great pyramids and the ziggurats. But over time, as the life spans of men shortened, the knowledge became lost."

Despite her concern for the doctor's health, Rebecca was intrigued by his conclusions. Furthermore, the discussion helped take her mind off of her own personal pain.

"And what's more," Doc continued, "the tower also explains why we see so many different people groups on the earth. Once they were separated, each of the groups that spoke the same language no doubt began inter-breeding. After a while, natural selection weeded out those traits that were not best suited for the new environments in which the people now found themselves. The genetic variation within their DNA became more and more specialized because the population was now isolated, similar to how a breeder of dogs mates certain dogs together to make a desired trait become prominent. This makes perfect sense, considering that modern genetic science has proven there's really only one 'human race.' The term 'race' is merely a social idea."

"Doc, please, you really need to rest. You shouldn't get yourself so worked up," Rebecca pleaded.

Closing his eyes, the professor nodded. "Yes, I suppose you're right." Looking up at her again, he grabbed her hand in his. "Only one more thing."

Rebecca looked down at him adoringly. "You just can't shut your mind off, can you? Even if your body is screaming at you for rest."

He simply grinned. "That's one of my more delightful qualities. While I'm resting, I want you to research the Table of Nations in the Bible. It's found in the book of Genesis near the account of the Tower of Babel, I believe. It shows which of Noah's descendants founded what nations around the world. I never put two and two together until I saw the effects of Babel firsthand. But if I'm right, you'll find that it matches actual historical and genealogical records from other non-biblical sources."

"Okay, Doc. I'll check it out. Now get some rest," Rebecca said.

"Yes, Nurse," he replied. "By the way, we did get the core, didn't we?"

"Yes."

"Good," he said with a sigh. "And Jeffrey and the others are okay?"

At the mention of her husband's name, Rebecca looked away from the doctor as tears began to fall again.

Seeing the look of grief in her eyes, Dr. Eisenberg squeezed her hand gently. "Tell me—
What happened, Rebecca?"

After several seconds, she was able to control her emotions enough to explain. "What is there to tell? When I needed him the most, he chose to rescue Lisa instead. She means more to him now than I do. I've been replaced."

Dr. Eisenberg looked up at her, his own expression filled with sorrow. "Dear Rebecca, I'm so sorry you had to find out like that. This is all my fault. I knew I should've told you earlier, but Jeffrey asked me not to. I never should've brought you into all of this."

"Why *did* you ask for me to be your assistant?" she asked. "Especially since you *knew* Jeffrey and Lisa were having an affair."

"That is precisely *why* I wanted you to come," he stated. "I felt it would be better for you to hear it straight from Jeffrey. I thought the way he was treating you was wrong, and I wanted to force him to face up to the consequences of his actions. And, I thought there might even be a chance that by having you around, he would see what a wonderful woman you are and realize that he was making an enormous mistake."

Rebecca smiled feebly at his words. "Thank you, Doc."

"You're most welcome, my dear," he replied. "Rebecca, don't beat yourself up over this. It wasn't your fault. Jeffrey has made his own choices, just as you have made yours. Stick to your convictions. Promise me that no matter what happens, you will remember what I said."

Suddenly, a voice echoed in her head, the memory distinct and vivid. *Always remember what you learned during your time on Ka'esch. Keep it in the forefront of your mind so that your faith will not waver during the difficult times that lie ahead.*

Feeling as if a bucket of ice-cold water had been thrown in her face, she sat bolt upright. With a clarity that shocked her, she now understood that *this* was the "difficult time" to which Sikaris, the angel she had encountered on Ka'esch, had referred. Although her current emotional state had caused her to begin doubting the truth, it would be her knowledge and experience that would keep her faith from wavering. *Forgive me, Lord,* she prayed. *How could I doubt, after all I've learned and seen? How could I question you? I don't know why you've allowed things to happen like this, but I know that you will see me through it. Some have called*

religion a crutch. Well, maybe it is. But when you live in a broken world,
you need a crutch. Without it, you are left with only hopelessness and despair.
Lord, it hurts so much. I want to hurt them back for what they have done.
Yet I know you would have me forgive. Help me, Lord. I can't do it on my
own. Help me to forgive…

Looking back down at her friend with new tears in her eyes, she
answered softly, "I will, Doc. I will."

32

STRANDED

"ALL I'M SAYING is, doesn't it make you a little nervous that he's walking around with a massive sword that can shoot lightning out of the tip?" Jerome said to Jeffrey as the two men stood near the central shaft in the control room.

"I don't think there's anything we can do about it right now," Jeffrey countered. "Besides, that sword may come in handy yet."

"Yeah, well I'm just glad I happened to pick up his laser pistol back at the tower. At least now we still have a bargaining chip if things get ugly," Jerome replied.

Akwen, seated at the control board, suddenly swore violently. "Something's wrong," she said.

"What do you mean, 'something's wrong'?" Jeffrey replied, and he and Jerome strode over to stand behind her and Lisa.

Anxiously staring at the readouts in front of her, she responded. "Da engines have begun to slow down, but we are not even halfway trough our programmed jump."

"Is it because the core is damaged?" Lisa asked, Akwen's concern beginning to infect her as well.

"No, I don't tink so," Akwen said. "Elmer, plug into da computer and see if you can figure out what it is."

The droid responded immediately to the command. Within seconds, it swiveled its head toward them and reported. "The virus that had been controlling the ship on previous jumps has taken over once again. The premature termination of our programmed jump has put an undue strain on the damaged core."

"What does that mean?" Jeffrey asked, not at all happy about the droid's prognosis.

Suddenly, the walls began to lighten, while the pyramid and its occupants began to become translucent.

"How can we be fading now?" Jerome asked in fright. "The engines are still running!"

"What's going on?" Goliath said as he leapt up the last few steps. "I thought we weren't due to arrive for at least another half hour!" Following on his heels was Mack, his face gripped by fear.

"We're just trying to figure that..." Jeffrey began. Before he could finish his sentence, the walls became completely transparent, giving the onlookers a view of the earth below. They all froze in place, transfixed by what they saw. As the engines continued to slow down, they watched the orb below change as they traveled through time. Because of the movement of the clouds and sun, the overall effect was disorienting. They continued to watch in wonder and horror.

Initially, the earth seemed similar to what they had observed on their previous jump. Massive banks of clouds covered large portions of the planet. Then it all began to change. The portions of land that were visible began to shrink as the waters surrounding them rose higher and higher. Within seconds, the entire globe was covered with water.

The engines slowed further, causing the changes on the earth to slow proportionally. All at once, several large lines appeared over the water.

"Good Lord, what are those?" Jerome asked.

"They look like...like huge geysers," Jeffrey speculated.

"But they're splitting up the earth like a huge jigsaw puzzle!" Mack stated.

Before anyone else could comment further, the land began appearing again. However, as the water receded, the landmass that began to take shape was unrecognizable. In sync with the water, the clouds also shrank, giving a clearer view of the surface. Then several things happened at once. As the engines came to a complete stop, the geysers disappeared, as did the dark clouds. The world that remained sparkled like the purest blue sapphire. Beneath the modest cloud cover, an enormous, green, C-shaped super-continent stretched across the globe with smatterings of islands on each side. From their vantage point, they could see neither ice nor deserts anywhere on the planet.

"Uh…what…what just happened?" Mack asked, his eyebrows knitting together in confusion.

"I'm not sure," Jeffrey said. "But somehow, I don't think the earth below us is anything like the one we know. We need to be prepared for whatever this new dimension has in store for us. Once we land, we'll get that core swapped and get out of here."

Suddenly, the engines began to reverse, sending the vessel and its passengers down towards the center of the strange landmass. Thick vegetation covered almost the entire surface of the continent. Massive trees sprang out of the lush forests. Long, meandering rivers cut through the terrain and huge lakes dotted the landscape. Before long, the travelers found themselves heading straight for an enormous city that loomed out of the jungle.

"Akwen, I don't like the looks of this," Jeffrey called out. "I don't want to end up near any cities. I'm tired of dealing with natives. Can you get us away from here?"

Nodding in agreement, Akwen grabbed the control yoke. "Elmer, try to get me some control. Anyting would be great!"

"Hurry!" Lisa called out as the outline of the city grew larger. Several precious seconds passed in silence as the droid worked.

"Dr. Nancho, I have been able to slice into the program success-fully," Elmer announced. "However, I was only able to free up the lateral controls before the virus shut me out."

"Dat will have to do," Akwen said. Pulling hard on the stick, she moved the pyramid so that it headed south of the city. "We are getting too low. I need to set it down now!"

Locating a small grassy area on a nearby hill about two miles south of the city, Akwen landed the craft. As the beams of white light dissi-pated and the walls returned to normal, the passengers began to relax.

"Man, I swear, if this keeps up, this pyramid is going to send me to an early grave," Mack commented.

As the fresh air entered through the opening above them, he and the others stood motionless. The incredible fragrances that drifted down on them were intoxicating. As they began breathing in the foreign air, their eyes widened in pleasant awe.

"Wow!" Mack called out. "The air is incredible! I feel so...so alive!"

For several seconds, they could do nothing else but stand and breathe. Even the normally stoic giant appeared amazed by the effects of the air.

"What do you think is causing this?" Jerome asked as he took in another deep breath.

"I don't know," Lisa replied. "It almost feels like there's more oxygen in the air."

"Whatever it is, I *like* it," Mack added. "I feel strong enough to pull the ears off of a gundark!"

As they reveled in the new sensation, Rebecca dashed into the room as fast as her wounded leg would carry her.

"Becky, isn't it—" Mack began. However, the moment he saw the expression on her face, his lips froze in mid-sentence.

"Hurry! We have to get out of here. NOW!"

"Why? What's wrong?" Jerome asked.

"Didn't you see it? Don't you realize what's about to happen? It could start at any minute!" Rebecca practically screamed in panic.

"Slow down," Jeffrey said in a reassuring tone. "What did you see?"

Rebecca ignored him and looked directly at Akwen. "How long will it be before the core is recharged?"

As the African woman looked down at her control board, her brows furrowed. "Uh oh...dat's not good."

Alarmed, Jeffrey leaned over her shoulder. "Akwen, don't do this to me. What's wrong now?"

"Oh man, I've got a bad feeling about this," Mack said as he shook his head, his unkempt hair clinging to his face.

"Noting is responding!" Akwen said in frustration. "And I don't just mean dat we have no power. I mean dat da entire system has been shut down."

"All the more reason we need to get the other core installed," Jeffrey said.

Akwen just shook her head. "No, you don't understand. We came out of da jump early, remember? Da damaged core still had power. What I am telling you is dat da virus has shut us down completely. We are stranded."

Silence fell as Jeffrey and the others considered her statement. Finally, Rebecca spoke, her voice laced with fear. "It's worse than you all realize."

"What are you talking about?" Mack asked fearfully. "How could it be worse?"

"You probably wouldn't believe me if I told you. So follow me."

She led the others down the stairs and toward the front of the pyramid. As they reached the entrance, Rebecca pointed to a long rectangular shape resting on a hill several miles away.

Fear seeped into their blood as recognition set in. "It can't be..." Jeffrey whispered.

"Yes, it is," Rebecca confirmed. "It's Noah's Ark."

AFTERWORD

DINOSAURS LIVING WITH humans? Levitation devices? Only one Ice Age? A supernatural origin of languages? An earth that is younger than ten thousand years? You can't really believe this stuff, can you?

I'll admit, when I first heard of some of these theories, I was very skeptical as well. However, part of the problem is that most of us have been raised to believe in evolution. Even cartoons and Hollywood movies are part of the propaganda machine. But the more you delve into the subject of human origins, the more you encounter mystery upon mystery that runs counter to the evolutionary explanation.

I am not specifically referring to information that comes from a religiously motivated source. Plenty of books out there touch on some of these mysteries, yet are from a secular point of view. If you encounter any of these, you may be surprised at how the authors are usually at a loss for how to explain these phenomena.

Whether discussing the Antikythera device, the Great Pyramids, or the Piri Reis map, secular scholars will, at best, usually just say that it is a mystery we don't understand—or, at worst, they will offer up some bizarre explanation attributing these things to aliens or extra-dimensional beings.

But what none will ever suggest is that perhaps these mysteries can be explained by altering our presuppositions. What if humans were highly intelligent in the past? What if evolution is false and we really *were* created? What if the earth really isn't billions of years old? If one allows for the existence of God and takes biblical history at face value, then suddenly the evidence looks very different.

ANTI-GRAVITY

Before I go any further, I want to say a few words about the concept of anti-gravity, or gravity control, as some call it. While I truly believe that the earth is young, that dinosaurs lived with humans, and that the other topics mentioned in this book are true, the existence of anti-gravity is one topic I am neither certain of nor dogmatic about. The arguments I presented in chapter 26 for gravity-control technology are indeed factual, and I believe it is possible that humans could have used this technology to construct many of the massive structures we see around the world. The possibility of gravity control also solves many mysteries of the past, such as the fact that Mayans didn't use wheeled carts, as far as we know, yet they had wheeled toys, or the fact that ancient cultures built pyramids and ziggurats with such massive blocks. However, I don't want anyone to discount any of my other arguments due to the uncertainty of the existence of this technology. As a sci-fi novelist, I chose the theory I felt made for the most interesting story. So I simply ask that you indulge me a little in this area!

CHOOSING A SCIENTIFIC MODEL

The more I study the topic of the origin of life, the more I am struck by the fact that those who promote evolution blur the lines between Operational and Origins science. Creationists and evolutionists have the same evidence. They have the same fossils, the same rock layers, the same animals to examine. The difference lies in the interpretation of the evidence.

Both views try to make sense of the evidence, but since they are dealing with events that happened in the unobservable past, neither view can be scientifically "proven." The only thing we can do is analyze what each view proposes and try to decide for ourselves which view is best. To help explain how to do this, let me quote at length from Dr. John Morris:

> Having completed the formal statement of each model, predictions can now be made. These are not predictions of the future, but instead, predictions about the data. In effect, each adherent must say, "If my assumptions are correct, I predict that when we look at the data, we will see certain features." The model that better predicts the evidence is more likely the correct one, but neither model can be ultimately proved or disproved.

> We evaluate the predictions by looking for internal inconsistencies. Is the model consistent within itself? Does the model need secondary modifications in order to be consistent? Furthermore, does it fit all the data? Are there facts that just do not seem to fit at all? Finally, on a more basic and intuitive level, does the model in question work when applied to science and life? Does it make good common sense, or does it require imaginary components? Can I live with its implications? Does it satisfy my personal need for purpose and hope? Does it lead to a suitable and pragmatic philosophy of life? This process of evaluation allows us to select an appropriate model, one that works in science and in life.[54]

If examined carefully, the theory of evolution makes several predictions that simply do not match reality. Although many books out there detail how these predictions fall short (see my list of suggested resources), I will give just a couple of examples.

LIVING FOSSILS

By its very definition, evolution requires change over time. And we are not just talking about the minor changes we see with animals adapting to environments through natural selection. The changes that evolution *predicts* would occur would be one kind evolving into another over millions of years.

However, what we see in the fossil record is often the opposite. The fact that animals in the fossil record can even be recognized and categorized attests to the fact that animals *don't* change as much as evolutionists require. Furthermore, there are clear examples of animals that remain unchanged for *millions* of years (according to the evolutionists' own timescale). Let me give an example.

The coelacanth is a fish thought to be extinct for seventy million years. Evolutionists *predicted,* based on their model and interpretation of the coelacanth fossils, that they had lungs, a large brain, and four bottom fins about to evolve into legs. They believed it was a connection between fish and reptiles—and students were taught this for years.

In fact, the coelacanth was used as an index fossil, meaning that any rocks containing a fossil of one were dated as at least seventy million years old. However, all that changed in 1938 when a *living* coelacanth was caught deep in the Indian Ocean, northwest of Madagascar! Since then, hundreds of these fish have been caught.

Evolutionists were stunned because the live fish looked exactly like the fossils! Furthermore, in 1987, a German team led by Hans Fricke filmed the coelacanths in their natural environment and discovered that all the evolutionists' predictions were wrong. They didn't use their fins to crawl on the bottom of the ocean, they didn't have lungs, and they didn't have large brains.[55]

Other examples of "living fossils" have been discovered as well. Not only do they clearly show that the evolutionary model does not make accurate predictions, but they also confirm how little information scientists can actually glean from fossils.

THE AGE OF THE EARTH

Another example of how the predictions made by the evolutionary model do not match what we observe in science regards rates of change used to determine the age of the earth. If evolution is true, then the earth MUST be billions of years old. For if the earth is young, then not enough time would pass for mutations to produce the millions of changes necessary for one animal to evolve into another. Therefore, a logical prediction would be that all the rates we can measure would yield ages consistent with that statement. But that simply is not the case.

In chapter 24, Rebecca lists several observed rates of change that support a young earth when calculated using uniformitarian assumptions. Due to story-flow considerations, I chose to only include a few brief examples. However, I would like to include a few more of these here.

As you read the following, keep in mind that the evolutionists' own philosophy of uniformitarianism (which basically means that the rates at which we observe today have been the same throughout history) is being used. So although the ages that are calculated are quite large in terms of a young earth, the method itself is full of assumptions that would quickly reduce those numbers. The point here is that any *one* of these rates should prove that the earth cannot be billions of years old.

Let me give you an analogy that may help you understand this concept.

Imagine that you are walking through the woods and you find an old house that looks to be abandoned. You grow curious and try to guess how long it has been vacant. You begin studying the outside of the house and, based on the type of architecture, you realize the house is typical of houses constructed in the 1920s. Therefore, the MAXIMUM time the house could have been abandoned was less than ninety years ago.

Next, you enter the house and find covers on all of the chairs and dust on the floor. Lining the shelves are books. You search through several and find one that has a publication date of 1960. You now adjust your estimate of when the house was abandoned to less than fifty years ago.

You continue into the kitchen and discover a blender sitting on the counter. You check the make and model, and after doing a quick Internet search, discover that particular model was produced in 1980. You now adjust your estimate to less than thirty years ago.

And so it goes. Any new evidence you find that produces a date younger than a previous bit of evidence must logically cause you to adjust your timescale. Keep that in mind as I present these next points.

EROSION OF THE CONTINENTS

According to the uniformitarian model, the formation of the continents we see today has been in its current configuration for tens of millions of years, and the continents themselves have been around for 3.5 *billion* years. Erosion is slowly cutting into the rocks of the mountains of the continents. The eroded sediments enter the ocean by way of streams and rivers. The rate at which this occurs is 27.5 billion tons of sediment per year.[56]

Scientists have measured the volume of the continents above sea level to be 383 million billion tons. Using the erosion rate that we observe today, and taking into account the movement of the plates due to plate tectonics, every continent on earth would be eroded down to sea level in fourteen million years.[57] Again, this is the *maximum* age, using uniformitarian assumptions.

SEDIMENTS IN THE OCEAN

Considering the amount of sedimentary material entering the ocean each year (27.5 billion tons per year), we can measure how much sediment is currently on the ocean bottom, then calculate how long it would take for it to reach its current level.

It has been determined that there are 410 million *billion* tons of sediment currently on the ocean floor. By simply dividing the numbers, we can determine that it would take a *maximum* of fifteen million years.[58] This, of course, is using uniformitarian assumptions. If the earth is really as old as many say it is, then the oceans ought to be filled with massive amounts of sediments. Here is another prediction that does not fit the evidence.

HELIUM IN THE ATMOSPHERE

Helium forms under the earth's surface and, because it is lightweight and very small, it moves through the pores in rock until it makes its way to the surface. Once there, it mixes with the other gases in the atmosphere. The rate at which helium is added to the atmosphere is an incredible thirteen million helium atoms per square inch each second! Helium also escapes from our atmosphere into space at the theoretical rate of 0.3 million helium per square inch per second. Therefore, it is not difficult to see that helium in the atmosphere is increasing rapidly.

Now if we *assume* there was no helium in the atmosphere at the beginning, and *assuming* the rate is the same that we observe today, and *assuming* no helium has been added or removed in some other way, then we can calculate that all the helium in the atmosphere would build up to its current level in no more than two million years.[59]

EXISTENCE OF COMETS

Comets are composed mostly of ice, and they move through long, oval orbits around the sun. As a comet moves through space, it releases gas and dust, which forms its tail. There are two types of comets: short-period comets, which complete an orbit in less than two hundred years, and long-period comets, which take more than two hundred years to complete an orbit.

As these comets move around the sun, they lose some of their mass. We can accurately measure how much material is lost over time, and by applying that rate, we can determine that many comets are not old. For at the rate at which we observe them losing their mass, these comets, especially the short-period ones, would soon cease to exist. Many of them would do so in less than ten thousand years.[60] The fact that they *do* exist poses a serious problem for evolutionists.

In order to solve the dilemma of long-period comets, scientists have proposed the existence of a *hypothetical* spherical cloud (called the Oort Cloud) that lies about one light-year from our sun. They have no evidence for this comet factory, but because of their assumptions regarding the age of the universe, they believe it must exist.

Dr. John Morris, in his book, *The Young Earth*, puts it very succinctly. "Did you follow the logic? Assumption: The solar system is old. Observation: Comets live for only a short time. Conclusion: Youthful comets are continually coming in from a faraway unseen source."[61]

In this case, not only is the prediction wrong, but the only way the evolutionists can make the evidence fit with their theory is to introduce a rescuing device, the Oort Cloud. Perhaps it does exist, but there is no evidence for it other than the existence of comets and the belief in billions of years. This is not good science.

SHRINKING OF THE SUN

For more than 170 years, scientists have been measuring the sun. They have determined that it is shrinking at a rate of 0.1 percent each century, or about five feet per hour.[62] This makes sense, of course, considering that the sun is burning its fuel! Even when one uses the most conservative data, it becomes clear that just several million years ago, the sun would have been so hot it would have destroyed all life on earth.

CONCLUSION

As Rebecca says a couple of times in the book, if you are a skeptic, I don't expect to be able to convince you in such a short time. I know there are many other arguments and counter arguments I could address, but my goal is not to write an exhaustive treatise on these issues; rather, it is to whet your appetite. I want to spark your interest and challenge you to do your own research. Just look into some of the items mentioned in the story. Read some of the books and materials listed in the resource page at the back of this book. Many of the arguments I present are not my own, but were taken from resources written by scientists and researchers from some of the world's largest and most respected creation ministries, such as Answers in Genesis and the Institute for Creation Research.

I hope I have at least sparked your interest in this subject and caused you to consider some of your own beliefs and biases. The material presented in this novel is but the tip of the iceberg. I wanted to footnote my story so that you, as the reader, would know what is fact and what is fiction. Numerous books have been written on each of the topics I have touched on, and I encourage you to look into them further. When you begin to study the evidence from a non-evolutionary perspective, or at least from a perspective that is open-minded regarding the possibility of God's existence, it is amazing how the pieces of the puzzle begin to fall into place.

Finally, I cannot end without pointing out that if the Bible's history is true, then that gives us confidence that what it says about Jesus is also true. A belief in a young earth will not grant you entrance into heaven, nor will the belief in a literal, worldwide flood, or even a belief in God's existence. The Bible says that Jesus was more than just a good teacher, as some modern critics would characterize Him. Instead, it declares Him to be the one and only begotten Son of God who came to the earth to die for our sins. The most important question you can answer in life is: What is going to happen to you when you die? The Bible answers that question: Those who die without accepting Christ will suffer for eternity, while those who accept His offer of salvation will enjoy eternal life with Him. No one is guaranteed another second of life on this earth. Decide what you believe and act on that decision.

Keith A. Robinson

SUGGESTED MATERIALS

WEBSITES

http://www.apologeticsfiction.com

A website dedicated to promote fiction that supports the Christian faith, including works by Tim Chaffey, Nick Daniels, and other novels by Keith A. Robinson.

http://cssmwi.org

The website for the Creation Science Society of Milwaukee, a Creation ministry located in the southeastern Wisconsin area. This site contains videos and other materials supporting the creation model, as well as a list of public speakers about the topic of creation and evolution, including Keith A. Robinson.

http://www.AnswersInGenesis.org

The official website of Answers in Genesis, one of the largest creation ministries in the world.

http://www.icr.org

The official website of the Institute for Creation Research.

http://www.discovery.org

The official website of the Discovery Institute, the "think tank" for the Intelligent Design movement.

http://www.creationscience.com

This website contains the complete, FREE, online edition of *In the Beginning: Compelling Evidence for Creation and the Flood* (seventh edition) by Dr. Walt Brown.

http://www.evolution-facts.org

This website contains the complete, FREE, online edition of *Evolution Cruncher* by Vance Ferrell. This paperback is based on a 1,326-page, three-volume "Evolution Disproved Series."

http://www.christiananswers.net/creation

This website has lots of great material, including the entire video, *A Question of Origins,* available to view FREE online.

http://www.leestrobel.com

Lee Strobel was a former atheist and has now written several books investigating the Christian faith, including *The Case for the Creator.*

BOOKS AND MAGAZINES

The Young Earth: The Real History of the Earth—Past, Present, and Future by John Morris

The Puzzle of Ancient Man: Evidence for Advanced Technology in Past Civilizations by Donald E. Chittick

Frozen in Time: Wooly Mammoths, the Ice Age, and the Biblical Key to Their Secrets by Michael Oard

Life in the Great Ice Age by Michael and Beverly Oard
The New Answers Book—Ken Ham, General Editor
The New Answers Book 2—Ken Ham, General Editor
After the Flood: The Early Post-flood History of Europe Traced Back to Noah
    by Bill Cooper
The Case for the Creator by Lee Strobel
Answers Magazine: Building a Biblical Worldview (especially Vol. 3, No.
    2, April–June 2008, and Vol. 3, No.4, October-December 2008)

DVDS AND VIDEOS

Incredible Creatures that Defy Evolution, Vols. 1, 2, and 3 with Dr. Jobe
    Martin—Exploration Films
Unlocking the Mystery of Life—Illustra Media
Icons of Evolution—Illustra Media
The Privileged Planet—Illustra Media
The Case for the Creator—Illustra Media
A Question of Origins—Eternal Productions (This entire video can be
    viewed online FREE at http://www.christiananswers.net/creation).

For other products, visit the Answers in Genesis website mentioned
above.

ABOUT KEITH A. ROBINSON

Author of *Pyramid of the Ancients:*
A Novel about the Origin of Civilizations

Photo by Cindy Donegan

Keith A. Robinson has dedicated his life to teaching others about the evidence for creation and against evolution. He began his research into the Creation/Evolution debate back in 1998 when he taught the subject in an adult Sunday school class.

Since then, the "origin of life" debate has been his passion and his calling. He has presented his research findings to school district administrators, public school teachers, university students, and church members.

Since the release of *Logic's End,* his first novel, he has been a featured speaker at Christian music festivals, and has appeared as a guest on numerous radio shows. In addition, he is also the extensions director of the Creation Science Society of Milwaukee.

With the completion of his second novel, *Pyramid of the Ancients,* he is now devoting his time to finishing the third installment of the *Origins* trilogy, tentatively entitled *Escaping the Cataclysm,* which is scheduled to be released in 2011.

In his spare time, Mr. Robinson is a full-time public school educator and professional freelance musician. He currently resides in Kenosha, Wisconsin, with his two sons, Alejandro and Sebastián, and his 110-pound old-English sheepdog named Osa.

NOTES

CHAPTER 9

1.. *Wikipedia,* "Olmec," http://en.wikipedia.org/wiki?Olmec (accessed December 20, 2009).

CHAPTER 14

2. John Morris, *The Young Earth: The Real History of the Earth—Past, Present, and Future,* Rev. and Exp. Ed. (Green Forest, AR: Master, 2007), 16.
3. Ibid.

CHAPTER 15

4. This chronicle was begun by John de Trokelow and finished by Henry de Blaneford. It was translated and reproduced in the Rolls Series, 1866. IV. Ed. H. G. Riley. (cit. J. Simpson, British Dragons. B. T. Batsford Ltd., 1980), 60.
5. Ibid., 118. See also "The Fighting Dragons of Little Cornard," *Folklore, Myths and Legends of Britain* (Reader's Digest, 1973), 241.
6. Bill Cooper, BA, *After the Flood: The Early Post-Flood History of Europe Traced Back to Noah* (Chichester, West Sussex: New Wine Press, 1995), 143–144.
7. (4) Ibid., 152.
8. (5) Ibid., 156.

382 KEITH A. ROBINSON

9. (6) Bill Johnson, "Thunderbirds: Did the American Indians See 'Winged Dinosaurs'?" *Creation* (March 2002), 28–32; "Serpent-bird of the Mayans," *Science Digest* (November 1968), 1.
10. Job 40:15–19.
11. Job 41:13b–15a, 22, 27–28, 30.
12. *Proceedings of the National Academy of Sciences of the United States of America,* http://www.pnas.org/content/96/17/9705/full (accessed September 29, 2009).
13. *Genesis Park,* http://www.genesispark.org/genpark/ancient/ancient.htm (accessed September29, 2009).
14. Anton Moortgart, *The Art of Ancient Mesopotamia,* 1969, plate 2.
15. *CEN Technical Journal* 12, no. 3 (1998), 345.
16. M. Schweitzer and T Staedter, "The Real Jurassic Park." *Earth* (June 1997), 55–57. See report in *Creation* 19(4), 42–43, which describes the careful testing that showed that hemoglobin was present.
17. K. Davies, "Duckbill Dinosaurs (Hadrosauridae, Ornithischia) from the North Slope of Alaska." *Journal of Paleontology* 61, no. 1 (1987), 198–200.
18. *Geelong Advertiser* (July 1845), reprinted in the same newspaper in 1991.
19. Roger Patterson, *Evolution Exposed,* 2nd Ed. (Hebron, KY, 2007), 45–46.

CHAPTER 16

20. World Mysteries, http://www.world-mysteries.com/sar_1.htm (accessed September 29, 2009).
21. See also: Charles Hapgood, *Maps of the Ancient Sea Kings: Evidence of Advanced Civilization in the Ice Age* (Philadelphia: Chilton, 1966), 98.
22. Donald E. Chittick, *The Puzzle of Ancient Man* (Newberg, Oregon: Creation Compass, 2006) 81.
23. Ibid., 11–12.

24. Lionel Cassin, Robert Claiborne, Brian Fagan, and Walter Karp, *Mysteries of the Past.* Edited by Joseph J. Thorndike, Jr. (New York: American Heritage, 1977), 287.

CHAPTER 19

25. Michael and Beverly Oard, *Life in the Great Ice Age,* Edited by Gloria Clanin (Green Forest, AR: Master Books, 2005), 56.
26. D. Paillard, "Glacial Cycles: Toward a New Paradigm." *Reviews of Geophysics,* (2001), 325–346.
27. Ken Ham, Editor, *The New Answers Book* (Green Forest, AR: Master Books, 2006), 210.
28. Michael J. Oard, *The Frozen Record: Examining the Ice Core History of the Greenland and Antarctic Ice Sheets* (El Cajon, CA: Institute for Creation Research, 2005), 31–34.
29. Ham, 213.
30. L. Vardiman, "A Dark and Stormy World," *Answers Magazine* (October–December 2008), 78–80.
31. L. Vardiman, *Climates Before and After the Genesis Flood: Numerical Models and their Implications* (El Cajon, CA: Institute for Creation Research, 2001).
32. Morris, 69.
33. Monty White, *Creation* (September 1996) 16–17).
34. Morris, 42.
35. Steve Auston, *Creation Ex-Nihilo,* 10, no. 3 (1995), 335–343.
36. Funkhouse and Naughton, J. Goephis. Res. 73:4606, 1968.
37. Morris, 66.
38. Ibid., 79–80.
39. Walt Brown, PhD, *In the Beginning: Compelling Evidence for Creation and the Flood* (Phoenix, AZ: Center for Scientific Creation, 2001), 302–306.
40. Morris, 89–90.

CHAPTER 26

41. Chittick, 130.
42. Alberto Carpiceci, *Art and History of Egypt: 5000 Years of Civilization* (Florence: Bohechi, 2000), 71.
43. Ibid., 68.
44. http://www.world-mysteries.com/mpl_2.htm (accessed September 29, 2009).
45. Chittick, 289–192.
46. Rene Noorbergen, *Secrets of the Lost Races: New Discoveries of Advanced Technology in Ancient Civilizations* (Collegedale, TN: Norcom, 1992), 196–197.
47. Ibid., 197.
48. http://www.coralcastle.com (accessed September 29, 2009).
49. Chittick, 108–110.
50. Chittick, 155–157.
51. Sir W. M. Flinders Petrie, *The Pyramids and Temples of Gizeh* (New York: Scribner & Welford, 1883), 84.
52. Ibid., 177.

CHAPTER 28

53. Chittick, 147–148.

AFTERWORD

54. Morris, 21–22.
55. Brown, 29, 76–77
56. S. E. Nevins, "Evolution: The Oceans Say No!" *Impact*, 8 (1973); Ariel A. Roth, "Some Questions about Geochronology," *Origins*, 13, 2 (1986), 64–85.
57. Morris, 92–93.
58. Ibid. 93.

59. Ibid. 87–88.

60. Brown, 33.

61. Ibid., 20.

62. John A. Eddy and Aram A. Boornazian, "Secular Decrease in the Solar Diameter, 1863–1953," *Bulletin of the American Astronomical Society,* Vol. 11, No. 2 (1979), 437.